Taming a Fortune

JUDY DUARTE
NANCY ROBARDS THOMPSON
ALLISON LEIGH

First Published in Great Britain 2017
By Mills & Boon, an imprint of HarperCollins*Publishers*
1 London Bridge Street, London, SE1 9GF

TAMING A FORTUNE © 2017 Harlequin Books S. A.

House Full Of Fortunes!, *Falling For Fortune* and *Fortune's Prince* were first published in Great Britain by Harlequin (UK) Limited.

House Full Of Fortunes! © 2014 Harlequin Books S. A.
Falling For Fortune © 2014 Harlequin Books S. A.
Fortune's Prince © 2014 Harlequin Books S. A.

Special thanks and acknowledgement are given to Judy Duarte, Nancy Robards Thompson and Allison Leigh for their contributions to *The Fortunes of Texas: Welcome to Horseback Hollow* continuity.

ISBN: 978-0-263-92952-2

05-0217

Our policy is to use papers that are natural, renewable and recyclable products and made from wood grown in sustainable forests.The logging and manufacturing processes conform to the legal environmental regulations of the country of origin.

Printed and bound in Spain
by CPI, Barcelona

A HOUSE FULL OF FORTUNES!

BY
JUDY DUARTE

Judy Duarte always knew there was a book inside her, but since English was her least favorite subject in school, she never considered herself a writer. An avid reader who enjoys a happy ending, Judy couldn't shake the dream of creating a book of her own.

Her dream became a reality in March 2002, when Mills & Boon Cherish released her first book, *Cowboy Courage*. Since then she has published more than twenty novels. Her stories have touched the hearts of readers around the world. And in July 2005 Judy won a prestigious readers' Choice Award for *The Rich Man's Son*.

Judy makes her home near the beach in Southern California. When she's not cooped up in her writing cave, she's spending time with her somewhat enormous but delightfully close family.

To my daughter, Christy Duarte,
who has been an awesome critique partner,
brainstorm wizard and editor. You are a creative
and talented author who will soon hold your first
of many of your published books in your hands.
I love you, T.

Chapter One

"Justin! Get down from there!"

At the sound of the baritone voice spiked with irritation, Angie Edwards looked up from the cash register, stopped totaling her mother's grocery purchases and looked across the Superette to see a little red-haired boy high atop the stock clerk's ladder.

She was just about to rush over to the child before he fell when she spotted Toby Fortune Jones standing near the bottom rung, waiting for the little imp to climb down.

Toby, who owned a small ranch just outside of town and volunteered his time as a coach at the YMCA in nearby Vicker's Corners, had become a foster parent to the three Hemings children last fall.

Who would have guessed that the hunky rancher had such a paternal side? Just seeing him with those kids each time they came into the Superette gave Angie pause. And it warmed her heart, too.

What didn't warm her heart, however, was her mother checking up on her. Again.

"Don't forget that you're always welcome to come stay at my house if you need to," Angie's mother said, drawing her back to the task and the conversation at hand.

Angie loved her mom—she truly did—but there was no way she'd ever consider living with the woman again. There were times she couldn't get her mom off the telephone or, in this case, through the Superette checkout line fast enough for comfort.

"That'll be fourteen dollars and seventeen cents," Angie said, after she'd finished totaling her mother's purchases.

Why would Doris Edwards, who now lived and worked in Lubbock as a real-estate agent, drive all the way into Horseback Hollow to buy fifteen dollars' worth of groceries?

To check up on Angie and give her another lecture, no doubt. Thank goodness no one had gotten into line behind her yet.

"You're twenty-four and you can't work at the Superette forever." Her mother reached into her purse for her wallet. "Not that you've worked anywhere longer than a few months, but how are you ever going to make ends meet if you're only putting in four hours a day? Your rent will be due soon. I hope you have enough money set aside to cover it."

She did, but just barely. However, she'd learned early in life that it was best not to share her worries or concerns with her mom. The woman stressed about things entirely too much as it was. And nothing Angie did would ever be good enough for a hardworking powerhouse like Doris Edwards.

"I'll be fine. Really." Angie glanced around the grocery store, hoping the owners—Julia Tierney or her parents, Mr. and Mrs. Tierney—weren't within earshot. When she saw that they weren't, she slowly released a sigh of relief. "I knew this was a part-time position when I accepted it."

"You put in your application at The Hollows Cantina like I told you to, right?" As Doris pulled out a twenty-dollar bill, Angie nodded her confirmation that she had reluctantly applied.

"Well, at least that's something promising. From what I've heard, it's going to be an upscale place to eat."

If truth be told, Angie really had no interest in waiting tables. She'd already done that gig and, as much as Angie liked to cook, the restaurant business wasn't for her. Unfortunately, working part-time at the Superette and filling in as a receptionist at the flight school and charter service barely enabled her to make ends meet. Thank goodness she'd moved recently and had worked out a deal with her new landlord.

"You realize," Doris added, "that with the Fortune name behind the cantina, and with Jeanne Marie Fortune Jones being related to royalty and all... Well, you know what that means. People with money will be eating there. So it'll be a good place for you to network and make some connections. Then again, if it's a husband you want, your prospects will be better there than here. After all, if you want to catch a big fish, you have to go where they're swimming."

Angie blew out a sigh. Her mother had been pushing her to get the college degree she'd never gotten for herself. And since Angie usually found jobs through friends or through a temp agency in Vicker's Corners, her mother had decided she lacked the ambition to succeed in life. So Doris had recently started pushing a white-lace and gold-band solution.

But Angie wasn't looking for love. Not until she had a good idea of who she really was and where she was going in life.

She just wished her mother's voice wasn't so loud, and that she wouldn't make those kinds of comments in public.

"Why don't you come over for supper tonight," her mother said, as she reached for her grocery bag. "If you do, I'll fix meat loaf."

Angie would rather have a root canal than spend the evening with her mom, especially if she was making meat loaf. The woman had never been known for her domestic skills. Or her parenting skills, for that matter. In fact, Angie had probably cooked more of the family meals growing up than she had.

But it wasn't the quality of the food that would keep her away. It was the heartburn and the headache she expected to get from the mealtime conversation. As usual, her mom was sure to point out that Angie's only hope—at least, as far as Doris could see—was for Angie to snag a gainfully employed husband. And there was no reason to believe tonight would be any different. They'd had this conversation at least twenty times in the past couple of months.

To be honest, Angie feared that at least some of what her mother believed might be true. Not that she needed a man to rescue her. That certainly wasn't the case. But for some reason, Angie just couldn't seem to get fired up about anything, which she found troubling. Because at twenty-four, you'd think she'd know what she wanted to do with her life.

Angie had never been good with decisions of any kind, as was evident by her résumé, which read like a copy of the Yellow Pages. But why pour herself into something when her heart wasn't in it? She always figured she'd know what she was meant to do with her life when she felt some sort of spark or passion. Until then, she'd just keep trying a little bit of everything and commit to nothing.

The sound of broken glass sounded from the first aisle, followed by a little girl's shriek.

"I'm sorry!" This came from a boy—maybe the one who'd been on the ladder. "But it wasn't my fault, Toby. Kylie pushed me into the stack of mayonnaise. I didn't mean to knock the jars over."

Angie reached for the small microphone to the right of her register. "Ralph? We'll need a cleanup at the front of aisle one."

Poor Toby. His foster kids were usually pretty well-mannered, but they were obviously having a bad day. At least, the middle boy was.

"Thank goodness you don't have *that* problem to worry about, Evangeline." Her mother shot a look of annoyance at the mayonnaise mess and then at the three children arguing over who was at fault. "Women like us were *not* meant to stay at home and raise a passel of rug rats. I can't imagine what Toby was thinking when he took in that brood."

The soft dark hairs on the back of Angie's neck bristled at her mother's familiar rant against children. *Just ignore it,* Angie thought. She knew better than to engage Doris in a conversation like that, especially in public.

"I'm sorry, Mom. I can't do dinner tonight. I already have plans." Angie just hoped her mother didn't ask what those plans might be because she'd probably spend the first half of her evening looking in her pantry trying to decide what to eat and the second half sitting in front of the television, wearing out the remote.

"Oh, really?" Doris perked up. "What are you doing tonight?"

So much for hoping her mother wouldn't ask.

As the next customer began to place his groceries on the conveyor belt, Angie tore her gaze from her mom and glanced at Toby, the man who'd gotten in line behind her. In spite of those gorgeous baby blues and the kind of face that made even strangers want to confide in him, Toby looked a bit frazzled today.

Funny. He usually looked so capable and put-together.

"I'll have to give you a call and we can talk more later," Angie told her mother. "We don't want to hold up the line."

"Sure, honey." Doris glanced over her shoulder. When she spotted Toby, she offered him a sympathetic smile. "You've certainly got your hands full."

"Just enough to keep life interesting—and fun."

Toby tossed Doris a boyish grin, then winked at Angie as if the two of them were in on a secret.

Being included, even in a make-believe secret, was enough to lift Angie's spirits and to trigger a smile of her own.

"We're going fishing," Brian, the older boy, said. "That is, if there're any fish left by the time we get to Cutter's Pond."

Toby placed a hand on the boy's shoulder. "Nonsense. Everyone knows the bigger fish are busy fattening themselves up and waiting for just the right person to come and catch them up." Toby winked at Angie again, and she realized he must have overheard her mother's comment about fishing for a suitable mate while working at The Hollows Cantina.

As her cheeks warmed, she looked at the small space under the cash register, wishing she could stuff her five-foot-seven-inch body into the square opening.

But why stress about it? It wasn't as though she'd set her sights on Toby as a viable romantic option. He was practically the guy next door.

She'd known the Jones family—make that the *Fortune* Jones family—forever. She'd gone to school with Toby's sister Stacey, although they'd never run in the same circles. She'd even double-dated with Toby's brother Jude a couple of times, but there'd never been any sparks, so nothing had ever come of it.

Toby was probably the only one of Stacey's hunky brothers Angie hadn't considered dating.

Not that he wasn't just as handsome as the others. Angie looked at his tall frame, lean and muscled from years of ranch work and extracurricular sports coaching. Yep, Toby Fortune Jones could definitely compete with his brothers in the looks department.

But Toby always seemed so confident and so sure of himself. And people who knew exactly what they wanted and went after it always intimidated her. Plus, the whole "Mother Teresa meets Dudley Do-Right" personality only made Toby seem all the more out of reach.

A guy like Toby would never be interested in someone like her. He'd want a woman who was down-to-earth, a woman who had her ducks in a row.

Someone who had dreams and plans to fulfill. Someone who wouldn't ever stress about what job she was going to try next.

Angie's mother reached for her grocery bag, causing Angie to break her bold perusal.

"Must be nice to have so much free time on your hands," Doris said to Toby. "Have fun."

Angie could see the disapproval evident on her mom's face. Doris Edwards didn't believe in burning daylight simply for fishing or spending time with one's family.

"We will," Toby told her. "You have a nice day, Mrs. Edwards."

As Doris headed to the parking lot, she turned back to look at what Angie was wearing behind the check stand. "And, honey," Doris said reproachfully, her voice quieter yet still loud enough for anyone within five feet of her to hear, "try to dress a bit more conservatively. Nobody is going to take you seriously with all those curves popping out everywhere. You look like you just got off a shift at a roadhouse honky-tonk."

Doris's smartphone rang, thankfully cutting off her insult to Angie's snug-but-comfortable jeans and her white T-shirt. "Gotta take this. You know, the client always comes first."

Angie started the conveyor belt as her mother breezed out the door in a conservative shoulder-padded power suit. She tried to smile through the mortification that warmed her cheeks and strained the muscles in her face. "Chips, soda, cookies… Looks like someone is planning a picnic."

Toby tossed her a playful grin. "Fishing on the lake is hungry business."

"It should be a nice day for it," Angie said, as she began to check out Toby—or rather, his groceries.

Not that there wasn't plenty to check out about the man himself—if she were looking.

Brown hair that was stylishly mussed, but not out of place. Dazzling blue eyes that were both playful and bright. Broad, strapping shoulders. Arms that looked as though they could pitch a mean curveball—or hold a woman tightly all night.

"I don't want to go to Cutter's Pond," Kylie complained, breaking Angie from her wayward thoughts. "You're just going to kill those poor fish. And I don't even like to eat them."

Brian rolled his eyes. "Don't be such a stinking crybaby, Kylie. We never get to do anything fun without you complaining."

Toby glanced at Angie and gave a little shrug. "Sometimes it's hard to find an activity or an outing they can all enjoy. It seems that someone always has an objection."

Angie smiled. "To be honest, I can't blame her a bit. I never did like putting a worm on a hook."

"You had to go fishing, too?" the little red-haired girl asked.

Angie offered her a sympathetic smile. "When my father was alive, he would take me to Cutter's Pond. And while I could usually count on getting sunburned and bit by a mosquito or two, there was always something special about spending time with my daddy."

"But I don't have a daddy," the girl said.

Angie's cheeks warmed. She'd only wanted to help, but had probably made things worse.

"You might not have a dad," Toby said, as he gave one of Kylie's lopsided auburn pigtails a gentle tug, "but you have *me*."

Toby's hands might be skilled at lassoing horses and throwing a football, but the poor man couldn't do a little girl's hair to save his life.

Still, these kids were lucky to have Toby. If he hadn't stepped up to the plate when their aunt had gone off the deep end and lost custody, they might have been separated and placed in different foster homes.

Justin, the boy who'd climbed the ladder, said, "Too bad we don't have a babysitter for Kylie. She's gonna wah-wah like a little crybaby and ruin our whole day." Justin made fake crying noises and rubbed his eyes to emphasize his overly dramatic point.

Maybe Angie could help out after all. "I only have to work for a half hour or so, and then my shift is over. If you don't mind leaving Kylie here with me, I'd be happy to hang out with her while you and the boys go fishing. We can do cool girls-only things that boys don't get to do."

"That's nice of you to offer," Toby said, "but you don't have to do that."

"Yes, she does!" Kylie gave a little jump and a clap.

Uh-oh. What had Angie done? Had she overstepped her boundaries—or bitten off more than she could chew?

"*Please,* Toby?" Kylie looked at her foster dad with puppy-dog eyes. "Can I stay here with Angie? Can I *please?*"

"If you're sure you don't mind." Toby's gaze zeroed in on Angie, and her heart spun in her chest.

What was that little zing all about?

Had that come from the way Toby was looking at her? Or from having second thoughts about what she'd just offered to do?

After all, she didn't know anything about kids. She'd been an only child and Doris definitely wasn't the maternal type. Plus, unlike some of the other girls she'd grown up with, she'd never even had a babysitting job.

But now that she'd made the offer, she couldn't very well backpedal.

"Of course I don't mind." Angie reached under the checkout stand for a stack of coloring pages and pulled out the top sheet. "The Superette is having a poster contest this month. All the kids have to do is color this picture and turn it back in for the judging. I have a few markers Kylie can use. Then, after I clock out, we'll be on our way for the best girls' day ever!"

Toby shot her an appreciative smile. "All right. We'll

probably only be a couple of hours. Where should I pick her up?"

Angie hadn't given much thought to what she'd do with Kylie, but since she didn't have any money to spend, they'd have to find something cheap to do at home. "I live in the small granny flat behind Elmer Murdock's place. Do you know where that is?"

"Sure do. Mr. Murdock owns the yellow, two-story house next to the post office. I didn't know anyone was living in that…unit in the back."

It wasn't common knowledge. In fact, she hadn't even mentioned the move to her mother yet.

Should she explain her living situation? Or better yet, make an excuse for it?

She decided to do neither.

After totaling Toby's purchases, Angie took his cash and gave him his change. Then she watched him leave the store with the boys, walking with that same swagger the other Fortune Jones boys possessed.

No, she'd never considered dating Toby in the past. And for the briefest of moments, she wondered why she hadn't.

After a fun but unproductive day at Cutter's Pond, Toby and the boys climbed into his truck. If they wanted fish for supper tonight, Toby would have to make another stop at the Superette and purchase a few fillets. As it was, he decided to make things easy on himself and to take the kids to The Horseback Hollow Grill for a couple of burgers. But first they'd have to pick up Kylie.

It had been nice of Angie to offer to babysit. The

afternoon had been a lot more pleasant with only the boys. Not that Kylie was a problem child. She was a sweetheart most of the time, but... Well, she had a tendency to get a little teary when things didn't go her way. But he supposed he couldn't really blame her. It had to be tough for a little girl growing up in a boys' world.

As he pulled his black four-wheel-drive Dodge Ram along the curb in front of the old Murdock place, he scanned the front yard, which looked a lot better than it had the last time he'd driven by. The once-overgrown lawn had been mowed recently and a sprinkler had brought the grass back to life.

The old house was still in need of repair—or at least, a fresh coat of paint and some new shutters. But that wasn't surprising. Elmer Murdock was well over eighty years old and living on his marine-corps retirement pay.

"Can we get out, too?" Justin asked.

"I don't see why not." While they'd all had a blast fishing, Toby knew the boys had been stewing over what kind of things might constitute a "girls-only" day. Apparently, the mystery of womanhood began early in a male's life.

He shut off the ignition, got out of the pickup and made his way to the path that led to the back of the house, where Mr. Murdock had built separate quarters for his widowed mother-in-law decades ago.

The "granny flat," as Angie had called it, was even more run-down than the main house. The small porch railing had come loose and was about to collapse, although the wood flooring had been swept recently.

A pot of red geraniums added a splash of color to the chipped and weathered white paint.

Brian and Justin lagged behind by several feet because they'd stopped to check out two different birdhouses in a maple tree. The birdhouse on the left was pretty basic, but the one on the right was three stories with a wraparound porch and looked like something straight out of his mother's *Southern Living* magazine.

Toby continued to the front door and knocked loud enough to be heard over the sound of Taylor Swift belting out her latest hit. He cringed, although he knew that, as a proud Texan, he should favor country music, even crossover pop artists like Taylor Swift. But his well-guarded secret was that he couldn't stand the stuff. He preferred his music with a lot more soul and a lot less twang.

When the front door swung open, Kylie, her face smeared with green goo, greeted Toby with a bright-eyed smile. "Guess what? Mr. Murdock and Angie had a nail-painting contest and I got to be the judge. And see, Mr. Murdock won because he painted the cutest little horse on my big toenail." She lifted her right leg high in the air in an effort to put her toe in front of his face.

"Yeah, well, Mr. Murdock cheated," came Angie's reply. "He took an hour to do it, using a magnifying glass and his model-airplane paint, which, by the way, isn't washable. That horse will never come off."

Toby couldn't actually see Angie, since she had her back to the door and was leaning over the arm of the sofa, a white container in one hand and a green sponge in the other.

Both amused and touched by the sight, Toby couldn't help but chuckle.

"Ooh, gross," Brian said, when he spotted his sister's face. "What happened to you?"

"I'm getting pretty—just like Angie."

Both boys began to hoot and howl.

Toby couldn't say that he blamed them. Kylie, who was a cutie-pie when she wasn't whining, looked like a pint-sized version of the creature from the black lagoon, walking around with a green face and her fingers and toes splayed out wide so the paint would dry.

The little red-haired girl stepped aside to allow them into the small house, just as Angie straightened. As Toby's eyes landed on Angie's face, it appeared as though she'd climbed from the same lagoon.

She smiled as if having green goop smeared all over wasn't the least bit unusual. "We didn't expect you back so soon."

"It certainly appears that way." Toby couldn't help but laugh.

"Just for the record, I did not cheat. You never established any ground rules." Elmer Murdock sprang up from the sofa Angie had been leaning over, the same green mud on his face. And Toby didn't know whether he should hoot with laughter or try his best to hold it back.

Was this the formidable retired marine who'd instilled fear in most of Horseback Hollow High School's youth with his loud shouting during football practices?

And for some reason, the old leatherneck didn't seem to be the least bit embarrassed at being caught having a facial.

Mr. Murdock slapped his hands on his hips and zeroed in on Angie. "I didn't complain about *you* cheating when you used way more material on that Bird McMansion than I did during our birdhouse-building contest."

Toby quickly grabbed his ball cap from his head and pulled it lower over his face to cover his smirk. Was this the one-and-only Elmer Murdock?

His brothers would never believe this.

"You built that huge birdhouse outside?" Brian asked Angie. "I didn't know girls could build like that."

"Girls can do anything. Especially *this* girl." Angie pointed to her green-covered face. "I got an A in woodshop when I was in high school. Give me a hammer, wood and nails, and I can build anything."

"Can you help me build my car for the soapbox derby?" Brian asked.

"Only if you want to win," Angie replied. Then she pointed to the sofa. "Have a seat, guys. Mr. Murdock has a few more minutes for his face to dry, but it's time for us ladies to wash off our masks. We'll be back in a Flash, Gordon."

"Hey," Brian said. "*Flash Gordon.* That's funny."

Toby crossed his arms and shifted his weight to one hip. Wow, Brian had been pretty quiet and distant ever since the state had stepped in and removed the kids from their aunt's custody. But he'd warmed up to Angie in about three minutes flat.

As Angie led Kylie across the small living area that served as both kitchen and sitting room, Toby couldn't help but watch the brunette who wore a pair of cutoff jeans that would have put Daisy Duke to shame pad across the floor. Her hips moved in a natural sway, her long, shapely legs damn near perfect. He remembered Doris Edwards's cutting potshot at the Superette and thought that from where he was standing, there was absolutely nothing wrong with Angie's curves.

He continued to watch her from behind until she and Kylie disappeared into the only other room in the house and shut the door.

Justin was sitting next to Mr. Murdock and reaching out his fingers to the wrinkled weather-beaten cheek. "Is that mud?" he asked the old man.

"Justin," Toby scolded, "keep your hands to yourself."

"Yeah, but this is sissy mud," Mr. Murdock answered casually. "It's supposed to clear your pores and detoxify your skin or some such bull. I'll tell you what, we never worried about our pores when we were covered in mud back in that wet foxhole in Korea. All we cared about was not getting our fool heads blown off."

"Wow, you got shot at in a war?" Brian asked as Justin started using the white container to apply stripes to his own eight-year-old face in a war-paint fashion that would make any Apache proud.

"Mr. Murdock," Angie yelled from the bathroom at the end of the small hall, "stop talking so much. You need to keep still and let the mask dry. Every time you talk, you crack it."

Mr. Murdock clamped his thin lips together in their perpetual grimace.

As Toby scanned Angie's small living area, he couldn't help but take note of the freshly painted blue walls that had been adorned with the oddest forms of artwork—

the label side of a wooden produce crate that advertised Parnell's Apple Farm, an old mirror framed with pieces of broken ceramic, a coatrack made out of doorknobs...

She'd placed a whitewashed bookshelf against one wall. Instead of books, it held various knickknacks. A bouquet of bluebonnets in a Mason jar sat on top. The furniture was old, and while the decor was kind of funky, the house had a cozy appeal.

"So you're running the old Double H Ranch?" Mr. Murdock asked Toby, lasting only a couple of minutes before he broke Angie's orders to stay quiet. It was hard to take the crotchety old man seriously with the green mud caked onto his face and his lips barely able to move.

"Sure am," Toby replied, warming up to his favorite subject—his ranch. "We have more than three hundred head of cattle now, and I've been doing some breeding."

"I used to do some roping back before I enlisted, you know. Could probably still out-rope most of you young upstarts. I should swing by your place and we could have a little contest."

What was it with this old man and contests? Apparently his competitiveness went well beyond the high-school football field.

Before Toby could politely decline the challenge, the door swung open and the girls came out.

Angie had apparently swapped the denim shorts for a yellow floral sundress, yet she was still barefoot, her toenails painted the same pink shade as Kylie's— minus the horse.

"We had a really good day," Angie said, her face clean, her eyes bright.

"We did, too," he said.

"Did you catch anything?"

"I'm afraid not."

"I used to catch all kinds of stuff out at Cutter's Pond," Mr. Murdock chimed in, while the boys continued to stare at the old swamp monster look-alike as if he were a real hero come to life. "Still hold the record for the biggest trout ever caught in Horseback Hollow. Nobody's beat me yet."

"Okay, Mr. Murdock, you should be dry." Angie patted her landlord on his shoulder. "You can probably go home and wash your face now."

"Roger that," the old coot replied as he shuffled toward the door and back to the main house. The former marine looked like a strong Texas wind would knock him over, and Toby doubted the man was in any shape to rope a tractor on his ranch, let alone a longhorn steer, although he'd never say so out loud.

Instead, he nodded at the interior of Angie's little house, at the freshly painted blue walls. "I like what you've done with this place. You certainly have a creative side."

"You think so? Thanks." She scanned the cramped quarters, too. "The house was empty for nearly twenty years, so it was pretty stuffy and drab when I moved in. I spent a couple of days cleaning and airing it out. I've also learned how to decorate on a shoestring budget, which has been fun."

"I can see that. You've done a great job. Where did you find this stuff?"

"Some of it was already here—like the furniture. I picked up the paint on sale when I was in Vicker's Corners the other day. Someone had ordered the wrong color, so it was practically free. I've also been picking up odds and ends at garage sales. Then I figured out a way to make them pretty—or at least, interesting."

"I'm impressed. You're quite the homemaker."

She brightened, and her wholesome beauty stunned him. Not that he hadn't noticed before, but he'd never seen her blue eyes light up when she smiled like that.

"To tell you the truth," he added, "I was surprised to hear that you'd moved in here. The windows had been boarded up for ages, and the weeds had grown up so high that most people forgot that there was a little house back here at all."

"Mr. Murdock and I were talking one day at the Superette, and he mentioned that he needed to hire someone to do some chores for him. I told him I had some free time. And when I spotted the little house, I asked if he'd be interested in renting it to me."

"I'd think you would have preferred to find a place that wouldn't have required as much work."

She shrugged. "Let's just say that, like Mr. Murdock, I love a challenge. Besides, his sons live out of state, so he's all alone. Plus, this way, I can look out for him and let him think he's looking out for me."

Toby had always thought Angie was a bit shallow, although he couldn't say why he'd come to that conclusion. Probably because he'd heard a few people say that she was flighty. But apparently, he'd been wrong. There was more to her than he'd given her credit for.

He also owed her for taking care of Kylie today, although something told him she wouldn't accept any money for doing it. So it seemed like the most natural thing in the world to say, "We're going to have burgers at The Grill. Would you like to join us?"

And it seemed even more natural for her to respond, "Sure. Why not?"

Chapter Two

The Horseback Hollow Grill, which was attached to the Two Moon Saloon, wasn't much to shout about when it came to eateries. But it was one of the only options in town. Fortunately, they served the juiciest burgers and dogs, fresh-cut fries and a mean grilled-cheese sandwich.

As Angie climbed from Toby's lifted truck, she couldn't help but smile. If her mom could see her now, the poor woman would be torn between deep anxiety and despair.

First of all, she'd be dancing on clouds to see Angie enter a restaurant with one of the Fortune Jones men, even if it was only The Grill. Doris assumed all the Fortunes were wealthy beyond their wildest dreams, although local rumor had it that the Horseback Hollow branch of the family hadn't struck any gold.

According to what Angie had heard, Jeanne Marie Fortune Jones had been adopted. And when her birth brother, James Marshall Fortune, had found her last year, he'd given her a portion of his stock in the family company. But when she found out those shares were supposed to go to his kids, she'd refused it.

Nevertheless, even with a boatload of cash, a man with three kids wasn't the catch Angie's mom had been hoping she'd snag.

Of course, this wasn't a date by any stretch of the word. Toby had only included her in the family plans because he was a nice guy. And Angie had accepted because she'd had nothing better to do and was on an especially tight budget these days.

As they entered the small-town restaurant, where artificial flowers in hammered coffeepots sat on old-style tables with rounded edges encased in silver metal, Angie realized they weren't the only ones in Horseback Hollow who'd decided to pick up a quick meal tonight. The place was certainly hopping.

Toby nodded toward an empty booth by the window, one of the few places to sit that weren't taken.

"Can we play in the game room for a while?" Justin asked.

Angie remembered the small arcade in back—if you could call it that—from her own school days. Back then, The Grill was *the* place to hang out if you were a teenager in Horseback Hollow. It probably still was, so she couldn't blame the kids for their eagerness to drop coins into the video-game machines.

"What do you guys want to eat?" he asked.

"I'd like grilled cheese," Kylie said, "but only if they have real bread and square cheese."

Angie cocked her head slightly. "What's she talking about?"

Toby chuckled. "We stopped at a place in Lubbock one day, and they brought out a sandwich that had been made with focaccia bread and several fancy kinds of cheese. It was the restaurant's claim to fame, and it cost a pretty penny, but Kylie didn't like it. By 'square' cheese, she means good ole American slices, individually wrapped."

"Aw." Angie smiled. "I'll have to remember that."

"I want a corn dog and fries," Justin said.

"Got it." Toby turned to Brian. "How about you?"

"I want a cheeseburger, but I don't want onions or lettuce or pickles. But ask if they'll give me extra tomatoes."

"Since we've got that out of the way, here you go." Toby reached into his pocket and pulled out a small handful of quarters. "Why don't you start with these? I'll get some change after the waitress takes our order."

While the kids dashed off, Toby waited for Angie to slide into the booth, then did the same.

As she settled into a middle spot, he removed his ball cap, as any proper Texan gentleman would do, leaving his brown hair disarrayed and close to his head. She was tempted to reach out and finger-comb it.

Or maybe she just wanted to touch it and see if it was as soft as it looked.

Odd, though. He didn't appear to be the least bit… mussed. He actually looked darn near perfect.

As if completely unaware of her perusal—and why

wouldn't he be?—he reached across the table for the menus and handed her one, ending her silly musing.

But as she opened it up and scanned the offerings—burgers, hot dogs and sandwiches—her options, while too few by some people's standards, still seemed too difficult to narrow down.

This was the part about eating out that she dreaded. She could never decide on what to order, especially when there were other people with her.

Since she didn't want Toby to think that she was indecisive, she did what she'd learned to do on her other dates. Not that this was a date.

Or was it? Did *Toby* think it was a date?

The waitress, a tall brunette in her early forties, approached. "What'll it be?"

Toby placed the kids' orders, then asked Angie, "What would you like?"

She gave her standard reply. "I'll have whatever you're having."

But when Toby ordered the double bacon cheeseburger, the large onion rings, fried pickles and jumbo peanut-butter milk shake, she realized she'd have to rethink her strategy if she ever went to another restaurant with him again.

Where was she going to put all that food?

"Maybe you'd better not bring me those pickles," she told the waitress.

The woman nodded, then made a note on her pad. After she left them alone, things got a little quiet. Actually, too quiet, since Angie tended to get bored easily.

So she said, "Looks like the kids will be busy for a while."

He smiled. "I remember when those games were brand-new. Fifteen years later, and they're still entertaining kids."

"You might not believe this," Angie said, "but I was a whiz at Ms. Pac-Man. There weren't too many people who could outscore me."

"Not even Mr. Murdock?"

At that, Angie laughed and shook her head. "Please don't tell him. I've never met a man more competitive than he is. If he finds out, I'll be forced to defend my title."

"Wow! A *titleholder?*" Toby tossed her a heart-strumming grin. "Who would have guessed that I'd be sharing a meal with a real live champion?"

"Yeah, well, it'd be nice to have a more worthwhile claim to fame than 'Top Scorer on Ms. Pac-Man.'" Angie settled back in the booth. Even the praise over what little she had achieved in life didn't do much in the way of soothing her embarrassment over her mother's public criticism.

"I'm sure you have plenty of things to be proud of," he said.

Their gazes met and held for a moment. Her smile faded, and she broke eye contact.

She was also a champ at changing subjects.

"The kids certainly seem to be settling in," she said.

"They seem to be. It was tough for a while, though. Justin was acting out and getting in trouble at school, but he's doing better now. And Kylie no longer has nightmares. Brian still holds back a bit, although I can understand that. It's hard for him to trust adults. Each

one he's ever had to depend on has abandoned him—
one way or another."

She'd heard a few scant rumors about the kids, but
she didn't know what was true and what wasn't.

"What happened to their mother?" she asked.

"She was diagnosed with cancer right after Kylie
was born and died just before her first birthday. Justin
was only two at the time, so Brian's the only one who
was old enough to remember her."

"What about their dad?"

Toby glanced toward the arcade, where the kids
continued to play. Still, he kept his voice low. "From
what I understand, he wasn't the kind of guy who could
handle responsibility. When Ann, their mom, found
out that she was pregnant with Kylie, he left her. And
no one has heard from him since."

"That's so sad." Angie had always been close to
her father, and when her parents had split up, it had
crushed her. Losing her dad to cancer two years later
had been even worse.

"After Ann died," Toby continued, "the kids went to
live with her sister. But Barbara wasn't prepared for the
challenge of raising two toddlers and a five-year-old.
She drank as a way of escape. And the kids seemed
to exacerbate her stress—and her need for the bottle."

"When did the state step in?" Angie asked.

"Last year, when Justin's behavioral problems in
school escalated. The authorities were called in to
investigate, and that's when they found out how bad
things were at home. Shortly after that, Barbara was
arrested. At that point, she was ordered to get in-patient
treatment and the children were placed in separate fos-

ter homes. I hated the thought of them being split up. Family is important. And they'd lost so much already. So I volunteered to take them in."

"That was a big step for a bachelor."

He shrugged. "My mom was adopted. It just seemed like a natural way to pay it forward."

There it was again. Toby's altruistic personality. Everything about him was too perfect. Even his slightly mussed hair, which she was still tempted to reach out and touch.

It had a bit of a curl to it. Was it *really* as soft as it looked?

Oh, good grief. Get a grip, girl. She forced herself to stop gawking at him and to keep the conversation going. "So how long have you had them? About six months?"

"Yes, and I'll be the first to admit that it was a big adjustment. But it's getting easier. I actually like having them around. The ranch was too quiet before. You probably can imagine what it was like for me, growing up with all my brothers and sisters. I'm used to noise. Sometimes I feel as if I can't concentrate unless the decibel level is over ninety-five."

Actually, Angie couldn't imagine what any of that had been like. She didn't have any siblings. So her house had always been as quiet as a tomb, unless she had friends over.

"It was the talk of the town when you got custody of the kids," she said. "Most people didn't think it would last."

"My buddies certainly didn't think it would."

"How about you?" she asked. "How are you holding up?"

"I'm doing all right, but it's put a real cramp in my social life."

Angie smiled. "You mean with the guys—or romantically speaking?"

"Romance? What's that?" Toby laughed. "Actually, if I were even in a position to be looking for a relationship, I'd be in a real fix. Most women go running for the hills when they hear I have three children, even though the situation is supposed to be temporary. Other women look at me as if I'm some kind of hero. But even then, when they're faced with the reality of dating a man with the responsibility of three kids, they don't stick around long."

Point taken. Toby was making it clear that he wasn't looking for a relationship. Therefore, Angie now knew this clearly wasn't a date.

"Yet here you are," she said, "out with the kids having burgers, when you could be having a few beers at the Two Moon Saloon and dancing with Horseback Hollow's most eligible bachelorettes. From what I remember, you were always a pretty good dancer."

"I still am. Maybe I'll prove it to you sometime." Now, that was a challenge Angie looked forward to. And while the boyish grin on his face suggested that he was teasing, for a moment, for a heartbeat, she'd suspected that he'd been a wee bit serious.

And if they were ever to lay their secrets out on the table, she'd have to admit that she wouldn't mind dancing with him, holding him close, swaying to the slow beat of a country love song, her body pressed to his...

"Seriously, though," he said, drawing her back to reality, "if I wanted a beer, they'd serve me one in here. But I have enough on my plate without having to worry about dancing and courting the ladies, too."

"I hear you." And she did—loud and clear. He'd said it twice now, which was just as well. *Really,* it was. "I'm not looking for love, either—although my mother seems to think I should be."

"Doris is really hard on you. Why is that?"

"Because she's lost all hope of me making a financial success of my life. So if I can't be the money-making ballbuster she envisions, the least I can do is marry one."

"Well, then, Doris can rest assured that you'll be safe from me. I'm definitely not raking in the dough."

Safe from him? Toby couldn't be more obvious if he was wearing a blinking neon sign. She wanted to say, *Okay, I get it. You're not interested in me.*

But she supposed it wasn't necessary. Neither one of them was in any position to enter into a romantic relationship right now—with anyone.

"I wouldn't let your mother drag you down," Toby said. "You seem like a happy person. So whatever you're doing must be working for you."

Well, not exactly. While she wasn't miserable, she'd be a lot happier if she had a full-time job—or at least some direction.

"I'm doing just fine," she said.

Before Toby could respond, Kylie ran up to the table. "Brian won't let me have a turn driving the race car. He said it's 'cause I'm a girl. And 'cause my feet won't reach the pedals. But they will if he lets me sit on his lap."

"I have an idea," Angie said, as she slid out from behind the booth. "I'm going to show you how to play a better game. One that you can play all by yourself."

"You're coming in pretty handy," Toby said.

Angie laughed. "I'm just paying for my supper."

"At this rate, I'm going to owe you breakfast, too."

For a moment, just like the comment about dancing together had done, the overnight innuendo hung in the air. And while they both might have laughed it off, there'd been a brief moment when their gazes had met, a beat when she suspected that neither of them had taken the promise of an early-morning breakfast lightly.

Toby hoped the waitress brought their food soon. Not only was he hungry, but he was down to his last few quarters and wasn't about to ask for any more change than he had already. Since taking in the kids six months ago, his coin contributions alone could go a long way in refurbishing some of those old games and buying a new one.

He took a sip of his milk shake and watched the kids and Angie return to the table—out of quarters again, no doubt.

"You're pretty good at Ms. Pac-Man," Brian told Angie, as she slipped back into the booth.

"Thanks." She winked at Toby. "I used to be a lot better, but I'm getting rusty in my old age."

"You aren't that old," Justin said, taking her far more seriously than she'd intended. "Maybe if you came here to practice more often, you'd be supergood again."

Angie laughed. "I'm afraid my days of playing in the arcade are over."

"That's too bad," Justin said. "I'll bet you could hold the world record."

"I'll have to remind my mother that I actually have some talent the next time she worries about my future prospects."

"Here you go," Toby said, as he rationed out a few more of the coveted coins to the kids.

Then they dashed off, leaving him and Angie alone again. It was nice getting to know her, getting a chance to see a side to her he'd never realized was there. He didn't think he was the only one in town to have misconceptions about Angie Edwards. Heck, even her own mother didn't seem to appreciate her.

Toby hadn't liked the way her mom had talked to her today, especially in front of other people. But he supposed that wasn't any of his business. He'd always had a sympathetic nature. In fact, his brothers often ribbed him, saying he was a sucker for people who were down on their luck. Some of that might be true, although he didn't see Angie that way.

Sure, maybe she wasn't a superambitious go-getter. But she seemed to have a good head—and a pretty one at that—on her shoulders. And something told him that she'd find her groove in life soon.

"You know," he said, "it's not too late to go back to school."

"No, it isn't. But you're looking at a woman who'd joined the Toastmasters Club, the Teachers of Tomorrow, Health Careers and Future Farmers of America when I was in high school. I was even a member of the French Club one semester. I couldn't decide on a direction then, and I'm no closer to having one now. So I can't imagine spending the time and money to take classes without a goal in mind. So far, my motto in life has been 'just keep on keeping on.'"

"Well, if it makes you feel any better, I think that motto suits you pretty well. You're a lot of fun to be with. And you have a great ability to adapt. I'm sure you'll figure something out."

"Yes, but as each week passes, my mother gets more and more stressed about my future."

"How about you?" he asked. "Are you worried about it?"

She tossed him a pretty smile. "I'm doing just fine."

He didn't doubt that she was. "Then that ought to settle it."

She took her glass, wrapped her full lips around the straw and took a slow drag of her milk shake, making him think about somewhere else her mouth could be...

What in blazes was wrong with him? Angie Edwards wasn't the woman for him. He needed someone who was solid and stable, someone who was willing to take on three kids. And while Angie could probably handle anything life threw at her, she didn't seem like the type who would stick around for the long haul.

And even though everyone in town, including his family, thought that his taking on the Hemings kids was a temporary thing, Toby had gotten attached to them, and he wasn't planning to give them up unless their aunt insisted on taking them back. And even then, he wasn't sure if he'd step back without a fight. But from what he'd gathered from the social worker, their aunt Barbara wasn't the maternal type.

So if he had any chance of keeping them, he needed a partner who would be just as committed to the kids as he was.

Still, that didn't mean Angie wasn't an attractive woman. What she might lack in commitment, she more than made up for with sex appeal.

Yet the more time he spent with her, the more intriguing he found her.

Why hadn't he looked at her that way before? Well, of course he'd noticed her looks. He wasn't blind. But he'd never been the kind of guy to date someone just because of her physical appearance. He'd been interested in the woman on the inside.

Of course, after talking with her this evening, he had to admit that he was curious about what made her tick.

Even though they'd both grown up in Horseback Hollow, he really didn't know very much about her— except in the way that most folks in small towns knew stuff about each other.

Up until today, he and Angie had never said more than a few words to each other in passing.

Before he could ponder it any further, the waitress brought their food. While she was placing the plates on the table, Toby excused himself and went after the kids.

Moments later, they were all seated at the booth. The boys began to dig in, but Kylie merely looked at her plate and frowned.

"What's the matter?" Angie asked.

"It's too much. I don't want it."

"Oops," Toby said. "The boys are such good eaters that I sometimes forget about her. She isn't actually all that fussy, but I think she gets overwhelmed when her plate is too full."

"What if you share with me," Angie said. "Would that help?"

When Kylie nodded, Angie took a knife and, with a careful slice, cut the grilled cheese into quarters instead of halves. "I like smaller triangles. Don't you?"

The little girl smiled.

Angie reached for a section. "Can I have some of your fries, too?"

Again, Kylie nodded.

Toby would have to remember that trick.

Next, Angie took the knife, then sliced her double bacon burger in two. "When the waitress comes by I'm going to ask her for a to-go box."

"What are you going to do?" Toby asked. "Take that home for lunch tomorrow?"

"Actually, I thought I'd offer it to Mr. Murdock. He likes a late-night snack when he watches television. And I thought it would be a nice surprise."

So she was thoughtful, too—especially with kids and the elderly.

Toby took a bite of his burger, relishing the taste. No one made them better than The Grill.

"Can you hand me the mustard?" Angie asked.

Toby reached for the bottle that stood next to the menus on the table and handed it to her, thinking she was going to apply it to the portion of the burger she intended to eat. Instead, she poured a glob onto her plate, dipped one of the French fries into it and took a bite.

"Most people prefer catsup," he said. "Miss Edwards, you're proving to be quite a novelty."

She smiled. "'Always keep 'em guessing.' That's my motto."

Toby laughed. "You have a lot of mottos, I'm learning."

She tossed him a pretty smile.

"Can I try that?" Justin asked. "Pass me the mustard, too."

"I'm not going to be able to eat all these onion rings," Angie said. "Does anyone want to help me out?"

"I've never had them before," Brian said.

She passed her plate to him. "You should at least try one. You might be missing a real treat."

Ten minutes later, Kylie had eaten three-quarters of her sandwich. Justin had finished off his corn dog and decided that he preferred dipping his fries in mustard rather than catsup. And Brian had wolfed down most of Angie's onion rings.

Then the kids dashed back to the arcade with the last of the quarters, leaving the adults sitting amid the clutter of nearly empty plates, wadded napkins, dribbles of soda pop and a melting ice cube.

Toby studied Angie in the dim light of the least romantic restaurant in West Texas.

Why in the world hadn't he taken the time to get to know her sooner, when his life hadn't been complicated by three children?

He supposed one reason he'd steered clear of her

was because his brother Jude had once dated her. And for that reason, Toby had considered her off-limits.

Yet, when the kids returned to the table, high from their final top-ranking scores on Ms. Pac-Man, the sound of Angie's infectious laughter, as well as the way she pulled Kylie onto her lap and gave her a squeeze, made Toby think he'd better have a talk with his newly engaged brother.

There were a few questions he needed to ask Jude. Because maybe, just maybe, this funny and beautiful woman wasn't entirely off-limits after all.

Chapter Three

Ever since Angie had joined him and the kids for dinner on Saturday night, Toby hadn't been able to stop thinking about her. By Monday morning he was racking his brain, trying to come up with an excuse to see her—other than stopping by the Superette to pick up groceries, although he was tempted to do just that.

Then, while driving the kids to school, he had a lightbulb moment.

Brian, who was seated in front, was craning his neck and peering out the windshield at a plane flying overhead.

"Look at that one," he said, pointing it out to his younger brother, who sat in the back with Kylie. "Wouldn't it be cool to fly an airplane?"

And bingo! Toby had the perfect solution.

"How would you like to talk to a real pilot and see some planes up close?" he asked Brian.

The oldest boy had been unusually quiet and introspective since moving in with Toby, but when he glanced across the seat, his mouth dropped open and his eyes lit up in a way they'd never done before. "That would be awesome. Do you know one?"

"My cousin Sawyer and his wife, Laurel, own the new flight school and charter service. Laurel is actually the pilot. She was even in the air force."

"No kidding?" The boy's jaw dropped, and his eyes grew wide. "For *real?*"

Most people in town were more impressed with Toby's connection to the Fortune family, rather than the lovely woman one of his cousins had married. "Yes, for *real.* I'll give Sawyer a call this morning and ask for a tour."

"For all of us?" Justin asked.

"And for me, too?" Kylie chimed in. "If it's a girl pilot, I want to see her."

Toby laughed. "Yes, we'll all go. After I drop you guys off at school, I'll try to work out a good time for us to go. But no promises on when that might be."

And that was just what Toby did. Once the kids had gotten their backpacks, climbed out of the truck and headed for their respective classrooms, he called his cousin.

Sawyer's father, James Marshall Fortune, had been a triplet. His two sisters had been given up for adoption when they were very young. Josephine May was raised in England by the Chesterfields, a family that was both rich and royal. Jeanne Marie, Toby's mom, was raised in Horseback Hollow by loving parents who were common folk. But what they lacked in finances, they made up for in love.

Last year, Sawyer had met Laurel Redmond in Red Rock, where they fell in love. On New Year's Eve, they married in Horseback Hollow, where they now made their home. Sawyer and Laurel opened Redmond-Fortune Air, which served folks in this area. Laurel used to work with her brother, Tanner Redmond, who owned the Redmond Flight School and Charter Service back in Red Rock. They originally opened a branch of that company here, but with Tanner's blessing and Sawyer's capital, Laurel bought out her brother's stock and recently went out on her own.

When Sawyer answered the phone, Toby told him about Brian's interest in airplanes, then asked if he could bring the kids by the airfield sometime for a tour.

"Absolutely," Sawyer said. "Laurel flew a couple of businessmen from Vicker's Corners to Abilene this morning for a meeting, but she should be back before three."

"Is Angie Edwards working for you today?" Toby asked, as casually as he could.

"As a matter of fact, she comes in at one-thirty and will be here until four. Why?"

"No reason. I'd heard she was a part-time receptionist." Toby glanced at the clock on the dashboard, realizing he had a lot of chores to get done today. But no telling when Angie would be working at the flight school again.

"The kids get out of school at three," he told Sawyer. "So we'll head over to the airfield then."

And that was just what he did.

As had become his routine, Toby waited in front of the school when the bell rang. Only this time, he'd gone home so he could shower, shave and put on a new shirt and his favorite jeans.

"Did you talk to your cousin?" Brian asked, as he climbed into the truck.

"I sure did. And Sawyer said to come by today."

Whoops and cheers erupted from the backseat. Even the usually quiet Brian was beaming, confirming that Toby had just hit a home run.

So what if fulfilling a young boy's dreams to get to see the inside of a cockpit hadn't been his only motive? Besides, the kids had been talking about Angie nonstop—especially Kylie—and they were going to be just as excited to see her as he was. If he happened to talk to a beautiful woman and casually slip in a dinner invitation while they were at the airfield, then so be it.

"But let's set some ground rules," he told the kids. "You're going to have to mind your manners and not touch anything you're not supposed to. No running off—that means *you,* Justin. And the minute we get back to the ranch, you're going to have to sit down and do your homework. No complaints. Got it?"

A chorus of "got it"s and excited chatter filtered over the seat to him.

Fifteen minutes later, as the anticipation built in the cab of the truck, Toby turned down the county road that led to their destination.

Prior to the addition of Redmond-Fortune Air, the Horseback Hollow Airport hadn't amounted to much more than a small control tower, a couple of modular buildings, one of which housed Lone Star Avionics, several hangars and a relatively small airstrip.

But the brand-new building Sawyer and Laurel had built, with its gray block exterior, smoky glass windows and chrome trim, added some class to an otherwise small-town, nondescript airport that served both Horseback Hollow and nearby Vicker's Corners.

After parking next to Sawyer's new black Cadillac Escalade, Toby led the kids up the walkway and through the double glass doors into the reception area.

Angie, who was busy typing some letters at the reception desk, brightened when they came in. "Hey, look who's here!"

She greeted each child with a hug, but stopped short when she reached Toby. After all, what was required? Certainly not an embrace. And a handshake was much too formal.

They both settled for a smile, which worked out just fine.

"I heard you were coming." She turned to a guy in green coveralls who was seated near a potted ficus tree and reading a newspaper. "Pete, is Sawyer still out back?"

"Yep. He'll be in shortly." Pete lowered his newspaper and nodded at Toby. "How's it goin'?"

"Not bad."

Pete Nelson, a tall, lanky mechanic, worked for Lone Star Avionics and sometimes did side jobs for Sawyer and Laurel. Ever since Sawyer and Laurel opened up for business, the other employees at the airfield usually came over to use their break room, as well as the new fridge, microwave and coffeemaker.

"Taking a break?" Toby asked the thirtysomething air-force vet, trying to keep the hint of jealousy from his voice. After all, if he worked at the airfield, he'd be taking breaks in the office when Angie was here, too.

Hell, Toby didn't even work at the airfield, and he was looking for reasons to stop by the sexy brunette's places of employment.

"Just having a quick cup of coffee," Pete said. "Then it's back to the hangar."

"Hey, Justin," Brian said, as he wandered toward a table with a plastic-enclosed display of miniature-sized scale models of airplanes. "Look at this."

Kylie followed the boys, just as Sawyer entered the building.

"Hey, Toby." He extended his arm, and they shook hands. "Sorry I wasn't here when you arrived."

"No problem. We've been checking out the reception area." And the receptionist, who'd just bent over to reach into the lowest drawer of the filing cabinet.

Toby hadn't noticed before, but Angie was wearing a short black skirt. Well, it hadn't looked so short until she'd bent over and those long, tanned, shapely legs stretched out.

Wow.

Sawyer continued to talk, although Toby couldn't quite wrap his mind around what he was saying. Still, he nodded as if he'd heard every word.

When Kylie, who must have gotten bored looking at the miniature planes with her brothers, wandered over to Angie, Toby was about to call the little girl over to him and tell her that Angie was busy. But without missing a beat, Angie set her up at the desk with a stamp pad and paper, then went back to stooping and bending and flashing those long, shapely legs.

"Aw, so that's the way the wind is blowing," Sawyer said, calling Toby out.

"The *wind?*"

Sawyer lowered his voice to a whisper. "It's not the airplanes you're interested in. It's Little Miss Google. I'd wondered why you wanted to know if she was working today."

Toby tore his gaze from Angie, ran his fingers through his closely cropped hair and focused on Sawyer. "What are you talking about? Who's Little Miss Google?"

"Evangeline Edwards, our part-time receptionist and jack-of-all-trades."

Toby never had been good at lying, so he zeroed in on the subject he'd rather discuss. "Why do you call her Little Miss Google?"

"Because she's a walking version of the website. If you want any information about anything at all, there's a pretty good chance she knows it."

While Toby had never considered Angie to be dumb, she hadn't struck him as being exceptionally knowledgeable, either.

Had he missed something?

"You don't believe me? Watch this." Sawyer called across the open reception room. "Hey, Angie, Captain Schroder called a few minutes ago. Laurel wasn't around for me to ask, but he's flying his client's new Cessna Nav into Horseback Hollow. He wants to know how many feet per minute his descent should be."

Angie didn't look up from her work. "If his true air-

speed is 75 knots, which is standard for most Cessna
Navs on approach, our headwind component here is
usually 15 knots. That would make his ground speed
60 knots, which you'd multiply by five for a rate of descent of 300 feet per minute."

"Thanks. I'll let him know." Sawyer gave Toby a
little jab with his elbow, then tilted his head and lifted
a single eyebrow as if to ask, *What'd I tell you?*

Toby had no way of knowing if what Angie had re-
cited was true or not, but he figured it must be. Pete
the mechanic hadn't argued the point. Of course, he
still had his nose in the newspaper.

Moments later, Laurel Redmond Fortune came
through the same back door Sawyer had entered. The
lovely blonde greeted Toby with a hug, then gave her
husband a kiss. "I'm going to grab a quick cup of coffee in the break room, then I'll give you guys that tour
we promised."

"Take your time," Toby said.

As Laurel left the room, Pete lowered the newspaper he'd been reading. "Did you guys know that Herb
Walker got busted for drunk-and-disorderly conduct
last night outside the Two Moon Saloon?"

Sawyer gave Toby another little elbow jab, then
said, "I wonder what kind of bail his wife will have
to post for him."

"Normally, it would be twenty-five hundred dollars," Angie said, "but seeing how today is Monday and
Judge Hanson doesn't approve of drinking on Sundays,
drunk and disorderlies from the night before usually
have to post four thousand."

Angie's position on her knees, as she placed the last

of the papers in the very back of the lowest drawer, gave Toby an excellent view of the rear end Doris Edwards had criticized days earlier. But Toby was so busy picking up his jaw off the floor that he was having trouble concentrating on those lovely curves.

How did she know those random facts?

When Sawyer and Pete started to laugh, Angie finally looked up and clued in to what was happening. "Were you guys doing that Google thing again?"

"What's a drunk and disorderly?" Kylie asked, reminding the adults that the kids were still hanging around.

"It's what Aunt Barbara got arrested for," Brian answered, displaying knowledge beyond his age.

The laughter suddenly ceased, and the adults sobered. Fortunately, Angie swooped in for the save. "Hey, Brian, Mr. Fortune said you could go sit in the cockpit of his brand-new Gulfstream. You can even touch every button and lever. And Mr. Nelson won't mind a bit putting them all back into place after you guys mess with them to your heart's content."

As a whoop went up from the kids, Angie cheekily smiled at her boss and the mechanic.

About that time, Laurel came out of the break room with her coffee. "Let's go, kids."

"I call first on talking on the headset to the people in the control tower," Justin said.

"I get to sit in the pilot's chair first," Brian countered, as he followed Laurel out the door.

"Wait for me," Kylie yelled as she tried to keep up with her brothers, who were already headed toward the hangar with Laurel.

The mechanic and Sawyer both gave Angie a look that promised they'd get even with her. But as far as Toby could see, they'd messed with Angie first.

It was nice to see that she gave back as good as she got.

"Laurel's going to need my help," Sawyer said.

"Mine, too." Pete set aside the newspaper, grabbed his disposable cup and followed Sawyer outside, leaving Toby and Angie alone.

Finally.

"How do you know so much?" he asked.

"I used to watch *Jeopardy!* a lot with my dad when he was sick, and trivial facts tend to stick in my brain. Plus, I did a lot of internet research when I was trying to decide upon a college major." She glanced at the clock on the wall, noting that it was four.

She straightened her desk, then shut down her computer. As she reached for her purse, she added, "Learning various oddball things is also a perk to changing jobs frequently. So I ended up knowing a little something about everything. Obviously, the flight stuff, I learned here."

As she pushed back her chair, he couldn't help noticing those long, tanned legs emerging from the skirt that no longer seemed too short.

"What about the drunk and disorderly?" he asked. "Is that from a job or from firsthand experience?" *Please don't let her be a party girl,* he found himself thinking.

"Do I look like the drunk-and-disorderly type?" She turned back to Toby. She must have noticed his gaze on her legs, because she crossed her arms and said, "Don't answer that."

"Sorry."

She didn't seem to be actually annoyed, though, because there was a spark of humor in her voice when she added, "Before that temp agency folded, they sent me to work at Señor Paco's Bail Bonds for a few weeks."

That was a relief. Not that he planned to actually date her.

Or did he?

"Aren't you going out with the kids to see the new plane?" she asked.

He'd much rather learn about Angie's control panel than some stupid airplane's, especially since it was four o'clock and she was leaving.

Who knew when he'd see her again, which brought out an unexpected sense of urgency, prompting him to blurt out, "Do you want to come over for dinner tonight?"

Dinner? At the Double H Ranch? With Toby and the kids?

The invitation had come out of the blue, and judging from the expression on Toby's face, Angie suspected that the question had surprised him as much as it had her.

"I'm not sure what we'll be having," he added. "I'll have to stop by the Superette and pick up something. But the kids need to eat tonight. And if you're not busy…"

"Actually, I have to stop by there to pick up my paycheck anyway. Do you want me to do the shopping for you?"

"That would be great." Toby reached into his back pocket, pulled out his wallet and peeled out a couple of bills. "Here's forty bucks. Pick up whatever you think the kids will like."

Great. The choice was hers, then?

Not only had she agreed to have dinner with him and the kids, she'd also agreed to plan the menu, which meant she'd be stuck trying to decide what to cook for a hungry man and three picky children.

What had she been thinking?

At least he'd given her the money to pay for the groceries. She wasn't sure how she would have been able to afford them if he hadn't.

"Do you know how to get to the ranch?" he asked.

She tossed him a smile. "I'm sure I can find my way there."

Ten minutes later, she was walking up and down the aisles of the Superette, grabbing packages and cans in record time.

Julia Tierney, who'd been working the check stand, laughed when Angie started laying items out on the conveyor belt.

"What's so funny?" Angie asked her friend and boss.

"Girl, I haven't seen you make such quick decisions on what to buy since that time you came running in here after that chili-pepper-eating contest with Mr. Murdock. You grabbed the first bottle of Mylanta you could find and drained it right in the middle of aisle three."

Sometimes, when Angie didn't have time to think about it, she could be rather decisive. And her tummy had been on fire that day.

She shook off Julia's teasing. "I'm picking up dinner for Toby and his kids this evening. And since I'm sure everyone's probably hungry, I don't have time to roam the aisles, stewing about what to cook."

Julia glanced at the items she rang up. "Pizza sauce, mozzarella cheese, pepperoni slices, mushrooms, ham, peppers, onions, ice cream, strawberries, instant bread mix. Looks like you'll be having homemade pizza."

"I figured it would be safe, especially if the kids can make their own."

"That's clever," Julia said. "I couldn't have come up with a better idea myself."

That was quite the compliment. Julia had always dreamed of going to culinary school or maybe getting a degree in restaurant management, but when her father suffered a heart attack, she'd decided to stick close to home and help out her parents with the store. So she'd given up her dream.

However, now that her father was better, it looked as though her dreams would finally come true. When Wendy and Marcos Mendoza finally opened up The Hollows Cantina in the next month or so, Julia was going to manage it.

"Yeah, well, I've learned that if you can't choose just one thing, it's best to have plenty of options available."

"Good idea," Julia said, as she totaled Angie's purchases.

"How are things going with the new restaurant?"

"Great. I love what Marcos and Wendy have envisioned, and it's really coming together. In fact, I was going over some of the job applications we've gotten and saw yours. We won't be scheduling interviews yet, but I wanted you to know that you're at the top of the pile."

"Thanks. That's nice to know." Angie helped Julia bag her purchases. "Who's going to take over for you here?"

"My mother's sister just retired from a cable-television company in Lubbock. So she's going to move in with my folks and help out for a while. I think it's all going to work out nicely."

"I'm glad to hear that."

"So tell me," Julia said. "This thing with Toby and the kids... That's a little intriguing."

Only because Julia was in love with Liam, Toby's brother. And she had stars in her eyes and thought everyone else should, too.

"We're just friends," Angie said.

Of course, she'd caught Toby staring at her legs a few times earlier today. And unlike a lot of other men she'd caught gawking like that, he'd seemed to be interested in more than just her appearance.

"Didn't I once hear you say that you never liked limiting your options?" Julia asked.

Yes, that was Angie. Her father had always told her that life wasn't an Etch A Sketch. That she ought to weigh each decision carefully, especially when it came to choosing a career—or a spouse.

Otherwise, she could find herself stuck in a really bad place.

She supposed that was why she'd never been able to settle on a college major or to find a job that interested her for very long—or a man worth making any kind of commitment to.

Angie didn't respond to Julia's question. Instead, she thanked Julia, took the two bags of groceries and headed for her car.

No, Toby Fortune Jones wasn't in the running when it came to considering romantic possibilities.

But if he wasn't an option, then what was he?

The answer came to her as she placed the pizza fixings into her car and prepared to head for the Double H Ranch.

Toby Fortune was one fine cowboy who was far too attractive for her own good.

Chapter Four

After Toby finished overseeing the homework hour, he told the kids they could watch television before dinner. Then he went into the kitchen to check the pantry. It wasn't as though his cupboards were bare. He could certainly rustle up something to add to whatever Angie planned to cook.

He'd no more than scanned the canned goods in the pantry when he heard a car pull up. Knowing it had to be her, he went outside to greet her.

As she climbed out of the driver's seat of a black Toyota Celica that had seen better years, let alone days, she reached into the back for the first of two eco-friendly bags. Her hair had been pulled back in a ponytail when she'd been at Redmond-Fortune Air, but it hung loose around her shoulders now—soft, glossy and teased by a light evening breeze.

She wasn't wearing anything different—just that black skirt and white blouse. Yet tonight, for some crazy reason, he found himself a wee bit... Hell, he didn't know what to call it—starstruck, stagestruck, dumbstruck...?

"Here. Let me help you with those." He reached for the bags, and she handed them over.

As they headed for the house, he said, "I'm sorry for not having stuff on hand to cook. When I lived by myself, I could go weeks without grocery shopping. But since the kids have been living here, it seems like I need to restock my fridge every other day."

She tossed him a carefree smile. "You should probably shop at one of those warehouse stores where you can buy in bulk and use a flatbed cart to haul your purchases to the checkout line."

"If I didn't have to drive clear to Lubbock to find one, I would. But then again, the kids wouldn't get to come into the Superette all the time and see you."

Toby chanced a glance at the woman walking next to him, wondering if she knew the kids weren't the only ones who'd miss seeing her.

"The kids are fun," she said. "I like it when they come in."

What if he didn't have children? Would she like it when he came in?

"Nice house," she said, as they entered the living room, which always managed to stay tidy because there wasn't a television set or a video game in sight. "I've always liked the ranch style."

Toby slowed his steps long enough to scan the white walls, the open-beamed ceilings, the distressed hardwood floors, the stone fireplace, as well as the leather furniture. "Thanks. I've been meaning to add a little color, maybe some Southwestern-style pictures on the wall, but I haven't gotten around to it yet."

"I'm sure the kids take up most of your free time."

"You got that right." He carried her purchases into the kitchen and placed the bags on the white tile countertop.

"What are we having?" he asked.

"Pizza. And just the way everyone likes it."

"Great idea. But I've never told you my pizza preference." There had to be some things even Ms. Google didn't know, unless she was psychic.

She tossed him a breezy smile. "I'll bet I even have your specific preference covered."

Something told him not to take her up on any wagers or else he'd end up in some wacky competition with her, just like Mr. Murdock.

But then again, Toby had always liked a good challenge. And Angie Edwards would prove to be one heck of one—if he were to pursue her.

"Hmm," she said, as she studied the directions on the box of instant bread-dough mix. "This might not be enough. Do you have any flour?"

"It's in the pantry. I'll get it. Is there anything else I can do to help?"

"You can wash the veggies, chop them up and put them in separate containers. Do you have a cutting board and knife?"

"Sure do."

While Toby got busy on his assignments, Angie began kneading the dough. Next they sliced the pepperoni and grated the cheese. Before long, they were moving around the kitchen seamlessly, almost as if they'd worked together a hundred times.

"So let me ask you something," Angie said.

Oh, no, here it comes, he thought. *She wants to know why I keep showing up at her workplaces and inviting her to hang out with me and the kids.*

"How do you do it?" she asked.

"Excuse me?"

"I couldn't help noticing your refrigerator door. It's plastered with papers—Kylie's artwork, Justin's B+ in spelling, the graph Brian created in math, not to mention that bulletin board with the YMCA flyers posted all over it. Then there's a list of dance classes and the schedule for swim lessons. I'm amazed that a single dad is so supportive of his kids. But what really blows me away is that LEGO-themed calendar you have on the wall."

"When I was a kid, our fridge was always covered in stuff like that. And my mom used to display all our awards and trophies throughout the house. She kept a bulletin board in the kitchen, too. Right next to the telephone. But why does the calendar surprise you?"

"Because almost every square this month is full. And just look at this list of YMCA classes. Nearly all of them are circled."

"You think that's too many?"

"Not for the kids. It's great for them. But the YMCA is in Vicker's Corners, which is a bit of a drive from the ranch. And I'm worried about you. I was an only child, with two parents. And it was all they could do to get me to school, the sitter and to any medical appointments."

"I have to admit, it's tough sometimes."

She crossed her arms, as if she was going to scold him, but she smiled and her eyes sparkled in mirth. "Toby, you're doing it to yourself. It's only April, and you have them in swim lessons? It's not even summer vacation yet."

"I know, but Justin can't swim. And he wants to go to camp in June. So I figured we'd better get started on those lessons so I won't have to worry about him." Toby shrugged and added, "Besides, I don't mind running them around. They've had it rough ever since their mom died. And they've missed out on a lot of things— like parents and a happy home. I just want them to see what it's like to have a normal family life."

"I think that's wonderful. So don't get me wrong. I'm happy for them. And I think it's awesome that you're providing them with so many opportunities, especially when you're the only one available to drive them back and forth. It's just that I know how much you must be sacrificing, and I'm not even talking about the cost of those activities."

Toby thought about the old beat-up car sitting in his driveway and the fixer-upper granny flat in which she lived. Apparently money was an issue for her.

He was pretty sure that Angie couldn't care less about his family's financial situation—or rather, the wealth most folks seemed to think they had by way of their rich relations. But he had reason to believe her mother didn't feel the same way.

So just in case he'd misread Angie, he figured it wouldn't hurt to let it be known that if a woman was looking for a wealthy "catch," she wouldn't find him living on the Double H Ranch.

"I want the kids to stay busy, even if that keeps me hopping. I hired a foreman early on to take on a lot of my work and responsibilities, which put another strain on the finances, especially since the Double H doesn't bring in that kind of money yet. So I've had to scrimp in other ways."

"Yes," she said. "I know."

He cocked his head slightly. So he'd been right? She was not only smart, but a psychic, too? No, that couldn't be right.

"What do you mean?" he asked.

She pointed to the bag of flour on the counter, which he'd picked up at the Superette because it was half the price of the name brand.

"Oh. You mean because I bargain-shop."

She laughed. "You didn't get a deal. That flour is too inferior for any proper baking, and it was aging on the shelf. So the price was discounted, but it still isn't selling—except to people who don't know anything about cooking."

"Oh, yeah? It seems to work well enough." Toby reached into the bag, grabbed a handful of flour and blew the mound directly into her pretty little upturned face. "See? It's light and airy."

"Oh, you…" Angie sputtered through the white dust covering her lower face, then quickly picked up a mushroom she'd been chopping and threw it directly between his eyes.

The vegetable struck him dead center. He laughed,

and she reached into the bag of flour—no doubt wanting to dust his face a ghostly white, just as hers was.

He grabbed her wrist to stop her, and she twisted, trying to pull free. Then, as their eyes met, she stopped. He stopped. For a moment, everything stopped—time, breathing, heartbeats....

No, not heartbeats. He could feel her pulse pounding in her wrist, under his fingertips.

Their gazes remained locked, and something passed between them. Before he could figure out just what the heck it was, Kylie ran into the kitchen, breaking the tension, as well as the silence.

When she spotted Angie, her eyes widened. "What happened to your face? It's a great big mess."

"I know." Angie laughed.

So did Toby. "She might be a champ at playing Ms. Pac-Man, but she's no match for Mr. Ranch-Man."

"Cute," Angie said. "Very cute."

He tossed her the dish towel closest to him. She caught it, then walked to the sink, dampened it and wiped off her face.

"Is dinner ready yet?" Kylie asked.

"Almost, honey." Angie grabbed a slice of Kylie's favorite American cheese. "Snack on this and I'll call you guys in just a couple of minutes."

"Okay." Kylie took the cheese, then dashed out of the kitchen and back to the family room.

Deciding to get their earlier conversation back on track, Toby said, "Actually, just to set the record straight, the Horseback Hollow Fortunes aren't rich like our cousins from Red Rock, Atlanta or the U.K. So taking on the kids did put me in a financial bind at first, but not for long. Someone apparently wanted to help out and donated money to cover those expenses and then some."

"That's amazing. What a generous gift."

"It certainly was. I wish I could thank them, but it was an anonymous donor."

"Could it have been their father or maybe one of their long-lost relatives?" she asked.

Toby snorted. "I doubt that. I'm more inclined to think that it was one of *my* long-lost family members."

"Who? Or would you rather not share that with me?"

"My best guess and number one suspect is James Marshall Fortune, Sawyer's father and my mother's brother. I think it was his way of indirectly giving my mom some of those shares of stock she returned to him last year. But I'm not going to push too hard to find out. If the donor wants to remain anonymous, then I'll respect that."

"Nevertheless, I still think it's wonderful that someone wanted to help the kids."

"That's how I see it, too. The money was actually given to me through an attorney in Lubbock, along with a note saying that it was to offset the costs I incurred by taking in the kids. But that I should spend it as I saw fit. That's what made me think the donor had to be my uncle." Toby raked his hand through his hair. "I wrestled with my pride for a while and was tempted to refuse it. But then I realized the kids really deserved it. And it would provide a better life for them. So I decided not to look a gift horse in the mouth."

"I assume it was a substantial amount."

"Enough to see them each through high school and

to pay for their college. So I put the money into a trust fund for them. It's invested and provides a monthly income that helps cover their expenses and pays for extra things like swim lessons and dance classes. Summer camp, too. Stuff like that."

"Wow. That's awesome." She tossed him a dazzling smile, then added, "*You're* awesome, Toby."

Angie gazed at him as if he'd just been awarded the Medal of Honor. And while he found her admiration touching, it also felt undeserved. So he lobbed a playful smile at her in return. "Yep. A horrible bargain shopper, but an awesome man."

Toby leaned toward the bag of cheap flour again and Angie threw up her arms in protection. "No, no, I give up. You are not only a good man, but a fine steward of your money. You make excellent shopping decisions. You should be on that coupon show on TV."

"Now I know you're full of it," Toby said, laughing along with her.

Teasing had been a way of life in the Fortune Jones household, and he liked that Angie was the kind of woman who found it so easy to banter.

"Okay," she said. "The ingredients are all set."

"Do you want me to call in the kids?"

"Go right ahead. I'll turn on the oven and get the drinks." Angie went to the refrigerator door, paused and stared at the most recent flyer. "Speaking of saving money, it looks like they're offering two free weeks of classes at the Y this month. Maybe I should check into that. I've always wanted to see what yoga is all about."

Toby didn't know if she was talking to him or to

herself, but apparently there was yet another interest she wanted to add to what had to be a lengthy list.

She tossed him a pretty smile. "Who knows? Maybe I'll become a yoga instructor someday."

"Speaking of people who run around too much," he said, returning her smile with a teasing grin, "what about you?"

"Me?" Angie tilted her head slightly and furrowed her brow. "What about me?"

"You seem to change jobs a lot. Why not find a good, full-time position and stick with it?"

"I will someday. But I want something that I can feel passionate about. Maybe, if I keep trying different things, I'll eventually find the career I'm best suited for."

He hoped she came across it soon—for her sake.

And maybe for his. She really was easy to talk to, and the kids adored her. If she were more settled, he'd like to see where this relationship—if he could even call it that—would go.

But he couldn't risk allowing himself or the kids to get too close to someone who could be gone working on an oil rig or joining the military or going to cosmetology school or wherever the wind took her next month.

Unless, of course, Angie had already worked on an oil rig and had crossed that off her to-do list.

If he didn't have the kids and didn't need her help, he'd...

He'd what? Cut her loose?

That might be the wisest thing to do.

So why did he feel like reeling her in?

Because she was beautiful. And fun to be around. In fact, if he didn't have the kids to think about, good ole dependable Toby might even consider doing something wild and crazy—like having a one-night stand or a weekend fling with her.

Talk about something totally out of character for a guy like him.

But yeah, if he were footloose and fancy-free, that was exactly what he'd do.

As he took another glance at Angie, saw the glimmer in her eyes, caught a whiff of her citrusy scent...

Well, heck. If he had a babysitter willing to spend the weekend at the ranch with the kids, he just might consider taking Angie for a night or two on the town in Lubbock anyway.

The pizza-making station had been a smashing success. Altogether, they'd created three medium lopsided pizzas, one supersized with only meat, and one that was perfectly formed with every single topping.

Once the homemade creations came out of the oven, the kids could hardly wait for them to cool before they scarfed them down.

"Thanks for dinner," Toby said. "It was awesome."

"It sure was," Justin said. "I never made pizza before. It was fun."

"I'm glad you liked it." Angie turned to the boys. "Hey, guys. I don't suppose I could get you to do me a favor. After we get the kitchen cleaned up, I was hoping you'd teach me a few tricks on your PlayStation. I need a crash course."

"Sure!" Justin turned to his older brother, and the boys pumped their fists in the air.

"Seriously? You want a lesson from the kids?" Toby asked. "And why the big rush?"

"Mr. Murdock won his grandson's PlayStation from him in a poker game."

Toby lifted his eyebrow. "He gambled with a kid?"

"Long story. Anyway, he's been beating me left and right on Madden."

"Oh, great," Toby said, a spark of humor in his tone. "I thought I'd brought in adult reinforcement, but I've ended up with a fourth kid."

"Come on," Justin said. "Let's go, Angie."

"We have dishes to do first," she reminded him.

"No, you go ahead," Toby said. "I'll take care of the cleanup."

"Are you sure you don't mind?"

"After you pulled off such a successful dinner? Heck no. Besides, I'd hate to see Mr. Murdock get the best of you again."

She laughed, then took off with the boys.

Twenty minutes later, Toby reminded them that it was a school night.

"Aw, man," Justin said.

Angie wrapped her arms around his shoulders and gave him a squeeze. "You heard what Toby said. Maybe I'll come back another night, and we'll play again."

Toby let the kids stay up long enough to eat a bowl of ice cream topped with fresh strawberries for dessert. Then it was time for them to go to bed.

Overall, it was one of the best evenings Angie had ever had. At least since… Well, since she'd had din-

ner with Toby and the kids a couple of nights ago at
The Grill.

Kylie approached the chair where Angie was sitting and placed a hand on her knee. "Will you read
my Disney princess book to me before I go to bed?"

"I don't mind." Angie looked at Toby for the ulti-
mate okay.

"It's all right with me. Each night at bedtime, I read
a story to her. After that, I read a chapter out of *Treasure Island* with the boys. We're at a pretty exciting
part, so it'll be nice to get back to where we left off."

What a nice family ritual. Angie was glad she'd
been given a chance to take part in it.

By the time she'd read the princess story twice, gotten Kylie two glasses of water to drink and checked in
the closet and under the bed for dragons three times,
Kylie finally drifted off to sleep.

As Angie quietly sneaked out of the little girl's
room, she wondered if she should wait for Toby, or
just let herself out. Fortunately, she didn't have to make
a decision.

Having finished his bedtime duties, Toby was already back in the living room, picking up ice-cream
dishes and putting the sofa cushions and throw pillows back in place.

"Listen," he said, "I can't thank you enough for your
help with the kids. When I do handle bedtime by myself, it takes another hour."

"The kids really are amazing." And Angie meant
that from the bottom of her heart. She couldn't believe
her mom had referred to those sweet, adorable children as "rug rats."

"Look at *you*," Toby said. "You're the one who's *amazing*. I can't believe how quickly the kids have taken to you. Brian even talked to you about the girls in his class, and Justin didn't try to sneak off to the barn once while you were here. And Kylie... Well, I can't even tell you how great it's been for her to be around a woman. My mom and my sisters help out whenever they can, but they've got such full schedules and lives."

Did he think Angie didn't have much of a life? Or was she reading too much into what he was saying?

"Anyway," he said, "you're great with kids. Are you planning to have some of your own someday?"

"I haven't really given it much thought." She'd never been around children all that much. And her mom hadn't made any big deal about motherhood— or parenthood, for that matter. So she'd never really considered it one way or the other.

She did have to admit, though, that being around Toby's kids had made her see motherhood in a brand-new light.

"I suppose I'd have to think about getting married first," she said. "And that's never been a priority."

Toby seemed to straighten at that. "You mean to tell me that you're twenty-four, incredibly beautiful, fun and smarter than an internet search engine, and there hasn't been a single guy who's come along and made you think about bridal showers and wedding cakes and the whole nine yards?"

Toby thought she was beautiful? And fun? And smart?

"I...uh...thought about it once, but it didn't work out." She hoped he wouldn't ask for details. She hated talking about it. And there'd been so many witnesses that inevitably the subject always seemed to crop up when she least wanted it to.

"What happened?" he asked.

So much for hoping.

"I dated this guy once. David. He wasn't especially handsome, but he was bright and had a great personality. I really liked him, so we dated a couple of months—which was longer than most of my relationships last. But one night, he ruined everything."

"What did he do?"

"He insisted upon taking me to the Two Moon Saloon, and when we arrived, a lot of my friends were there. Even my mom showed up, which should have been a major clue that something was off-kilter. But apparently, come to find out, my mother had been coaching him."

"Your mom *coached* him? What happened?"

"Apparently, with her help and encouragement, David planned this elaborate and romantic proposal in front of an audience. Everyone was expecting me to say yes. So I did. And then two days later, I gave him the ring back."

"Why didn't you want to marry him?"

"Everyone asked me that same question. The truth is, I didn't know. And I still don't. Heck, I can't even commit to a brand of shampoo long enough to take advantage of a two-for-one sale. How could I have made a lifelong commitment like that without feeling something?"

"You didn't feel anything for him? I thought you said he was a great guy."

"Yes, but I never had the zing. You know what I mean?"

"I'm not sure that I do."

"It's that heart-spinning, soul-stirring rush that you get when you know the other person is 'the one.'"

"I can't say that I've ever felt that way," he said.

"Yeah, well, I've never felt it, either. But I've read about it. And if I ever make that kind of forever-commitment to someone, I want to feel it. And I didn't have it with David."

"So you broke up with him."

"Um. Yeah. But I should have ended things way before I did." She blew out a sigh.

Toby didn't say anything. He just stared at her. But she knew what he must be thinking. It was the same thing everyone else always thought about her—that she was unreliable and scattered and wouldn't know a good decision if it fell from the top shelf of a Superette display case and landed straight on her head.

Suddenly embarrassed that she'd revealed so much, she realized she'd better regroup, which was her standard operating procedure when things got sticky or icky or whatever.

So she grabbed her purse and decided to bolt before she could change her mind, climb into Toby's lap and tell him that she was already feeling more for him than she'd ever felt for David.

And before he could respond by reiterating that he wasn't looking for a girlfriend or a potential mom for his foster kids.

"Anyway," she said, "I have to get home before it gets too late or I'll have Mr. Murdock out looking for me."

"Thanks again for dinner."

"You're more than welcome. I'll see you around town sometime."

She was just about to make her escape when he tossed her a smile that sent her heart spinning and set off a little…?

Oh, no. It couldn't be.

Surely, it wasn't.

But it certainly felt like a zing.

Chapter Five

Angie had been kicking herself the past two days for bolting from Toby's house the other night. He'd never even commented on her story about David, yet assuming he'd think the worst of her, she'd left before he could say anything.

Wasn't that typical? When the going got tough, Angie skedaddled.

But why had she been in such a hurry to escape? If he hadn't considered her to be flighty before, he probably did now.

She just hoped she hadn't ruined their friendship, because she really enjoyed her time spent with him and the kids. She was just about to close down the register and clock out when the subject of her thoughts for the past forty-eight hours approached with the kids in tow.

"We're getting ice cream," Kylie announced, as she placed a frozen chocolate bar on the conveyor belt.

"I thought an after-school treat was in order," Toby said.

If he'd wanted to avoid her, he could have stopped by The Grill for that ice cream. So obviously he hadn't thought that badly about her.

"What're you guys up to today?" she asked, as she rang up his purchase.

"I need to take Justin to the YMCA for his swim lesson," Toby said. "But Kylie's dance practice was moved up earlier in the day, which is a problem since I can't be in two places at once. And so, I wondered if there was any chance you'd be getting off soon."

"As a matter of fact, I am."

"I don't suppose you could do me a huge favor."

When he gazed at her with those big baby blues, she said, "Sure."

Anything, she thought.

"Can you either take Kylie to dance or Justin to the Y?" he asked.

"Actually, I'd planned to stop by the Y and check out that yoga class today. So I can take Justin with me, then bring him to the ranch when we're done."

"Great. That would sure help me out. And this time, I'll have dinner ready for you."

"Meals at the ranch could become habit-forming," she said.

"Maybe, but everything seems to go better when you're around." He flashed her a smile, and there it went.

An almost definite zing.

Twenty minutes later, Angie dropped Justin off with his swim instructor, a lanky teen who barely looked old enough to drive. She wondered if he was qualified to be giving lessons and certified in CPR, but she decided he must be or the Y wouldn't have hired him.

"I'm going to take my class now," she told Justin. "You'll probably get finished a few minutes before me, so change into your dry clothes, then meet me by the vending machines. I'll buy you a candy bar as soon as I get there."

"Cool."

She remembered Toby telling her that the eight-year-old wasn't a very strong swimmer, so she wanted to make sure that he didn't hang around the pool without supervision. He also had a habit of wandering, so she figured a bribe to stay at a designated location was a good idea.

Satisfied that Justin was in good hands—and that she'd thought of everything, Angie headed to the front desk to find out where the yoga class was being held.

A young woman, clearly the receptionist, pointed her down the hall.

Angie turned in that direction, her gaze scanning the entry of the building, just as Mr. Murdock pushed open the double doors and walked inside.

He was wearing a red T-shirt with Semper Fi printed in yellow letters in front. He also had on a pair of green-and-white Hawaiian-print swim trunks and blue flip-flops.

"Hey," she said. "What are you doing here, Mr. Murdock? Are you a member of the Y?"

"Just joined yesterday. My doctor says I gotta exercise. So I'm heading out to the aquatics area. Thought I'd swim a few laps. How about you?"

"I just dropped off Justin, Toby's boy, for his swim lesson. And while he's there, I'm going to take a yoga class. They're offering free classes this month."

"You and Toby are getting pretty tight," Mr. Murdock said, lifting a single gray brow in that paternal way of his.

"We're just friends. I've been helping out with the kids."

"Humph." Mr. Murdock folded his arms and rested them on his ample belly. "Is that what you call it?"

Okay, so she'd been questioning that herself, too. But she wasn't about to admit it—especially in public.

"No need for you to be jealous, Mr. Murdock." She gave the old man a wink. "My heart will always belong to you."

"Glad to hear that, Girly. I'm getting pretty used to having you around the house." Then he winked back at her and shuffled off toward the pool, leaving her to scope out that yoga class—which she'd better hurry to or she'd be late.

When the class was over and she'd released her last pose, Angie didn't stick around to talk to anyone. Instead she hurried to meet Justin and buy him that treat.

But when she reached the vending machines, he was nowhere in sight. Were there other places to get snacks in the building that she hadn't known about? Some that were outside?

Oh, no. Not by the pool. She'd tried to tempt him with a treat to keep him away from the water.

She quickly made her way out to the aquatics area,

which was directly behind the building. But after a quick scan, she still didn't see him.

Darn it. Where was he? She should have known better than to have taken that yoga class. She should have sat by the pool and watched his swim lesson instead.

Panic set in, raising her heart rate to the level of a full-scale cardio workout. She hurried into the building, but she didn't dare ask if anyone had seen him.

What if word got out that she'd lost him? Not only would that further perpetuate everyone's belief that she was unreliable, but social services might get wind of it. What if they investigated Toby and somehow found him lacking because he'd entrusted a child with a flaky, irresponsible friend?

Mere seconds later, both of those concerns paled when she still hadn't found Justin. Where could he be?

When she spotted the swim instructor coming out of the men's locker room, she nearly accosted him when she asked, "Have you seen Justin Hemings?"

"No, not since his lesson ended ten minutes ago."

Oh, God. He could have been kidnapped, whisked away from here by some predator. And all on her watch.

Angie rushed back to the aquatics area for one last look, the teenage instructor now fast on her heels.

The area had pretty much cleared, except for Mr. Murdock, who sat on the edge of the pool's shallow end, his feet dangling into the water, his face red, his breathing labored, his hand clutching his chest.

Oh, dear God. Poor Mr. Murdock was having a heart attack. What else could possibly go wrong?

"Call 911," she told the swim instructor. "That man needs an ambulance."

Then she ran to her friend to let him know that help was on the way. When she reached him, he pointed to the pool, where Justin's body lay at the bottom.

"No!" she screamed, as she leaped into the water, clothes and all. She grabbed the child, pulled him to the surface and dragged him to the steps. "I've got you, honey. I've got you."

Justin, whose eyes opened and grew wide, appeared dazed. Or was he confused? He looked at Mr. Murdock, gasped, then called out, "What was my time? Did I win?"

"Win?" Angie shrieked. "Win what?"

"Me and Mr. Murdock were having a contest to see who could hold their breath the longest."

In her panic to save the boy's life, Angie had nearly forgotten about Mr. Murdock. But several bystanders, as well as YMCA employees, had now gathered around the older man and were trying to help.

"Are you okay?" one woman who appeared to be in management asked the retired marine.

"The paramedics are on their way," the teenage swim instructor said.

"You won…that round," Mr. Murdock told Justin, his voice coming out in short little pants. "But give me…a second. We'll go…best two…out of three."

A *contest?* They'd been having a fool competition?

Angie, who'd always prided herself on being cool, calm and collected in a crisis, practically shouted, *"Nobody* is going back in that water. You two nearly scared the living daylights out of me. And the whole time you were only competing in a stupid challenge. I can't blame Justin for acting childish. But really, Mr. Murdock, you should know better."

Before the elderly man could respond or even catch his breath, the ambulance arrived, along with a hook-and-ladder truck. Two firemen brought a gurney to the pool, while a female paramedic carried her bag and placed it next to Mr. Murdock.

The tough old man waved her away, especially when she tried to attach an oxygen mask to his face.

Justin seemed none the worse for wear, thank goodness.

"Can I have a ride in the ambulance?" he asked one of the firemen.

"That depends," the fireman said, nodding toward Mr. Murdock. "Is this man your grandfather? And did you ride with him here today?"

"No, they're not related," Angie clarified. "And we're *not* riding in the ambulance. We need to go back to the ranch."

"Then can I see how you turn on the siren?" the boy asked.

"Maybe after we get this gentleman loaded up," the fireman said.

"Who, *me?*" Mr. Murdock asked, apparently realizing that the 911 call had been made for him. "I ain't going nowhere in no damn ambulance. And I don't need no siren. My ticker is just fine. I only got a little winded after a friendly competition with the boy."

"A competition?" the paramedic asked. "Maybe we should start at the beginning. What's going on here?"

Justin explained what had happened, going so far

as to tell them how Angie had tried to save his life, even though it didn't need saving.

"Mr. Murdock beat me the first round," Justin said, "but he taught me how to let the bubbles out my nose to keep the air in my lungs longer."

"Well, I don't think Mr. Murdock's lungs are doing so great right about now," Angie mumbled in frustration. Her worry now switched to the old man.

Mr. Murdock finally ripped the oxygen mask out of the female paramedic's well-intentioned hand and threw it about ten feet into the pool.

Then he pointed an arthritic finger at the poor woman only trying to do her job. "I *said* I don't need medical attention. What I need is a Scotch and a cigarette."

Angie wanted to tell the old man that she didn't think his lungs could take the extra stress of inhaling tobacco right this second. But before she could, he turned to her and said, "You done good, Girly. No one was drowning, but if the kid had been, your response time was the quickest I've ever seen."

A wet Mr. Murdock in a saggy bathing suit shuffled to his feet and dripped his way to the changing rooms with the paramedics still following him.

A 911 call was big news and everyone inside the YMCA had now gathered around the pool area to watch. There was no getting around it. She was going to be the talk of the town before nightfall.

Angie, her yoga outfit drenched in water and stuck tight to her skin, pulled Justin into her lap and held him close. Thank God everything had turned out okay.

Still, as she glanced at the oxygen mask floating to

the deep end of the pool, she sighed. What a day. She might have had the best of intentions, but she'd really screwed up.

How was she ever going to tell Toby that she'd nearly lost Justin—and that she just might be as flighty and irresponsible as everyone seemed to think that she was?

Toby had just pulled the chicken off his outdoor grill when the headlights of Angie's Toyota flashed, letting him know she was turning up the drive that led to his house.

He'd put Brian in charge of making the salad with the promise that if the kid could master assembling some easy dishes in the kitchen, Toby would teach him how to man the grill next time.

And it had worked like a charm.

When Angie and Justin climbed from the car, Toby called out, "You guys are just in time for dinner."

Neither of them spoke as they slowly made their way to the patio at the side of the house.

That seemed a bit odd.

Toby flashed Angie a smile, which she didn't return. And that was his second clue that something had gone wrong.

Why was her hair all wet and slicked back?

Uh-oh. Her clothes were wet, too.

Before he could ask, she said, "We had a bit of an incident at the pool."

"What happened?"

When she didn't give him a speedy reply, Justin answered. "Me and Mr. Murdock were having a breath-holding contest, and Angie thought I was drowning. So she jumped in the pool to save me."

Justin glanced at Angie, then at Toby, his eyes wary as though he was bracing himself for a scolding. But Toby was still waiting for Angie to say something.

Apparently, thinking he was off the hook, Justin brightened and really opened up. "It was pretty sweet, though. The firemen and paramedics came—with sirens and everything. But best of all, I beat Mr. Murdock at holding my breath. And then he cussed. And Angie yelled at both of us. And even though the fireman said I couldn't ride in the ambulance, but I could look inside, Angie wouldn't let me. But that's okay, because—"

Toby interrupted the boy's rambling dialogue and said, "Kiddo, why don't you go get some dry clothes on before dinner. I'll let Angie tell me the rest of the story."

There was no telling what all had transpired at the YMCA earlier, but knowing Justin's history of wandering off and Mr. Murdock's fierce competitive streak, Toby was able to piece a lot of it together.

After Justin ran inside, Toby turned his full attention to the soaking-wet woman. She'd better get out of her clothes, too.

Whoops. Now that was an intriguing thought. And an arousing one, seeing how the Lycra now covered her like a sexy layer of skin. But as tears filled her eyes, his thoughts cooled to sympathy.

Justin said she'd been angry earlier, but she appeared to be hurt now. Crushed, actually.

Uh-oh. This was bad.

What in blazes had happened?

"I'm *so* sorry," she said. "It's all my fault. I shouldn't have gone to that yoga class. I should've just stayed out by the pool with him. And then, when he wasn't where he was supposed to meet me, I thought of all the terrible things that could have happened to him, and I panicked. I guess you could say I had a meltdown, and everyone saw the whole thing."

"It couldn't have been that bad," he said.

"Oh, no? If I'd been on an E.R. reality show, the TV ratings would have shot through the roof. It was terrible, and I completely lost it."

She started rambling then, just as Justin had. And while her sweet face still looked confused in the aftermath of her unnecessary panic attack, the snug workout pants sent his testosterone soaring, and he nearly dropped the platter of grilled chicken he was holding.

Damn. If he didn't have his hands full, he'd pull her to him, wet Lycra and all, just to offer his comfort and whatever else he could.

"Salad's ready!" Brian yelled out the side door. "I'm starved. Can we start eating?"

"You go ahead and eat with the kids," Angie told him. "I'm not hungry. I need to go home and get out of these wet clothes. If you want to talk more about it, we can do that in the morning."

Then she turned toward her car.

"Wait!" Toby called to her back.

When she turned around, he said, "I'll give you some dry clothes and a glass of wine. You look like you could use both. And after dinner, you and I can sit down and enjoy some quiet time—adults only. Then you can tell me what happened. Or, if you'd rather, you can forget all about it."

Whatever would make her smile again.

That was, unless she wanted to get the hell away from him and the kids as fast as her toned legs would carry her.

And quite frankly, he wouldn't blame her if she did. After all, he'd known all along how it would end. And he'd implied as much to her a few days ago when they'd discussed his nonexistent love life.

Women saw him as some sort of Captain Rescue at first. And then they ran for the hills as soon as they came face-to-face with the reality of dealing with three kids, each of whom still had some issues after living in a dysfunctional household with their aunt Barbara. But they seemed to be getting through all that, especially since Angie had started coming around.

"You know," she said, "a glass of wine sounds great. Besides, if I go home now and run into Mr. Murdock, I just might ring his little ole leatherneck."

Toby laughed. At least her sense of humor was coming back.

He shifted the plate into his left hand, then slipped his arm around her shoulders. She leaned into him, and he gave her a gentle squeeze.

A guy could get used to comforting her, even when she was soaking wet. In fact, Toby might have just stood there, holding her all night, except he had children to feed.

"Come on," he said, as he led her to the kitchen, where the kids had gathered.

Once inside, he assigned them all chores so they

could eat sooner. "Check the rice steamer, Brian. Kylie, set a place for Angie. She's staying for dinner."

Kylie, who was down on her hands and knees, looked up from the floor, where she was picking up some dropped silverware. "I already set the table. Well, all but the forks and spoons."

Toby was about to warn her to get fresh utensils from the drawer, then he figured he may as well forget it since the housekeeper had been here today and had mopped the floor. So at least for tonight, the three-second rule for germ-free drops had become a three-minute rule, as far as he was concerned.

While the kids did as they'd been asked, Toby took Angie to his bedroom, where he began opening drawers, looking for something she could wear, something that might fit.

When he caught her looking at the king-sized bed in the center of the room, he wondered if she was thinking the same thing he was.

And just what *was* he thinking?

Right now, he didn't dare put it into words. Instead, he haphazardly handed her a worn-out Houston Texans T-shirt, along with a pair of his old cross-country shorts from Horseback Hollow High, which he figured would be too big.

If he had his way, he'd prefer to see her stay in those tight pants and sports tank. But they were wet. And even if they were dry, he had to find something else for her to wear—and quick.

It was killing him to see her looking so sexy and so vulnerable at the same time, especially since she was just an arm's distance and mere steps away from his bed.

"While you change," he said, "I'll get the wine."

Minutes later, everyone was sitting in their places when Angie came to the table. The kids must have picked up on her solemn mood, because they were so quiet you could hear a pin drop—or a man's heart beat, his blood race.

She'd rolled his shorts up at the waist to make them fit her. The shirt barely reached the hem of the shorts, making it look as though she wasn't wearing anything underneath.

Man, he needed to get a grip. There were kids present.

And thankfully, the kids soon began to chatter, because Angie remained quiet through dinner, sipping her wine and picking at her food.

When everyone else had eaten their fill, Toby said, "Okay, guys, no TV tonight. It's already time to pick up your rooms, take your baths and get ready for bed."

It really wasn't all that late, but Toby had waited long enough to get Angie alone.

With her being as pensive as she'd been at dinner, he hadn't expected her to help out with the evening routine the way she'd done the other night she'd been here. But she surprised him by stepping right up to the plate, which was nice. The kids liked having her around.

He did, too. But he'd have to be careful that nobody got too attached. Especially him.

When Toby finished reading the next chapter of *Treasure Island,* Angie was still with Kylie, so he went to the kitchen and started to clean up. He'd just loaded the dishwasher when she entered the room, her shoulders slumped.

"Come on," he said, wiping his hands on a dish towel. "The rest of this can wait until tomorrow."

After refilling her wineglass, he grabbed a cold beer out of the fridge for himself. Then they walked into the living room. The house was noticeably quieter with all the kids tucked in.

She took a sip of the chardonnay before practically collapsing on the sofa. He recognized the signs of an adrenaline dump. Or maybe she was just emotionally exhausted.

He sat next to her, and it seemed only natural to reach out, to touch her shoulder, to finger her hair. "Okay, tell me what's bothering you."

She let out a ragged sigh. "I feel as though I've let you down."

"Why would you think that? The way I see it, you took your responsibility seriously. I'm actually impressed."

"Thank you, but I never should have let him out of my sight in the first place." She closed her eyes.

"Don't blame yourself. The same thing happens to me at least four times a week. Justin is impulsive. He has a history of running off and doing his own thing, which led to some of the behavioral problems he was having at school. We've been working on correcting it, but he's eight. It happens. I should have better prepared you."

She shuddered, and he adjusted his body so he could pull her even closer. He reminded himself that she was upset and vulnerable now, but she felt so good in his arms. He stroked her back, his fingers unhampered by any bra straps. And with those long, tanned legs bare to her thighs, she was practically naked.

Aw, man. It would be so easy to take advantage of the situation. But should he?

Then what?

She had her head cradled against his shoulder, and he was tempted to kiss the top of her head—a gentle kiss meant to comfort. But something told him he wouldn't want to stop at gentle.

Or at the top of her head.

And kissing her would take their relationship to a level neither of them was ready for, not when three kids stood in the balance.

So he reined in his lust and didn't kiss her at all. But he probably should have taken the opportunity while he'd had the chance, because it seemed as though she was pulling away from him and getting to her feet before he knew it.

She was leaving? So soon?

"It's been a long day," she said. "I need to go."

He followed her to the door. He hated to see her go, but the fact that she was wearing his shirt and shorts gave him some comfort. If he wouldn't be sleeping with her, maybe his clothes would.

"Thanks for dinner and for understanding," she said, as she grabbed the oversized purse and the wet shoes she'd left just outside the front door.

When she straightened, their eyes met.

A good-night kiss crossed his mind, but he pondered the wisdom of doing so for a beat too long, because she said, "I'll talk to you later."

Then she headed for her car.

As he stood on the porch and watched her go, the sway of her hips and those long, shapely legs taunted him. He kicked himself for his lack of courage, his foresight and his strong sense of family values—or whatever the hell had convinced him to do the right thing and keep his lips and his hands to himself.

He'd had two opportunities to kiss Angie tonight, neither of which he'd taken. He tried to tell himself that he'd done the right thing, that he'd made the right call, but his libido wasn't buying it.

But wouldn't you know it? Once he'd lost his chance to kiss her, he wanted her all that much more.

Chapter Six

After Angie left, Toby went into the bathroom to take a shower and spotted her wet workout clothes hanging over his towel bar. He'd assumed she'd taken them with her, along with her purse and the wet shoes she'd left outside by the door, but apparently, she'd forgotten them after she'd changed.

He'd return them, of course, which would give him an opportunity to see her again soon.

That was a good thing, right?

Less than twenty minutes ago, he'd been tempted to kiss her. In fact, he'd been tempted to do more than that, right there on his living-room sofa—and despite having a house full of kids.

But that *wouldn't* have been good. He blew out a sigh.

As long as those three children were depending

upon him, he'd better not even think about having a woman spend the night. And since he hoped they'd be living with him until they each went off to college, he'd better get used to sleeping alone—unless he tied a cowbell around each of their necks.

The image of him doing that was actually kind of funny, and he might have even chuckled out loud if being twenty-six and facing the possibility of ten years of near celibacy wasn't downright unsettling—and unthinkable.

Surely it wouldn't come to that.

He ran his hand through his hair, then turned on the water in the shower, adjusting the temperature to warm—hoping cold sprays wouldn't be the only ones in his future.

Something told him this was going to be a long night, and that sleep would be a long time coming.

And he'd been right.

The next day, as soon as school let out, he surprised the kids by driving to the Superette and telling them they could each pick out a snack. As they unbuckled their seat belts, he reached for the plastic bag holding Angie's now-dry workout clothes.

Then he herded the happy kids into the mom-and-pop grocery store, riding pretty high in the saddle himself. No matter what he told himself, being with Angie always brightened his day.

Trouble was, once he got inside and the kids took off, he didn't see her at any of the checkout registers.

Where was she? He could've sworn that she worked at the market on Thursdays. But it was tough keeping up with her schedule. Had he been wrong? Was she working for Sawyer and Laurel today?

Dang. Was this what his life would be like if he were to actually date her? Would she always be working at some odd job, changing shifts frequently, possibly moving to another city?

She didn't have a history of stability, and no matter how many family conversations she livened up or how many heated looks passed between the two of them, nothing was going to change that fact.

Just when he began to realize he'd have to take the plastic bag back to his truck, Justin ran up and asked, "Can I have one of Angie's cupcakes? She put little race cars on top and everything."

"Slow down, Justin. What are you talking about?"

"I'll show you." The boy turned and dashed off toward the bakery section.

Toby followed him to the display case—and to Angie, who stood behind it, wearing a white apron tied around her slim waist.

"See?" Justin said, imploring Toby to tear his gaze from Angie and to look at the tray of cupcakes behind the glass enclosure, each one blue and topped with candy sprinkles and a tiny toy race car.

"You're a baker, too?" Toby asked her.

"It's a long story. The baker called in sick, so I stepped in. And when I spotted the toy cars stashed in one of the cupboards in back, I thought they might add a little more pizzazz. Apparently, the customers agreed because we sold the first batch already and the second is going fast."

"So can I have one for my treat?" Justin asked again.

"I want the one with the purple car," Kylie chimed in.

"All right," Toby said. "We'll take 'em."

"Do you want to eat them here?" Angie asked. "Or should I box them up for you?"

Justin, always one for instant gratification, said, "I want to eat mine right now."

Toby laughed. "I'll never hear the end of it if I make them wait."

Angie carried the cupcakes to one of the two small bistro-style tables, where the morning customers enjoyed their doughnuts and coffees. She set them before Justin and Kylie, then passed out a couple of napkins, just as Brian walked up with a highly caffeinated energy drink in his hand.

"I'm gonna just have this instead of a snack," Brian said, as he sat down at the table.

"Oh, no, you won't." Toby snatched the can out of the boy's hand. "Kids aren't supposed to drink this crap. It's not good for you."

"Mike Waddell drinks it all the time at school," Brian argued.

"Maybe so," Angie said, as she set a cupcake in front of the boy. "But Mike Waddell got detention last week for jumping out of his seat seven times during that movie in science class. He also had eight cavities at his last dentist appointment."

As the kids dug into their cupcakes, Toby followed Angie behind the bakery display case and lowered his voice. "How did you know that about Mike Waddell?"

"We live in a small town, Toby. People talk. Especially Brian's teacher, Mrs. Dawson, and Wendy Cummings, the dental hygienist." Angie glanced at the plastic bag he still held. "What's that?"

"The clothes you left in my bathroom." He handed them to her.

She flushed, then scanned the area as if they were making a drug deal and she didn't want to get caught. Then she stashed the bag in one of the drawers near the cash register.

Was she embarrassed? Whatever for? It wasn't as though she'd spent the night at the ranch and left her panties behind, although the thought of her doing that made him smile.

She lowered her voice. "And that's another thing people have been talking about and why I'm really back here in bakery and not out in front."

Because people thought she and Toby were…sleeping together?

"What are you talking about?" he asked.

"Several people who came through the checkout line asked me about the incident at the pool. They'd heard from a neighbor, who'd heard from a cousin, who… Well, you know how small towns are."

Yes, he did. And there wasn't much he could do to stop a rumor like that from getting out. But heck, if he was going to be the subject of gossip, it was too bad he couldn't have had a night to remember it by.

"Finally, around ten this morning, I asked Mrs. Tierney if she could man the cash register for a while," Angie said. "And so she let me work back here instead."

"All because of a little misunderstanding?" Toby shook his head. "That reminds me, though. How is Mr. Murdock?"

"He was here this morning, having coffee and holding court. He gave everyone a firsthand account of what happened. He…uh…also mentioned to Mrs. Rhodes, who was on her way to The Cuttery for her shampoo and set, that I've been helping you out a lot with the kids."

Should that be a secret? Toby wondered. Apparently Angie thought so because the pink flush on her cheeks deepened.

"Actually," he said, "you've been a godsend. And I really appreciate your help more than you can imagine."

"Even after yesterday?" she asked.

He laughed. "I told you before. I've had my share of bad days, too. It happens."

Angie glanced at the kids, who'd finished their cupcakes and were now racing their frosting-coated cars along the table, then looked at Toby and smiled. "To be honest, I've really enjoyed helping you, too. The kids are great, and I'm actually surprised at how much I like spending time with them."

What about their foster dad? Toby wanted to ask. *Do you enjoy spending time with him, too?*

But he knew better than to let things get personal, especially when he really did need another favor from her tomorrow. Besides, he'd picked up on what she'd left unsaid earlier.

If Mrs. Rhodes knew Angie was spending so much time with him and the kids, it wouldn't be long before all the other women getting their hair done at The Cuttery would start linking him and Angie romantically.

He really didn't mind what people said, but he didn't think Angie would like it, especially if her mom got wind of it. Doris Edwards had been pushing Angie to find a husband. And if the eligible men in town thought she was already taken, it might ruin her chance of going out with a guy who could offer her more than a cattle ranch and three foster kids.

Although the thought of her going out on a real date with someone else reared up inside of him, throwing him to the ground like an unexpected buck from a mild-mannered horse.

Maybe, in that case, he ought to keep her unavailable for a while—until he figured out where this thing was going. Or where he wanted it to go.

"I feel bad asking you this," he said, "but I'm in a bind. I'd ask Stacey, but she works and has her hands full with Piper."

"I'd be glad to help," Angie said. "What do you need me to do?"

"I have a meeting in Lubbock tomorrow afternoon, and I'm not sure when I'll get back. Is there any chance you could pick the kids up from school and take them home?"

"I have a few things to do, but it shouldn't be too hard to reschedule them. Let me work on that. In the meantime, don't worry about the kids. I'll pick them up from school. And I'll have dinner ready for you when you get home."

Well, what do you know?

He was back in the saddle again.

The meeting in Lubbock had gone later than Toby had expected, so he called Angie before he left town and told her to go ahead and feed the kids.

"Don't wait for me," he said.

"We're having spaghetti," she told him. "I'll keep a plate warm for you."

"Sounds good. Thanks."

"Did your meeting go well?" she asked.

"It sure did. I've been negotiating a deal on a piece of property that backs mine, and the man who owned it had refused to sell. But he passed away last spring, and his widow doesn't want to deal with it any longer. Her late husband thought it was a lot more valuable than it really is, so we had to agree upon a price."

"Great. We'll have to celebrate when you get home."

"Sounds good to me."

"Oh," she said. "I hope you don't mind, but I told the kids they could have a movie night after dinner."

"That's fine. I'll see you in a bit."

When the line disconnected, he turned on the radio, letting Gladys Knight fill the cab with her soulful voice as she sang about a midnight train to Georgia.

See, all you Texas country music fans. Willie Nelson isn't the only one who can sing about the Peach State.

The song had barely ended when his cell rang.

Toby glanced at the lit display, but didn't recognize the area code. Still, he turned down the volume on the radio, took the call and pushed the speakerphone button. "Hello?"

"It's Barbara Hemings, Toby."

The kids' aunt. He glanced in the rearview mirror, then pulled to the shoulder of the road and let the truck idle.

"Hi, Barbara." He wanted to ask her how rehab was going, but the woman sometimes became defensive, so he let it be. Besides, he had a feeling this wasn't going to be a social call, which was why he wanted to have his hands free in case he needed to make any notes about something she said.

"I heard about what happened at the pool the other day, so I put in a call to the case worker from child services. I'm waiting for her call back, but I thought you should know that just because I'm stuck in court-ordered treatment, I haven't stopped fighting for my kids."

They weren't *her* kids. And she'd had a lot of opportunities to fight for them, especially when she had custody, but she kept blowing it. However, arguing with her wasn't going to solve anything.

"I'm not sure where you're getting your information, Barbara, but that incident was blown all out of proportion. Justin was never in danger at the pool. The kids are all safe, and they're happy. And just so you know, I've already called Ms. Fisk and given her a heads-up about the situation. I'm sure she'll tell you the same thing when she calls you back."

"Toby, you're a young, single man with a tumbling-down ranch. And those kids can be a handful at times. There's no way you can handle them on your own."

Tumbling-down ranch? He'd turned the Double H around in the three years he'd owned it. And, thanks to the meeting he'd had thirty minutes ago, he'd be running more cattle next year, and that meant he'd be turning an even better profit—if things went according to plan.

"As I seem to remember," he reminded her, "you were single when you took the kids on, too. And my 'tumbling-down' ranch is a hell of a lot nicer than that cockroach-infested motel you had them living in when the state took them away from you."

"Yes, and that turned out badly. But I'm better now."

At least the woman was able to admit the obvious.

"Anyway," she added, "the kids need to be with family. And if they can't be with me for the next few months, then I want them with one of my relatives."

What family? If there were any Hemings relatives nearby, wouldn't they have stepped up by now?

"Do the kids even know these relatives?" Toby finally asked, his fingers gripping the steering wheel until his knuckles ached.

"No, but they're family, Toby. You of all people should understand about long-lost family."

She was talking about James Marshall Fortune coming to Horseback Hollow and finding his sister, Jeanne Marie, Toby's mom. Although, quite frankly, Toby was surprised that she even knew about that.

"I have a cousin in California," Barbara said. "I'm going to ask him to take the children until I get out of rehab."

Great. Another upheaval? And just who was her cousin?

"What's his name? What does he do?"

"His name is Rocky, and he's looking for work. His parole agent thinks he can find a job by the end of this month. His wife works at a hospital out there, but one of his conditions of parole is that he's not allowed to work at hospitals anymore, so that's out. But there are plenty of other places where he can get work."

His parole agent? He couldn't work in a hospital

anymore? If the cousin couldn't be trusted in a hospital then he sure as shooting couldn't be trusted with Brian, Justin and Kylie.

What made Barbara think that the children would be better off with some deadbeat cousin they didn't even know than they would be with Toby?

"I don't think that's in the children's best interest, Barbara."

"Honestly, Toby, it's not your decision. I thought you'd be a little more cooperative, but I guess the kids can't count on you for that."

The woman disconnected the call before Toby could throw the phone out his open window, which was what he'd wanted to do the moment he'd heard her voice.

He sucked the country air into his lungs and counted to ten, the way his pitching coach had taught him to do when he'd been on the mound.

Think. Whom did he call first? Ms. Fisk, the case worker? Or an attorney?

He glanced at the clock on the dashboard. Crap. It was too late to call anyone today. That would have to wait until tomorrow. He continued to sit in the idling truck for a while, his hands on the steering wheel, his thoughts on the troubling call.

Would the court decide that the kids were better off with a sketchy family member over a stable and caring guardian? It didn't seem feasible, but then again, anything was possible...

He did his best to shake off Barbara's threat, telling himself he didn't have time to worry about that blasted woman. He'd told Angie that he was going to be late, but he hadn't meant to completely abandon her with the kids.

After checking for traffic, Toby pulled back onto the road and accelerated.

At times like this it was nice to know he had someone to rely on, especially Angie.

People might think that she was flighty—and they might even be right. But either way, she was proving to be a real blessing.

A man could get used to going home to a woman like her.

Angie sure hoped Toby got home soon, because she was fading fast. She hadn't slept very well the past two nights, thanks in large part to the residual stress and worry from that 911 fiasco at the Y.

Even her mother had heard all about it and called, asking her what had happened. Sheesh. What a pain that conversation had been.

But at least Toby trusted her enough to ask her to help with the kids again.

It hadn't been easy to adjust her schedule to accommodate his, but she had. She'd worked a split shift at the Superette, going in early this morning. Then she'd left at ten o'clock to take Mr. Murdock to his doctor's appointment in Vicker's Corners. After that, she'd run over to Redmond-Fortune Air to type some letters for Sawyer. And it was back to the Superette for another two-hour shift, after which she purchased the ingredients she needed to make spaghetti for dinner.

She was nearly late picking the kids up from school, but she got there just in the nick of time. Then it was a quick stop at her house for the surprise she'd planned for the evening.

A couple of summers ago, she'd worked at an old movie theater outside of Lubbock. When the Red Raider Cinemas went out of business, the owner gave Angie a projector and several old movie reels. She'd always wanted to have an old-fashioned movie night under the stars, but she'd never gotten around to planning one. That was, until tonight.

Too bad she was about to nod off from exhaustion. She could really use one of those energy drinks Brian had wanted yesterday afternoon.

Hopefully, Toby would be home soon. He'd told her not to wait dinner for him, and they hadn't. At this rate, she was going to start the movie without him, too. Otherwise, she'd probably curl up on his sofa and nod off before he even got home.

She'd fixed him a plate and left it on the stove. Then she'd cleaned up the kitchen. She'd made popcorn, but had to make it the old-fashioned way, since Toby didn't have any kind of popper. She'd just salted a large bowl for them to share when Brian came in.

"We're all done," he said. "Me and Justin hung up the white sheet, just like you told us. And Kylie made beds for us on the lawn. You ought to see it."

Angie followed the boys out of the house, where they'd set up the makeshift outdoor movie theater. And, just as Brian had said, Kylie had, indeed, made them a giant bed—with every blanket, sheet and pillow she could possibly find.

"Did you leave any of the beds made up in the house?" Angie asked her.

"Nope," Kylie said. "Even Toby's blankets and pillows are out here."

That wasn't quite what Angie had in mind, which meant there was going to be a big mess to clean up afterward, when she doubted she'd have the energy to deal with it. But she wasn't about to scold the kids when the whole idea had been hers in the first place—and when they'd tried so hard to follow her instructions.

Besides, look how happy they were.

"Okay," she said. "Let's get this show on the road."

She'd just finished setting up the projector with the *Star Wars* film threaded in the proper slots, when Toby's Dodge rolled into the driveway.

"What's all this?" Toby asked, as he stepped out of his truck.

"Movie night!" Justin yelled, as he barged out of the back door in his pajamas and dived onto the bedding on the lawn, calling his spot.

Toby looked nearly as tired as Angie felt—probably realizing they'd have four beds to make up before anyone could go to sleep tonight.

Angie hoped she hadn't blown it by throwing the impromptu cinema party in his backyard.

Toby nodded to the old projector. "Where in the world did you get that thing? Wait, don't tell me. Does it have something to do with an old job?"

His grin and a glimmer in his eye teased her in a way that didn't make her feel quite so bad about her history of random employment. But she sidestepped his question and asked one of her own. "You look tired. Would you rather we do this another night?"

"And disappoint the kids?" Toby's grin blossomed into a smile, easing her mind. "No way. Let me get out of these clothes and put on something more comfortable."

Angie had been so busy reading into Toby's expression, which hadn't matched the upbeat tone of his voice when he'd called her earlier, that she'd failed to notice that he wasn't wearing his trademark jeans, T-shirt and cowboy boots.

He was dressed in black slacks, a button-down shirt and expensive dress boots. He looked sharp—and ready for a night on the town without the kids.

She wondered what it might be like to actually go out on a date with him—if they had a sitter.

That was, if he'd actually ask her to be his date.

As Toby headed into the house, Brian and Kylie followed Justin's lead, rushing outside in their pajamas and choosing their own spots to spread out on the blankets.

But Angie's thoughts were on Toby.

"I'll get the popcorn," she told the kids. "Showtime is in five minutes."

She made her way into the house slowly. She didn't want Toby to think that she was following him.

But what if he'd wanted her to?

Oh, get a grip. She was so sleep-deprived, she was becoming delusional.

She was about to carry the first load of refreshments outside when Toby stepped into the kitchen.

"Thanks," he said, his eyes contradicting the simplicity of his single word as they bored deeply into her own.

She tried to downplay the intensity in his gaze, as well as her efforts to provide a fun evening for the kids. "It was no big deal."

"Actually, it's a big deal to me. You have no idea how much I need this right now."

She thought Toby was going to pull her in for a hug, and she would have willingly gone—if he'd made the first move. But as her heartbeats pounded off the seconds and he didn't make the attempt, she realized it was probably more likely that one of the kids would come flying in the door to ask what was holding them up.

So she handed him the bowl of popcorn and grabbed the five ice-cream-filled mugs by their handles and led the way out the back door.

"So what are we watching?" Toby asked as he settled into the only spot the kids had left open, which happened to be right beside Angie.

"Star Wars I," Justin said.

"No, dude, this is *Star Wars IV*," Brian said snarkily, as if Justin was an idiot.

"How can it be number IV when this is the first *Star Wars* they ever made?" Justin challenged back.

Angie quickly explained the nuances of the *Star Wars* episodes before the boys came to blows across the blankets.

"So you're both right," she said.

The boys conceded, going back to their ice cream.

"Is that my bedsheet?" Toby asked as he studied the improvised movie screen nailed to the side of his barn.

"Well, the boys' sheets are dark blue, and Kylie's has a *My Little Pony* print," Angie defended.

"Why is there a big brown spot on it?" Toby asked, glossing over the fact that the boys had put nail holes into his sheet.

"Justin dropped his end in some manure while I was on the ladder trying to nail it in place," Brian explained.

"I'm sorry," Angie said. "I didn't know they were going to use real nails. And I didn't realize they'd dropped it in cow… Well, in…you know. I just thought you had stained sheets."

Toby looked at her as if she'd been the one to drop the manure outside the barn in the first place.

"Did you try the popcorn yet?" she asked, trying to get the conversation heading in a different direction. "I put extra butter on it for you."

Toby reached into the bowl. "That stain on the sheet makes it look like Luke Skywalker has melanoma on his face."

"What's 'melanoma'?" Brian asked.

"It's a kind of skin cancer," Angie answered.

The pillows looked so comfortable. Maybe she could just put her head down for a second and rest her eyes, maybe even doze off for a moment or two.

"My mommy died of cancer," Justin said.

"Is Luke Skywalker gonna die of cancer, too?" Kylie asked.

Oh, no. Angie hadn't meant to mention the C-word.

"Nobody is going to die tonight," Toby said, trying to save the day.

But that didn't make Angie feel much better. If her brain hadn't been so sleep-deprived, she might have thought before opening her mouth.

Here she was, trying to do something fun and nice for the family, but then she'd screwed everything up by reminding them of their dead mother.

No matter what she tried to do, it seemed that she only made things worse. Maybe Toby and the kids would be better if she ran for the hills and stayed out of their lives forever.

They'd be better off. But as she scanned the yard, taking in the sweet kids and the handsome cowboy who'd taken them in and given them a home, she wondered how she'd ever just walk away from them without looking back.

Or did she dare risk it all and stick around until she finally got things right?

Chapter Seven

The kids settled back on the blankets to watch the movie. Toby and Angie did, too, stretching out next to each other.

By the time Han Solo was telling Leia that he was in it for the money, Toby leaned over and whispered to Angie, "Is there any more popcorn?"

He hadn't eaten lunch, so he'd pretty much wolfed down the spaghetti Angie had set out for him, but it really hadn't quite filled him up.

"I'll run in and make some more," she said, getting to her feet.

He hadn't meant to put her to work. "You don't have to do that."

"Actually, I was about to fall asleep. It'll help me stay awake."

Toby followed her into the kitchen. She may not

need any help, but he saw an opportunity and decided to take it. With the kids so engrossed in the movie, he didn't know when they'd get another chance to be alone. And the longer he'd lain next to her, the more he'd craved some one-on-one adult time with her.

When she realized he'd followed her into the kitchen, she said, "I'm so sorry about bringing up the C-word earlier."

"Don't even give it another thought. Everyone slips up now and then. Besides, I was the one who brought up melanoma in the first place. And if it makes you feel better, the social worker told me that the kids need to talk about their mom. It's better for them to process her death in a normal, healthy way. When they lived with their aunt, they saw a bad example of hiding emotions behind the bottle."

Just thinking about Barbara reminded him of the unsettling conversation they'd had. He'd almost forgotten about it once he'd gotten home. Angie had a way of getting his mind off his trouble, which was one more thing he liked about her.

Should he tell her about the call?

He didn't consider the idea very long. He didn't want to dump any more on her than he had to, no matter how easy she was to talk to. She wasn't in this thing for the long haul anyway.

Besides, why did he want to think about Barbara when he had Angie in front of him now, standing at the stove, heating oil and popcorn kernels in a covered skillet?

When the corn began popping against the lid, she

moved the pan across the burner—back and forth, faster and faster—her breasts swaying with the motion.

Aw, man. If he didn't stop gaping at the mesmerizing sight, those kernels wouldn't be the only thing popping.

"Is the popcorn done yet?" Justin yelled from the open doorway.

If you were talking about being hot and bothered, Toby was certainly close to done.

"Just about," Angie called out to the boy. "I'll bring it out to you in just a minute."

Justin ran back to the movie, and Toby decided he'd better do the same before his thoughts got the better of him.

A few minutes later, Angie joined them in the yard, bringing the replenished bowl with her and settling back into her spot next to Toby. Even the action scenes, with swishing lightsabers, zooming X-wing fighters and intergalactic battles, didn't keep Toby from wanting to reach out and grab more than a handful of popcorn.

But he managed self-control.

By the time the credits started to roll, he looked over and saw that Kylie and Justin had fallen asleep.

"I guess we'll have to carry them in to bed," he whispered to Angie, who'd nuzzled into the pillow next to his.

But she didn't answer.

He leaned over and, while tempted to brush back the strands of hair that had fallen across her face and tell her the movie was over, he let her sleep.

Brian, thank goodness, picked up his blankets and

pillow and made his way into the house on his own. But Toby had to carry the smaller kids one at a time.

Thanks to Kylie's overzealous efforts to make them all cozy for the movie, the mattresses were completely bare. Remaking all the beds seemed like way too much work to do. So instead, he went back to the grass, retrieved a couple of blankets and put one over each of the sleeping children.

When he returned outside and saw Angie curled up under the stars, the corner of his comforter tucked under her chin, he stood there and watched her for a while.

Now what? Wake her up? Send her home?

Invite her inside?

He looked back at the house. Considering the bare mattress that awaited him inside, he figured, what the heck.

She looked so soft, so comfortable. Why not let her nap? He could certainly use a little snooze himself.

So he lay down next to her, just as they'd done when the movie had first begun. Then he pulled a blanket over the top of them. Surely one of them would wake up in an hour or so. At that time, they could each go their own way, she to her house and he to his own room.

And no one would be the wiser.

Toby might not be able to invite Angie to actually spend the night in his bed, but this seemed like the next best thing.

Angie wiggled backward, not quite ready to wake up from her dream.

When had her bed gotten so small and cramped?

Her back was pressed up against a warm wall, her bottom nestled against something hard.

Her waist was tethered down.

She didn't feel trapped or claustrophobic, though. Nor did she feel compelled to move away. Rather, she snuggled deeper into the cocoon of comfort.

Whatever had been clamped on her waist slowly traveled upward until it reached under her shirt and began to fondle her breast.

Ooh. Nice. She sighed and arched in contentment, her dream getting better by the minute.

A warm breeze whispered along her neck, as lips brushed against the sensitive skin below her ear.

She leaned her head back to provide more access to the mouth that was giving her such delicious pleasure.

Swish.

Swack.

Swish.

What was that flapping sound?

Angie didn't want to stir, didn't want to ever wake up, but the annoying sound wouldn't go away. She cracked her eyes open and saw something big and white floating up in the wind, then smacking down against the side of a huge, red barn.

A barn that looked a lot like Toby's.

Why was her bed in Toby's backyard?

Wait. Whose pink-pony-covered pillow was wrapped in her arms?

And whose hand held her left breast? Whose fingers had tightened over her taut nipple?

"You feel good," a sleep-graveled, baritone voice whispered against her ear.

Toby?

This wasn't a dream, was it?

Swish. Swish. Splat.

Were those water droplets that just sprinkled her face?

"What the—" Toby shot up, and his hand left her breast. "Oh, hell. The sprinkler."

Angie stared at Toby through wet lashes, fully awake now and trying to piece together why they'd been sleeping together outdoors, why he'd been holding her so intimately. But more water from a nearby sprinkler shot her in the face again, and Toby grabbed her arm, pulling her toward the house.

"We have to get this stuff inside. Everything's going to get soaked."

Angie, still dazed from her erotic sleep-induced bliss, didn't take the time to decide whether Toby had been fully awake or dreaming. Instead she snapped out of it long enough to run for the movie projector, pull the hefty old machine off the relocated patio table and lug it, extension cord and all, inside the kitchen, trying to dodge the shooting sprays of water as she went.

She set the reels on the table, just as Toby dropped the first load of wet blankets on the kitchen floor.

"Why are you guys all wet?" Kylie asked, walking into the kitchen before Angie could process what had happened outside on the lawn.

Angie waited for Toby to answer because she didn't think the words would form in her throat.

But a red flush on Toby's face as he reached down for one of the damp pillows and placed it in front of his waist suggested that her hormones hadn't been the only ones getting an early-morning workout.

She didn't know whether to laugh at his discomfort or run out of the room in embarrassment because, whatever had just happened—sleep-induced or fully conscious—their friendship had just taken a tremendous turn in an unexpected direction.

Maybe it was best if she got out of here.

She was usually good with smooth exit strategies, but she couldn't seem to get her brain to engage.

As much as she'd like to pretend this morning hadn't happened, she hated to leave Toby to face the music alone. And judging from the pink tint blossoming underneath his stubble-covered cheeks, he didn't quite know what to make of it, either.

"The sprinklers came on early this morning," Toby mumbled, not dropping the pillow. "So Angie and I were trying to get all this stuff inside."

"Why didn't you bring it in last night?" Justin asked, making his way into the crowded kitchen, oblivious to the strong but awkward sexual attraction swirling in the room like a Texas dust cloud.

"Sweet," Brian said, padding in to join them, his red hair sticking up on one side of his head. "You guys had a sleepover."

Oh, great. That wasn't going to look good in the social worker's report—if one of the kids happened to mention Toby having a woman spend the night while the kids were home.

Angie reached up to smooth her own sleep-tousled hair.

Maybe she should tell the kids she'd been out for a morning jog and had decided to stop in for breakfast.

She glanced down at her bare feet. No, they were

too smart to fall for that. She needed to nip this thing in the bud before everyone in town heard that she and Toby had slept together—which, technically, they had.

"It wasn't really a sleepover," she said. "I just dozed off while watching the movie."

"Then can Mike Waddell kinda fall asleep over here next Saturday after our baseball game?" Brian asked.

The energy-drink kid? Angie could only imagine the hyperactivity that would come along with that night. But at least the focus was now off her.

"We'll talk about it later," Toby said, finally releasing the pillow.

"If Brian gets a sleepover, then can I have a slumber party?" Kylie asked.

"How many girls do you want to come to your slumber party?" Angie asked.

"My teacher said that, if we have a party, we have to invite everyone from the class so we don't hurt anyone's feelings. And we have twenty-three kids in our class. But I don't want to invite Destiny Simmons because she told everyone my hair looks funny because I don't have a mommy to do it right."

That reminded Angie that Kylie needed a real mother figure, someone permanent. And not a fly-by-night female role model who'd nearly made love to a man outdoors in broad daylight, with three impressionable kids inside the house.

"Twenty-three kids?" Toby asked. "But that's counting the boys, too. You can't invite them to a girls' slumber party."

Kylie pointed at Angie. "But *you* had a *girl* over for a slumber party."

The tiny red-haired cherub in the princess pajamas had brought the conversation full circle without missing a beat.

And just as quickly, Toby opened the pantry door and changed the topic. "Hey, guys. We need to get our chores done early today. Why don't I make pancakes for breakfast? You can help me by setting the table and getting the juice out of the fridge."

Smart move. New focus.

While the children were distracted with setting the table and getting the orange juice out of the refrigerator, Angie decided it was the perfect time to sneak out of here.

She was such a coward. But she was doing what she did best—leaving before things got uncomfortable again.

So she slipped out the back, quietly shutting the door. When she walked by the kitchen window, Toby spotted her and lifted his eyebrows.

She gestured, then mouthed, "I have to go." It was a lame excuse, especially since she really had nowhere to go on a Saturday morning. But she couldn't very well stay here and play house with Toby and the kids.

He nodded as if he understood. Yet guilt, embarrassment, fear and other emotions she hadn't yet pegged all tumbled around in her throat, threatening to cut off her air supply.

She put her thumb to her ear and her pinkie to her lips, giving him the universal sign for telephone. Then she mouthed, "I'll call you."

Again, he nodded.

Then she climbed into her car before she could debate whether she really had any business calling Toby at all.

Ten minutes after Angie drove away, the cordless phone on the counter rang and Kylie answered it before Toby could make a grab for it. Was Angie calling him already? He could understand her wanting to get the heck out of Dodge this morning. He'd been tempted to jump in her car and go with her just to escape the curious eyes pelting him with unspoken questions.

What had he been thinking, spending the entire night with Angie like that? Better yet, what had he been thinking setting those damn sprinklers on a timer to go off at six in the morning? If they hadn't blasted them with water, Toby knew exactly what he would have done to Angie's sweet, warm and tempting body this morning. He wouldn't have stopped with a hand on her lush breast—that was for sure. Instead, they'd gotten sprayed with water like a couple of dogs someone had to turn the hose on to keep from going at it on the front lawn.

"Yeah, Aunt Stacey," Kylie said. "He's right here, fixing pancakes for us and Angie."

Obviously, Kylie still hadn't realized that Angie had left. Or that Toby was still staring out the kitchen window after her like a sad, abandoned puppy.

He tried to reach for the telephone before Kylie could tell his sister anything else, but his hands were full of slimy eggshells, which he'd have to rinse off first.

"Uh-huh," Kylie continued. "Angie and Toby had a

sleepover last night. And Toby got my pillow all wet, but that's okay because he said I get to invite my class over for a slumber party."

With his hands clean, but still wet, Toby took the phone from Kylie. "Hey, Stace. What's up?"

"Why did Kylie put *you* on the phone?" Stacey asked. "I wanted to talk to Angie."

"She's not here," Toby said, a bit more defensively than he'd intended.

"She left already?" Justin asked. "Aw, man. I wanted to ask her to help me build a spaceship out of LEGO."

"We'll see her later," Toby told the disappointed boy.

But the truth was, he didn't know when they'd see Angie again. Or if Angie would even want to see him after the way he'd been pawing at her this morning.

"Later, huh?" Stacey asked. "I heard the two of you have been spending a lot of time together lately, but I had no idea you guys were at the sleepover stage."

Toby covered the mouthpiece. "Brian, stir the pancake mix. I'm going to talk to my sister for a sec. But don't use the stove until I get back."

After giving all the kids an assignment, Toby walked into the living room so they wouldn't hear his line of defense.

Not that he'd done anything wrong. Had he? Maybe if he just explained what had happened…

Hey, wait. He didn't owe anyone an explanation.

When he reached the living room, he asked, "So how's Piper?"

Everyone knew Stacey adored her nine-month-old daughter, so he figured he'd change the subject to one of toothless grins and sleepless nights.

"She's fine," Stacey said. "Growing cuter and smarter every day."

"And how about Colton?" he asked, hoping he could get her talking about her new fiancé, one of the neighboring ranchers. "Have you guys set a date yet?"

"Colton is doing great, but don't try those distraction tactics on me. I'm one step ahead of you, big brother. You are *not* getting out of this one. What's going on with you and Angie Edwards?"

His sisters, Stacey and Delaney, were protective over all their brothers, but particularly Toby since his family always accused him of being a softy—and a sucker for a sob story. Not that Angie was a sob story.

"Nothing's going on," he said. "Angie's been helping me out with the kids. That's all."

"Are you paying her for babysitting services? Because I heard Angie's always looking for a new job. She never seems to stick with one very long."

"Not that it's any of your business, but no, I'm not paying her. She's doing it to be nice and because she likes the kids. And for your information, Angie is a very hard worker. Just because she hasn't found a career she likes doesn't mean she isn't a good person."

"I never said she wasn't, Toby. I was just telling you what I've been hearing around town. I went to high school with Angie, remember? She used to date a lot back then."

Toby felt a jostle of jealousy stir up again in his veins.

"What do you mean she used to date a lot? Like she was…" Toby didn't want to say anything that would be demeaning to Angie, but he didn't know how else to ask.

"Well, she didn't have a reputation for being fast or anything like that, but she was known as the Queen of the First Date."

"What does that mean?"

"It means she would go out with a guy if he asked her, but usually, they never made it to a second date. I don't know if it was fear of commitment or what, but she never went steady with anyone or took any of the guys seriously. She for sure never had sleepovers with anyone before. Or at least none that I heard about."

The envy died down a little bit inside him. At least he couldn't fault Angie for being choosy.

"Listen, last night wasn't a sleepover. It was just an accident. Nothing, uh, really happened."

He hoped his sister hadn't caught the hesitation in his voice.

"Aha!" she said. "Define 'nothing.' And 'really.'"

"I'm not defining anything." Toby looked back to the kitchen to make sure none of the little ears had made their way within hearing distance.

Stacey clicked her tongue. "You wouldn't be getting so defensive if your relationship was strictly platonic. So how far have you guys gone?"

Toby couldn't believe Stacey had just asked him that. "This isn't high school, Stace. We're not playing truth or dare. I'm not talking about my sex life with my little sister."

"So you're saying there *is* a sex life to talk about," she said, a spark of excitement lighting her voice as if she'd tricked a leprechaun into revealing the location of his pot of gold.

Embarrassment was an understatement. Toby remembered holding the wet pillow up to cover his arousal this morning when the kids came into the kitchen. He wished he had something to hide behind now.

He wasn't going to admit to anything. He'd said too much as it was and figured silence was his only option.

"So," Stacey said, apparently changing tactics, "the reason I called was to tell you that Mom and Dad are having a family dinner at their house tonight. And we'd like you to bring Angie."

"Why, so you guys can check her out and pump her for information? No way."

"Mom told me and Delaney you'd say that when we came up with the idea."

Great. His family was already plotting and scheming.

"That's why," Stacey continued, "Delaney is calling Angie right now and asking her to come over for dinner. Too bad she didn't pick up the phone a few minutes earlier. We could've killed two birds with one stone."

"I'm not coming to dinner tonight," Toby said. "And I'm not inviting Angie."

"Why not? If there's nothing going on between you two, then why try to keep her away from your family?"

Stacey had a point. Unfortunately, with the sparks that were jumping between him and Angie lately, he doubted a blind man would believe there wasn't anything going on between them.

And knowing his family the way he did, he was

sure they'd figure out something was up the second he, Angie and the kids walked in the door.

Hell.

"Okay," he finally conceded. "But let me invite her. And I'll only do it if you guys promise not to interrogate her."

"My, aren't you the protector. She's lucky to have you in her corner."

Toby didn't know about that.

"Oops," Stacey said, "Piper just smeared green beans all over herself. Gotta go."

Good, Toby thought. He was glad Stacey's baby had made a mess she'd have to clean up. That was what his sister got for butting into Toby's business.

He just hoped he didn't have an even bigger mess to deal with now.

Angie saw Toby's name displayed on her caller-ID screen. She'd been too chicken to call him after she said she would. What was the proper length of time one should wait to call the man they'd intimately nestled against all night long? Three days? Maybe there was an article in some women's magazine she could reference.

Ugh. She needed to get this over with. He was probably calling to tell her that they needed to see less of each other. That he wasn't looking for a relationship. He'd made that more than clear. The sooner she bit the bullet, the sooner she could get over him. Unfortunately, she didn't think she'd ever get over the feeling of his fingers stroking their way up her waist. Or his husky voice telling her how good she felt.

She tried to sound more upbeat than the groan stuck in her throat would allow when she said, "Hello?"

"Um, hey."

Couldn't he even manage a proper greeting? He must already be experiencing remorse at what they'd done and guilt over what he was about to tell her.

She should make it easy for him and call things off first, but she couldn't bring herself to say the words for him.

"Did my sister Delaney call you yet?" he finally got out.

"Not that I know of. But I haven't looked at my missed calls since I got out of the shower."

Why would Delaney be calling her? Had the rumors started already? Was Toby trying to do damage control? Maybe they needed to get their stories straight about her spending the night out at the Double H.

"Good. I wanted to talk to you before she did."

Uh-oh. This didn't bode well.

"It sounds like my family is doing a dinner thing tonight and they want me to bring you."

"Why would they want me there?" Unless they thought something was going on between her and Toby. Of course, she didn't know why his family would think that when she, herself, had no idea if there was anything going on between the two of them.

"They, uh, well, they're just curious about you since we've been spending, uh, so much time together and, you know…" Was Toby nervous? His voice tripped over the words like a shy schoolboy asking her out to prom. He was usually so confident. What had happened to all his swagger and self-assuredness?

"So they want to check me out?" She actually wanted to ask if they were trying to determine if she was good enough for their Fortune Jones standards. Angie had the feeling she wouldn't pass that test.

"It's really not a big deal. It's just a little family get-together. And I made Stacey promise that they wouldn't interrogate you or anything."

"Yeah, that's not exactly selling me on the idea, Toby." In fact, the implication that he probably had to wrestle the promise from his sister made it seem that much more likely that what his family had planned was a full-scale inquisition.

"Well, I figure we could either go to the dinner together and show a kind of united front, or we can sit back and wait for them to come into the Superette one by one and hound you for information."

That was a good point. She didn't relish being the subject of the Fortune Joneses' scrutiny, but she'd rather it be in the privacy of their family ranch than in public at her place of employment. She didn't mind working in the bakery on occasion, but she'd hate to have to hide back there for good.

"Plus," Toby continued, "the kids will be there and Stacey is bringing Piper. If we stick close to at least one of the children, we should be safe, right?"

Angie didn't know if he meant they'd be safe from the prying questions from his family or safe from their own raging hormones.

But she just wasn't sure she should go. She wanted to spend more time with him, but would this just make things more complicated? He sounded as if he was eager to have her there, which wasn't how a man would act if he was trying to break it off with a woman.

"Let me think about it," she finally said.

"Fair enough. I'll be at the baseball field most of the afternoon, so just give me a call on my cell when you decide."

She had no more than set her phone down on the counter when a preprogrammed ringtone sounded. The foreboding theme song from *Jaws* indicated it was her mother.

Doris had called her twice last night, and if Angie didn't talk to her mom now, the woman would think something was going on and make another surveillance trip into the Superette.

"Hi, Mom," Angie finally said, ending the crescendo of doom.

"Evangeline, I've been trying to get ahold of you since yesterday. Where have you been? On a date?"

Did her mom suspect?

Probably not. Doris didn't keep in touch with many people she'd known from when she'd lived in Horseback Hollow. They were too small-town for Doris's perceived cosmopolitan lifestyle. Not that Lubbock could be considered an epicenter of sophistication by most people's standards, but her mom liked to think she was a big deal now.

"I've just been really busy. Nothing new or exciting going on here."

"Good, because if you don't have plans tonight, there's a dinner dance at the country club here in Lubbock, and Margie Suttelheimer's grandson is going to be there. He's a corporate attorney, and his second divorce was just finalized last month. Margie assured me his prenup was ironclad. His ex barely got a dime, so he's still worth millions."

Angie had never made a quicker decision.

"I'm sorry, Mom. I've already made plans for tonight."

She'd just have to tell Toby that dinner with the Fortune Jones clan was on.

At one minute after nine, Toby went out to the barn for some privacy. Using his cell phone, he placed a call to Ms. Fisk at child services, only to reach a recording that said she was out of the office. So he left her a voice-mail message.

Next he called the Lubbock attorney who'd first contacted him about the money that the anonymous donor had given him and he'd placed in trust for the kids. Jake Gleason specialized in estate planning, so if push came to shove, Toby would retain someone else to handle the custody issue. But for right now, he needed some professional assurance that Barbara had only been blowing smoke.

Unfortunately, Jake hadn't been able to do much to ease his worry. "It's hard to second-guess what the court will decide in cases like yours. One judge may consider stability a priority and look at how well the kids are doing under your care and not want to move them. But another might prefer to keep kids with their family members."

Jake did, however, give Toby the names of a couple of family-law attorneys.

As morning wore on, the only thing that had given

Toby a lift had been thoughts of Angie. Her bright-eyed smile and upbeat nature had a way of making him feel as though everything would work out fine—one way or another. So he hoped she still planned to join them at his parents' house.

By the time lunch was over and afternoon rolled around, he'd picked up the phone a couple of times to call her, just to make sure they were still on for dinner. After all, she'd been known to change her mind.

Finally, at three o'clock, he bit the bullet and called. When she answered, he asked, "Are we still on for that barbecue at my parents' house?"

"Sure. What time did you want to go?"

"I thought I'd pick you up around four."

"You shouldn't have to drive all the way into town to get me when your parents live closer to you. Why don't I drive to your place? Then I can fix Kylie's hair."

"That makes more sense. And Kylie would really appreciate a woman's hand with those pigtails. I can never seem to get them to hang evenly."

Angie laughed, and the lilt of her voice made him grip the phone tighter, as if he could draw her near and hold her close.

"While I was helping Mr. Murdock organize his closets, I found some ribbons in an old sewing basket. He said I could have them, so I'll bring them with me. I also baked brownies to take with us. I'm ready now, so I may as well head on over to your place."

"That sounds like a plan. I'll round up the troops, and we'll be ready when you get here."

"By the way," Angie said, "who's going to be at that family dinner?"

"My parents, of course. My sister Delaney and my

brother Galen. Stacey is the ringleader, so she and her fiancé, Colton Foster, will be there, along with her baby, Piper. I imagine my brother Jude and his fiancée, Gabriella Mendoza, will be coming. And of course Liam and Julia Tierney."

"It'll be fun to see Julia outside of the Superette," Angie said. "And it will be nice to see Stacey and Delaney again."

Toby hoped she still felt that way after his sisters began plying her with questions about their supposed relationship.

"It might be best not to mention my brother Chris," Toby said. "Unless someone else brings him up first."

"Why?"

He waited a beat, wondering why he felt inclined to even mention it.

"It's not as though there's a big family rift," he explained, trying to downplay things and to choose his words carefully. "It's just there were some hard feelings about him leaving Horseback Hollow and moving to Red Rock."

"That's really not a secret. There's been some talk around town. And Sawyer and Laurel made a comment about it at the flight school."

"What did they say?" Toby asked.

"Nothing really. They don't discuss things like that in front of their employees. But they said something in passing, and I connected a few dots. So I know that Chris is working for Sawyer's dad at the Fortune Foundation. But that's about it."

Toby didn't know much more than that, either, although he'd been tempted to go to Red Rock and talk to his brother face-to-face. But with him now having three kids, all of whom were in school and involved in outside activities, he wasn't free to make a trip like that without a lot of juggling and some careful orchestrating.

"I'm assuming that your parents aren't happy about his move," Angie said.

Toby didn't usually air family laundry in public, but he and Angie had become pretty close lately, so sharing his concerns came easily. "When my mom asked us to accept our roots by taking on the Fortune name, my dad was a good sport about it. But when Chris announced he was moving to Red Rock, my dad hit the roof. He felt as though my brother had completely jumped ship by leaving town and going to work for James Marshall Fortune. Things really hit the fan then."

There'd always been issues between Chris and their dad over the years, although Toby never had thought they were all that serious. But apparently, he'd been wrong.

"Don't worry about me saying anything at dinner tonight—or to anyone else," Angie said. "I may have my faults, but being a gossip isn't one of them."

"Thanks. I appreciate that."

Silence filled the line for a beat, then Angie said, "I'd better let you go. I'll see you in a little while."

As soon as they ended the call, Toby rounded up the kids and told them to wash up, change their clothes and get ready to go to Grandma and Grandpa's house.

They might not be related by blood, but his parents and siblings had accepted them into the Fortune Jones fold, just as though they were. And the kids, who'd been starved for love and affection, had been thrilled to have a family to call their own. So the last time they'd visited, his mom had suggested they not be so formal. "Why don't y'all call us Grandma Jeanne and Grandpa Deke?" she'd said.

The kids, who'd never really had parents, let alone grandparents, had jumped at the chance to become a part of Jeanne's brood. In fact, if you didn't know, you'd think there'd been a long line of redheads somewhere in the Fortune Jones family tree.

Toby did, however, realize that it could all come to an end one day if Barbara made good on her threat, and his gut twisted at the possibility. But he shook off the negative thoughts and tried to focus on the fact that the kids were thriving. And that their school would back that up if need be.

"Can I pack my backpack with things me and Piper can play with?" Kylie asked.

Toby smiled. Most little girls loved dolls, but having a real baby to play with? "Absolutely. Just let Aunt Stacey check out the toys first. You know how careful she is about the things Piper puts in her mouth."

"I will," Kylie said, as she dashed off to her room.

Toby glanced at the clock on the mantel. While the kids were getting ready, he'd take a shower. Angie would be here before he knew it.

Chapter Eight

Nearly an hour later, Angie arrived at the Double H wearing a white sundress that was wholesome, yet strappy and sexy at the same time—especially when paired with brown cowboy boots.

"Look what I have," she said, lifting a platter of gooey-looking brownies in one hand and a fistful of colorful hair ribbons in the other.

"Nice," Toby said, although he was far more focused on the sweet and lovely lady who stood in front of him, her blue eyes bright, her brown hair lying soft and glossy along her almost bare shoulders.

"Where's Kylie?" she asked.

"In her room. I'll call her." But before Toby could open his mouth, Kylie came dashing into the entry to greet Angie.

The two of them took off, and before long, Kylie

returned, wearing a pair of cowboy boots, just like Angie, her hair in princess-perfect pigtails.

"Let's go," he said.

It took only ten minutes on the county road to reach his parents' ranch. After driving through the white wooden gate, Toby followed the graveled road to the house and parked near the barn, next to the other cars and trucks.

"Looks like everyone beat us here," he said.

"Are we late?" Angie asked.

"Not really. But I have a feeling the women in my family were eager to be here when we arrived."

"Why?"

"Curiosity, I suppose." Toby shut off the ignition. "They know we've been seeing a lot of each other, and I'm afraid their imaginations are getting the best of them."

He could argue—and, in fact, he had argued—that he and Angie weren't dating, that she was merely helping him out with the kids. But sexual attraction and mutual interest were definitely flaring beneath the surface, and he wasn't so sure he'd be able to keep that a secret, especially here.

They all got out of the truck. As usual, the kids managed to pile out a lot faster than they ever climbed in.

"Don't forget to wipe your feet at the front door," Toby called out to them. "And don't barge in. Hang on until Angie and I get there."

"We won't," they called back in near unison.

Toby waited for Angie, as she reached into the cab and pulled out a denim jacket. Then she slipped into it, covering the white sundress that revealed a lovely set of tanned arms and shoulders. But as afternoon wore into evening, he knew there was a chance it could get chilly, so he couldn't blame her for being prepared.

Next he watched as she reached into the cab for the platter of brownies she'd brought.

"I'm sorry," she said, as she realized he was standing near the truck, waiting for her. "I didn't mean to be a slug."

"No problem." He actually liked watching her. But if he stared at her any longer, thinking about how much he wanted to pull her close, to kiss her before entering the house, it was going to take a whole lot more than an evening breeze to cool him off.

They walked together, meeting up with the kids at the front door, which was flanked by large pots of colorful flowers.

Out of habit, Toby took care to wipe his boots, just as he'd asked the children to do.

"My mom always made a big deal about us coming inside with muddy feet." He chuckled as he reached for the doorknob to let them all into the house. "I guess some habits are hard to break."

Toby's mom, with her silver hair pulled into a bun and dressed in her usual stretch-denim jeans and a pale blue sweatshirt, greeted them in the foyer. She gave Toby a warm embrace, then took the time to address each of the kids.

"Now, don't you look pretty, Kylie. Look at those yellow ribbons in your hair. And my goodness. What in the world have you stuffed in that backpack?"

"Toys to show baby Piper. Is she here?"

Jeanne Marie placed a hand on Kylie's head and smiled. "She certainly is. Aunt Stacey just gave her some bananas and peaches for a snack, which she's washing off her face and hands now. Why don't you go into the kitchen and see if she's ready to play."

"Oh, good," Kylie said, as she dashed off.

"And you boys are in for a big treat," Jeanne Marie told Brian and Justin. "Grandpa Deke fixed the rungs to the tree house and gave it a new coat of paint yesterday. And when Uncle Galen saw what he'd done, he attached a rope swing to one of those sturdy ole branches. You probably ought to go check it out."

"Cool," Brian said, as both boys hurried off.

Well done, Toby thought. His mother adored the kids, but it was plain to see that she had something up her sleeve. She'd sent them off happily so she could devote her full attention to Angie and to the interrogation process.

Now, with the children out of the way, she welcomed Angie with a warm shake of the hand. "I'm so glad you could join us. Toby tells me how helpful you've been to him this past week."

"It's been my pleasure. The kids are great. And in all honesty, Toby's so good with them, I'm not sure he even needs my help at all."

"Don't let her downplay her efforts," Toby said. "She's been awesome, whether it's playing beauty salon with Kylie or planning a make-it-yourself pizza night or watching a movie under the stars. And I would have really been up a creek yesterday without her."

"You don't say." His mom smiled, those blue eyes glimmering. "I'll tell you what, Toby. Why don't you check out that tree house and make sure Galen secured that swing right, while I take Angie into the kitchen. Since she's such a good helper, I'm going to rope her into helping the girls and I finish up with the burger fixings."

And just like a mama fox, Jeanne Marie had dispensed with Toby.

He could argue and insist that Angie stick close to his side, he supposed. But Angie was a big girl and had proved that she could hold her own. Besides, he wanted to check out that old fort he and his brothers used to play in. And on top of that, he trusted his mom and his sisters not to go overboard.

So he took his leave, walking out to the backyard, where his own interrogation undoubtedly awaited.

Angie followed Toby's mother out to the kitchen. She'd always liked the woman, but then, who in town didn't?

Jeanne Marie might come across as plain and simple, but there was more to her than met the eye. She had a quick wit, a gentle spirit and a kind heart. She also loved her husband and children dearly and was fiercely devoted to them.

Since working at the Superette, Angie had picked up on all of that. She'd even found herself a bit envious of the family's closeness. How could she not be?

She'd always wanted to be part of a big, happy family, but she'd been an only child. She and her daddy had been close, but he'd died five years ago.

Now that Angie was an adult, her mom sought the closeness they'd never quite had before. But Doris

Edwards was so determined to make Angie into the woman she wanted her to be that it was easier to avoid her, which was sad.

"I brought some brownies," Angie said, holding out the platter of chocolaty squares covered in caramel frosting and toffee pieces.

"You didn't need to do that," Jeanne Marie said, as she led Angie through the large-but-cozy living room. "But it was awfully nice of you. I try to have plenty for everyone to eat, but I have to admit, this family can really put away the desserts. So I doubt you'll have anything to take home except a few crumbs."

When they reached the kitchen, Angie saw Piper sitting in a walker on the floor with Kylie playing beside her. The little red-haired girl had made fast work of emptying out the entire contents of her backpack on the hardwood floor.

"You girls remember Angie," Jeanne Marie said to both Stacey and Delaney.

"Of course." Stacey, a bright-eyed blonde with a light spray of freckles on her nose, smiled. "We're so glad Toby finally brought you out to meet his crazy family."

Angie and Stacey had graduated from high school together, although they really hadn't run in the same circles. Stacey, who'd gone on to nursing school after graduation, had been more of an academic and tended to hang out with the smarter kids. And Angie had been all over the campus, hanging with the members of whichever social club she was trying out that semester.

"Thanks for including me." Angie placed the brownies on the sideboard, next to a Bundt cake in a covered dish and a plate of lemon bars. Toby's mom had been right. They were certainly dessert-friendly in this household. She hoped everyone was as sweet as the offerings on the countertop.

"Can I help you guys with anything?" Angie asked, noticing that Stacey was putting the finishing touches on a cheese-and-vegetable platter.

"Julia and Gabi are setting the tables outside," Delaney said, as she stirred something that appeared to be potato salad. "And we're almost done in here."

"Why don't you pull up a chair?" Stacey nodded to one of the empty barstools on the other side of the kitchen island. "Tell us what you've been doing with yourself since high school."

"Now hold off a moment," Jeanne Marie said. "It's only fair to offer Angie a glass of wine or some iced tea first. The least we can do is let our guest wet her whistle before you launch into a full-blown question-and-answer session."

When Jeanne winked at Angie, and her daughters laughed, easing the awkward tension, Angie couldn't help but join in the merriment. If Stacey and Delaney could make light of their overly curious natures, then so could she. Besides, she had nothing to hide.

Well, nothing except the fact that she had the hots for one of their brothers.

"I think I'll take an iced tea," Angie said, "but you guys keep doing what you're doing. I'll get it."

She'd no more than crossed the kitchen and was reaching for the pitcher when Justin rushed into the room, his eyes bright, his excitement impossible to ignore. "Angie, I was telling Uncle Galen about your candy brownies, and he wanted me to bring them out to the tree house so we can all try them."

If there was anyone who loved sweets more than the Fortune Jones family, it was Justin Hemings. And since he'd been eyeing those brownies and asking for a taste ever since she'd arrived at the Double H, Angie knew when he was still trying to finagle an early treat.

"You tell Uncle Galen that we have so many desserts to choose from that it's best if he waits until after dinner. That way, instead of having only one treat, he'll be able to try them all." Angie pointed to the counter holding the sweets.

Justin hurried over to look at his many options. His eyes darted from side to side, unable to settle on a favorite.

"Did you make all of these?" he asked Angie. Before she could answer, he looked at Jeanne Marie and continued. "Angie makes the *best* cupcakes with little race cars on the top. And she makes us pizza with our very own favorite toppings. And she puts extra butter on the popcorn because that's how Toby likes it best. She's the best cooker in the world. I'm going to tell Brian about the desserts. C'mon, Angie. You gotta come see the tree house."

And with that, Justin shot out the open sliding door, running as fast as he talked.

Angie looked at Toby's sisters, who both seemed eager to pounce on her with questions, but Jeanne Marie saved her by saying, "Let's go see the tree house. Then you can meet my husband. That will give my daughters plenty of time to strategize about what they want to ask you."

Grateful to have escaped what she was sure would have been a barrage of questions, Angie tossed them each a smile and went outside with Jeanne Marie to a built-in barbecue, where Deke was preparing to grill hamburger patties and hot dogs.

"Honey," Jeanne Marie said, "this is Angie Edwards, Toby's friend."

Deke, a tall, rugged man with a thatch of thick gray hair, turned to Angie and greeted her with a hint of a smile. "It's nice to meet you. We like it when the kids bring their friends home."

"I'm glad to be included," Angie said. "Where's that tree house I heard so much about?"

Deke pointed about fifty yards from the house to a huge tree where Toby stood with his brothers Jude, Liam and Galen. The men were watching Brian swing while laughing at something Liam said.

"The boys found that ole fort the first day Toby brought them to the ranch," Deke said. "But we hadn't realized how rotten some of that lumber had gotten until Justin fell and bumped his head a couple of weeks ago. So we wouldn't let them play on it until I could find the time to replace some of those old boards."

"Well, it looks as though they appreciate your time and effort," Angie said. "In fact, if I wasn't wearing a dress, I'd join them on that swing."

Jeanne Marie laughed. "And I might take a turn with you. When our sons were little, we used to have overnight campouts in that fort."

"You slept outside with them?" Angie couldn't imagine her mom doing something like that.

"I did until they stopped being afraid of the bogeyman. After that, whenever they had those campouts I stayed inside and enjoyed the peace and quiet with their daddy."

Deke grinned and gave Jeanne Marie a little pat.

It was heartwarming to see such a loving couple. She'd never seen her parents show each other any affection.

"Honey," Deke said to his wife, "can you please go in the house and get a clean platter for me to put the cooked meat on?"

"I'll get it," Angie offered. "Everyone else has a job to do. I better earn my dinner, too."

"Then you go on ahead," Jeanne Marie said with a laugh. "We wouldn't want you to feel excluded."

Angie started toward the house, just as Julia Tierney was coming outside with a pitcher of lemonade and a stack of red plastic cups.

"Hey," Julia said. "I heard you were coming. It's nice to see you outside of the Superette."

Angie smiled. "It's nice to be here. In fact, I've only been on the ranch a few minutes, but everyone has been so warm and welcoming. You're lucky to be a part of this."

Julia, who'd recently become engaged to Toby's brother Liam, had a glow about her these days. "I've really been blessed. I've fallen in love with the greatest guy in the world, and he has a wonderful family."

"You know," Angie said, as she stepped aside, "I'd better let you put that lemonade down before you drop it. Besides, I finally have a job to do and don't want Deke to think I'm lagging."

Julia smiled. "I'll talk to you later."

As Julia passed through the doorway and onto the patio, Gabriella Mendoza followed behind her, carrying a platter of lettuce leaves, tomato slices and other hamburger fixings.

Gabi was also sporting a diamond engagement ring these days, courtesy of Jude, another of Toby's brothers. The two had met after Gabi's father, Orlando Mendoza, had been seriously injured in a plane crash.

Orlando had been a pilot for the Redmond Flight School when the accident happened. And Gabi had flown out from Miami to be with him as soon as she'd gotten the news.

"Hi there," Gabi said. "It's good to see you again."

"Same here," Angie said. "How's your dad doing?"

"Much better. Thank you for asking."

"I'm so glad to hear that." Angie again stepped aside to let Gabi pass, then entered the kitchen, which was a bustle of activity as Stacey and Delaney laid out plates of appetizers to go outside.

"Your dad asked me to bring him a clean platter for the cooked meat," Angie said.

"I'll get that for you." Stacey went to a side cupboard and pulled out a large, ceramic platter. "But before you go, I do have a question for you."

Angie smiled. "Okay, shoot."

"In high school you were Queen of the First Date and president of just about every club they offered," Angie assumed Stacey was going to point out the obvious—that Angie couldn't commit to anything—until she added, "At times I was a bit envious."

No kidding? She hadn't meant to insult her? Stacey had actually admired her?

"I'm curious," Stacey said. "When you told Justin not to choose anything too soon, how did you come up with that strategy?"

It was a strategy, although no one had actually pegged it as such.

The other women in the kitchen—Julia and Gabi were now back—continued to move about, but their movements slowed and their side conversations stalled.

Angie had never tried to explain it to anyone before, but for some reason, she opted for candor now. "My dad used to tell me to be careful when making a choice, because once I made it, I couldn't change my mind. So I took that to heart. I try everything once, knowing that when I find something I'm passionate about, I'll stick to it."

Trouble was, she wasn't entirely convinced of that. If it turned out she was wrong, she could end up in some eternal revolving door of new beginnings and never find a happy ending.

"But you don't believe that, do you?" Delaney said. "I mean, everyone makes mistakes. It's not like you can't start over and have a second chance."

Angie had never talked about her childhood to anyone before, but being here with Toby's family had a way of making her lower her guard.

"Yes, I know that—intellectually. However, I grew up in a household with parents who remained in an unhappy marriage for my sake. And they drilled it into me that once a commitment was made, you had to stick to it."

"That's kind of sad," Delaney said.

"I know. My mom hated small-town life, so living

in Horseback Hollow nearly sucked the life out of her. And as a result, her unhappiness nearly sucked the life out of my dad."

"Is that why your mom eventually moved to Lubbock?" Delaney asked.

It was common knowledge that Doris acted as though she was better than everyone in town. And that she'd filed for a divorce and moved to Lubbock the day after Angie had graduated from high school.

Still, even when her mom had lived with them in Horseback Hollow, she'd commuted to work in Lubbock, which meant she was gone most of the time. And to be honest, she'd left Angie and her father emotionally even before that—or so it had seemed.

"My parents were mismatched from day one," Angie said. "And, if anything, it's made me not want to make any big decisions that I might regret for the rest of my life, especially when it came to a college degree or a lifelong profession."

"C'mon, Angie," Delaney said. "Don't you think you're taking your dad's advice to an extreme?"

"Maybe," Angie conceded. "But I've had a lot of cool jobs, tried a variety of things and learned a lot along the way. I can also handle just about anything thrown my way."

"I've heard about some of your job experience," Jeanne Marie said, as she entered the kitchen and breezed right into the conversation.

"What have you heard?" Angie asked.

"That you're more than qualified to do *my* job." Jeanne Marie laughed as she carried the big bowl of potato salad out the back door to the tables set up in the yard.

Angie looked at Toby's sisters and whispered, "What's your mom's job?"

The girls both laughed, and Angie began to wonder whether any of them would answer. Finally, Delaney said, "She was a professional stay-at-home mom."

Angie was at a loss. She could never be a stay-at-home mom. Not like Jeanne Marie.

When the girls finally got their giggles under control, Stacey asked, "Do you need any help deciding what to do with our brother?"

"No, not really. We never seem to have any time to talk about it. So I have no idea what he's even thinking."

Angie did, however, have a very memorable moment of waking in his arms—before the sprinklers ruined it all.

"You mean you've never had a proper date?" Stacey asked.

"I'm afraid not. The kids are always with us. And to tell you the truth, I don't know if Toby *wants* to date me."

"Oh, believe us," Stacey said, "he wants to."

Delaney beamed. "Just leave it to us. Stacey and I are just the ones who can make that happen."

A date? With Toby Fortune Jones?

Angie didn't know if she should run for the hills—or thank her lucky stars.

As the meat sizzled on the grill, setting off the aroma of barbecued burgers and hot dogs, Toby stood next to his father and Colton Foster, Stacey's fiancé.

Deke had roped his future son-in-law into helping

him man the grill, and the two ranchers had been discussing the rising cost of feed corn, as well as the new bull Deke intended to purchase.

But Toby couldn't seem to focus on the discussion at hand. Instead he kept thinking about the one going on in the kitchen, where the women had gathered with Angie.

"Excuse me," he said, as he stepped away from his dad and Colton.

The two men continued to talk while Toby strode across the patio to the insulated cooler that held a variety of drinks, including the ice-cold bottle of beer he snatched for himself.

So far, the family dinner at his parents' house seemed to be going well. The women had begun to carry out the food and place it on tables that had been set up on the lawn, which meant it would be time to eat soon.

Jude, Liam and Galen had gathered near the tree house, where they were probably still reminiscing about their childhood or predicting the likelihood of the Rangers making it to the World Series this year.

But Toby's mind was on the kids and the fear that he might lose them. He could honestly say that if Barbara were a loving and maternal woman who'd made a few mistakes and was trying hard to straighten her life out he wouldn't be so uneasy. After all, he probably valued family ties more than anyone. It was just that he'd never seen a maternal side to Barbara.

He thought about sharing his worries with his family, but he didn't want to talk about it in front of the kids. Maybe it was best to wait until after he'd talked to Ms. Fisk on Monday—assuming she'd return his call the day she returned to the office.

Either way, he couldn't very well stew about it all weekend. So he'd better shake it off for now and start mingling before people started asking him what was bothering him.

As he stood in the center of the yard, a beer in hand, debating which of the two male groups to join, a squeal of feminine laughter rang out from the kitchen.

What in the heck were the women talking about in there? He hoped the topic of conversation wasn't on him and Angie.

Should he check? Did Angie need him to bail her out?

No, they were all laughing, so it had to be something else. His presence would only remind them of the questioning they'd planned upon his and Angie's arrival. So it would be best—and safer—if he hung out with the men.

Opting for the rowdier group near the tree house, Toby returned to the cooler, reached in for a couple more Coronas and carried them out to his brothers.

Upon his approach, a big ole grin stole across Galen's face. "You're just the guy I wanted to talk to."

"What about?" Toby asked.

"About you and Angie. I hear things are heating up."

Toby wasn't sure where Galen had come up with that. He glanced at Jude and Liam, both of whom were smirking, and realized it was now his turn to get the third degree. But there wasn't much to tell—or much he was willing to talk about.

He offered up the extra two Coronas he held instead. "You guys want a beer?"

Liam and Jude both took one.

Galen crossed his arms, his grin bursting into a full-on smile. "Don't change the subject, little bro. We just want to know what's going on with you and Angie, especially since Justin told us you two had a sleepover last night."

Aw, hell. Toby had been afraid that was going to happen.

He blew out a sigh. "As nice as that might sound, I'm afraid Justin blew that all out of proportion. Angie stayed over, but it's not what you're thinking."

"Hmm." Liam crossed his arms. "So if it would have been nice, does that mean you're interested in her?"

So what if he was?

Still, Toby wasn't going to admit anything. If he did, he'd never hear the end of it. And besides, he and Angie hadn't even talked about whether they wanted their relationship or friendship or whatever the hell it was to progress to a level like that.

"You know what I think?" Toby said to Liam. "You guys have fallen in love, so you think everyone else ought to be feeling the same way."

"I'm still single and unattached," Galen said. "And I think there's definitely some big-time sparks going on between you and Angie."

"Okay," Toby said. "I'm attracted to her. She's fun to be with. But that's about all there is to it."

"Why aren't you pursuing anything more?" Galen asked.

All kinds of reasons. The kids, for one. Angie's inability to commit to anyone or anything, for another. But then again, that hadn't seemed to matter when they'd woken up in each other's arms this morning.

Of course, there was also the matter of Jude dating her in the past. And Toby didn't want to cross any weird fraternal boundaries or become romantically involved with a woman his brother had once been… intimate with.

Wouldn't that be one huge disappointment?

"Speaking of Angie," Toby said to Jude, "you dated her, didn't you?"

"I guess you could call it that. We only went out a couple of times. It ended pretty abruptly."

"What happened?" Toby asked.

"When Angie's mom saw her out with me one evening, she flipped out. Apparently, she thought Angie could do a whole lot better. Doris tried to lower her voice, but I overheard her refer to me as a 'Horseback Hollow Casanova' and ask if I'd gone through all the women in my own age bracket and had started on a new generation." Jude blew out a sigh. "Okay, granted, there was a six-year age difference, but come on. A whole generation?"

Knowing her mom, that didn't surprise Toby. So if he and Angie ever did start dating, he and Doris would have to set some definite boundaries.

"So it ended quickly," Toby said. "But how serious were you?"

"It never would have gotten off the ground. She was a little too indecisive for me." Jude laughed. "Don't get me wrong. She's a nice girl, and we had fun. But

I made the mistake of asking her which movie she wanted to see. If I hadn't picked one myself and taken her by the hand, we probably would have stood outside the theater all night."

Toby had never really seen that side of Angie. She always seemed to know just what she wanted when she was with him and the kids.

Feminine voices grew louder as the women gathered outside and his mother announced that it was time to eat.

"Brian and Justin," she called to the boys in the tree house, "go on in the house with Kylie and wash your hands."

As the boys hurried to do as they were told, Jude asked Toby, "Has Angie decided upon a career yet?"

"No, she hasn't."

"Don't let that stop you," Galen said. "Look at her. She's smoking hot."

His oldest brother certainly had that right. Toby studied the lovely brunette crossing the lawn in that white sundress. She had on the denim jacket now, as well as those cowboy boots. So she'd covered up her arms and shoulders. But she still looked good.

In fact, she looked amazing in whatever she wore—especially a wet yoga outfit.

"Let me know if you're not interested in her," Galen added. "If that's the case, I might ask her out myself."

Just the thought of Galen moving in on Angie sent Toby's senses reeling.

"All right, I'm interested," he admitted. "So back off."

Before his brothers could tease him further, he

headed for the tables and found seats for him, Angie and the kids.

As was typical of a Fortune Jones dinner, everyone ate their fill, including the variety of desserts. All the while, they told stories about growing up together, sometimes teasing, usually smiling or laughing.

When Toby could finally call it a day, he rounded up the kids and told them it was time to head home.

"Why don't you let Brian and Justin spend the night here," Galen said. "I think I'll camp out in that tree house for old times' sake. And it would be nice if the boys kept me company."

Before Toby could respond, Stacey chimed in. "And Piper would like to have her very first sleepover. Why don't you let Colton and me take Kylie home with us?"

"A sleepover?" Toby asked. "Piper is only nine months old."

Stacey smiled. "You're right. She doesn't stay up past seven. But then I'll get a chance to play with Kylie."

What was going on? Galen and Stacey were offering to keep the kids?

"I don't know about that," Toby said. "They don't have their pajamas or toothbrushes."

Galen elbowed him. "Come on, Toby. Real cowboys don't sleep in jammies. They sleep in their boots and clothes. What's the matter with you?"

Stacey edged forward. "Kylie can sleep in one of my old T-shirts. I also have a brand-new toothbrush she can use. What do you say?"

He didn't know what to say. The offer stole the words right out of him.

"Come on, Toby." His little sister gave him a wink. "You deserve a good night's sleep."

It took him a moment to realize what his crazy family was up to. And he didn't know if he should kill them or kiss them. But when he took a look at Angie, when he spotted the wide-eyed wonder, the look of surprise…

Well, it wasn't just the kids who were whooping it up and begging for the night to come.

Toby's hormones were right there with them.

Chapter Nine

As Toby's pickup headed down the county road that led to the Double H Ranch, Angie bit down on her bottom lip and stared out the windshield. It was the first time they'd actually been alone, and for some reason they both seemed to be at a loss for words.

Sure, they'd had a few stolen moments before, but this was different. There were no children to worry about walking in on them, no job to hustle out to, no errands to run.

It was just the two of them.

The silence in the cab was almost overwhelming, and if that weren't enough, Angie's heart was zipping through her chest, racing around as if it wanted to beat her and Toby back to his place.

But then what? Things were sure to be more awkward there.

Would he tell her good-night the minute they got out of the truck? Or would he invite her into the house?

He hadn't uttered a word since they'd left, so she had no idea what he was thinking. But whenever she stole a glance across the seat, the expression he wore suggested that he felt just as on edge and nervous as she did.

She'd like to put him—or rather both of them—at ease, but she was so far out of her element that she didn't know where to begin.

What she could really use was an icebreaker, but she couldn't seem to come up with anything clever to say or do. So she just sank into the leather passenger seat, trying to keep her eyes off the handsome rancher who'd been captivating her thoughts more and more each day.

When they finally turned down his drive and neared the ranch house, she spotted her car parked right where she'd left it. The old Toyota looked a little sad and lonely sitting there, and Angie was going to feel the same way if she drove off in it.

Think, girl. Say something.

"So," she finally said, the sound of her voice breaking into the silence. "What are you going to do with an evening all to yourself?"

At that, Toby turned, glanced across the seat at her and smiled. "It's been so long since I've had a night without the kids that I have no idea."

Angie tucked a strand of hair behind her ear and tossed him a carefree grin. "Then if I were you, I'd turn on the TV, choose a channel that doesn't play cartoons and eat ice cream straight from the container."

Toby shut off the ignition. In the dim light of the

cab, she caught a glimmer in his eyes and a flirtatious tilt in his smile.

Now there went a definite *zing*.

He stretched his arm across the seat, and his smile deepened. "If you were me, would you invite someone in to watch television and help you eat the rest of the chocolate ice cream?"

"Actually, that's exactly what I'd do. But instead of the ice cream, I'd offer her wine because she probably avoided anything alcoholic at the barbecue for fear she'd slip and say something that your sisters might misconstrue. But I'd also promise to let her control the remote."

Toby laughed. "The wine, I can do. But I'm pretty territorial about my remote."

Not bad for an icebreaker, huh?

Angie smiled, then reached for the door handle and let herself out of the truck. They walked together to the porch, and when Toby opened the front door for her and flipped on the light switch, she stepped inside.

The house was quieter than it had ever been, at least since she'd started coming to visit. Only now, the solitude made things awkward again. Without the kids around to act as buffers, she and Toby had to face each other and whatever they were feeling.

He led her to the kitchen, where he opened the fridge and pulled out the bottle of wine for her and a longneck beer for him.

"I had a lot of fun tonight," she said, as she removed a goblet from the cabinet. "Your family knows how to have a good time. And they're down-to-earth."

"If by 'down-to-earth,' you mean 'meddling,' then,

yes. They are." Toby filled her glass. After popping the top off his drink, he leaned against the counter in a sexy cowboy slant.

"They weren't meddling," Angie said. "They were a little curious, maybe. But friendly. And look at how helpful they were, offering to take the kids for the night so that you could have a break."

Toby chuckled, then lifted the Corona to his lips and took another swig.

Oh, sweet goodness. Those lips. Angie had never been so jealous of a drink container.

When he lowered the bottle, his gaze zeroed in on her. "You know why they offered to keep the kids, don't you?"

She hadn't wanted to speculate, but now that he'd brought it up, she supposed, deep down, that she'd known what they'd been up to. They'd wanted to give her and Toby some time alone.

Or rather, a *night* alone.

Gosh. It was sure getting warm in here. Had someone left the oven on while they'd been gone?

She slipped off her denim jacket and placed it on the back of one of the barstools. All the while, Toby continued to lean against the counter, watching her.

Why was he looking at her like that—as if there was a big ole elephant in the room and he was determined to circle around it and come right on over to her?

His gaze was only making her warmer, and if he didn't stop, she was going to melt into a puddle.

Hoping the wine would help her cool down, she took a gulp.

"Come on." Toby reached for her hand, his fingers

threading through hers and sending a flurry of little zings rushing all the way to her core. Then he led her to the living room.

Thank goodness they were walking. Her knees had turned to rubber, and she wasn't sure they'd hold her up much longer if she didn't shake them out and get the blood flowing again.

She could use some cool air, too.

When they reached the living room, he led her to the leather sectional, where she took a seat. Then he sat next to her, even though there'd been plenty of room to spread out.

That was a good sign, yes?

Or was it a bad one?

She wasn't quite sure. But either way, the heat from the kitchen had followed them into the living room, and she took another swallow of wine.

"My family was definitely meddling," he said. "They could have kept the kids last night—or the weekend before. But they wanted to spend some time with you first, to see us together, before they made the offer."

"So they were vetting me?" she asked.

"That's about the size of it."

"Hmm." Angie stared at her chardonnay as if it was the most fascinating wine she'd ever tasted. Then she took another sip. If she continued to drink at this rate, she'd finish what was left in the bottle—and be on the floor soon after that.

"I guess I should be flattered that they approve," she said.

He placed his arm along the backrest, close enough

for her to feel his body heat along her bare shoulders. "How could they not approve of you? You're bright, funny, sweet and genuine." He paused, then fingered a strand of her hair. "And you're so damn beautiful."

Zing! Zing! Zing!

Now her glass was empty. Where had all that cold wine gone?

"Aw, hell," he said. "I'd wanted to spend some time with you away from the kids. But now that I've finally got you alone…"

When he trailed off, she studied his averted gaze, his pained expression.

What had he been about to say?

That he wasn't interested in her? That she was nice as far as babysitters went, but there was no point in her being here if the kids weren't?

"But *now* what?" she prodded.

Whoa. Where had the double-shot of courage come from? Did she really want to hear what he'd been about to say?

Her heart went haywire while she awaited his answer.

Toby removed his hand from her hair, from the back of the sofa and leaned forward.

Uh-oh. Bad sign?

Then he raked his fingers through his own hair. "It's just that now it all feels forced. And expected. It's like every member of my family knows exactly what we're doing right this second."

Angie chuckled, the sound coming out in a nervous rush. "But we aren't doing *anything*. And even if we do decide to do something, whatever happens or doesn't happen is our secret. Nobody has to know."

Toby's brows furrowed, and a look of annoyance crossed his face. "Of course no one will know. Do I look like the type to kiss and tell?"

"Toby," Angie said, her tone the same one she used when one of the kids was out of line. "I'm not sure if you're the type to *kiss,* let alone talk about it."

Their eyes met for a moment, and then a slow grin spread across his face. "Oh, I'm the type, all right." Then he lowered his mouth to hers.

Angie turned into his embrace, eager to kiss him with the passion that had been building over the past week until it threatened to consume her now.

And she wasn't disappointed.

His lips were soft, yet demanding. And his taste, while cool and refreshing, was hot and arousing.

Breaths mingled, tongues mated and the kiss deepened, intensifying until they were making out on the sofa like a couple of teenagers who had the run of the house for the very first time.

As Toby tugged at the strap of her dress, slipping it off her shoulder, he stroked her skin, igniting a fire and an ache deep in her core. Her breath caught, and her zing meter burst, like a flash of sparklers on a Fourth of July night.

As she leaned back and sucked a gulp of air into her lungs, Toby trailed kisses down her neck, along her shoulder. The warmth of his breath, the skill of his lips, caused her back to arch. And she was…his.

Toby had wanted to get Angie into his arms ever since the day he'd seen her wearing those cutoff shorts and walking around with bare, freshly painted toes.

And judging from the wispy little pants and whimpers coming from her sweet lips, she'd been wanting him just as badly.

At least, she certainly wanted him now.

The ride home from his parents' house had just about done him in. He'd never been so tense in his life. Not just because the physical attraction between the two of them had built to astronomical proportions, but because they'd soon have a big decision to make.

If they took things to a physical level tonight, there'd be no going back. And he needed to know that they were both on the same page.

As much as it pained him, he pulled his mouth from hers and ended the kiss.

"I...uh..." He cleared his throat. "We..."

Hell, he didn't even know what to say. Seconds ago, when they'd been kissing, he'd been in complete control of his tongue. But now he could barely form a simple word.

Angie merely looked at him with passion-glazed eyes.

Finally he managed to spell it out. "If you think you might have second thoughts about where this is heading, now would be a good time to say it."

"If you're afraid I'll change my mind or have any regrets," she said, "don't be."

That was the answer he'd wanted to hear. So he captured her mouth in another heart-soaring, star-spinning kiss.

Somehow, without removing her lips from his, she managed to lift a knee, and in one swift movement, she straddled his lap and faced him.

As they continued to kiss, he ran his hands up and down the slope of her back, along her hips, caressing her curves, memorizing them.

The lovely sundress, once so damn sexy, was now in the way. Should he unzip it and do away with it?

As she began to rock back and forth, a movement that was sure to drive them both over the brink, he realized they could very easily make love right on the sofa if he didn't change tactics. So again he drew his lips from hers.

"Let's take this into the bedroom," he whispered. But instead of releasing her, he held her tighter, leaned forward and slowly got to his feet.

She wrapped her legs around his waist, holding on as he carried her to his room. He kissed her along the way, hoping not to step on any of the LEGO pieces or dolls that sometimes littered his hallway.

He meant to hold himself in check, but he couldn't seem to help himself from tumbling with her onto the bed.

As they stretched out, hands reaching, lips seeking, she sobered and pulled away. "Toby, wait."

Oh, no. She wasn't going to stop him now, was she? If so, this was one hell of a time for her to prove everyone right and change her mind.

"I'm not on the pill," she said. "And I don't have any…you know…protection with me. I wasn't really anticipating this."

Did she think *he* was?

He couldn't help but smile, as he rolled to the side, taking her with him. "I hope you don't think I was expecting this to happen, either, or that I planned to bring you back here and ravish you." He'd hoped to, yes. But he hadn't planned to. "I do happen to have some condoms, though."

She smiled. "So we have that hurdle covered."

"And just so you know, I've been weighing the pros and cons of where moving forward might take us."

"Maybe you're overthinking things," she said.

Had that come from the woman who seemed to overthink every little decision she'd ever had to make?

"It's really quite simple," she added. "Either you want me or you don't."

He ran a knuckle along her cheek. "That part *is* simple. I want you more than I've ever wanted another woman in my life."

Dang. Had he really admitted that to her? And was it actually true?

Yeah, he was afraid that it was.

"But then what?" he asked.

"If you're sure about what you want, then everything else will fall into place."

How could he argue with *that* logic?

Toby chuckled and slowly shook his head. Who would have guessed that Angie would be the one helping him make a decision?

But, in truth, he feared he'd decided he wanted her—and wanted this—long before now. And judging by the way she'd sat up, unzipped her dress and began to lift it over her head, so had she.

Toby reached into his nightstand drawer and pulled out the box of condoms he'd picked up at the pharmacy when he'd been in Lubbock yesterday.

Okay, so maybe he *had* done a *little* planning. And

after waking up with her on the lawn this morning in a state of arousal, he'd realized that purchase had been a good investment, since he'd thought—or rather, he'd hoped—an occasion like this might arise.

When Angie had completely undressed, she stretched out on the bed, her perfect breasts, her lush curves a tempting sight he'd never forget.

She was beautiful and sweet and, at least for this moment in time, completely his.

She reached for his belt buckle, letting him know that she was ready for him to join her, and he quickly removed his clothing, too.

"You're so beautiful, Toby. So perfect."

Him? She thought *he* was perfect? She was the beautiful one. The perfect one. And as he lay down beside her again, he used his mouth and his body to tell her just that.

When he entered her, making them one, she arched up to meet his thrusts. And as she peaked, as her nails dug into his shoulders, she called out his name, sending him over the edge of control.

They came together in one amazing kaleidoscope of color, then held on to each other, riding the ebb and flow of the wonder-filled moment to the very end.

Finally, as their breathing slowed to normal, Angie opened her eyes and smiled. "That was amazing."

"To say the least." Toby pressed a kiss on her forehead. "And I have to admit, it was probably one of the best decisions I've ever made."

"Sometimes," Angie said, as she ran a leg along his, "the right decision can't be made with a list and a spreadsheet. Sometimes you just have to follow your heart."

He'd followed his—right into Angie's arms. Trouble was, he feared she'd captured his heart and that he might never get it back, even if she decided she was no longer interested in what little he had to offer her.

After walking naked through the quiet house to the kitchen for the carton of ice cream to share in bed, they made love several times before finally falling to sleep in the wee hours of morning.

The next day, as sunlight peered through the open shutters of his bedroom window, Toby awoke with Angie in his arms, the tousled sheet doing very little to cover her naked body. There was no telling when they'd have the house to themselves again, so he decided to wake her with a kiss.

But before he could nuzzle her neck, the bedside telephone rang, dashing his romantic thoughts.

Angie shot up in bed, pulling the sheet with her, as if the ringing phone had not only awoken her but reminded her their night in paradise had ended.

Toby snatched the telephone receiver after the third ring. "Hello?"

"Hey," Justin said, his voice so loud Angie could undoubtedly hear. "What are you doing? Grandma made us wait until eight o'clock to call you, but we've been up since six."

Bless his mom for putting a time restriction on the morning wake-up call, but would waiting another thirty minutes have hurt?

Angie began to inch off the bed, a pink tint brightening her cheeks. She had a history of running off on him when they'd been caught in an intimate position, and Toby wasn't going to let her slip away from him this time. Not after last night. So he made a grab for the sheet she was tugging along with her, and she tumbled back to the mattress, practically landing on him.

A muffled "oomph" sounded from her lips, as he locked his arm around her and pulled her close.

"What was that noise?" Justin asked.

Before Toby could make up a reasonable explanation, Brian yelled, "Don't forget to tell Toby about the baseball game!"

"Oh, yeah," Justin said. "The reason I called was because Uncle Galen has tickets for the Lubbock Hubbers game today and said he would give them to us. So can we go? And can we invite Angie? Galen has five tickets, and the game starts at one. So can we? Please?"

Toby wondered how his brother had magically come up with exactly five tickets to a minor-league baseball game the morning after his sisters had concocted a plan to get him and Angie alone together for the night. Somehow, it didn't seem like a coincidence.

He put his hand over the mouthpiece and whispered, "You want to go with us to the ball game?"

Angie's second of hesitation was all he needed to make the decision for her. After all, she'd been the one to tell him to follow his heart. So now, in the aftermath of their incredible night together, he was going to keep following his. And he was going to encourage her to do the same.

"Okay, kiddo," he told Justin. "I'll call Angie at *her house* and ask her if she wants to go with us. Then I'll go by *her house* to get her before I swing by Grandma and Grandpa's house to pick up you guys."

He wondered if he'd gotten his point across that Angie wasn't with him.

But Justin didn't seem to care either way. All he said was "Don't forget to bring our gloves. I'm going to catch the first foul ball!"

"I won't forget."

When they'd said goodbye and the call ended, Toby went back to his very first catch of the day—a beautiful brunette he hoped wouldn't run off on him anytime soon.

Chapter Ten

Toby, Angie and the kids had a blast at the baseball game on Sunday, although Kylie, who'd eaten too much cotton candy, popcorn and too many mustard dogs, had thrown up in Toby's truck on the way home. But both Angie and Toby had gotten used to unpleasant surprises like that—and to rolling with the unexpected punches of life with children.

In fact, it seemed only natural for them to settle into a routine, with Angie spending more time at Toby's than at her own place.

However, Toby was expecting a visit from child services and thought it best to downplay their relationship. Angie, of course, agreed with him, especially since she wasn't sure how involved she wanted to be with him and the kids anyway. So she didn't spend the night with him again. But that didn't mean they weren't able to steal a kiss or enjoy a tender-but-secret embrace whenever they could.

For the next week, they tried to be discreet about the change in their relationship, but their happiness was hard to contain, and the secret began to leak out.

On the following Monday, while the kids were in school, Toby took lunch to her while she was working at Redmond-Fortune Air. She'd stayed so late at the ranch the night before, making out with him on the front porch after the kids went to sleep, that by the time she'd driven home, she'd barely gotten any sleep. And she'd hurried to work without having breakfast.

When Toby had called that morning and learned her alarm hadn't gone off, he'd known she'd be hungry. So he came sauntering in to the flight school carrying a take-out bag from The Grill.

Angie's heart melted at the sight of him, and her stomach growled at the aroma of pastrami and fries.

"What's in the bag?" Sawyer asked his cousin.

"I figured you weren't making enough money to feed your employees," Toby said. "So I brought Angie's lunch."

"Well, it's nice to see you've stopped using the kids as a pretense to schmooze with my most valuable employee."

"I brought one for you, too." Toby tossed one of the wrapped sandwiches to his cousin. "Maybe this will keep your mouth too busy to talk."

Sawyer laughed as he snatched the flying pastrami. "You're going to be buying a lot of extra lunches if you think you can keep the whole town from talking."

Sawyer had been right about that. Angie had heard

a few murmurs while she'd worked at the Superette the next day, although no one came right out and said anything directly to her.

Of course, Mr. Murdock did when she was getting ready to leave for work on Wednesday morning.

"Why don't you take my car," he said, pulling out his set of keys. "Leave yours here, and I'll change the oil for you. When I'm finished, I'll come down to the market and we'll trade."

"That's really sweet of you, Mr. Murdock. Thank you."

"I thought it'd be a shame if you had car trouble and got stranded on the road." He burst into a grin, then winked at her. "No telling how many miles you've logged on that car by driving out to that ranch at all hours of the day and night."

She could have downplayed the whole thing, but she realized people weren't dumb, especially the ones who knew her so well. The fact was, she was falling for Toby. And that was going to be tough to hide.

But would their happiness last? She hoped so, but she feared they were living in their own little bubble and that reality would eventually intrude.

She just hadn't realized it would happen so soon.

That very afternoon, following her yoga class and Justin's swim lesson—which, thankfully, went off without a hitch!—she entered Toby's kitchen to find him gazing out the window, his hands braced on either side of the sink.

The cordless phone sat on the counter beside the forgotten chicken-and-rice casserole she'd left for him to pop into the oven.

This wasn't good.

Angie told Justin to do his homework and to tell the other kids they'd be eating in thirty minutes. Then she placed the casserole in the preheated oven herself.

When Toby still hadn't moved or otherwise acknowledged her presence, she walked up behind him, slid her arms around his waist and pressed her face to his back. "I'm here if you want to talk about whatever's bothering you."

Toby turned and gathered her into his arms. "I know. And I love having you here. It's just that…" He blew out a sigh. "I got a call from child services. I need to talk to you about it, but not until after the kids go to bed."

The sound of a heated argument rising up in the family room about whose turn it was to use the computer forced Angie to lower her arms and ease out of their embrace.

"Do you want referee duty?" she asked. "Or would you prefer to make the salad?"

"I'd rather putter around in the kitchen alone until I can manage a happy face."

Uh-oh. That phone call hadn't been a good one.

She placed a hand on his cheek, felt the light bristle of his beard, then drew his lips to hers for a quick kiss. "I've got your back, Toby. Don't worry about the kids. I'll keep them busy until dinner is on the table."

Then she walked to the family room, where an old laptop had been set up for the kids to use for homework assignments.

I love having you here, he'd said.

Did that mean he loved *her?* Or that he just loved having her help?

They'd spent so much time together since they'd made love, which would lead Angie to believe that Toby definitely wanted to be with her. Yet, they hadn't had the opportunity for a repeat performance of that magical night, so she was feeling more insecure than she would've liked.

But within minutes of entering the family room, her insecurities disappeared. She was too busy setting time limits on the computer, helping Kylie with her word search and explaining the different biospheres to Brian. Then, of course, she had to explain to Justin that while she didn't mind inviting Mr. Murdock to dinner so he could share more war stories, tonight wasn't a good night for them to have company.

It was funny, though. When she was with Brian, Justin and Kylie, all of the other pressing details in life seemed so inconsequential. These sweet kids needed her and were way more important than her shift at the Superette or her mother's wish to see her married off.

As she herded the children and their freshly washed hands toward the kitchen table, she noticed that Toby had managed to slap on a smile of sorts.

However, he'd also added strawberries to the Caesar salad. Yuck. He knew better than that.

She suspected the telephone call with child services must have really knocked him off-balance because, despite his forced smile and attempts at conversation over dinner, he asked Brian several times what game they'd played during PE today. And then he promised Kylie that she could invite her three best friends to The Cuttery for a beauty makeover day tomorrow, just like Madison Rodriguez had done when it was her birthday.

How was he going to pull that off? Angie had already told him she was having brunch with her mom in Lubbock tomorrow, so she couldn't help him.

She supposed he'd have to ask Jeanne Marie, Deke or one of his sisters to help out, which made Angie feel a little insignificant. But she scolded herself for the crazy thought and shook it off.

What was the matter with her? She deserved a break, didn't she? And besides, shouldn't his mother or his sisters help him out once in a while?

As soon as dinner was over, she handled the bedtime duties alone, while Toby stayed in the kitchen to clean up.

When she finally returned, she stood in the doorway and watched him go through the motions, his mind still clearly on anything but what he was doing, as he wiped the casserole dish over and over again.

"I think that's as dry as it's going to get," she said. "Just leave everything and come with me."

When she reached out her hand to him, he laid the baking dish and towel on the counter. Then he let her lead him outside to the porch, where they took seats on the cushioned patio bench.

While she listened to the ranch sounds at night— cattle lowing, crickets chirping—she waited for him to share what had been weighing on his mind.

Finally, he said, "Ms. Fisk, the kids' case worker, called. Their aunt Barbara isn't ready to leave rehab, but she's been pushing hard to have the children shipped out of state to live with her cousin, a guy who's out on parole and who's never even met them."

The news slammed into Angie like a line drive to

the chest, and her stomach twisted. Toby stood to lose the kids? What would that do to them?

What would it do to *him?*

Oh, God. What would it do to her? She'd grown to love them, to care for them. To want the best for them....

"Did the case worker think that could happen?" she asked. "I mean, they're doing so well."

"She said it was unlikely, but that it could happen. I've read about cases that went badly. And bottom line? I'm just their foster dad. I'm not their blood kin, so I don't have much legal standing."

Angie took his hand in hers, letting him know that she was here for him, that she was worried and hurting, too.

"Did you tell the case worker your concerns?" she asked. "Did you mention how well they're doing, and that uprooting them wouldn't be good for them?"

"I laid out every argument I could think of. And she agreed with me, but her hands are somewhat tied. Apparently, that long-lost cousin in California wants to petition for adoption. And Ms. Fisk thinks the court would rather see the kids in a permanent home than in foster care."

Angie's stomach tossed and turned as she tried to make sense of it all.

"Why would a guy in California suddenly want to adopt three kids he's never even met?" she asked. "That seems like a mighty big step for someone to take."

"I agree. And I hope the judge will consider that question, too. That trust fund could very well be motivating both Barbara and her cousin to seek custody, especially since she knew about my mom's long-lost brother and her connection to the Fortunes. She'd also heard about the incident at the YMCA."

Angie stiffened, and her fingers, still held in the warmth of Toby's hands, grew cold. "You mean she heard about the day I flipped out and the paramedics were called?"

If she'd somehow caused a black mark upon Toby's case, she'd never forgive herself.

"I don't think the incident at the Y had anything to do with Barbara's call to child services and the petition for adoption. But someone in town has been feeding her rumors. And knowing her, the one rumor that she may have heard, the one that may have really caused a stir in her, was the one about the kids' trust fund."

"But you're the trustee. Don't you control the money?"

"That's the problem. I'm the trustee, but the kids' legal guardian is in charge of the monthly payments they receive—and they're substantial. Those classes and all the extras I've been providing them aren't free. Barbara may not know all of the details, but I'm certain she's after whatever money is available to her."

"That's too bad." Angie thought about how her own mother seemed more interested in earning a dollar than in being a stay-at-home mom.

"I'd never planned on using that money for myself," Toby said. "That's why I set it up for their guardian to have control of the monthly income. I didn't mind who had access to it, as long as they were looking out for the kids' best interests. But I hadn't realized Barbara's problems and issues went deeper than her alcohol dependency."

"And now there's her cousin to contend with," Angie added. "Who knows what kind of problems he has. Or what kind of parent or guardian he'd be."

"I've done some online research," Toby said. "And I can't believe any judge in their right mind would think that guy should have custody of them. The last thing they need right now is to move to a home with a man they don't know, a man who's on parole and can't even work at a hospital anymore because of whatever crime he was convicted of. And while I realize he may have paid his debt to society, those poor kids have had enough instability and unhappiness in their lives."

"So what are w…?" Angie cleared her throat, then coughed before she fully pronounced "we." The kids and Toby had become a big part of her life recently, but she wasn't entirely sure where she fit into their lives—at least, in the long run.

She cleared her throat again, then continued with the corrected version of her question. "So what do you plan to do?"

"If it comes to fighting for custody, Ms. Fisk thinks I can win, but she isn't sure. And a 'maybe' isn't good enough for me. It's not a risk I'm willing to take. So I'm giving the court another option. I'm going to talk to an attorney in Lubbock who specializes in family law. And then I'm going to petition for adoption myself. I'll show that I'm much better suited to raise those kids than some ex-con way out in California or a greedy aunt who can't seem to follow the rules in rehab."

While glad that Toby had a game plan and that he

felt more hopeful now than when she'd first arrived, Angie's shoulders slumped and she couldn't stanch the wave of disappointment that swept through her.

She might not have known where she fit into Toby's life, but apparently he did.

He'd just spelled out exactly what he planned to do, saying, "I."

And never once had he used the word *we*.

If there was one thing Angie hated, it was being late when meeting her mother. But she'd tossed and turned all night, thinking long and hard about Toby's dilemma, as well as her own. And she hadn't fallen asleep until almost dawn.

Needless to say, she'd overslept. So she quickly showered, dressed and pulled her hair into a ponytail. She figured she'd apply a quick coat of lipstick when she stopped at the first traffic light in Lubbock.

She'd no more than tossed her purse onto the passenger seat of her car when Mr. Murdock stepped out on his back porch, his cup of coffee steaming in his hands. He was wearing a bright yellow shirt that read Not As Mean, Not As Lean, But Still A Marine.

"Good morning, Mr. Murdock." She gave him a little wave as she slipped behind the wheel and strapped on her seat belt.

"Slow down, Girly." Mr. Murdock took his time as he lumbered down the steps, obviously intent on talking to her.

She'd told him yesterday that she was meeting her mom for brunch this morning. Didn't he realize that if she was even ten minutes late she was in for a lecture even the best mimosa couldn't dull?

When he finally made his way beside her idling car, he asked, "You tell your mama you're living here yet?"

"No, but I promise to do it today." And she would, even if it meant her mother would again offer to put a down payment on a condo in Lubbock for her.

Angie could hear it now. *There's no way I'll tolerate my only child living in some old-timer's run-down granny flat in Horseback Hollow.* In fact, her mom would be scrolling through the online MLS pages before the eggs Benedict arrived.

"Well, that's the thing, Girly. I don't see any need for you to mention that to old Doris."

Old Doris? Angie couldn't help but chuckle. If her mom could hear the eightysomething-year-old veteran refer to her as *old,* she'd be searching the internet for deals on Botox injections.

"Why the change of heart?" Angie asked her landlord. Just last month, Mr. Murdock had insisted that she stand up to her mother and become her own person.

Angie had tried to explain to the competitive man that she was passive-aggressive by nature. And that it was easier to nod her head and then do whatever she wanted to do anyway. So she was surprised that the old marine didn't want her to do battle at brunch today.

"Last night, while I was down at the VFW, Pete told me that the Jones boy was adopting those three kids."

"You shouldn't listen to gossip, Mr. Murdock. Especially from Pete. Wasn't he the one who told you that Ethel Gardiner was as bald as the cue balls in the Two Moon Saloon?"

"Yep. He did."

"And then you pulled on her hair, thinking it was a wig, and she smacked you silly."

"That slap won me five bucks." Mr. Murdock stood tall and puffed out his chest. "Her hair might have been dyed the shade of Pepto-Bismol, but I knew it wasn't no dang wig."

Angie wanted to laugh, but with her foot on the clutch, ready for her to slip the car into Reverse and back out, she was afraid a fit of giggles would cause her to stall the engine.

Besides, she didn't have time to waste getting off on tangents, so she steered the topic back to the original.

"What does Toby adopting those kids have to do with me telling my mother that I rent the granny flat from you?" she asked.

"Well, the way I figure it, since you spend about all your time at his ranch helping him with those young'uns, he'll convince you to move in with him before Old Doris ever finds out you ever lived here."

Thankfully, Mr. Murdock had the grace to turn and walk back to his house so Angie wasn't forced to come up with any sort of reply or denial. Instead, she backed out of the driveway and drove to Lubbock, hoping she didn't get a speeding ticket while she was at it.

As usual, Mr. Murdock had a funny take on things. But there was no way Toby would ask her to move in with him, especially now that he was seeking permanent custody of the kids. In fact, it looked as though their relationship—whatever there was of it—was going to have to take an even bigger backseat to the kids.

But she understood why. And she'd go with the flow. She'd have to deal with her disappointment later.

When she finally arrived at the quaint cottage-style bistro in Lubbock, Angie saw her mother's sedan parked in front. She found an empty space a few shops down the street, yet didn't immediately climb out of the car.

Dealing with Doris Edwards was nothing new. She'd been ignoring her instructions and advice for years. So why did she feel like backing out of the parking space and driving in the opposite direction—as far as she could from Lubbock *and* from Horseback Hollow?

The only thing stopping her from doing so now was a promise she'd made Toby. She'd told him she would pick up the children at the ball field and take them to dinner at The Grill so he could meet with some of his family this afternoon and talk about the adoption plans.

So she couldn't flake on him—or the kids, who would be looking forward to seeing her.

Steeling herself with a deep breath, Angie entered the restaurant and spotted her mom, joining her at a small table in back.

"You finally made it," Doris said. "I thought for sure that old wreck you drive around had broken down somewhere on the highway."

And there was the first insult of the day. But, hey, brunch wouldn't last more than an hour.

"I'm sorry I'm late," Angie said. "How are you, Mom?"

"I've never been better. And you'd know that if you came to see me more."

Insult number two.

"I wish I could come to town more often, but I've been busy lately."

"So I've heard. I talked to Ethel Gardiner on Monday. And she said that you've been spending a lot of time with Toby Fortune Jones and those kids he has running around his house."

Angie crossed her arms, suddenly not the least bit sorry about Mr. Murdock's bet with Pete. Ethel Gardiner deserved to have her pink locks tugged after spreading gossip.

"For the record," Angie said, "Toby's an amazing guy. Not many men would give up so much to take care of three children who weren't their own."

"That's just it," Doris argued. "Those kids *aren't* his own. It's unnatural. I mean, maybe if he used some of his family money and spent more time making something out of that ranch of his and less time playing daddy, he could be the right man for you."

Angie wanted to tell her mother that Toby didn't have any family money, but it really wasn't any of her business. So instead she signaled the waitress and ordered a much-needed cappuccino.

She normally would've spent twenty minutes reading every detailed item on the menu and trying to decide what to order. But since she wanted to get out of this restaurant as quickly as possible, she pointed to the frittata special—which was the first thing listed on the menu.

Her mother ordered plain yogurt, and Angie wondered why the woman would even bother coming out to eat if that was all she was going to have.

"You know," Angie said, "if you drove out to the

ranch and spent some time with Toby and the kids, you'd see things differently."

Had Angie actually suggested that? What would Toby say? He might claim to be easygoing, but having her mom around would probably be the kiss of death for their relationship—or whatever it was they had.

"Your defensive response is telling," Doris said.

"Telling?" How could it tell Doris anything when Angie didn't know what she was feeling herself?

"It sounds like you're trying to sell me on a ready-made family. You're not, are you? I mean, look at your history. You've avoided any kind of commitment in the past—and not just when it comes to relationships."

Angie couldn't argue with that.

"Besides," Doris said, "if you can't commit one hundred percent to those kids, then you shouldn't waste your time with their foster dad. It wouldn't be fair, especially if those children have lost as many people as everyone says they have."

Angie didn't normally see eye to eye with her mom, but those last words resonated loud and clear.

She didn't want to give anyone false hope, especially those kids.

"Plus, dear, you were meant to be so much more than just a mother."

Was she? She'd always thought that she was destined for more. After all, Doris had been telling her that for years. But she could still hear Jeanne Marie's words, still feel the way they'd warmed her heart.

...you're more than qualified to do my *job.*

Angie had been good at it, too. And she liked the kids. She'd even turned down some afternoon shifts at the Superette so that she could help Toby more with the carpooling.

But the Mama Angie gig had only been going on for a couple of weeks. Could she continue doing it for the next ten or fifteen years?

And did she even want to?

When the waitress brought their breakfast, Angie stared at the frittata placed in front of her. Why hadn't she ordered the stuffed French toast instead?

For some reason she found herself retreating back to her usual on-the-fence mode.

Was she up to the job of raising children?

Talk about long-term commitments.

What if the kids bonded with her, and then she skipped out on them?

Or maybe even worse, what if she stuck it out, like her mother had done when Angie had been growing up, and the decision to stay in an unhappy situation only made her life, as well as those of everyone around her, miserable?

No, in this case, her mother had called it right. Angie had never been able to commit to anything up until now. And those children needed stability in their lives more than anything.

Of course, Toby had never given her any reason to believe he envisioned her as a part of his long-term family plan. And the fact that he hadn't lanced something soft and fragile inside.

In what ways had Toby found her lacking?

Certainly not as a lover—or as a teammate, babysitter or friend.

But did he question her ability to make a lasting commitment to him and the kids? If so, she couldn't blame him for that. Because as much as she'd come to care for that precious little family, she had those same worries herself.

"I know you've never taken my advice in the past," Doris said. "And it's no secret that you pretend to listen—and that you think I'm pushy."

For some reason, Angie couldn't let that one go without commenting. "Listen, Mom. I love you. And I appreciate the fact that you believe you have my best interests at heart. But this is my life, not yours. You may have made some bad choices in the past, but they were yours to make—and yours to live with. Right or wrong, I intend to do the same thing. If you want to offer a bit of advice, that's fine. But then drop it. Please."

Doris sat there for a moment, then cleared her throat. "I'm sorry, Angie. Believe it or not, I really don't mean to interfere. I'll try to be more respectful of you in the future. And I'll be supportive of whatever you decide to do—even if it means going out to the ranch for a visit."

"Thank you. And for the record, I truly care for Toby and those kids. I actually love them. But deciding what to do about that isn't a simple decision for me to make. And no matter what I choose to do, I'll do it with my eyes and my heart wide open, knowing that if I make the wrong decision, if I end up hurt or disappointed in the long run, then so be it."

Doris placed her napkin in her lap, signaling it was time to eat and to put unpleasant matters behind them. "Since you understand the importance and are giving it a great deal of thought, I can respect that. So I'll drop the subject. I just hope that you will be able to make that decision quickly."

Her mother had never been more right.

Angie was facing the most critical decision she'd ever had to make—one that could prove to be life-changing and heartbreaking. And one she couldn't afford to stew about.

But instead of only having to consider the effects of her choice on her own life, her own heart, she had to consider what it would do to three children and to Toby, as well.

That being said, she really had to follow her heart, even if it was breaking. And that meant there was only one possible choice.

She had to step back and let them go.

And the sooner she told Toby the better.

Chapter Eleven

Toby's meeting with his family had gone even better than he'd hoped. When he'd laid out his dilemma and his plan, they'd all agreed to support him in a full-scale custody battle—if it should come to that—and in his attempt to adopt Brian, Justin and Kylie.

The only concern that had come up was the cost of legal fees, which could get expensive, but Toby had already talked at length to Jake Gleason, the attorney who'd drawn up the trust. So he was able to explain to his family that he, as the trustee, was allowed to tap into the principal at his discretion for any unexpected needs the kids might have. He'd also been able to assure them that securing a permanent home qualified as such a need.

So now Toby was on his way to The Grill. He intended to have a heart-to-heart talk with Angie while the kids played in the arcade. He wasn't looking forward to it, but he had to do it.

Over the past twenty-four hours, he'd been preoccupied with thoughts of the custody hearing and the adoption, but not so much that he hadn't sensed a very subtle difference in Angie. And he'd picked up on it again in the distant tone in her voice when they'd talked on the phone earlier.

He sensed that she was withdrawing from him, just as he'd suspected she would. And he really couldn't blame her. His life had taken a sudden and complicated turn, one their budding relationship wasn't prepared to handle.

Asking her to babysit or to fix Kylie's hair was one thing, but assuming that she'd want to take on even more responsibility or to actually become a permanent part of his and the children's lives was something completely different.

For one thing, she was still trying to find herself and her way in the world. How could he ask her to take on a burden she clearly wasn't ready for? Besides, she might want to have her own kids someday, and a large family was... Well, it was probably more than a woman who'd grown up as an only child would ever consider.

On top of that, they hadn't been dating very long.

Dating? He couldn't even call it that. One amazing night of lovemaking, no matter how amazing it might have been, wasn't the kind of romantic relationship Angie deserved. Not when the bulk of their time together was spent dealing with sick kids, spilled milk and squabbles over whose turn it was to use the laptop or the TV remote.

Heck, Toby had never even taken her out on a real

date, had never provided her with candlelight and roses. There'd been no nights on the town, no holding hands in the movie theater or dancing until dawn.

So allowing things to continue in the way they'd been going wasn't fair to her.

Knowing Angie, she was probably trying to figure out how to end things between them without hurting or disappointing the kids. So Toby would just have to make things easier on her. And, in the long run, he'd make things easier on all of them.

While the kids played in the arcade, oblivious to the custody battle that loomed, Toby would thank Angie for all she'd done for him. Then he'd let her off the hook, making the decision for her. If she wanted to stick around for dinner, they'd have one last meal together, then she'd go her way, and he and the kids would go theirs.

It sounded easy enough. He just hoped his voice didn't crack and reveal the ache in his heart that set in whenever he thought about her walking out of his life for good.

When Toby arrived at The Grill and spotted Angie's Toyota in the parking lot, his heart skipped a beat, and his breathing stalled. She'd probably been here awhile, since he was ten minutes later than he'd told her he'd be.

Yet he continued to sit in his truck, his hands on the steering wheel, wishing there was another way around what he had to do, but knowing there wasn't. Finally, he mustered his courage and opened the driver's door to let himself out. Then he headed for the front entrance.

When he stepped inside The Grill, he was met by Bonnie Sue Hillman, a petite blonde waitress.

"Angie is in the big booth in back," Bonnie Sue

said, "and the kids are in the arcade, going through quarters like crazy."

"Thanks. Have they ordered yet?"

Bonnie Sue laughed. "Angie's only been here for about fifteen minutes, and it takes her a lot longer than that just to study the menu."

As Toby made his way to the booth where Angie sat, another waitress stopped at her table. She said something to Angie and nodded. Then she whipped out her pad and pencil.

Toby approached, just as Angie said, "Brian will have the cheeseburger—well-done, no onions, lettuce or pickles. But he'd like extra tomatoes. And can you bring a side of mustard for his fries?"

As the waitress made note of it, Angie added, "Justin would like the corn dog, but instead of fries, he'll have onion rings with a side of ranch dressing. Kylie wants the grilled cheese with American—not cheddar. And can you please ask the cook to cut it into four triangles? If not, I can do that. She'd also like a bowl of strawberries—if you have them. When Toby gets here, he'll want the double bacon cheeseburger, fried pickles and a peanut-butter milk shake. He can share the onion rings with Justin. And I'll have the patty melt on rye and an iced tea with lemon."

Bonnie Sue, who'd followed Toby to the booth with a handful of menus, blew out a little whistle. "That's gotta be some kind of record. You'd think Angie's been ordering food for you guys for years."

It sure seemed that way. She'd picked up on a lot of their habits in a few short weeks. But then again, they didn't call her Little Miss Google for nothing.

Still, it tugged at his heart that the woman who'd

fallen into his life seemed to have somehow picked *him* up after that fall.

Angie looked up and spotted Toby. "Oh, you're here. I'm sorry. I probably shouldn't have ordered for you."

"No, that's fine. I'm glad you did." He slid into the booth and placed his hat on the seat beside him.

"How did it go?" she asked.

"Great. My family is behind me one hundred percent."

"I knew they would be."

Toby studied his hands, which rested on the table.

"Is something wrong?" she asked. "Do you want to talk about it before the kids come back?"

All right. This was the opening he needed. Now all he had to do was form the words.

He took a deep, fortifying breath. "Things will probably get pretty intense over the next few weeks and months."

"I know."

He paused a beat, then pressed on. "I realize you didn't sign on for all of this. And I want you to know that I understand. At this point, you can bow out gracefully before anyone gets hurt."

There. He'd said it.

Now all he had to do was wait and see what she would do with the ball he'd lobbed into her court.

Angie hadn't been sure how to tell Toby that she'd decided to back off, that she needed some space and time to herself. Then he'd broached the subject himself.

Not only that, he'd practically spelled it all out for

her, making it easy. But now that he'd given her a free pass…

Well…was taking a step back what she really wanted?

In truth, she hadn't been ready to walk away yet. But because she was afraid she'd change her mind down the road, which would devastate the kids, she'd thought it would be best to do it now.

And apparently, Toby felt the same way.

Yet now that he was cutting her loose, she felt an incredible sense of loss and fear that she stood to lose everything she'd ever wanted or needed if she didn't speak up…

Speak up and say what? That she didn't want to completely bow out?

That, in fact, she might not want to bow out at all?

"You're not saying anything," Toby said. "What are you thinking?"

"That I'd planned to take a step back and give you guys time to yourselves, but not because of the problems you're facing."

"Then why?"

"It's complicated."

Toby leaned forward. "I'm going to fight to keep Brian, Justin and Kylie. So things aren't temporary anymore. I'm making a commitment to them—one I hope the courts will make permanent. And as much as the kids—and I—would like you to be a part of that, I wouldn't even think of asking you to stick around for the long haul. It would be asking too much, and it wouldn't be fair."

Good. That was what she'd wanted to explain to him.

But the way he'd said it, the way he'd implied that it was just him and the kids from here on out—a family through thick and thin—made her feel as though she was the odd man out. And she wasn't so sure she wanted to be on the outside looking in.

She lifted her eyes, caught his gaze zeroing in on hers. Glossy. Intense.

His words told her he was letting her go and that he thought it was for the best.

Okay, she got that. But his pained expression said something entirely different to her heart.

Or did she just want to read something into all the emotions she saw brewing in his eyes?

"What's the matter?" he asked. "I thought you'd be relieved to have an opportunity to ease out of this relationship."

She should be. She'd come here intending to end things between them after dinner, then return to her own little corner of the world—the part-time job at the Superette, the twenty hours a week at Redmond-Fortune Air, the small little granny flat behind Mr. Murdock's house that she called home....

But was that cute little granny flat where she really called home?

Not when she woke up each morning in her own bed, thinking about Toby, seeing his face, hearing his voice. And whenever she thought about going home, it was always to the Double H, where Toby, the kids and one big mess or another always awaited her.

Come to think of it, no matter where she was—brunch with her mom, the Superette or at the airfield, her thoughts revolved around that precious, ragtag family. Even in her spare time, she planned meals she thought they'd like to eat and worked out better ways to balance their busy after-school schedules.

Just this morning, when she'd fixed her hair before her shift at the store, she'd wondered if Kylie was wearing the new headband Toby had bought her to use on days Angie wasn't there to braid her hair. She'd also wanted to tell Justin to practice his spelling words one more time and to remind Brian not to forget his backpack.

She'd gone so far as to pick up the phone to call Toby and offer her suggestions, but she'd been afraid that she was getting way too involved, especially if she was going to distance herself.

But as she looked at Toby now, as she saw his anguished expression, as she realized how difficult this was for him...

It was breaking his heart, and for that reason, it was breaking hers, too.

He was all on his own and facing a custody battle, one he might lose. But that wasn't the only thing hurting him.

Call it a zany sixth sense, but Angie could see it as plain as the summer sun at high noon. He was struggling with letting her go.

And she was struggling, too—right along with him.

All she wanted to do was to make his pain go away, to settle his fear, to strengthen his resolve.

And for some crazy reason, she didn't even question the fact that she might be wrong in her assumption about what he was feeling for her.

The solution to the problem, to *their* problem, had

never seemed so clear or so simple. All she had to do was to follow her heart.

Without a thought to the repercussions, the words rolled out of her mouth as loud and clear as the church bells on Sunday morning. "Toby, I think we should get married."

He blinked, and his lips parted. "What did you say?"

"Those kids need a loving, two-parent home. And you and I are the ones who can provide it for them. I want us to be a family. And if we go before the court together, I don't think the judge will turn us down."

"You mean you'd marry me because of the kids?"

Angie laughed. "I want to marry you because I love you. And because I love the kids, I want us to be a family."

Toby reached across the table and took her hand in his. "You love me?"

"Yes." How could she not? He was everything a woman could ever want in a man—loving, loyal, a family man... And he was the most handsome man in all of Texas—if not the whole world.

"Are you sure about that?" he asked. "You're not going to change your mind?"

"I've always known that when the perfect choice came along, I'd know it and that I'd jump on it. And that's what I'm doing. When I'm with you and the kids, I don't feel the least bit insecure or indecisive or flighty. I feel in control, at home, and..." She paused, realizing that was one word she needed to hear Toby say himself.

"And what?" Toby asked. "I hope you feel loved,

because I'm crazy about you." He slid around to her side of the booth and slipped his arm around her. "And I'm going to spend the rest of my life proving to you just how much."

Angie leaned into him. "I must admit, I felt loved and cherished on Saturday night."

He brushed a kiss on her cheek. "Honey, if we weren't out in public, I'd make you feel loved and cherished right now."

She laughed. "Something tells me our private times together, as nice as they'll be, aren't going to be easy to find. But I'll put some thought into it and figure out something."

"One thing I can do is to call Stacey and ask if she knows any reliable sitters we can hire on a regular basis. We're going to set aside one day a week as date night. I'd also like to plan some romantic weekend getaways."

Angie's heart swelled until she thought it might burst wide open. "I'm going to like being married to you, Toby."

"I'm glad, because the more I think about it, the more I like the idea of being married to you."

"It's too bad the junior college doesn't offer a crash course in motherhood," she said. "There's a lot I need to learn. Maybe I should ask your mom to tutor me."

"You're doing just fine. You've picked up plenty already."

"I'm not sure about that."

"Oh, no? You know which girls in Brian's class think he's cute and how many breaths Justin takes when he swims the length of the YMCA pool. It took you all of fifteen seconds to figure out how to juggle the timing of Kylie's gymnastics lesson and still get the boys to baseball practice on time. You're a natural—and a fast learner. You've also come to know me pretty well."

She smiled and bumped his shoulder with hers. "Oh, yeah?"

"You can read my mood like nobody's business. You knew that I really wanted to beg you to stay with me and the kids, even though I was trying to do the gentlemanly thing and give you a way out. And, maybe even more importantly, you know how to set my blood on fire."

She leaned in and gave him a long, heated kiss that could have set The Grill on fire if he hadn't drawn back.

Toby ran his finger along her lips. "But you need to know something. No matter what happens with the kids, even if I lose them, I still want you for my wife."

"We won't lose them," Angie said. "I've set my heart on it."

For the first time since Ms. Fisk had returned his call and told him Barbara had moved forward with her plan, Toby began to relax. With Angie in his corner, how could he lose?

Before either of them could comment further, the kids dashed back to the table announcing their high scores and asking for more quarters.

"What do you think?" Angie asked Toby. "Should we tell them?"

Justin pressed in front of his brother and sister. "Tell us what?"

"Angie and I are getting married," Toby said.

"No kidding?" Brian asked. "Sweet."

"Woo-hoo!" Justin shouted, drawing the other diners' attention to their table.

Kylie clapped her hands and gave a little jump. "Can I be in the wedding?"

"Absolutely," Angie said. "You're all going to be in the wedding. We wouldn't have it any other way."

"So when is it?" Brian asked.

"We'll have to wait at least three days," Angie said. "That's Texas law."

Toby chuckled. "I suppose you picked that trivial piece of info up at one of your temp jobs?"

"As a matter of fact, I spent a few weeks working at a bridal shop in Vicker's Corners."

Miss Google strikes again.

"So how soon can I call you my wife?" Toby asked.

Angie tossed him a flirtatious grin. "How does next Saturday sound?"

"That long, huh?" He slipped his arm around her again and drew her close. "Saturday is fine with me. But don't you think you'll need more time to plan a wedding?"

"Yes, but I'd like to keep things simple. You may not believe this, but I can practically see it all unfolding in my mind."

"You're right. That *is* hard to believe, but I don't doubt it." He leaned over and kissed her again.

"Hey," Justin said. "Before you guys start smooching again, can you look and see if you have any more quarters?"

Toby laughed, then dug into his pocket and pulled out several. "Take these."

When the kids dashed off, Toby turned his attention back to Angie. "So you're not going to drag your feet and make me wait while you stew over bridal magazines and reception venues?"

"No, I won't have to. When I make up my mind, and my heart's in it, I don't drag my feet. I can tell you right now that I'd like to be married in your parents' backyard. And that I want Stacey and Delaney to be my bridesmaids. I've never had sisters, so I'm looking forward to having two right off the bat."

"I'm sure they'll be happy about that."

"Good. Then since we're both on the same page, I don't see a problem."

"Neither do I."

Well, other than having to wait until next Saturday to make love with her again. But he was going to work very hard at getting her alone before that.

"I don't suppose you've thought about a guest list," he said. "Saturday won't give us time to send out invitations."

"We'll keep it simple—mostly family, if that's okay. But with it being so soon, we'll have to call and invite people."

"I'd like my brother Chris to be there, but that's going to be tricky."

"Because of the hard feelings within the family?" she asked.

"Yes. Chris has always been both a black sheep and a lone wolf. I've understood that and known when to give him his space. After things blew sky-high, I knew he needed to do some airing out. So I gave him the time he needed, figuring that he'd contact me when he was ready to talk and move back into the fold."

"So will you call him?" Angie asked. "You could use the wedding as an excuse."

"It might be best to extend the invitation through Sawyer. That way I'm respecting his decision to distance himself from Horseback Hollow and from the rest of the family. Yet it's also a way to let him know that I still love him and want a relationship with him. I have a feeling he'll reach out to me at that point, even if he doesn't come."

"Do you think he'll stay away?"

"I hope not, but Chris has always had to do things his way. In the meantime, my dad will need to do some bending, too. So if I want to see any fences getting mended, I'd better start working on him."

"If anyone can talk some sense into your dad, I'll bet you can." Angie gave him a kiss. "Now let's get busy. I have a lot of work to do—and nine days doesn't give me much time."

She was right. But when it came to waiting for Angie to move into the ranch and become his wife in every sense of the word, nine days seemed way too long.

Toby had an appointment to meet with his new attorney in Lubbock on Monday at eleven o'clock. So while he was in the city, he decided to stop by the real-estate office where Doris Edwards worked.

Needless to say, she was surprised to see him.

"Do you have a couple of minutes?" he asked.

"Certainly." She led him down the hall to a small break room. "Would you like a cup of coffee?"

"No, thanks. I can't stay long, but I have a question for you."

"What's that?"

"I'd like to ask for Angie's hand in marriage."

Doris sat up a little straighter. "That's a bit of a surprise—and a little old-fashioned. What if I were to tell you no?"

"We'd get married anyway. I just thought I'd pay you the respect you deserve—and to ask that you do the same for us."

"I see." Doris sat back in her seat. "So have you proposed to Angie yet?"

"Actually, it was her idea. She's the one who first popped the question." A slow smile tugged at his lips. "She's going to call you when she gets off work today and talk to you about it."

"Have you set a date?"

"Saturday."

"So soon?" Doris stiffened. "Are you eloping?"

"We're going to get married at my parents' ranch. We're only inviting family and a few close friends, although I suspect it won't be as small as it sounds."

Doris perked up. "Will the Fortunes from Red Rock be attending?"

"They'll be invited, as well as those from Atlanta and the United Kingdom. But with it being such short notice, I'm not sure who'll be able to make it."

"In that case, don't you think it would be better to wait at least a month? That way, you'll have more time to plan a nicer event. I might even be able to get the *Lubbock Avalanche-Journal* to run a spread in the society pages."

"We don't want to wait."

"Oh, dear. She's not pregnant, is she?"

Toby groaned inwardly. Doris Edwards was certainly going to be a trial, but Angie was worth it.

"No, she's not pregnant. But don't worry—even though we only have a few days to plan, the wedding is going to be nice. My entire family is pitching in, and we'd like you to be as involved as you want to be."

"Of course I'd like to be included." Doris began to click her manicured nails on the table—plotting and planning, no doubt. "I'll also need to purchase a new dress to wear." She bit down on her bottom lip, then looked at him with hope-filled eyes. "Do you think your aunt Josephine May Fortune Chesterfield will come all the way from England? Goodness, I'll bet the cost of *that* flight will be incredibly expensive."

Toby reached out and placed his hand over his future mother-in-law's, stopping her from fidgeting. "Listen, Doris. There are a few things we need to get straight. I may be a Fortune by blood, and while my ranch is doing just fine and I'm financially stable, I'm not wealthy by any means. And I probably never will be. But I love your daughter with all my heart. We may never have the money that some of my family members have, but in everything that matters, Angie and I are rich beyond measure."

Doris smiled. "I understand. But you can't help me for being a little starstruck. I mean, the Chesterfields are almost royals in the U.K."

Toby didn't know about that, but at least Doris seemed to support his and Angie's union.

"Do you think it would be all right if I stopped by to see Jeanne Marie and Deke after I get off work today?" Doris asked. "I'd love to offer my services—and to do whatever I can to offset the cost of the wedding. I'm not rich, either, but I did set aside some cash for my baby girl's big day."

Toby didn't dare tell her that Sawyer had already offered to do the same thing. Or that Sawyer's dad, James Marshall Fortune, had agreed to pay for their honeymoon in San Antonio, the flight courtesy of Redmond-Fortune Air.

Doris might accept that Toby wasn't as rich as some of the other Fortunes, but she'd certainly place a boatload of value on his family connections.

"I'm sure my parents would be glad to have you stop by this evening," Toby said, as he stood, preparing to leave.

His talk with Doris had gone better than he'd hoped. She seemed to be looking forward to the wedding.

He just hoped she wouldn't place any unnecessary stress on Angie, especially on their special day.

Angie, Stacey and Delaney were going to shop for dresses in Vicker's Corners on Tuesday afternoon. Angie's mom, who'd been both supportive and excited about the upcoming ceremony, was coming along, too.

Who would have guessed that Doris would actually be looking forward to her role as mother of the bride?

Angie had a feeling her excitement might have something to do with knowing that there would be quite a few Fortunes present and that one of Toby's handsome brothers would be walking her down the aisle. But either way, it would make the day go by a whole lot smoother.

Her mom was also planning to purchase the bridal gown, which was nice. And as long as Stacey and Delaney were there to prevent her from going tulle-crazy, it should work out okay.

Before driving to the bridal shop to meet everyone, Angie stopped at Mr. Murdock's house to tell him about the upcoming wedding and to let him know that she'd be moving out in less than a week.

"So that Fortune Jones boy has finally talked some sense into you, did he?"

Angie smiled at the old man she'd grown so fond of in the past couple of months. "Yes, he certainly did."

Mr. Murdock turned and headed to the lamp table, where he kept his telephone.

"What are you doing?" she asked, a little disappointed that he'd walked off while she was still sharing the news of the biggest and best decision she'd ever made in her life.

"I need to call Pete," he said.

"Your VFW buddy? Why?"

"Because I told him you'd be tying the knot by the end of the month. But he thought those young'uns would scare you off. So now Pete owes me five bucks and two of his lucky bingo cards."

"Oh, no. Please tell me you didn't make a bet on my love life."

"Girly," Mr. Murdock said with a big ole grin, "I'd bet on you any day of the week."

Coming from him, that was a huge compliment.

He picked up a glass of amber-colored liquid from the table. "Can I get you some Scotch?"

"No, thanks. And you shouldn't be drinking it, either. You really need to cut back. Remember what your doctor said?"

He glanced at the glass, scrunched his face as though he was really giving it some thought, then returned the drink to the table.

She didn't think he'd go so far as to pour it out, though. She suspected that he was going to finish it as soon as she left.

"Listen," she said. "There's something else, Mr. Murdock. I'd like to ask you to be in our wedding."

"Huh?" He scrunched his craggy face, as if thinking it over, then pointed an arthritic finger at her. "I know you young kids today are all okay with this gender-role-reversal business, and I'll go ahead and be your brides-man or man of honor or whatever you equal-rights hippies are calling it nowadays. But I ain't wearing no pink tuxedo."

Angie suddenly wished she'd accepted the glass of Scotch so she could lift it to her face and camouflage her twitching lips. "I wasn't asking you to stand up with me in the bridal party, Mr. Murdock."

"No?"

"I want you to walk me down the aisle."

Chapter Twelve

Saturday finally dawned, bringing a cloudless sky, a lazy breeze and a buzz of excitement. It was a perfect day for a wedding.

As two o'clock approached, the guests began to arrive and mingle. Toby stood off to the side, taking it all in and feeling as though he'd been blessed beyond measure.

He surveyed the once-familiar yard, which had morphed into a festive, ranch-style setting for the outdoor ceremony, thanks to the rented lattice gazebo, the white chairs lined up on the freshly mowed lawn and the small stage where the DJ was setting up his equipment next to the portable dance floor.

Marcos and Wendy Mendoza, who planned to open The Hollows Cantina at the end of June, had volunteered to cater the event as a wedding gift. They'd flown in from Red Rock two days before and were already laying out their spread on the linen-draped tables that had been adorned with the bouquets of flowers Angie and his sisters had created yesterday.

Come to find out his new bride had once worked for a florist in Vicker's Corners. With all the random skills Angie had acquired at her temp jobs, she was proving to be surprisingly handy.

As Toby marveled at all the work everyone had done in order to get the family homestead ready and decorated for a wedding, he shook his head in amazement.

Last night, his parents had hosted a rehearsal dinner with many of the Fortunes in attendance. Not all of his newfound relatives had been able to drop everything and come to Horseback Hollow, but quite a few from Red Rock and Atlanta had actually made the trip. Even Amelia Fortune Chesterfield had flown in from England.

But there was one family member noticeably missing—his brother Chris.

Toby had planned to talk to Sawyer, but a few minutes ago, his cousin had stepped away from the crowd to take a phone call. When Toby saw that Sawyer had put away his cell, he crossed the yard and made his way toward the man whose charter service had been busy all week flying guests into town.

"You're just the guy I wanted to see," Sawyer said.

"Same here. Did you talk to my brother?"

Sawyer reached into his lapel and pulled out what appeared to be a greeting card. "He asked me to give you this before the wedding."

Toby studied the pale blue envelope, then slipped his finger under the flap and tore it open. After removing the card, he read the printed words that wished the bride and groom all the best as they started their lives together. It was signed: Love, Chris.

Sawyer again reached into his lapel. This time, he withdrew a white business envelope. "He also wanted me to give you this. Open it."

Toby did, finding ten crisp one-hundred dollar bills inside. The amount of the gift was staggering, and while he appreciated his brother's generosity, he actually would have preferred just the card and having Chris attend the wedding in person. But he wouldn't mention his disappointment to Sawyer.

Instead, he said, "Chris must be doing well in Red Rock."

"I think so. And he's sorry he couldn't be here, but he figured, under the circumstances, his presence would only put a damper on your special day. And that's not the kind of wedding memory he wanted you and Angie to have."

As much as Toby would like to argue, Chris had a point.

"He also said to tell you that, if you ever need anything, he's just a phone call away."

Toby nodded, knowing that his brother's heart was softening. And that it was in the right place. "Thanks for being the go-between, Sawyer. I really appreciate it."

"I just wish I could have done more to help smooth things over."

"He'll come around. Eventually." Toby folded the envelope in half and slid it into his own lapel pocket.

"Would you look at all of this?" Sawyer lifted his hand and gestured to the decorated ranch and to the happy people milling about. "Who would have guessed that you and Angie could have pulled off something like this so quickly?"

"She worked her tail off," Toby said. "We both did. But we had a lot of help. And we appreciate your contribution, too."

"Flying you to San Antonio for your honeymoon was the least Laurel and I could do. I just wish you and Angie were able to stay for more than a few days."

"Our attorney said we need to demonstrate that we're the best caretakers for the children, so we didn't want it to look like we were ditching them the first chance we got. Four days will be enough."

Plus, they would miss the kids while they were gone. Maybe, in late summer, the five of them could take a family honeymoon to Six Flags.

"When my dad offered to pay for your hotel room," Sawyer said, "he hoped you'd choose a more exotic locale for your honeymoon."

"San Antonio is a beautiful city. Besides, we won't have to leave the state. And if we need to, we can get home fairly quick."

"That makes sense."

"But speaking of San Antonio," Toby said, "it's only a short drive from there to Red Rock. I think Angie and I will rent a car and stop by the Fortune Foundation to see Chris while we're in the area. It's time I talked to him in person."

That family rift had gone on too long. And it was time to mend fences.

"Uh-oh," Sawyer said. "You're being paged."

Toby scanned the grounds and spotted Jude, who was motioning for him, indicating it was time to get this show on the road.

"I'll talk to you later," Toby said. "Thanks again for everything."

Sawyer placed a hand on Toby's shoulder and gave it an affectionate squeeze. "Congratulations, cousin. I hope you and Angie will be as happy as Laurel and I are."

"I'm sure we will be."

Toby crossed the yard, then took his place at the gazebo, near the minister. His brothers—minus Chris—and Brian followed behind him, lining up at his side.

Just as Angie had promised, the kids all played a special part in the ceremony. Brian took pride in his role as a junior groomsman, while Justin felt honored to be the ring bearer, especially since it had been explained that his was the most important job of all. And Kylie, of course, was delighted to be the flower girl.

Now all the hard work and last night's practice was coming into play.

As the music began, signaling the start of the processional, Justin started down the aisle, balancing the small white satin pillow that had been in the Jones family for generations in one hand and tugging Kylie's flower-bearing arm with the other.

The guests laughed at the struggling pair of red-heads who eventually took their positions in front of the minister.

"There's still flowers left in my basket," Kylie stage-whispered to Justin.

With that, her brother snatched the basket out of her grasp and emptied it, dumping rose petals all over Toby's black cowboy boots. Then he pointed to the pile and smiled. "Now when Angie walks down the aisle, she'll know where she's supposed to end up."

Several of the guests covered their mouths to hold back their giggles. But apparently Doris Edwards didn't find it funny, because she turned her "grand-dame of Lubbock" eyes on anyone who seemed to be laughing at her daughter's expense.

Doris hadn't made it out to the Double H for a visit yet, but she'd purchased Angie's wedding dress and had paid the extra fees for the rush alterations. So she was definitely coming around.

Of course, she'd been on her best behavior last night at the rehearsal dinner. She'd also just happened to bring along some colorful brochures of houses and various other properties she had listed for sale. Apparently Toby's soon-to-be mother-in-law was in her element socializing and networking with his Fortune family members.

Next in the procession came the bridesmaids—Julia Tierney, who was engaged to Liam, and Gabi Mendoza, Jude's fiancée, followed by Toby's sisters, Stacey and Delaney.

But all thoughts of in-laws and family members

dissipated in the light afternoon breeze when the first chords of the bridal march were played.

The moment Toby spotted his bride, his breath caught at the sight of her. She wore a strapless, form-fitting satin gown that hugged her womanly curves, and when she flashed him a dazzling smile his lungs filled with so much pride he could have floated to the moon and back.

As she began her walk down the aisle on Mr. Murdock's arm, he realized his life was about to change in the most amazing way ever. And he couldn't wait until they became one—from this day forward, now and forever...

When Angie reached the gazebo, Mr. Murdock, who wore his much-too-snug dress uniform, handed her off to Toby.

"Who gives this woman away?" the minister asked.

The retired marine, who'd stepped back to his place of honor in the front row, drew up to his full five feet four inches, placed his hand on Doris's shoulder and roared out in his best drill-instructor voice, "Her mother and I do."

Toby had to bite back a laugh when Angie's mom leaned away and looked at Amelia Fortune Chesterfield, who represented the British Fortunes, as if wanting to silently communicate that she wasn't even remotely related to the elderly man.

Yet when Angie slipped her hand in Toby's, when she gazed into his eyes, all thoughts of laughter ceased. He was about to marry the most beautiful, loving woman in the whole world. And when she smiled back at him, he didn't think he could say "I do" fast enough.

Angie had never been happier. And her confident smile lasted all through the minister's opening words and continued through their vows. She'd just married the most perfect man ever made, and she'd never been more certain of a decision in her life.

The moment they were finally pronounced man and wife and Toby kissed her, the Hemings kids, dressed in their bridal finery, let loose with whoops, hoots and whistles.

If anyone thought the outburst was out of place, it would be her mother. But when Toby's family joined in with cheers and applause of their own, Angie couldn't see how her mom could possibly complain.

As the happy guests finally quieted down, the minister said, "May I be the first to introduce you to Mr. and Mrs. Toby Fortune Jones."

Again, the applause and cheers rang out.

The music began, signaling it was time to proceed back down the aisle, and Angie blew a kiss to her mom.

As soon as she and Toby had cleared the last row of chairs, he asked, "Are you glad it's over?"

"The ceremony? Yes. But our lives are just beginning, and I've never been happier."

"Neither have I."

"For the record," she admitted, "I'm looking forward to saying goodbye to our guests and having you all to myself, though."

Toby stroked his fingers along the delicate satin

on her back. "That dress is beautiful, and it couldn't look better on any other bride. But I can't wait to get you out of it."

As he brushed a kiss on her lips, and the photographer snapped another picture, Angie wholeheartedly agreed. The wedding night couldn't come quickly enough.

While the photographer went to gather up all the family members for some formal shots, Toby pulled her behind an elm tree, not far from the tree fort.

"Listen, about our honeymoon," he started.

Oh, no. Would they have to cancel? Had something come up with the kids or the babysitting arrangement? Oh, well. They'd just have to make do. She refused to be disappointed on the happiest day of her life.

"Since we'll be so close to Red Rock," Toby said, "I thought we could take one afternoon to visit Chris."

"That's a great idea."

Toby told her about the card and the monetary gift. "I think it's time to find out how he's doing and how he's feeling about things. He isn't the black sheep some people see him as."

Angie glanced down at the platinum band sparkling on her finger. She was Toby's wife now—and as much a part of the Fortune clan as everyone else. So she was doubly invested in making sure all members were happy and getting along.

"Maybe Chris would just like to get to know his uncle better," she said.

"You might be right. But he's probably also attracted to a new and different lifestyle. He went to college, so he has ideas on new ways to do things. And my dad's an old-school sort. Chris doesn't think Dad respects him. And my dad thinks Chris has gotten too big for his britches. In reality, they're probably both right."

"Do you think you can help them make peace with each other?"

"I'm sure going to try."

A snapping twig sounded, and the photographer called out. "Here they are."

As the rest of the family followed behind, the photographer asked them to gather in the shade of the tree, but he continued to snap random shots at the crowd anyway.

"Is this everyone?" the photographer asked.

No, it wasn't everyone, but that was okay. With all the couples who'd been hooking up lately, there was bound to be another wedding and reception soon. And they could get a bigger group photo then.

Jeanne Marie moved in next to Toby and, between smiles for the camera, whispered, "I'm so sorry Chris isn't here. I feel as though a part of me is missing."

Angie's heart ached for her new mother-in-law. And while Brian, Justin and Kylie weren't technically her children, she could understand a mother's distress.

"Angie and I are going to stop and see Chris in Red Rock while we're gone," Toby told her. "I'll talk to him."

"Thank you, son." She leaned in and kissed Toby right as another flash went off. "While you do that, I'll start working on your dad. And when these wedding pictures come back, I'll make a photo album to send to Chris. Maybe it'll remind him how much his family loves and misses him."

"Good idea."

"Can I have your attention?" the photographer asked. "I'd like to get one shot of everyone together. Let's gather around this tree. It'll make a good backdrop."

"Hey!" Justin chimed in. "Let's take it by the tree house instead. That way, some of us can climb up there and look down on you guys."

The photographed ignored the child, but Angie didn't. "Before the day is over, Justin, I'll have him take a family shot of the five of us near the tree house."

"How come we can't all be up in it?" Justin asked.

Angie caressed the top of his head. "Because I don't think I'd be able to climb very well in this dress."

"Five bucks says you can." Mr. Murdock, who stood beside her, nudged her with his elbow. "And another five says that I'll beat your time getting up there."

Angie laughed. "I'm not taking that bet, Mr. Murdock. This is going to be a wager-free wedding."

Before long, the reception launched into a full-scale party, with the food and drinks flowing freely.

When the DJ called the bride and groom to the dance floor, he said, "Since they didn't have a song picked out, I'll play a country classic."

"Seriously?" Toby called out. "Don't you have anything by Aretha Franklin? I'd take her over Patsy Cline any day of the week."

The whole dance floor fell into a hush, and Angie shook her head, realizing her husband had just said the one thing bound to agitate Texans quicker than a piñata at a five-year-old's birthday party.

"I'll see what I can do," the DJ said.

Moments later, as the music started, Toby and Angie stepped out onto the dance floor. Before long, other couples joined them—Stacey and Colton, Jude and Gabi, Liam and Julia.

Even Toby's cousin Amelia Fortune Chesterfield had found a dance partner in Quinn Drummond, who owned a ranch neighboring Toby's.

Quinn held Amelia close as Etta James crooned out through the speakers. The unlikely pairing of the proper British noble with a Horseback Hollow cowboy brought another smile to Angie's lips.

She nodded slightly and whispered, "Apparently, there's something about a wedding that makes for the strangest dance partners."

Toby drew her close. "And some of the nicest."

"You've got that right, cowboy." Then Angie wrapped her arms around her husband's neck and kissed him with all the love in her heart.

Two days later, in the honeymoon suite at one of San Antonio's swankiest hotels, Toby woke up with his wife in his arms, her back to his chest, her bottom nestled in his lap. Just hours ago, they'd made love again.

It seemed as though they couldn't get enough of each other, and he had a feeling that was how it was always going to be.

Today they planned to drive out to Red Rock, although he wasn't in any big hurry to let go of his lovely, naked wife.

"Are you awake?" he whispered against her hair.

"Um-hum." She arched and stretched. "I was just thinking."

Toby pressed a kiss on her bare shoulder. "What about?"

"About you and me and all the kids."

"All?" He chuckled. "I guess three would seem like a lot to an only child."

"Actually, I was thinking about the younger ones—the babies we're going to have."

"Babies? How many do you plan on having?"

"Well, none by myself. I was hoping you'd be involved."

He laughed. "I'm in this thing all the way, honey. So we can have as many kids as you'd like."

"I was thinking that six would be a good number."

"Six total?" he asked. "Or six more?"

Angie turned to face him, her smile radiant. "I'd like as many kids as we're blessed with."

"So the woman who once feared commitment is now daydreaming about having babies?"

"Yes. Little cowboys who are just like you—strong and handsome, loving and wise. And little girls who, like your mom, know that real wealth lies in love and family."

"Okay, but we'll need to have at least one little girl like you. One who's as inventive and creative and loving as she is beautiful." Toby pressed a kiss on Angie's brow. "Have I told you how much I love you?"

"Seven times throughout the night, but I'll never get tired of hearing you say it."

"Oh, yeah? Then you're really going to like it when I show you just how much."

Then he took her in his arms and did just that.

Toby had no idea what the future would bring, but right now, he was going to cherish every moment of the present.

* * * * *

FALLING FOR FORTUNE

BY
NANCY ROBARDS THOMPSON

Award-winning author **Nancy Robards Thompson** is a sister, wife and mother who has lived the majority of her life south of the Mason-Dixon line. As the oldest sibling, she reveled in her ability to make her brother laugh at inappropriate moments, and she soon learned she could get away with it by proclaiming, "What? I wasn't doing anything." It's no wonder that upon graduating from college with a degree in journalism, she discovered that reporting "just the facts" bored her silly. Since she hung up her press pass to write novels full-time, critics have deemed her books "funny, smart and observant." She loves chocolate, champagne, cats and art (though not necessarily in that order). When she's not writing, she enjoys spending time with her family, reading, hiking and doing yoga.

This book is dedicated to the memory of my sweet
mother-in-law, Juanita Eitreim.
I miss you every day.

Chapter One

"I'm sorry, sir, I've checked the directory three times. There's nobody by that name listed."

Strains of the new receptionist's voice carried in through Christopher Fortune's partially open door. He looked up from his in-office putting green.

What was her name again? He couldn't remember. It was only the start of her second week. Jeez, but she was shrill. He'd have to talk to her about her tone. Not good for community relations. But first...

He realigned his stance as the golf pro had taught him, making sure that his toes were parallel to the pin at the end of the fourteen-foot portable green. He set the putter in the hollow part of his left hand and placed the right hand so that his right thumb rested on the left side of the shaft. He pulled back to take his shot—

"Sir, I don't know what else to tell you." Now her

voice was teetering on exasperation. He couldn't hear what the other person was saying, but she was giving him a headache. "We have a Christopher Fortune, but nobody by the name of *Chris Jones* works here. Could he be the one you're looking for?"

The words made Christopher hit the ball a little too hard. It rolled off the end of the green and under the coffee table that was part of the furniture grouping at the end of the room.

Who was asking for Chris Jones?

Two months ago, Chris Jones had adopted his mother's Fortune family name and moved to Red Rock from Horseback Hollow, Texas. He'd dropped the Jones portion of his name when he'd accepted the new job. Now, he was Christopher Fortune, vice president in charge of community relations for the Fortune Foundation.

Christopher set down his putter, walked over and fully opened his office door to see what the ruckus was about.

What the hell—

"Toby?" Christopher said flatly when he saw his brother and his new sister-in-law, Angie, standing there. "What are you doing here, man?"

The receptionist, a slight woman with close-cropped black hair, looked so young that she could've easily been mistaken for a sixteen-year-old. She turned and froze, all wide dark eyes and pale skin, when she saw Christopher.

"Oh! I'm sorry, Mr. Fortune. I didn't understand that they were looking for you. They asked for Chris Jones."

Now she was blushing.

Christopher glanced at the name plate that was front and center on the reception desk.

"Don't worry about it, Beverly. It's fine."

"Hey, little brother," Toby said, extending a hand. "Good to see you."

Christopher shook Toby's hand. His brother immediately pulled him into an awkward hold that their sister, Stacey, was fond of calling a *man hug:* a greeting that started as a handshake and ended with the guys leaning in and stiffly slapping each other on the back a couple of times.

When they broke apart, Christopher stepped back, reclaiming his dignity just in time to see both elevator doors open and Kinsley Aaron, the Foundation's outreach coordinator, step into the reception area.

Her long, straight blond hair hung loose around her shoulders, framing her pretty face. God, she was gorgeous, even if she was a little too uptight for his taste. He straightened his tie and raked his fingers through his hair, trying to right what Toby's enthusiastic bear hug had mussed.

Kinsley had the bluest eyes he'd ever seen. Those eyes were two of the reasons he always remembered her name. Although, the dowdy way she dressed wasn't much of an enticement. He couldn't figure out why such a beauty chose to dress like a schoolmarm. She always covered up as much of herself as possible. Didn't she know her modesty only made him daydream about the gifts that were undoubtedly hidden beneath all that wrapping?

As Kinsley approached Beverly's desk, she arched a brow at him. For a split second he could've sworn she'd read his mind. But he knew it was a ridiculous thought. She was probably just curious about Toby and Angie, since she tended to take her job so seriously. After all, this was an office where visitors generally came seeking help, something that typically fell into her community outreach division.

Before Kinsley could start asking questions, Christopher turned to his brother and sister-in-law. "Why don't we go into my office? We can talk in there."

He made quick work of ushering them out of the reception area. This sure as hell wasn't the most ideal time or place for a family reunion. Especially when he was determined to keep his life in Horseback Hollow worlds apart from the new life he'd created for himself in Red Rock.

Before he shut the door, he cast one last glance back at Kinsley, who was still lingering by Bev's desk. They locked gazes, and Christopher felt that old familiar *zing* that always happened when he looked into those eyes. The virtual vibration lasted even after she looked away.

And she was always the first one to look away.

He was pondering that when Toby said, "Since you were too darned busy to come home for the wedding, I decided I'd bring my beautiful bride to see you. Angie, you've met Chris before. Chris, this is my wife. Can you believe it?" he said, grinning. "I have a wife."

"Good to see you again, Angie," Christopher said, keeping his tone all business and shaking Angie's hand.

"So, they call you *Mr. Fortune* around here?" Toby asked, a note of good-natured ribbing in his voice. But before Christopher could answer, Toby let loose a low whistle as he glanced around Christopher's new digs. "Would you look at this fancy place? I guess you're doing all right for yourself, little brother."

"It's a pretty sweet gig," Christopher said. "Actually, I wanted to work directly for Uncle James at JMF Financial, but how could I argue after I found out that he'd created a position just for me? I'm sure he could do something for you if you want. All you have to do is ask."

What Christopher didn't say was that the work was a little boring and "do-gooder" for his taste. But the salary they were paying him, which was commensurate with the Fortune name rather than his experience, more than made up for the lack of excitement.

If Christopher had learned one thing over the past two months it was that he had to create his own excitement, ensure his own future. It wasn't as if he'd been blazing trails in Horseback Hollow. Nope, back home, he'd been bored and broke.

And a nobody.

Now he had a job that people respected and the bank account to go with it. So he figured why not go for the trifecta and take on the Fortune name? It was his birthright, after all, even if his old man would be mad as hell when he found out.

But those were the breaks, weren't they? His father Deke's attitude was one of the things that had driven Christopher to Red Rock in the first place. Once he was settled, he'd gone to court and filed a petition to change his name. Once the judge had signed the order, Christopher Fortune said *Hasta la vista, baby* to Chris Jones and Horseback Hollow and claimed what was rightfully his.

Christopher glanced around his office, trying to see it through Toby's eyes. The Fortune Foundation had been founded in memory of Lily Cassidy Fortune's late husband, Ryan Fortune, who had died of a brain tumor nine years ago. The Foundation had started out in a small storefront on Main Street in downtown Red Rock but had since expanded and was now located in a stately three-story brick building just outside of town. Christopher had one of the corner offices with rich polished mahogany architectural wall paneling on the walls—or at least the ones that didn't have floor-to-ceiling windows with a to-die-for view of the local landscape. His traditional executive's desk and credenza still left enough room for the putting green, two chairs and a couch that were grouped conversation-style around a coffee table.

Hell, his office was bigger than his old studio apartment back in Horseback Hollow.

He directed Toby and Angie over to the couch. Until now, he hadn't even tried out the office's living room furniture.

"I just can't get over the change in you," Toby said.

Christopher turned to Angie, who was still as pretty as she had been in high school with her light brown hair, blue eyes and delicate features. His brother had done well catching her. He'd tell him so later if they had a private moment. But just as the thought crossed his mind, it was overshadowed by the hope that the newlyweds weren't planning an extended visit in Red Rock. Christopher had work to do.

He hoped this visit wasn't because Deke had sent Toby to do his dirty work. If any of his family got him it was Toby. But it would be just like Deke to send one of Christopher's brothers to hassle him.

But right now, Toby was talking to Angie. "The Chris I knew never wore anything but jeans and boots. I don't know who this suit is standing in front of me with those shiny pointy-toed shoes. How many crocodiles had to die to make those shoes?"

Christopher laughed, but it was a dry, humorless sound. "They're not made out of crocodile," Christopher said.

"It was a joke, Chris." Toby frowned. "No offense, but you're even acting differently. Just remember, I know where you came from."

Awkward silence the likes of which he had never known with Toby hung in the air. He didn't want to fight with him, and it seemed every time he opened his mouth he said the wrong thing.

That was the story of his life when it came to family. But Christopher wasn't about to sit here in his own office and let family drag him down to feeling bad.

"How was the wedding?" Christopher asked, hoping for neutral ground. He directed the question to Angie, who had been remarkably quiet.

"I would say it was the happiest day of my life, but each day I wake up seems to take that title," she said. "We wish you could've been there."

"Yeah, well, it's better that I didn't come. That way the focus was on the two of you. All sunshine and happiness. No dark clouds, you know?"

Angie looked at him with big blue eyes.

"Well, we certainly did appreciate your generous gift. A thousand dollars was…" Angie shook her head as if at a loss for words.

"It was too much," said Toby as he leaned forward and plucked a business card out of a brass holder sitting on the coffee table. "Ten crisp $100 bills. Leave it to my little brother not to miss an opportunity to show off— Wait. Christopher *Fortune?*" he read aloud from the business card. "Did they forget to print your entire last name on here?"

"No," said Christopher.

Toby held up the card. "Where's the *Jones?*"

Christopher shrugged, but didn't feel the need to explain himself.

"So, that's why the receptionist was having a hard time helping us." Toby gestured with his thumb toward the reception area. "It's true, then? They don't even know who Chris Jones is?"

"Don't take it personally, Toby," Christopher said. "I just needed to make a fresh start."

"How can I not take it personally? I mean, I get that you and Dad don't see eye to eye on your moving to Red Rock and working here at the Foundation, but come on, Chris. What the hell? Aren't you taking this a little too far?"

"Is that a question or an accusation?" Christopher challenged, holding his brother's gaze until Toby leaned forward again and put the card back where he'd found it.

This life was exactly what he wanted.

He wanted what the Fortunes had: money, power, respect. He had gotten none of that back in Horseback Hollow. What was wrong with claiming it now?

"I figure the family can't be any more disappointed in me now than they've always been. I never was any good to anyone around the ranch, anyway. Don't you think they'd consider the new and improved Christopher Fortune a vast improvement over Chris Jones, the son who couldn't do anything right?"

Toby looked down at his hands, then back up at Christopher. A somber expression crept into his eyes. "I don't even know what to say to that, except that Mom asked me to tell you she loves you."

Touché.

That was just about the only thing that Toby could've said to hit Christopher where he'd feel it.

The thing was, he didn't even sound mad. Just... disappointed. A look that said, *remember where you came from and don't let the Fortunes change you into something you're not.*

He hadn't forgotten and the Fortunes hadn't changed him. He would be the first to admit that embracing the Fortunes' world and starting on a desk job had taken some getting used to. He was surprised by how he sometimes missed not getting outside between the hours of nine and five. This indoor, sedentary job has been a challenge, but every time he looked at the view outside the windows of his executive's office or at his bank account balance, it got easier and easier.

"Y'all must be hungry," Christopher said. "Come on, let's go get a bite to eat. I'll treat you to lunch."

"Excuse me, darlin'." Kinsley Aaron frowned as she looked up from the notes she was taking while manning the third-floor reception desk for Bev. Christopher Fortune stood outside his office door, smiling broadly, no doubt thinking he was God's gift to women.

Darlin'? Excuse me?

Had they somehow time traveled back to the 1960s?

"My name is Kinsley," she said, doing her best to keep the bristle out of her voice. He may have been young and good-looking and a Fortune, but how dare he call her that?

"I know what your name is," Christopher said.

"Then why did you call me *darlin'?*" She didn't smile.

The man and woman who were with him looked a bit sheepish, perhaps a little embarrassed for him, before they ducked back inside his office. Actually, Christopher should've been embarrassed for himself. But did the guy do anything for himself?

The only reason he worked at the Foundation was because his uncle was James Marshall Fortune.

"Where is Betsy?" he asked

"Who is Betsy?" she returned.

"The new receptionist?" he answered with a tone better suited for talking to a small child.

Well, Mr. Man, two could play that game. "Nobody by the name of *Betsy* works here. Do you mean *Beverly?*"

Christopher shrugged. "Yes, the one who was here earlier." He motioned to the desk where Kinsley was sitting. "Where is she?"

If Bev was smart, she'd handed in her resignation and left.

Kinsley blinked away the snotty thought. She hadn't meant it. The Fortune Foundation was a fabulous place to work. Even though Christopher Fortune was full of himself, other members of the Fortune family had been very good to her. Not only did they pay her a decent salary to work as an outreach coordinator, a position she considered her life's work, but also she would be forever grateful that they had taken a chance on her.

She'd come to them with little experience, having not yet earned her degree. She was working on it, but with a full-time job and going to school part-time at night, it was going to take her a while before she completed her coursework.

"I'm covering for Beverly while she's on her break," Kinsley said. "She should be back in about fifteen minutes. In the meantime, is there something I can help you with?"

Christopher smiled and looked at her in that wolfish way he had that made her want to squirm. But she didn't. No way. She wouldn't give him the satisfaction.

What was with this guy? Better question, what was with her? Kinsley had always subscribed to the Eleanor Roosevelt philosophy: nobody could make you feel *anything* unless you gave them permission. Actually, the quote was nobody could make you feel inferior, but this adaptation felt just as authentic.

"Yes, will you please call and make a lunch reservation for three at Red for 1:15?"

At first Kinsley thought he was kidding. But as she squinted at him, it became quite clear that he was indeed serious.

News flash! She had not been hired as Christopher Fortune's personal secretary! And why did he want to eat at Red, of all places, today? She rarely went out to lunch, but today she had a 12:45 business lunch at the restaurant. She was meeting Meg Tyler, the Red Rock High School PTA president, to discuss the school's Cornerstone Club, an extracurricular student leadership organization, and to talk about the role the kids could play in implementing an anti-bullying program.

For a split second, Kinsley thought about calling Meg and asking if they could change restaurants, but then quickly decided against it. She'd been looking forward to lunch at Red. Why should she deny herself her favorite Mexican place just because he was going to be there?

Yeah, what was up with that? Why was she still feeling so shy around him? He'd started working with the Foundation about two months ago. They hadn't had much contact until recently, when Emmett Jamison had asked them to work together to establish a stronger online presence for the Foundation's community outreach program.

Why did she allow him to make her feel twelve years old? Worse yet, why did she shrink every time Christopher walked into the room? She didn't need his approval. So what if he was charismatic and good-looking? He skated through life on his looks and charm, much like her father had done when he was sober. At least she did her job better than he did.

Fighting the riptide of emotions that threatened to sweep her under, Kinsley stared unseeing at the notes she'd been writing before Christopher had come out of his office. She wasn't going to allow herself to be drowned by the past. Her father had been dead for six years, and she certainly wasn't twelve anymore. In all fairness, despite Christopher's bravado, he really didn't have the mean streak that had possessed her father when he had been drunk. That was when her dad had drummed it into her soul that she would never amount to anything. That she wouldn't be good enough, strong enough, smart enough, pretty enough. No man in his right mind would ever want her.

But that was then and this was now. She was well on her way to proving him wrong. She had a good job, and she was making her own way in the world. No matter how the scarred memories of her bastard of a father tried to convince her that she would never be enough, she needed to muster the strength to exorcise his ghost and set herself free. She needed to quit projecting her father and his twisted ways onto Christopher, who, like so many other men, had a way of making her feel overlooked, dismissed.

She knew her value and what she was capable of. That was all that mattered.

Because she was sitting at the reception desk filling in for Bev, she swallowed her pride and placed the call to Red. A few minutes later, Christopher and his posse emerged from his office and made their way to the elevator. But Christopher hung back. "Thanks for taking care of my family and me, Kinsley."

He looked her square in the eyes in that brazen way of his and flashed a smile. For a short, stupid moment part of her went soft and breathless.

"Mmm" was all she managed to say before she tore her gaze from his and he walked away to join his party.

Mmm. Not even a real word. Just an embarrassing monosyllabic grunt.

Kinsley sat at the reception desk waiting for Bev to return, pondering the shyness that always seemed to get the better of her whenever he was around.

Why?

Why did he have this effect on her?

It was because this job meant so much to her.

And maybe she found his good looks a little intimidating. But good grief.

So the guy was attractive with his perfectly chiseled features and those mile-wide broad shoulders. He had probably played football in college. One of those cocky jock types who had a harem clamoring to serve him. Not that Christopher Fortune's personal life—past or present—was any of her business.

Kinsley blinked and mentally backed away from thoughts of her coworker. Instead, she reminded herself that she had done the right thing by taking the high road and making his darned lunch reservation rather than trying to make a point.

Looks didn't matter. Not in her world, anyway. She had Christopher Fortune's number. He was a handsome opportunist who was riding his family's coattails. In the two months he'd been in the office he hadn't done much to prove that he had high regard for the actual work they were trying to do at the Foundation.

Obviously, he didn't *get it*. Guys like him never did.

But one thing she was going to make sure he understood in no uncertain terms—he'd better never call her *darlin'* again or there would be hell to pay.

Chapter Two

"Oh, look at the flowers." Angie sighed as Christopher guided her and Toby up the bougainvillea-lined path to Red.

"Just wait until you see the courtyard inside," Christopher said with as much pride as if he were showing off his own home. "Red is built around it. There's a fountain I think you'll love."

Angie stopped. "Red?"

"Yes, that's the name of the restaurant." Christopher gestured to the tile nameplate attached to the wall just outside the door, which he held open as he tried to usher them inside, but Angie stopped.

"Is this the same Red that's owned by the Mendozas?" Angie asked.

"One and the same," Christopher said.

"Wendy and Marcos Mendoza catered our wedding

reception." Angie sighed again as she looked around, taking it all in. "They have to be two of the nicest people I've ever met." She turned to Toby. "I can't believe we're here. Chris, did you plan this?"

He wished he could take credit for it, but until now, he'd had no idea what had taken place at their wedding. He'd been so intent on staying away to avoid clouding their day with bad vibes that he hadn't realized he didn't know the first thing about the event other than the fact that his brother had taken himself a bride.

Regret knotted in his gut.

"The Mendozas catered your wedding?" Christopher asked.

"Yes, they did a beautiful job," Angie said. "Everything was delicious. Oh, I hope that chicken mole they served at the reception is on the menu. I've been dreaming of it ever since."

A twinge of disappointment wove itself around the regret. Christopher knew it was totally irrational, but he had brought them here because he'd wanted to introduce them to something new, something from his world that he had discovered. Yet by a strange twist of small-world fate, Red was old news to them.

"This place is so beautiful," Angie cooed. "I could live here quite comfortably."

"I'll bet we could." Toby beamed at his wife. His love for her was written all over his face. Watching the two of them so deeply in love blunted the edges of Christopher's disappointment. He wasn't surprised that Toby had settled down. Of all of his siblings, Toby had been the one who was the most family oriented, especially after taking in the three Hemings kids. He was happy for his brother and Angie. He hoped things worked out and that they would be able to adopt the kids. But although Christopher looked forward to being an uncle, he couldn't imagine any other kind of life than the one he was living now.

On their way to lunch Christopher had seized the opportunity to show off his new town and lifestyle. He'd loaded the newlyweds into his spankin' new BMW and given them the fifty cent tour of downtown Red Rock.

Although there were certainly fancier restaurants in town, none spoke to Christopher quite the way Red did. Obviously the Mendoza appeal wasn't restricted to Red Rock, since Toby and Angie seemed to love their food as much as he did.

Christopher held open the door as Angie and Toby stepped inside. He breathed in deeply as he followed them. It smelled damn good…of fresh corn tortillas, chilies and spices. There was something about the mix of old and new that appealed to him. The restaurant was housed in a converted hacienda that had once been owned by a Spanish family rumored to have been related to Mexican dignitary Antonio López de Santa Ana. Santa Ana was known as the Napoleon of the West. Christopher had recently learned that the current owners of the property, Jose and Maria Mendoza, had been fortunate to purchase the house and land at an affordable price before anyone realized its historical significance. The place couldn't have been in better hands because the Mendozas had given the place its due reverence. That was especially true after the restaurant had been largely destroyed by an arson fire in 2009. Luckily, the family rebuilt and reopened after several months and had been going strong ever since.

Inside, the restaurant was decorated with antiques, paintings and memorabilia that dated all the way back to 1845 when President James Polk named Texas the twenty-eighth state of the Union.

In college, Christopher had complemented his business major with a history minor. So it was only natural that he liked the place for its history.

But the food...he *loved* the place for its food.

Red offered a mouthwatering selection of nouveau Mexican cuisine. The chef had a talent for taking traditional dishes such as huevos rancheros, the chicken mole that Angie was so crazy about and tamales, and sending them to new heights using fresh twists on old classics. The menu was bright and vibrant, familiar yet new and exciting.

Christopher had experienced nothing like it in Horseback Hollow. His mother, Jeanne Marie, was a great cook, but her repertoire was more of the meat and potatoes/comfort food variety. The food at Red was an exotic and surprising twist on traditional Mexican.

The chef was always coming up with new specials of the day and anytime Christopher was in, he asked him to taste test and share his opinion. Christopher loved being able to offer his input.

"Good afternoon, Mr. Fortune," said the hostess. "We're so glad you chose to join us for lunch today. Come right this way. Your favorite table is ready."

The shapely brunette shot Christopher a sexy smile before she turned, hips swaying, as she led the three of them to an aged pine table next to a large window where they could enjoy the comfort of the air-conditioning, but still look out at the well-landscaped courtyard. As far as Christopher was concerned, it was the best seat in the house.

After they were settled, the hostess handed each of them a menu. "Enjoy your lunch, and please let me know if you need *anything*."

She winked at Christopher before she turned to make her way back to the hostess station.

That was quite obvious of her, Christopher thought as he watched her walk away on her high-high heels with the grace and assurance of a tightrope walker. Her skirt was just short enough to draw the eye down to her firm, tanned calves. Now, that was a woman who knew how to dress. Unlike Kinsley, who hid herself under all that heavy tweed fabric that left her looking buttoned-up and shapeless. What a shame.

Suddenly, seeing Kinsley in a skirt and heels like that became his new fantasy.

"I see you come here for the good service," Toby said, a knowing glint in his eye.

"Of course." As Christopher turned back to his brother and Angie, a blonde caught his eye. She was was seated at a table to their left—and he couldn't help noticing that she resembled Kinsley—

Wait, that is *Kinsley.*

She was dining with a woman he didn't recognize. He had a view of Kinsley's profile. If she just turned her head ever so slightly to the right she would see him, but she seemed engrossed in her conversation. Just as he was contemplating getting up and going over to say hello, her server brought their food.

She must have gotten here before him and ordered already. Besides, he, Toby and Angie had just sat down. They hadn't even placed their drink order. He would wait.

When she'd made his reservation she hadn't mentioned that she'd be dining here herself, even though she knew he was going to be here right around the same time. Maybe she was afraid that he would think she was angling for an invite to join them. Most of the women he knew wouldn't have been shy about doing that. But Kinsley was different. Quiet, understated, more conservative.

She was a refreshing change from all the other women he'd met since he'd been in Red Rock. And there had been more than a few. Most of them were sassy and assertive, not at all afraid to reach out and let him know exactly what they wanted and how they wanted it. None of them was a keeper, either. They were all nice and fun, of course, but they left him wanting.

Kinsley, on the other hand, was a puzzle, and most definitely, he realized as he was sitting there, one he was interested in trying to solve.

Hmm. Why had he never thought about her like that before? He'd always thought she was pretty, and on occasion he'd tried to flirt with her, but until right now, he'd never really thought about what made her tick.

As if she felt him watching her, she glanced his way, and their gazes snared. He waved and she lifted a finger before turning her attention back to her lunch companion.

Despite this strange new Kinsley-awareness coursing through him, Christopher decided he should do the same and turned his focus to his brother and Angie.

But pushing her from his mind was harder than he had expected.

The view of the courtyard helped. It was spectacular, with colorful Talavera tiles scattered here and there on the stucco walls, Mexican fan trees and more thriving bougainvillea that seemed to be blooming overtime today in a riot of hot pink, purple and gold. But even the crowning glory of the stately, large fountain in the center of the courtyard couldn't keep Christopher's gaze from wandering over Kinsley's way.

"Too bad we couldn't sit outside," Toby said.

If the temperature wasn't pushing ninety, Christopher would've insisted that they sit out by the fountain. Even though the outside tables were shaded by colorful umbrellas, the humidity was a killer. He didn't want to sweat through his suit and then go back to work.

Not the image he wanted to portray, he thought, glancing at Kinsley.

"Is this okay?" he asked Toby and Angie. "We could move, but it's a killer out there."

"No, this is so lovely," said Angie. "I want to stay right here."

Before she could say more, Marcos Mendoza, the manager of Red, appeared at their table.

"Christopher Fortune, my man." Marcos and Christopher shook hands. "It's great to see you."

"You, too," said Christopher. "My brother Toby and his wife, Angie, are visiting. I couldn't let them leave Red Rock without dining at Red."

"Well, if it isn't the newlyweds." Marcos leaned in and kissed Angie on the cheek then shook Toby's hand. He hooked a thumb in Christopher's direction. "This guy is your brother?"

"Yep, I'll claim him," Toby said without a second's hesitation. His brother's conviction caused Christopher's heart to squeeze ever so slightly, but he did a mental two-step away from the emotion and everything else it implied: the problems between him and Deke; the way he'd left home; the fact that he'd allowed all the ugliness to cause him to miss his own brother's wedding.

"Christopher here is one of our best customers," Marcos said. "I can't believe I didn't put two and two together and figure out that the two of you were related. But different last names?"

"I go by Fortune. Toby goes by Fortune Jones." Angie flinched. Christopher hadn't meant to bite out the words. There was a beat of awkward silence before Toby changed the subject.

"Did you know that Marcos and Wendy are opening a new restaurant in Horseback Hollow?" he asked Christopher.

"Seriously?" Christopher said. He'd only been away a couple of months and he felt like a stranger.

"We're opening The Hollows Cantina next month. In fact, my wife, Wendy, and I are in the process of packing up and moving there with our daughter, Mary-Anne." Marcos paused, a thoughtful look washing over his face. He turned to Christopher. "So if you and Toby are brothers, that means Liam Fortune Jones is your brother, too?"

Christopher nodded.

Marcos smiled. "I've hired his fiancée, Julia Tierney, to be the assistant manager at the restaurant."

Christopher forced a smile.

"I had no idea that you were leaving Red Rock, or that Julia would be working for you," Christopher said.

"I kept it on the down low until I was sure that everything would pan out," said Marcos. "This is a great opportunity for my family, and having my own restaurant will be a dream come true. Really, we owe this happy decision to Julia. She is the one who talked us into opening a place in Horseback Hollow. Your future sister-in-law should work for the Horseback Hollow Chamber of Commerce—she can't say enough good about the place."

"Congratulations," said Angie. "We will be sure to come in after the Cantina opens."

"I have your contact information," said Marcos, "and I will make sure that the two of you are invited to the grand opening. The Fortunes are like family, and family always sticks together."

Toby shot Christopher a knowing look. "Yes, they do."

"In fact, Fortune," Marcos said to Christopher, "I'd better see you at the grand opening celebration, too. Especially now that I know that you're a native son of Horseback Hollow."

Christopher gave a wry smile. "Yeah, well, don't go spreading that around."

Everybody laughed, unaware or ignoring the fact that Christopher wasn't kidding.

"I need to get back to work," Marcos said. "So please excuse me and enjoy your lunch."

The men shook hands again and Marcos planted another kiss on Angie's cheek before he moved on to greet the next table of guests.

"When are Julia and Liam getting married?" asked Christopher.

"That remains to be seen," said Toby. "It's a big step that he's committed to one woman. Julia is good for him. She gets him, but doesn't let him get away with squat. I think she's about the only woman who could make an honest man out of him."

Nodding, Christopher gave the menu a cursory glance. He wanted to hear the day's specials, but it would take something extra appealing to sway him away from his favorite beef brisket enchiladas.

Toby looked up from his menu. "It looks like the marriage bug is infesting our family. I just heard that our cousin Amelia Chesterfield Fortune has gotten engaged to some British aristocrat."

"That just seems so odd," mused Angie. "She was dancing with Quinn Drummond at our wedding. It was the way they were looking at each other... The two of them seemed so happy. In fact, I would've wagered that something was blossoming between them. I just can't imagine that there's another man in the picture."

"Yeah, but I heard the news from Mama and she usually gets things right." Toby shook his head as if trying to reconcile the idea.

Their server was a woman named DeeDee. Christopher had seen her socially one time, but he hadn't called her again. He hadn't realized that she worked at Red. Within the first hour of their date, he'd realized DeeDee was after a whole lot more relationship than he was able to give. No sense in stringing her along, even if she was nice. The world was full of nice women and he needed to get to know a lot more of them before he settled down. He found his gaze sliding over to Kinsley's table yet again. It looked as if they were finishing up with their meals. "Well, if it isn't Christopher Fortune as I live and breathe," DeeDee said, a teasing note in her voice. She twisted a strand of her long red hair around her finger as she talked. "It's been so long since I heard from you, I thought maybe you'd fallen off the face of the earth or maybe you moved to some exotic, faraway land."

Christopher laughed, keeping things light. "It's good to see you, DeeDee. How long have you been working here?"

"It's only my second day."

"Which explains why I've never seen you here," said Christopher.

After a little more playful banter, DeeDee flipped her hair off her shoulder with a swift swipe of her hand and took their drink orders. Next, she described the day's specials, which didn't tempt Christopher's taste buds away from his usual order. After she left to get their drinks, Christopher recommended some of his favorites from the menu to Toby and Angie.

A few minutes later DeeDee returned with a bottle of champagne and three flutes. "This is for the newly-weds, compliments of Mr. Mendoza and the staff at Red."

"Oh, my goodness," said Angie. "Champagne in the middle of the day. How decadent. And how absolutely lovely. Thank you."

"Well, the way I see it," said Toby, "I'm only getting married once, and it's an occasion to celebrate. Right, little brother?"

Toby didn't wait for Christopher to answer. He put his arm around his bride and leaned in, placing a sound kiss on Angie's lips. If DeeDee hadn't been standing there, Christopher might have joked and told them to get a room. But really, it was nice to see Toby and Angie so happy.

"So this is your brother and sister-in-law?" asked DeeDee after she popped the cork and filled the glasses with the bubbly.

Christopher didn't want to be rude, but he didn't want to get too personal. "Yes," he said. "They're visiting, but I'm on my lunch hour so we should place our orders now."

"Of course," said DeeDee, snapping into professional mode. She wrote down their selections and headed toward the kitchen.

After she left, Christopher said, "I just can't get over the fact that you're *married.* But it suits you. It really does."

Toby gave Angie a little squeeze.

"Where do the adoption proceedings stand?" Christopher asked. Seven months ago, Toby had taken in the Hemings children: eleven-year-old Brian, eight-year-old Justin and seven-year-old Kylie. The kids had had nowhere to turn and faced possible separation when their aunt was ordered into rehab for a drinking problem and child neglect. Both Christopher and Toby had known the kids from the Vicker's Corners YMCA where they had worked as coaches. Most people would've run from that kind of responsibility— Christopher knew he certainly couldn't have handled it—but Toby hadn't thought twice before agreeing to take them in.

Unfortunately, the kids' aunt, who obviously didn't have the children's best interests at heart, had decided to try and take the kids from Toby and send them into another unstable situation in California. Her reasoning was the kids should be with relatives. Never mind that the relative she'd chosen was out of work and on parole.

That's all it took for Toby to decide he needed to legally adopt the children.

"Everything is still pending," said Toby. "Frankly, it's taking so long I'm starting to get worried."

"I just don't understand what the holdup is," said Angie. "They not only have a loving home with us, but they also have become part of the family. They call Jeanne Marie and Deke Grandma and Grandpa. They're calling your sisters and brothers Aunt and Uncle. How anyone could think that uprooting these poor kids is what's best for them is beyond me. It breaks my heart."

Toby caressed Angie's shoulder. "We are going to do everything in our power to make sure they stay with us."

"What can I do to help?" asked Christopher.

Toby shrugged. "At this point I don't know what else anyone could do."

"The Fortune name carries a lot of clout," said Christopher. "Maybe we can use its influence to get things going in the right direction."

Toby peered at him. "What exactly are you suggesting?"

Christopher gave a one-shoulder shrug as he rubbed the fingers of his left hand together in the international gesture for *money*. "Money talks, bro."

Toby frowned and shook his head. "Please don't even suggest anything like that. I don't want to be accused of doing anything unethical. That might hurt the situation more than it helps."

"Nonsense," said Christopher. "I think you're being very shortsighted if you don't take full advantage of your birthright."

Christopher saw Toby take in a slow deep breath, as he always did when faced with conflict. It was as if he were framing his response so that he didn't lose his cool.

"I appreciate your concern, Chris," said Toby evenly. "But the caseworker told me she's worried that the Fortunes themselves may be part of the problem. Since the Fortunes invaded Horseback Hollow so many strange things have happened. The authorities still think Orlando Mendoza's accident might have been directed at the family."

"Don't be ridiculous," said Christopher. "Why would anyone want to hurt the Fortunes? I mean, look at me. I'm living proof. Since I changed my name nothing bad has happened to me."

Christopher turned his palms up to punctuate his point.

"That is, if you don't count your running away from home and shunning your entire family as something bad."

Toby cocked an eyebrow at Christopher.

Christopher locked gazes with his brother and crossed his arms.

"Look, I know this Fortune Foundation gig is still new and exciting to you," said Toby, "so don't take this wrong. But someday you're going to learn that some things are more important than money."

Christopher glanced over at Kinsley, but she and

her friend were gone. His gaze swept the restaurant, but she was nowhere to be seen. How had he not seen her leave?

He picked up his champagne glass and knocked back the contents.

"Come on, Chris," said Toby. "When are you coming home? No one has seen you in months. They certainly have no idea that you've completely disowned Daddy's name."

Toby was usually the only one who could see Christopher's side in times when he and Deke disagreed, which was more often than not. Awkward silence hung in the air and, for once, Christopher didn't know how to fill it. He didn't want to fight with Toby, but he wasn't going back to Horseback Hollow. His life was here now, and he would prefer to keep his old and new lives separate. The contrast between the Joneses and the Fortunes was stark. Christopher couldn't take the chance of losing the respect he'd earned at the Foundation.

"Man up, Chris," Toby urged. "Take the high road and be the one who extends the olive branch to Deke."

"Yeah, well that high road has two lanes. Deke can bring that olive branch to me easier than I can bring it to him. I'm a little too busy right now to coddle a grown man."

Toby made a *tsk* sound. "An *old* man. Don't wait too long. You may be sorry if you do."

"Don't pull that guilt trip crap on me," said Christopher. "Just don't. But please do tell me why it's okay for Deke to resent me for making an honest living in a career I love. For making my own way. For not having dirt under my fingernails. No offense to you, but why should I have to grovel to him because the ranch life is not the kind of life I want? Until Deke understands that, I don't think we're going to meet anywhere, much less with an olive branch."

Truth be told, he would rather be known as James Marshall Fortune's nephew than as the son of Deke Jones, crusty old cattle rancher. Christopher hoped that Toby wouldn't make him come out and say that.

Toby stared at Christopher, looking thin-lipped and angry.

"So you've got the fancy suits, the brand-new car and a parade of women who think you're a big shot," said Toby, virtually rolling his eyes at what he obviously perceived as self-importance. "Looks like you've finally achieved your dream, haven't you?"

"You shouldn't knock it since you've never tried it," said Christopher. "No offense to you, Angie. I'm just saying."

Toby took his wife's hand and laced his fingers through hers. "No loss. Believe me, I wouldn't trade my life for yours. I couldn't possibly be any happier than I am with Angie and the kids. On that note, I think we'd better start heading toward home."

Toby pulled out his wallet and tossed a crisp $100 bill onto the table in payment for the food they hadn't managed to stay long enough to have delivered to their table. It was probably one of the ten that Christopher had given him as a wedding gift.

Christopher slid the bill back toward his brother. "Here, Toby. I've got this."

Toby stood. "No, you don't. If you *got this,* you would stop acting like such a pretentious jackass and come home and make amends with Dad. You may have given up on us, Chris, but we'll never give up on you. Take care of yourself and call me when you're ready to talk."

Chapter Three

With his long lunches and daily putting practice, was it any wonder Christopher Fortune didn't get much done? Kinsley mused after fielding a call from Emmett Jamison, the head of the Foundation. Even so, she'd covered for Christopher when Mr. Jamison had asked if she'd seen him. She'd explained that he'd taken a late lunch with family visiting from out of town. She didn't mention that he'd been gone nearly two-and-a-half hours.

She may not have agreed with the way Christopher conducted himself, but she wasn't about to throw him under the bus. That would just make her look bad in the eyes of Mr. Jamison.

She wanted him to see her as a problem solver, not the type of person who pointed fingers and ratted people out. Besides, with the Fortunes, blood was definitely thicker than water. If she wasn't careful the situation might get turned around and come back to bite her. She was sure if it came down to her or Christopher Fortune, Emmett Jamison would side with the man whose last name was on his paycheck.

Kinsley drummed her fingers on the desk. The Fortunes were all about family. She knew Mr. Jamison would excuse him for that. She couldn't deny that she envied Christopher and his huge support system. What was it like to come from such a large, protective family that would circle the wagons at a moment's notice?

Kinsley had no idea. Growing up the only child of an alcoholic father and a mother who couldn't stand up for herself didn't give her much experience to draw from.

She and her mother only had each other to intervene when her father was on a drunken bender. When they did stand up to him, there was always hell to pay.

Her grandmother—her mom's mom—had passed away when Kinsley was about eight, but Grandma hadn't had the wherewithal to extract her daughter from what Kinsley would later look back on and realize was a situation that had robbed her mother of her life.

But wasn't hindsight always perfect?

From the moment Kinsley was old enough to realize she could take care of herself, she vowed she would never personally depend on a man. For that matter, she preferred to not depend on anyone, because didn't people always let you down?

She'd only had two boyfriends, and both of them had proven that to be true. They were hard lessons, but she'd learned. And she prided herself on not repeating the same mistakes.

Family ranks or not, Emmett had said he was concerned because he had received a call from a woman named Judy Davis who was perplexed because she'd emailed the community relations office three times about a donation she wanted to make and still hadn't heard back. She was beginning to think the Foundation didn't want her money.

Kinsley made an excuse that there had been technical difficulties with the email account and had assured Mr. Jamison that she and Christopher would make sure everything was working as it should as soon as he got back...which should be any minute.

Technically, Christopher was being *difficult.* Right? Did that count as technical difficulties? She hoped so. Because it was all she had.

She would cover for Christopher this time, but they were definitely going to have a little heart to heart.

She wrote down Judy Davis's information and assured Mr. Jamison that they would follow up with her today and make sure she knew how much her donation was needed and appreciated.

Kinsley's cheeks burned.

She didn't appreciate being left holding the bag for matters like this, especially when it was something Christopher had insisted on handling. The new Foundation Community Relations email address had been her idea, but they had decided to split the work: as she went out into the community, Kinsley would get the word out about the new way to contact the Foundation; as vice president of community relations, Christopher had insisted on being the one to respond to the emails.

Thank goodness Kinsley had insisted on knowing the password. Christopher had agreed that it was a good idea for more than one person to have access to the account, but he had assured her that he would check it regularly. She had taken him at his word. Kinsley mentally kicked herself for trusting so blindly. People might have been reaching out for help or there could be more potential funding for the Foundation in these unread messages. Yet Christopher was too busy perfecting his putt...and she'd covered for him.

Feeling like a fool, Kinsley gritted her teeth as she typed in the URL to bring up the login page so she could sign into the account.

As a Fortune, Christopher was set for life. Unlike the other family members who worked at the Foundation, he didn't seem grounded in the realities of what mere mortals had to face in the world.

No, Christopher Fortune was fat, spoiled and smug—

Well, maybe not fat. Kinsley hated herself for it, but somehow her gaze always managed to find its way to Christopher's abs. The way his expensive, tailored dress shirts tapered in at his trim waist, she could plainly see that the guy didn't have an ounce of fat on his body.

No, he was all broad shoulders and six-pack abs— or at least she imagined he was sporting a six-pack under his buttoned up exterior. Who wouldn't be if they had time to work out daily? Actually, it didn't matter what Christopher Fortune was packing under his crisp cotton shirt. Mr. Vice President was still spoiled and smug. And completely irresponsible when it came to doing his job.

When the login page came up, she was relieved to see that it hadn't been that long since Christopher had checked the account. In fact, it had only been two days. She scrolled through the ten emails in search of Judy Davis's three messages. When she found them, she realized the three emails had arrived within a span of 36 hours.

Mr. Jamison had been under the impression that she'd been waiting a long time to hear back. Though it really hadn't been an excessively long time since Christopher had checked the account, it did need to be monitored regularly. Several times a day, in fact, to keep something like this from happening.

If that was too much for Christopher to handle, he needed to hand it over to someone who could keep a closer eye on it, Kinsley thought as she started to click on one of the unopened message.

But then she stopped. Instead, she had a better idea.

She took a screenshot of the emails that still needed attention and printed it out. Then she took a fluorescent yellow highlighter and marked each one that he needed to check.

She'd already covered for him. If she did his work for him, too, she would simply be fostering his habit of letting someone else pick up the pieces.

The thought took her back to another place and time that made her unspeakably sad. Maybe if she'd intervened a little more on behalf of her mother things would've turned out differently. She stared at the computer screen as the memory threatened to cut into her heart. But she shrugged off the feelings before they could take root. What had happened to her mother was entirely different from what was happening now.

No amount of wishing or dwelling would change the way things had played out. That's why Kinsley's job at the Foundation was so important. She couldn't change the past, but maybe, if she did her job well, she could make a difference for someone else.

Christopher Fortune didn't need saving. He needed a good swift kick in the rear.

Kinsley had her own workload to worry about. The last thing she needed was to try and reform Mr. Silver Spoon. He was a big boy; he could take care of himself. He needed to start pulling his load. She fully intended to tell him as much when he got back.

Well…in so many words.

She wasn't going to do anything to jeopardize her job. But she could still stand up for herself.

This would be a good time to make sure Christopher knew that, although she didn't mind helping him out with things like checking the Foundation's Community Relations email account and making his lunch reservations, she wasn't his secretary. She didn't intend to mince words about that.

She paper clipped Judy Davis's contact information on top of the highlighted list of unanswered emails and set the papers on the corner of her desk.

She knew it wasn't her place to call him out; she intended to do it tactfully. She'd make him think it was all his idea. But yes. They were going to have a little reality check when he got back. She glanced at the clock on her cell phone—was he even coming back to the office today?

She picked up the phone and dialed. "Hi, Bev, would you please let me know when Mr. Fortune gets back into the office? I want to schedule a meeting with him."

"Speak of the devil," Bev whispered. "He just walked in from lunch. Want me to see if he's available?"

"No, that's okay," Kinsley said. "I'll just walk down the hall and stick my head in his office."

Christopher swiveled his office chair so that it faced the window. He leaned back, stretching his legs out in front of him and resting his hands on his middle.

The more he thought about what had happened at lunch, the more he was sure Deke had sent Toby to do his bidding. It made him so angry he wanted to wrap his putter around the trunk of the magnolia tree out in front of the building.

It could've been a good visit with his brother. A chance to get to know his new sister-in-law a little better. But Deke had to insert himself, even if it was virtually, and mess things up.

His father was so good at messing things up.

But then Christopher had to wonder if his brother would've come to Red Rock if it hadn't been to prod him to go home. Well, it hadn't done any good. If anything it had given him more incentive to stay away. The Joneses couldn't stand anything that varied from their idea of normal. But Christopher had news for them all—this was his new normal.

He looked up at the sound of a knock on his door. He straightened up in his chair and turned back to his desk, moving the mouse to wake up his computer screen.

"Come in," he said.

He was delighted when he saw Kinsley standing in the threshold. Suddenly the afternoon was looking a lot brighter.

"Do you have a moment?" she asked.

"For you, I would clear my schedule."

She rolled her eyes. Not exactly the response he was hoping for, but he would've been surprised if he'd gotten a more enthused reaction.

"I'm just kidding," he said. Actually, he wasn't. "Come in. I'm not the big bad wolf. How was your lunch?"

She shut the door and walked over to stand in front of his desk. "It was fine."

"I saw you at Red," he said. "I was going to come over and say hello, but by the time we ordered you were gone."

"I only had an hour for lunch. I had to get back."

Since he'd seen her at the restaurant she'd pulled her hair back away from her face. And what a face it was; she had a perfect complexion that didn't require much makeup. In fact, he wasn't even sure if she was wearing any makeup. His mind wandered for a moment, imagining the curves that hid beneath the conservative clothes she wore. He smiled at the thought. But then he realized she wasn't smiling at him.

God, if he didn't know better, he might be afraid she'd read his mind.

"Is something wrong?" he asked.

"Since you asked," she said, "actually, yes, there is something wrong."

She held out a piece of paper. He reached across the desk and took it from her.

"What's this?"

She was standing there with her arms crossed—defensive body language. Her sensible blue blouse was buttoned all the way up to the top and was tucked into a plain lighter blue skirt that didn't show nearly enough leg. Legs, he thought, that would look killer in a pair of shiny black stilettos, ones like the hostess at Red had worn, rather than those low-heeled church lady shoes that looked like something out of his mama's closet.

"It's a message from a woman who has been trying to get a hold of you to make a donation to the Foundation," she said.

Christopher read the name and number scrawled on the paper. Judy Davis? He didn't know a Judy Davis.

"Who is she and when did she call?"

Kinsley crossed one ankle over the other, keeping her arms firmly across her middle. Good grief. If she twisted herself any tighter she was going to turn herself inside out.

"After she emailed you three times, unsuccessfully, she called Mr. Jamison to voice her displeasure. He called me while you were at lunch, none too pleased."

What the hell?

Christopher lifted up the paper with the message and saw a photocopy of what looked like a list of emails. Someone had taken a highlighter to it.

"Did Emmett do this?" he asked, gesturing at her with the paper.

Her cheeks flushed the slightest hue of pink, which made her look even prettier, if that was possible.

She cleared her throat. "No, I did. Christopher, you haven't checked the community relations email account in two days. She emailed us three times—"

"Three times over the course of what, 48 hours?"

he asked looking at the paper to check the time the emails came through.

"Actually, it's closer to 36 hours," she said. "I know she was a little impatient, but she wants to give us money and nobody contacted her in a reasonable amount of time. I can understand why she was a little upset."

Christopher watched Kinsley as she stood there, obviously irritated with him. The funny thing was, usually when people nagged him it made him mad, but he found her completely disarming. His gaze dropped to her full bottom lip.

He'd be willing to wager that those lips would taste better than that expensive champagne that Marcos had given them at lunch, and he was getting a little hot and bothered at the realization that he hadn't yet had a taste of Kinsley's lips.

He smiled as he added that task to his mental to-do list.

"I'll be happy to call her now," Christopher said, offering his best smile.

"That's a good idea. The sooner the better. I don't mean to tell you what to do, but you really should check that email account several times a day."

"I checked it three days in a row and there was absolutely no email," he said. "I've been busy. I know this is your brainchild, but people aren't exactly lining up to leave us messages."

Her brows knit. "Christopher, do you see that piece of paper I gave you? There are ten unanswered messages on there. Well, seven if you don't count the three from Judy Davis."

Her face was so expressive. Those lips were so full.

It was mesmerizing to watch her mouth as she talked. He realized he was sitting there grinning stupidly as she reprimanded him. Still, he wanted to laugh. Not at her, but at the situation—at the way the woman had somehow gotten under his skin, but in a good way. A sexy way. A way that made him want to walk over and unbutton the top button of her blouse to loosen her up a bit. Hell, he didn't want to stop there—

"Are you listening to me?" she asked.

"Every single word." He pursed his lips to remove the grin from his face.

Now her hands were on her hips. The stance drew her blouse tight across her breasts. The fabric between the middle buttons gaped a little bit. He forced his eyes back to her face. And she wasn't smiling.

Uh-oh. Busted.

"Then would you please tell me what I just said to you?" she said.

"You were talking about the messages from Susan Davis."

"Judy," she enunciated. "It's *Judy* Davis. For goodness' sake don't make matters worse by calling her the wrong name."

He looked down at the papers he was still holding in his hand. He shuffled the two sheets and saw that yes, indeed, the message said *Judy* Davis.

He smiled to mask his embarrassment. He never had been good with names. "I know her name is Judy. Says so right here." He waved the paper at her. "I was just seeing if you were paying attention."

She rolled her eyes again.

"You don't like me very much, do you?" he asked, eager to hear what she would say. Of course, he was daring her, and he got exactly the reaction he was hoping for.

She blanched. Her eyes flew open wide, and a look of innocence overtook her formerly contemptuous expression.

"I have no idea why you would say that," she said. "You're my coworker and I respect you."

Respect, huh?

But then she surprised him.

"And while we're on the topic of respect," she said, "I need to make sure that we understand each other in a couple of areas."

"Of course," he said. He gestured toward the chair in front of his desk. "Kinsley, please sit down."

She shook her head. "No, I'd rather stand, thank you."

Christopher shrugged. "Okay, suit yourself, but if you're going to stand I guess that means I will, too."

He stood and the slightly panicked and perplexed look clouded her face again. "You don't have to do that. Really, you don't."

"Of course I do. It makes me uncomfortable to have you towering over me."

"What? You're not going to tell me that you're one of those people who believes his head should always be higher than the heads of his subordinates?"

What was this? A dry sense of humor?

He walked around to the other side of the desk, careful to respect her personal space.

"No, but that's not a bad theory."

This time she looked at him as if he had just grown another head on his shoulder.

"You do know I'm kidding, right?"

"I wasn't sure."

"Kinsley. We've been working together for what—two months now? I would *hope* that you would know me better than that by now. You're great at what you do. But you need to loosen up just a little bit. This isn't brain surgery."

"It may not be brain surgery, but I take what I do seriously and I would like for you to take *me* seriously."

What?

Was that what she thought? That he didn't take her seriously? She was one of the most competent, capable people he'd ever worked with. He liked her poise, he liked the way she related to their clients and of course, he loved the way she looked. But maybe that was the problem....

The Fortune mystique didn't seem to work on this woman who was all business, all the time.

Why not?

Why was she immune when most of the women in Red Rock practically bowed down when a Fortune entered the room?

He liked that about her.

All she wanted was to be taken seriously. He understood. That's all he'd wanted from Deke. To be respected for what he did and how he did it.

"Point taken," he said.

She took a deep breath, held it for a moment and then silently released it. He saw her shoulders rise and fall as she did so.

"There's one more thing," she said.

Christopher gestured with both hands. "Please. Anything. You can talk to me."

"First—"

"I thought you said there was only *one* more thing?"

She gave him that look again, as if she were saying *really?*

"I'm sorry," he said. "I do respect you, Kinsley. But could you please unfurrow your brow for just a moment? Unfurrow your brow and smile. Will you do that for me?"

She stood there for a moment looking at him as if she still wasn't sure whether or not he was joking. He held his ground, looking at her expectantly. Finally, she forced a smile. It was the most pathetic and amusing attempt at one he'd ever seen.

"I mean a real smile."

She put her palms in the air, finally uncrossing her arms. "I don't understand what you want from me. But I'm going to tell you what I expect from you—I'm not your Girl Friday. I don't mind helping you, but I'm not your secretary. Secretaries make lunch reservations. Outreach coordinators, which is what I was hired to do for the Foundation, will check the email account if it's something you don't want to do. But you have to communicate with me, Christopher. I'm the one who had to deal with Mr. Jamison when he called wondering why we had dropped the ball. I told him we were experiencing technical difficulties with the new email account. But I don't want to lie, and I can't continue to cover for you."

Her voice was serious but surprisingly not accusatory. What amazed him even more was his reaction to what she was saying. He simply nodded and said, "You're right. We do need to communicate better. If you have suggestions on how we could do that, I'm happy to listen to what you have to say."

"Maybe we could have regular meetings and discuss where we're going with new venture...er, the Foundation's community relations and community outreach efforts?"

"I think that sounds like a wonderful idea," he said, trying not to acknowledge the voice inside his head detailing exactly how he would like to *communicate* with Kinsley.

The woman had asked for respect. He understood that and revered her even more for telling him that was important to her.

"I'm sorry if I gave you the wrong impression. Because you're a very important part of this team and I don't want you to ever feel uncomfortable."

There it was. An almost imperceptible shift in her demeanor, but he saw it. She had re-crossed her arms and was still standing there with her closed-off posture, but her brow was slightly less furrowed and her shoulders were somewhat more relaxed.

"I appreciate that," she said.

He resisted the urge to tell her that he knew there was a lot more to Kinsley Aaron than a pretty face and a potentially great pair of legs. There was something guarded and a little troubled about her and he wanted to know who or what had made her that way because she was way too young and pretty to be that uptight.

He silently vowed that he was going to find out. He was going to be the one to teach Kinsley Aaron how to loosen up.

Chapter Four

Two days later, Kinsley got a call from Emmett Jamison's assistant, Valerie, asking her to meet with Mr. Jamison at two o'clock. Apprehension knotted in her stomach.

Christopher had called Judy Davis right after their discussion. Kinsley had followed up and made sure that Christopher had placed the call. Christopher could be all wit and charm, so Kinsley had been certain that he would win the woman over. She hadn't given it a second thought.

Until now.

Now, Kinsley was nervous that maybe Judy Davis had called back with more complaints and, once again, she would take the fall. Well, she wasn't going to lie and she wouldn't go down without a fight. As she made her way to Mr. Jamison's office, she racked her brain for the words to defend herself if he was calling her in to level the boom.

She loved this job. She was good at it. She'd made great strides with the community outreach program. Really, her work should speak for itself.

When her heartbeat kicked into an irrational staccato, she took a deep breath and reminded herself not to jump to conclusions. Just because Mr. Jamison has never called her to his office before in the year and a half she'd worked there didn't mean the first visit spelled doom.

Valerie looked up and smiled at Kinsley as she approached.

"Hi, Kinsley," she said. "Have a seat. I'll let Mr. Jamison know you're here."

Kinsley had no more than settled herself on the edge of the maroon wingback chair when Valerie hung up the phone and said, "He said to come right in. He's ready to see you."

Kinsley dug deep to offer her most self-assured smile. "Thank you."

When she opened the door, Christopher was the first person she saw. What was he doing here?

He wasn't her boss. Yet he was her superior if you went strictly by job title. When he had started at the Foundation, his place in the chain of command hadn't been officially defined.

But here he was, sitting on the sofa in Emmett Jamison's office. Mr. Jamison occupied the chair across from Christopher. Notes of their laughter still hung in the air. They stood up and smiled at Kinsley as she walked in.

She hoped the convivial air was a good sign. Usually, people didn't sit and joke when they were planning on letting an employee go. She was eager to know what this was all about.

"Hello, Kinsley," said Mr. Jamison. "Thanks for taking time out of your day to meet with us."

That was a good sign.

"No problem at all," she said.

He gestured to the empty space on the couch next to Christopher. For a moment Kinsley silently debated whether she should sit in the chair next to her boss, but she walked over and took the seat he'd indicated.

After their talk the other day, Kinsley had forgiven the flirtation. Maybe it was because despite how incredibly maddening—and flirty—the guy could be, he seemed to have taken seriously her requests to be treated professionally. She couldn't ask for more than that.

She felt him watching her as she settled herself next to him. Okay, so maybe the old dog hadn't completely changed his ways. Or maybe she just needed to relax and own up to the fact that maybe she was the one with the problem. That maybe she found Christopher just a little bit more attractive than she would like to admit. *There.* She'd said it. And immediately blinked away the thought, wondering where it had come from.

"I want to thank both of you for the way you handled Judy Davis," said Emmett. "She called back to say she was delighted with the response she received. I think you charmed her, Christopher."

No doubt.

"But, Kinsley," said Emmett, "Christopher tells me you're the one who alerted him to the fact that there was a problem, allowing him to correct the situation.

That's great teamwork. It started me thinking that the two of you should collaborate on another community relations project."

Christopher had admitted that there had been a problem?

Kinsley checked herself to ensure that her expression didn't expose her surprise.

So he'd fessed up... Hmm... Maybe I need to give him more credit.

"Do you have something in mind?" Christopher asked.

"As a matter of fact I do," said Emmett. "Jed Cramer, principal over at Red Rock High School, told me that you, Kinsley, had lunch with his Cornerstone Club president the other day. He was telling me that there has been an increase in bullying among the students, and he's very concerned. He believes the Foundation can help since we've been successful in reaching teens through our community outreach program. Kinsley, you're really doing a wonderful job with that. I think this is a project that the two of you could really sink your teeth into. Together you could do some real good and put a stop to this bullying problem."

Emmett's eyes darted back and forth between Christopher and Kinsley. "Does this sound like something you would like to handle?"

Kinsley and Christopher both looked at each other and started to speak at the same time. Then they stopped talking and started again at the exact same time.

Finally, Christopher smiled and gestured to Kinsley. "You go first."

She felt her stomach flutter a little, but she ignored

it and simply said, "Thank you. Meg was telling me this is an unfortunate reality that's happening more and more these days. The challenge is getting the kids to speak up—not only the ones who are being bullied, but the ones who witness the bullying. A lot is going on here—self-esteem issues, cliques and a general feeling of wanting—no, needing—to be accepted."

Christopher was nodding his head. Kinsley paused to let him put in his two cents, but he remained quiet. So she continued.

"To reach the kids, we have to not only go where they are, but we also have to reach them on a more personal level. What would you think about the Foundation having a booth at the annual Red Rock Spring Fling?"

"I think it's a wonderful idea," said Emmett.

"I agree," said Christopher. "But we will have to move fast because it's happening toward the end of the month. How about if I check into the logistics of securing the booth?"

"That sounds like a plan," said Emmett. "The two of you can work together to plan the approach you'll take and the material you'll use. Here's more good news. We have about $20,000 in the unspecified reserve account. We had a board meeting yesterday and the board of directors approved your using some of that money to implement an anti-bullying program. How about if we make the Spring Fling our target launch date? Does that sound doable?"

Again, Christopher and Kinsley's gazes met. Maybe it was her imagination, but Kinsley could've sworn that something vaguely electric passed between them. For some reason, despite everything that had already happened, it didn't bother her like it would've before she and Christopher had talked. And that felt a little reckless. She refocused her attention on Emmett.

It was probably just the residual adrenaline rush she'd felt at Mr. Jamison's praise. He'd noticed her hard work. She was having a hard time keeping herself from smiling.

"It sounds doable to me," she said. "We will have our work cut out for us, though, with this timeline. But we can do it."

"Sounds like a very worthy project," said Christopher. "I'm definitely up for the challenge."

His words made Kinsley's breath catch in her throat, which was ridiculous. She needed to stop this nonsense. After her big declaration the other day, if she knew what was good for her she would just keep her mind on the job and stop thinking about how blue Christopher Fortune's eyes were and relishing the times when those eyes lingered and seemed to only see her.

What was wrong with her? Two days ago she had all but read him the riot act about treating her with respect, and here she was in her boss's office contemplating Christopher Fortune's eyes. She needed to get her head on straight. She would do this project and do it right without allowing inappropriate thoughts to get in the way. The last thing she wanted was to let a fickle man come between her and the only stability she'd ever really known.

If her mom had been strong enough to do the same, things would be so different today for both of them.

Well, she would just have to be strong…in memory of her mother.

"Fantastic," said Emmett. "I know the two of you will make a fabulous team. You complement each other. Christopher, you bring the charm, and Kinsley, I know you will keep Christopher on task. I have a very strong feeling I will be calling the two of you my dream team."

Dream team, Kinsley mused.

Why did that seem to work on so many different levels?

Over the next few days, Christopher realized just how many members of the Fortune family worked at the Foundation. The organization was run by Emmett and his wife, Linda Faraday, but working here had given him so many opportunities to meet his cousins: Susan Fortune Eldridge and Julie Osterman Fortune, who were doing great work with troubled teens; Nicholas Fortune, a financial analyst who monitored the Foundation's investments; and Jeremy Fortune, who was a doctor for the Foundation's medical clinic. Yet they always seem to have room for one more. He didn't want to be the slacker amid the bunch. He wanted to make sure that Emmett and Linda didn't regret hiring him. He vowed to be his most professional self.

Christopher had taken to heart Kinsley's request for him to treat her with respect. The anti-bullying project Emmett had assigned was the opportunity for him to prove himself—to Emmett, to his family and, of course, to Kinsley.

If he wasn't able to woo her with the Fortune name and charm that seemed to work on every other woman in Red Rock, he would win her over with his new-

and-improved work ethic. She was an inspiration. She made him want to be a better man.

He would show her that he wasn't just hired because he was a Fortune. Though she hadn't come right out and said it, he knew she must be thinking it.

The anti-bullying project was a worthwhile venture. It was an opportunity to do some good for the community. After two months of feeling as if he was spinning his wheels, he finally felt as if he had a foothold. Plus, it offered the bonus of extra time with Kinsley. It would be a chance for him to get closer to her, a chance for him to woo her and win her over.

Because they didn't have much time to put the display together, the two of them had been spending a lot of time together. They had agreed to a standing hour and a half meeting every afternoon so they could plan their approach.

He should've known by now that Kinsley would throw herself wholeheartedly into anything she committed to. Even so, he hadn't planned on her practically transporting her office to his. But for their first meeting, there she'd been with reams of files and at least a dozen three-ring binders that detailed the different branches of the Foundation's outreach program.

She'd brought so much stuff it required several trips to transport it all. Christopher had helped her carry the bulk of it. Now, the two of them sat across from each other in his office—since it was the larger space— with the information spread out across the coffee table.

"First, I think we should figure out what sort of printed material we need," Kinsley suggested. "I was thinking we could put together a brochure that offers tips about bullying prevention. Like what to do if you find yourself the victim of a bully, and what to do if you see someone else being bullied. We'll need to have these finished first because we'll need some lead time for the printing. What do you think?"

What did he think?

He thought she was one of the most beautiful women he had ever laid eyes on. With her long blond hair and complicated blue eyes, the saying *still waters run deep* came to mind. Kinsley might seem quiet and unassuming, but from what Christopher had experienced, there was a whole lot more going on beneath the surface.

"I think that sounds great," he said. "Do you want to write the copy for that? Somehow I have a feeling you would be a lot better at it than I would."

She had gorgeous skin. He just knew it would feel like silk... He balled his fists to keep from reaching across the table and running a finger along her jawline. She was a natural beauty, and he was willing to bet she didn't even know it.

"I'm happy to do it," she said. "In fact, I already have a couple of ideas for themes. Would you like to hear them?"

Smart. Beautiful. She just needed to know that she didn't have to be all business, all the time. He could help her with that. He felt himself smiling.

"I would love to hear them."

She surprised him by smiling back at him. "Well, the first one I thought of was *Take a stand. Lend a hand.*"

She paused and watched him. Though he knew she would never admit it, he could see in her eyes that she was looking for approval.

"That's great. It's catchy and concise."

Her blue eyes shone. "I'm glad you like it. I thought it served two good purposes. We're encouraging people to take a stand—that could mean standing up for yourself or stepping in when someone else is being bullied. And of course, the *lend a hand* part is all about helping those who are in distress. My research shows that one of the reasons people bully is because they're allowed to get away with it. When people speak up and then get together the bully loses his or her power."

He nodded. "That makes a lot of sense. It's important that we let people know it's okay to intervene."

"Exactly." Her eyes sparkled, and she spoke with such conviction he wondered if she was speaking from personal experience.

"I'm blown away by how much you know about this subject. Did you research it, or is this personal?"

In the seconds it had taken him to ask the question, the glint had disappeared from her eyes and her arms were crossed over her chest like body armor.

"It's just..." She shrugged. "It's really just common sense. But, hey, I have another idea. Are you familiar with the quote, 'Be the change you wish to see in the world'?"

"I am," he said.

"I thought it would be appropriate for something like this."

Christopher cocked his head to the side. "Why does that sound like something that would be your life's motto?"

Kinsley blushed a pretty shade of pink. "Oh, no, I can't take credit for that. It's a famous saying...."

As her voice trailed off, she looked down at her hands, which were tightly clasped in her lap now.

"I know you didn't invent it," Christopher said. "I was just saying it sounds like a good theory to subscribe to. I didn't mean to embarrass you."

Her head snapped up, and she looked at him with intense eyes. "I'm not embarrassed."

He was tempted to razz her about blushing, but he held back. "Kinsley, you've got to loosen up."

She stiffened. Her back was ramrod straight. Suddenly he wished he would've taken the teasing route.

"I don't know what you mean," she said.

She was fidgeting with the top button on her blouse. It wasn't the first time that Christopher had thought about reaching out and unbuttoning it. But that was a surefire way to get himself into a heap of trouble. He finally decided it was best just to move on.

"Either of those slogans would be good," he said. "Frankly, I'm partial to the first one. I think the kids might relate to it better."

She nodded, obviously just as relieved as he was to move away from his thoughtless comment about her needing to loosen up.

"I saw some rubber bracelets and pencils that we could have personalized with the slogan and the Foundation's phone number. We could have them sign an anti-bullying pledge card. And each kid who signs gets a bracelet and pencil as a sign of his or her commitment."

Christopher nodded.

"That's a great idea," he said. "I was doing some homework, too. How do you feel about some pricier giveaways?"

"What did you have in mind?"

"I was searching online and found a place that offers T-shirts, water bottles and dog tag necklaces. We could put the slogan on them and offer them to kids who stop by the booth."

Her brow was knitted again.

"What are you thinking?" he asked.

"That's a great idea, but it might get a little expensive if we gave something like that to everyone who stops by."

Christopher laughed. "I hope we get that much traffic at our booth. That would show a lot of community interest. But I do see what you mean. Plus, I don't want to giveaway throw-away swag."

"What is throw-away swag?" she asked.

"If it's free, the kids will grab it, but once they get home it won't have any value to them. We want the freebies we're offering to be worth something. So if we invest in higher-quality giveaways, purchase fewer of them and offer them as prizes, they will have more sticking power. See what I mean?"

"I do," she said. He followed her gaze and saw she was staring at his putting green. "Maybe we can use that as the game. Anyone who gets a hole in one wins one of the big-ticket items. We could offer less expensive prizes to those who take longer to putt the golf balls into the holes."

His putting green? Did she know how much that cost? Obviously not if she was expecting him to take it to the Spring Fling.

She laughed. "Now I have to ask you what you're thinking."

"I was contemplating one hundred teenagers with

muddy sneakers running up and down my putting green."

"And judging from your expression, am I right in guessing you didn't like the idea?"

He shook his head. "No, not really."

"Oh, right. Anything for the kids, huh?"

"Well, within reason. I was thinking we could have a price. You know, one of those things that they spin, like on Wheel of Fortune. Have different sections with prizes written in each. The kids can spin the wheel and wherever it lands, that's what they get."

"Or they could putt for a prize."

He laughed. "I see what you're doing there. What is it that you have against my putting green?"

"Me? I don't have a thing against your putting green. I just think you should share it."

"Do you golf?" he asked.

"No. I work."

His jaw dropped. *Touché*. The woman had a quick wit.

"Hey, my putting green helps me think."

She shrugged, but the mischievous gleam was back in her eyes. "Lounging by the pool helps me think. But you don't see me doing that during work hours."

"Are you suggesting that I'm a slacker?"

"I didn't say anything of the kind."

"No, but you insinuated it. My putting green and I, you see, we're really close. It's not the kind of thing I just indiscriminately lend out. I'm kind of monogamous when it comes to my green."

"Christopher Fortune monogamous? I'm not buying it. I'll bet I could make a hole in one before you could be monogamous."

"Is that a challenge?"

She looked at him, the amusement apparent on her face.

"I'd love to say yes, but I have no idea how to quantify that challenge. Besides, out of all the women you date, who would you choose? On second thought, don't answer that. I'm changing the subject into safer territory. I don't completely understand the fascination with golf. Can you enlighten me?"

"Come on." He stood and grabbed her hand, pulling her to her feet. "I'll show you."

"Christopher, I was just joking."

As he picked up the putter, he gave her his most wicked smile. He took her hand and led her to the putting green.

"Have you ever putted before?"

"When would I have time to do that?"

Their gazes snared, held. "Don't answer my question with a question."

He handed her the putter. "Go on. Let me see what you've got."

She laughed. "I'm afraid I might put someone's eye out."

His mouth twitched a bit, but he took care not to laugh outright. He was trying to be careful, going with the flow of the chemistry, afraid he might scare her off if he moved too fast or made the wrong move.

He positioned the golf ball on the tee. "Come here." He motioned to her, and she stood where he indicated. He stood behind her and hesitated for a moment, wanting to wrap his arms around her but instead he explained how she should position herself and hold the club.

When she was in place, she looked over her shoulder at him. "Like this?"

"Not exactly."

"Will you show me?"

Her gaze held his and he was sure she knew what she was asking. So he moved in closer, put his arms around her and positioned his hands over hers, holding very loosely and hesitating a moment to give her a chance to pull away. They were so close he could smell her shampoo...or maybe it was her perfume. Whatever it was, it smelled clean and fresh and edible...fruity with a hint of floral.

He breathed in as he drew her arms and the club back. His body completely engulfed her slender frame, making him feel big and broad as he leaned into her with his chest pressing into her back. He liked holding her so close, feeling her body next to his. For a moment, he pushed aside work and the Fortunes and proper decorum and allowed himself to imagine what it would be like to be Kinsley's lover.

Only for a moment. Then he had intended to dial it back to a safe emotional distance that added up to the respect and decency that she deserved. But after she let him pull back her arm and push it forward in a quick flick of motion, he felt her relax.

He didn't move. Neither did she. They stood there together, him engulfing her and her allowing herself to be engulfed, and the ball sank into the cup at the end of the green.

"Look at that." His voice was low and raspy in her ear.

She turned her head ever so slightly to the left. Her cheek brushed his. He turned to meet her, his lips brushing hers. It was a whisper of a kiss that made his blood surge and his need for her spike. Her lips tasted like peppermint and something indefinable— sweet and female. He didn't stop, despite good sense warning him that he should even if she wasn't showing any signs of objection.

It was a leisurely, slow kiss that started with lips and hints of tongue. Until he turned her around to face him so that he could deepen the kiss. She slid her arms around his neck and opened her mouth, fisting her hands into his hair.

Christopher responded by pulling her in closer. He couldn't remember the last time he'd felt so alive, felt so much need, so much want.

When they finally pulled away, they stood there blinking, both a little dazed and disoriented. Christopher was searching for his words. But Kinsley found her voice first.

"That was unexpected," she said. "Now that we've gotten it out of our systems, let's pretend like it never happened and get back to work."

Chapter Five

That kiss.

She couldn't forget that kiss. Even if she had insisted that they put it behind them and pretend like it had never happened.

She could still taste him. Still feel his lips on hers.

What was she supposed to do now?

Focus on the bullying prevention project that Mr. Jamison had assigned her to do, that's what.

Christopher had been out of town for the past two days. They had managed to maintain their cool and continue with their last planning meeting as if nothing had happened. It was both weird and a relief. They'd kissed. And then they'd acted as if nothing had happened. But that's how Kinsley had wanted it.

Or at least, she'd thought it was what she wanted.

After the emotional dust had settled, she was no

longer sure. If she didn't know herself better, she might let herself believe that she was hoping this chemistry brewing between them could morph into a good thing.

Right now, it was a dangerous thing.

Dangerous, seductive and reckless.

Growing up, Kinsley had witnessed firsthand the havoc a dangerous, reckless man could wreak on the life of a vulnerable woman.

If she knew what was best for her, she would get her mind off Christopher Fortune and get her head back into work.

Especially because he was back and they were meeting this morning at Red Rock High School to talk to the kids the principal had identified as leaders and potential candidates for an anti-bullying advisory board. Kinsley had thought it would be a good idea to ask some students to join forces with the Foundation's initiative to help kick-start the program.

Focus on the kids.

That's what she needed to do. If she did that, she would be just fine.

All that positive self-help talk went right out the window when Kinsley pulled into the parking lot and saw Christopher's car. Her stomach flip-flopped like crazy.

Glancing around the lot, she realized the only available spot was the one next to his car. She steeled herself and steered her old Toyota Camry into place.

For a split second, she grappled with the idea of parking across the street or driving around back to see if there was anything back there—away from Christopher's pristine new car.

But she let go of that thought as fast as it had floated into her mind.

She was who she was.

She had worked hard for everything she owned, including this seventeen-year-old sedan. It wasn't flashy, but it was clean and it ran well. As she eyed Christopher's shiny red BMW, she reminded herself that she had never been embarrassed of her station in life. No one had ever handed her anything. She'd never competed against anyone other than herself or pretended to be anyone other than who she was.

And she sure as shooting wasn't about to start now.

Killing the car's engine, she sat for a minute, thinking about the situation. She had enough on her plate with work and school. She didn't have time to worry about things that were beyond her control, such as whether she wanted to be Christopher Fortune's conquest du jour. And if the sad reality—that the only reason he was probably interested in her was because he couldn't have her—wasn't enough proof that this game was a very bad idea, then she deserved to crash and burn.

And possibly lose everything.

With that reality check firmly reframing her perspective, she got out of the car and made her way up the path toward the front doors of the old brick building that had housed Red Rock High School for more than fifty years.

A plaque next to the entrance proudly proclaimed that the building was considered a historical landmark and was registered with the Red Rock Historical Preservation Society. Over the course of the years, the building's interior had been renovated to serve modern needs, but the facade still exuded an ageless charm and held true to the history that this town celebrated so steadfastly. Ancient laurel oaks dripping with Spanish moss shaded the rolling front yard, as if they were standing sentry over the school and all the children inside. The sense of history, place and peace was one of the things that made Kinsley feel so at home in this town.

She pulled back the heavy glass-and-brass front doors and stepped into the cool air-conditioned space. Straight ahead, a long hall of polished hardwood lined by lockers on either side stretched before her. The reception desk was to her immediate right.

"Hello," said a smiling middle-aged woman. Kinsley figured she must be the receptionist, Carol. She'd spoken to her when she'd called to set up the meeting with the principal. "Are you by any chance Kinsley Aaron?"

"I am," Kinsley answered. "And you must be Carol."

"That's right." Carol offered a hand. Kinsley accepted it, appreciating the warmth she felt radiating from the woman.

"Come right this way. Principal Cramer and Mr. Fortune are in his office. They asked me to bring you back as soon as you arrived."

As Kinsley followed Carol past the desk and through a set of doors, she fished her cell out of her purse and checked the time, suddenly fearing she was late. But no, she was actually a few minutes early. That meant that Christopher had been even earlier. He might have had a lot of quirks, but habitual lateness wasn't one of them. In fact, punctuality was one of the things they had in common.

Thank goodness Carol stopped in front of a closed door and knocked before Kinsley's mind could continue too far on the journey of the other things she found attractive about Christopher.

Stop that. She silently reprimanded herself as a deep voice issued the message for them to "Come in."

As Carol pushed open the door, Kinsley realized she was frowning and quickly checked herself to make sure that she not only had her most pleasant business face on, but also that all errant, inappropriate and unbusinesslike thoughts were firmly contained.

There would be no more kissing Christopher.

Not even to get what remained out of their systems.

What a ridiculous thought. How had she ever thought something like that would help? Why had she allowed it to happen?

When she stepped into the principal's office, the first person she saw was Christopher. Her tummy flip-flopped again like crazy, throwing off her equilibrium. Each of her unwavering keep-it-businesslike resolutions flew out the window.

After the meeting with Jed Cramer, Christopher admitted to himself that he wasn't making much headway with Kinsley. Not on the romantic front, anyway.

When Kinsley had walked into the meeting at the high school, she might as well have been on another planet she was so distant.

Christopher was finally admitting to himself that what had started out as a game had turned into something more. He was trying to catch something unattainable.

This wasn't just about physical attraction. It was about not being able to get her out of his head.

This woman was special. She was different from anyone else he'd met. It wasn't like him to be so pre-occupied over a woman.

The kiss that they'd shared…and her subsequent parting words about them getting it out of their systems and moving on had plagued him since she'd walked out of his office that day. He'd thought about calling her while he was gone, but he wanted to give her some room. And, truth be told, he needed some space to sort out his own feelings, too.

He kept coming back to the fact that even though he couldn't explain why, he couldn't keep away from Kinsley Aaron the way he had from other women who had gotten too close. Not even after reminding himself of all the problems that could arise if they started something and things ended badly.

He was not ready to settle down. He'd worked too hard to gain his freedom from the ranch in Horseback Hollow to think of tying himself down now that things were just starting to work for him.

But even reminding himself that he and Kinsley would still have to work together if things went south didn't dull this driving need that had him careening toward her.

Since he'd come to Red Rock and started the job at the Fortune Foundation, he'd struggled to keep his professional and personal lives separate. Was he really willing to rethink his personal code for one woman who had somehow managed to get under his skin?

He scrubbed his hands over his eyes as if trying to erase the undeniable answer: yes.

They'd gone their separate ways after the meeting at the high school but had agreed to meet again in his office—the site of that amazing kiss—for their standing meeting.

Christopher glanced at the Waterford crystal clock on his desk. That meeting was set to start in ten minutes.

He had to hand it to her; Kinsley had a way with the kids. The way she'd dealt with the students Jed Cramer had gathered in his office had been amazing. She seemed to have this ability to reach teenagers, especially the girls, on their own level. By the time they left the high school, she had commitments from all seven students to serve on the Fortune Foundation Community Outreach Teen Advisory Board.

During their meeting today, he and Kinsley would work out a game plan for the teen advisory board, outlining exactly what role they wanted the kids to play.

This had come up so fast, and he had a million things to do after being out of town for two days, but he wanted to come into their meeting today with some suggestions. It seemed as if showing her that their project was a priority might be the best way to break through the wall of ice that had formed since the last time they met.... The day of the kiss seemed to have changed the way he looked at everything.

Christopher spent the next five minutes jotting down some ideas that came to mind. The next thing he knew, Kinsley was knocking on his door.

"Come in." He straightened his tie and raked his hand through his hair.

She walked in with her leather folio tucked under

her arm. The knotted tangle of emotions inside him threw him a little off balance.

I'll be damned.

For the first time in his life, Christopher was a little unnerved by the presence of a beautiful woman.

How had this happened to him?

Really, it didn't matter. She was here. He was here. They were going to break through this wall of ice even if he had to turn up the heat again.

"Good afternoon, Christopher," she said.

He rolled his hand in front of his body and made a show of bowing formally. "Good afternoon, Miss Aaron."

It worked.

She knit her brows. "Miss Aaron? My, my, are we a little formal today?"

Christopher smiled at her. "I thought that was the mood that we were going for here. You with your *Good afternoon, Christopher.*"

She hugged her leather folio to her chest and frowned at him. Okay, maybe glib humor wasn't such a good choice.

"Kinsley—"

She held up her hand. "If you're going to tell me to lighten up, just save it. We have a lot of work to do and not much time to do it. We better get busy."

Her voice was neutral. At least she wasn't annoyed or didn't seem to be.

Why was it that none of his usual methods of flirtation seemed to work on her?

Since they didn't, in an effort to keep things light, he decided to quit with the clowning and get down to business.

He gestured toward the coffee table, which was still cluttered from end to end with their previous notes and samples of collateral material. "We've been so prolific, it looks like we are running out of room."

He caught her eyeing the putting green. The thing that had started it all. "Yes, why don't we go into the conference room where we will have more space?" She tore her gaze away from the green and looked him in the eyes. "Plus, maybe we can use the whiteboard in there for outlining our ideas."

Christopher wasn't about to argue with her. He just wanted things to get back on even footing. He couldn't help but wonder if she felt safer with a conference table separating them.

"Sounds good to me," he said. "The whiteboard might come in handy."

With that she seemed to relax a little bit. He had to consciously keep his mouth shut as he forced his mind away from offering her a massage because her shoulders still looked so tense.

Instead, he held his office door for her as they exited and made their way toward the conference room. He was careful to give her enough personal space so that she didn't feel crowded or compromised.

Really, he wanted to make sure he understood the new rules they were playing by.

As he passed Bev's desk in the center of the reception area, she said, "Mr. Fortune, a package just arrived for you. Would you like me to put it on your desk?"

He paused and picked up the homespun-looking package, which was wrapped in plain brown craft paper and tied with twine, glancing first at the return address. Just as he feared, it had a Horseback Hollow postmark. The return address indicated that it was from Jeanne Marie Fortune Jones.

His mother.

A pang of guilt twisted Christopher's heart. He and his father may have had a hard time seeing eye to eye, but his mother was one of the sweetest, kindest women he'd ever known. Christopher new that his move to Red Rock had been hard on her, but he also knew in her heart of hearts she wanted what was best for him.

Unlike his father, who only valued Christopher as another set of hands to help out on the ranch. As he ran his thumb over the paper's rough-hewn surface, he knew that thought wasn't entirely true, even if it did make it easier to justify the way he left.

Christopher felt Kinsley's gaze on him. He looked up to see that she had paused in the hallway that led to the conference room. She was watching him expectantly.

"Thank you, Bev. I'll take this into my office so you don't have to get up. Kinsley, go ahead and start laying things out in the conference room. I'll meet up with you in a second."

Once he was behind closed office doors, he took a pair of scissors from the top drawer of his desk and cut the twine. He used the scissors to loosen the tape and cut away the excess paper, revealing a sturdy cardboard box. He lifted the lid and was a little disappointed when he saw that the package contained what looked like a photo album rather than the cookies he'd been so sure his mother had sent.

He opened the first page and saw a handwritten letter slid into a page protector that his mother had included at the start of the album. The letter said:

My Dear Sweet Chris,
Words can't even begin to express how much I miss you every day. Our family just isn't complete without you here. While I know it's important for you to set out and make your mark in the world, I just want you to know that you will always be welcome to come home when you're ready.
In the meantime, I wanted to send you some pictures to catch you up on everything that has been going on since you moved to Red Rock.
With all the love in my heart,
Mama

Christopher paged through the album and saw photos of various family members—Stacey and her baby girl, Piper; Toby and Angie's wedding portrait. He lingered over that picture, breathing through a stab of regret for not being there to support his brother on his big day.

The next picture he came to was a snapshot of the Hemings kids hugging his father, Deke. The crusty old jackass was dressed up in a plaid shirt with a bolo tie, that damn cowboy hat that he never went anywhere without perched on the crown of his head. He smiled broadly and regarded the kids with such a look of true adoration. Christopher remembered Toby and Angie mentioning that the kids had started calling his parents

Grandma and Grandpa. Sometimes a man didn't know how to be a father but by the mercy of God became an exemplary grandfather. Funny thing was, even though he resented the hell out of Deke for being such a lousy dad to him, he was glad to see the old man showing the kids some benevolence. Lord knew they had been through enough in their short lives; a little compassion would go a long way with them.

An odd feeling squeezed Christopher's chest. He tried to cough, to dislodge the emotion that was blocking his windpipe, but he couldn't manage to make a sound.

He closed the album and set it down on the corner of his desk. Kinsley was waiting for him in the conference room. He'd look at the photos later.

Much later.

Christopher's grumbling stomach was the first clue that it had gotten late. He glanced at his watch and was surprised to see that it was almost nine o'clock. He and Kinsley had been hashing out the copy for the bully prevention brochure since four-thirty that afternoon. He hadn't noticed how much time had passed until his stomach started to complain.

"I don't know about you, but I'm starving," he said. "We've made some good progress here. What do you say we take a break and go get a bite to eat?"

Kinsley swiped the hair out of her eyes and shot him a weary look. "No, thanks. I'm okay, but you go ahead. We're running up against a tight deadline here and I want to make sure this gets done."

Christopher propped his elbows on the table and watched her as she continued to jot down notes.

"Come on," he said. "You have to eat. I don't want you passing out on me."

Actually, the thought of her *on him* was more appetizing than food. But he kept his thoughts to himself. They had been working for nearly five hours and neither had said a word about what had happened between them the last time they were alone.

"I'll eat after this brochure is finished."

"Even if we get this to the printer by the end of the week we'll still be ahead of schedule. Don't you think there comes a point of diminishing returns after you've been at something so long? Especially if you're hungry."

Her lips puckered with annoyance.

"I'm not hungry. I want to finish my work."

He stood.

"Everyone around here knows how hard you work, Kinsley," he said. "You don't have to prove yourself."

She leveled him with a glare. "That's easy for you to say. But other people around here do have to work hard to get noticed. We don't have everything handed to us."

Ouch. Her words cut to the bone.

"Is that what you think?" he asked. "That just because I'm related to the Fortunes I've had everything handed to me, that life's been one big easy ride?"

She gave him a one-shoulder shrug that was more sexy than it was irritating.

"That just shows how much you don't know. You don't know me at all. So I would suggest that you not judge me until you know me better."

"Is that so?"

"Yes."

"So the guy in the expensive suit who drives the

fancy car and has the $3,500 putting green in his office and a different date every night is different from the Christopher Fortune who is standing in front of me now?"

Christopher cleared his throat. "You have no idea who I am on the inside or where I've come from to get where I am now."

"All I know is what I see," she said.

"Well, you've obviously formed your own conclusions," he said. "If you want to go on thinking the way you're thinking, then that's your right to do so. But if you are really as compassionate as you seem to be when you work with those teenagers, then have dinner with me tonight and get to know the real me."

She put her pen down and stared up at him with an unreadable expression.

"So what's it going to be?" he asked. "Are you going to stick to your preconceived notions? Or will you give me a chance to redeem myself?"

Chapter Six

She should be taking her own car, Kinsley thought as Christopher held open the passenger-side door of his pristine status mobile.

Actually, she should've maintained her *no, thank you* to dinner with him and kept working. But here she was, feeling an awful lot like the Country Mouse who had been ensnared in the City Mouse's grand trappings.

Oh, well, it had been her choice to come. It wasn't as if Christopher had kidnapped her.

Before he got in, he opened the back door on the driver's side and tossed what looked like a photo album onto the backseat. After he had settled himself behind the wheel, Kinsley gestured to the album and asked, "What's that?"

He glanced over his shoulder and stiffened as he looked where she pointed. His blue eyes looked pensive.

"It's nothing. Just a photo album."

"I love photos," she said, leaving the door open for him to say *take a look*.

But he didn't answer, just put the key in the ignition, started the car and backed out.

They drove in silence to Red Brick Bistro, but the place was dark and the parking lot was empty.

"What time is it?" Christopher asked. "Are they closed?"

The clock on the dashboard glowed *nine-twenty-five*.

"It looks like it," said Kinsley. "Maybe they're not open today."

Christopher shook his head. "That's one of the things that I just can't get used to. The restaurants close in Red Rock so early on weeknights. I would expect that from Horseback Hollow, but I thought Red Rock was a little more cosmopolitan."

"Why would you expect that in Horseback Hollow?" she asked.

His left wrist was draped casually over the steering wheel and his right elbow was propped on the center console. The stance caused him to pitch toward her ever so slightly. Despite everything, she was tempted to lean in so she could smell his cologne.

A lot of challenges came with working with Christopher Fortune, but his smell was not one of them. It wasn't just the cologne he wore; it was *him*. His own personal scent that had Kinsley breathing a little deeper and leaning in a little closer—even though she desperately wanted her personal space. The dichotomy was hard to reconcile. But he smelled of leather—probably from his car—soap and something else she couldn't define. It all added up to an alluring essence that made it difficult to stop everything female inside of her from roaring to life.

"That's where I'm from," he said. "It's a sleepy little town less than half the size of Red Rock. The sidewalks roll up at sundown and there's absolutely nothing to do. Well, okay, there's The Two Moon Saloon and The Grill, but I wouldn't take you to either of those places."

She blinked. "Why not?"

"Are you kidding? Neither is known for its ambience. They're just not the type of place you take a woman."

It vaguely occurred to her to remind him this was not a date. They were two colleagues who had worked late and were in search of a quick bite. But despite her better judgment, she liked the cozy feel of sitting there with him in the car, with him leaning in slightly, the amber glow of the streetlight casting shadows on his features. Cars passed on the road that ran alongside the parking lot, but in a way it felt as if they were the only two people in the world.

Strange that she would feel so safe and contented sitting in the confines of a car with a man she'd vowed to keep at a distance.

"Where is Horseback Hollow?" she asked, angling her body toward him.

Her peripheral vision caught sight of the photo album in the backseat. It reminded her that Christopher was an anomaly. In so many ways, he was all about flash and being a Fortune, but in other ways he was extremely guarded. That was evident when his brother and sister-in-law had arrived unexpectedly and he'd whisked them out in short order.

It almost seemed as if he had something to hide. Maybe he was embarrassed. Or maybe he was simply trying to keep the Horseback Hollow part of his life private.

"It's outside of Lubbock," he said. "It's about 400 miles from here. Believe me, it's worlds apart from what you're used to."

From what I'm used to?

What did he think her background was? She was born and raised in a small town about fifty miles away from Red Rock. It was a speck on the map. No one had heard of it and she was doing her best to forget it. She'd moved out as soon as she'd graduated high school. Growing up with a verbally abusive father who sometimes physically took his frustrations out on her mother wasn't exactly the life of royalty.

Both of her parents were gone now. A pang of regret swelled inside her that she hadn't done more to help her mother. The worst fights between her parents had always seemed to be centered around her. Sometimes her mother would put herself in between her father and her, and that's when her mother always got the worst of his wrath.

In her naïveté, Kinsley thought she was doing her mother the biggest favor by leaving since she had always seemed to be at the heart of some of her parents' worst fights. But little did she know she was actually leaving her mother even more in harm's way.

Kinsley was a levelheaded woman. She knew darn good and well that all the wishing in the world wouldn't change the past. So she did what she'd always done when the past crept up behind her and threatened to take her down—she pushed it out of her mind and looked forward.

That was her motto: look forward, not back.

But right now she was looking into Christopher's eyes, and she knew that wouldn't lead to anything good.

She shifted her weight so that she was leaning against the passenger door. As if picking up on her nonverbal cue, he shifted away, too.

The pang of regret surprised her.

"I have a feeling everything else around here is probably closed or close to closing," he said. "How about we go to Mendoza's and get a bite there?"

Kinsley didn't get out much. If she wasn't working, she was studying. If she wasn't doing either of those things, she was probably sleeping or attending classes to be a Lamaze coach for a teenage girl who she had met through the Foundation.

Work, school and volunteering didn't give her much time for frequenting places like Mendoza's nightclub. This was only the second time she'd been there. The other occasion was for the grand opening celebration nearly a year ago. Miguel Mendoza, the club's owner, had invited the entire staff of the Fortune Foundation, in addition to what seemed like the entire population of Red Rock, to the club's opening night celebration. Kinsley had considered it more of a work obligation than a night on the town. She had stayed long enough to put in a good showing but had left at the first opportunity.

She looked around, taking in the place, as she and Christopher claimed two places at the long, old-style cowboy bar.

It was hard to believe that just a year and a half ago the place had been an abandoned building. After Miguel, who was a former New York record company executive, had worked his magic, the club was all flash and neon.

A pink neon sign behind the bar that spelled out *Wet Your Whistle* in flowing cursive letters. Neon boot signs illuminated the raised wooden dance floor, where couples danced to music that was accompanied by videos playing on oversize screens located around the room.

At the back a doorway with a neon arrow pointed down over a sign that read *Play Time*. Kinsley wondered if the Play Time room still had the pool tables, dart boards, Skee-Ball and old-model video games that had gotten everyone so excited about the place at the grand opening. If she remembered correctly, there was even an old-fashioned fortune teller machine back there, too. It reminded her of one she had seen once when her grandmother had taken her to an arcade, on one of those nights when her mother had sent her out of the house because her father had been in one of his *bad places*.

That seemed like a lifetime ago. She filed the thought where she kept most of her childhood memories, in a very dark corner in the back of her mind where they wouldn't get in the way. She preferred to live in the here and now rather than dwelling on the past.

And right now, she recognized Miguel Mendoza, who was manning the bar himself tonight.

"Good evening," Miguel said over the music as he placed two cardboard coasters with beer logos in front of them. "What can I get for you?"

After they placed their orders—a glass of white wine for Kinsley and a beer for Christopher—Miguel poured the wine and set it in front of Kinsley, then pulled a frosty mug out of the small freezer and served up Christopher's beer from a tap right in front of them.

"Do I know you?" Miguel asked Christopher. "Maybe I've just seen you here, but I have a feeling we've met before. I'm Miguel Mendoza."

He set the beer in front of Christopher and offered a hand, which Christopher shook.

"Christopher Fortune," he said. "I don't know that we've ever been formally introduced, but I'm in here a lot."

Figures. Kinsley did her best not to roll her eyes, but then made herself step back and reframe her thoughts. He was a young, good-looking, wealthy, single guy. Of course he would want to blow off a little steam after hours at a place like this. That's what people with normal social lives did.

She supposed he could turn the tables on her and wonder why she never made time for fun. Sometimes she wondered that herself. But once she finished her degree and had saved a little money...

Then she would start her life.

However, at the rate she was going, she'd cross that bridge in the very distant future. The truth was she'd never been much of a barfly. That just wasn't her idea of fun. After she graduated she probably wouldn't feel the burning desire to go out and tear up the town any more than she wanted to now.

To each his or her own, she thought as she sipped her white wine. But she suddenly realized that both Christopher and Miguel were looking at her expectantly. She'd obviously missed something.

Christopher leaned in, much too close for her comfort. He placed a hand on her shoulder and whispered in her ear, "I just introduced you to the owner. You might want to say hello or something." He punctuated the suggestion with a quick raise and lower of his brows. It was one of those looks that wasn't cocky enough to be annoying. Cheeky was more apropos. In fact, it was almost endearing. She hated herself for thinking so.

"Hello," she said. "I'm Kinsley Aaron. I work with Christopher at the Fortune Foundation."

Miguel shook her hand and smiled. "That's what he tells me."

"I'm sorry," she said. "The music is a little loud. I didn't hear you the first time."

"I understand," said Miguel. "It's an occupational hazard. So since you both work at the Foundation, would you happen to know Sierra Mendoza Calloway? She's my cousin and she works there."

Kinsley and Christopher answered at the same time. She said yes; Christopher hedged as Kinsley did a double-take, but she did her best to keep her expression neutral. Inside, she was aghast. Sierra had just helped them secure some stock photos for the brochures they were putting together for the Spring Fling. He really didn't remember her? He probably did, he just didn't know her name.

Well, she wasn't about to embarrass him in front of Miguel.

"I adore Sierra," she said. "In fact, just the other day she helped me find a photograph that Christopher and I desperately needed for a brochure we're putting together for a project." She glanced at Christopher and saw a flicker of recognition register on his face.

"I'll be sure and tell her we met you," Kinsley said, turning back to Miguel.

"Please do," Miguel answered. "She's a sweetheart. It's too bad. We have so much family right here in town, yet we don't get to see each other as often as we should."

He looked to Christopher. "As a Fortune, I'll bet you understand how that is."

Christopher gave a quick shrug. "Actually, I've only been in Red Rock a couple of months, and I work with so many of my relatives we get to see each other plenty."

Miguel leaned on the bar. "Oh, yeah, where are you from?"

Kinsley saw the look of hesitation flash across Christopher's face. It was only there for a moment before he stiffened and said, "I'm from a small town outside of Lubbock. I doubt you've heard of it. I moved up here to take the job at the Foundation."

"Lubbock, huh?" said Miguel. "I'm familiar with the area. Try me."

"It's a little dot on the map called Horseback Hollow."

Miguel slapped his hand on the counter. "Get out! Are you serious? I have family there. My brother, Miguel, and his wife are getting ready to open a restaurant there, and my cousin Orlando Mendoza works at the Redmond Flight School."

"I was so sorry to hear about his accident," said Christopher. "It was good of his daughter Gabi to come and care for him."

Miguel looked a little embarrassed. "I haven't seen him since the accident. But I am glad to hear he's doing better."

"You know Gabi is engaged to my brother, Jude, right? She's going to be my sister-in-law. So, doesn't that make us related in some distant way?"

"What a small world. The Fortunes and the Mendozas have always considered each other family. So tonight, your drinks are on me."

"It is a small world," said Christopher. "It's great to meet you. Thank you for the drinks, my friend. But what we really came for was a bite to eat, which, of course, I will pay for. Could we see some menus, please?"

"Of course." Miguel pulled two menus out from behind the bar. "But just so we understand each other, your money is no good here. Money does not change hands among family."

Christopher shook his head and smiled. "I appreciate the generous offer, but really I would be happy to pay. We'll sort it out at the end of the evening."

"Please let me know when you're ready to order," said Miguel. His confident smile seemed to say that he'd already made up his mind. The bill was settled, and nothing Christopher Fortune could say would make a bit of difference.

After they placed their orders for burgers and fries, Miguel set another round of drinks in front of them and went to deliver their dinner request to the kitchen.

Christopher raked his hand through his blond hair. Kinsley was beginning to recognize that habit as a nervous tic.

"What the hell? Is everyone in this town related to someone?"

She couldn't help laughing at him a little. "Pretty much. If they're not a Fortune, they're a Mendoza and a lot of the Fortunes are married to Mendozas.

"May I give you a little bit of unsolicited advice?" Kinsley offered. The beer had loosened him up, and right about now he was longing to hear anything Kinsley had to say. He could be quite content listening to her read a dictionary out loud because it would give him license to drink her in. He could watch her lips move as she formed the words, study the graceful way her delicate jawline curved into her neck and imagine kissing her at that sweet spot where they intersected....

"Sure." Even if he was in for a Kinsley-style reprimand, he didn't mind. She had a firm but gentle way about her. She didn't grate on him the way Deke did when he spouted off with his holier-than-thou statements and rubbed Christopher's nose in I-told-you-sos.

He could tell Kinsley didn't suffer nonsense lightly, but she was also sensitive enough to temper what she said so that it didn't feel like a personal attack.

He appreciated that.

"You would do yourself a world of good to start remembering names. People around here get kind of funny about that. It's off-putting."

She wrinkled her nose and something inside him went soft...and then another part of him, farther south, felt as if it was about to go rock-hard. He held his breath for a moment to get a handle on his libido.

This wasn't college. She deserved his respect, especially after she'd made it perfectly clear where they stood.

He focused on the point she'd made. Remembering names was his weakness, and if he was going to succeed, he needed to fix that.

He still hadn't gotten used to the pop quizzes that jumped out at him just when he thought he had everything under control. All the more reason that he needed to be on the ball.

Sierra Mendoza Calloway was a perfect example. Even if they did call her Sierra Calloway around the office, he should've remembered her. He should've put two and two together. If he really wanted to make his mark in Red Rock, he knew he'd better pay attention and learn the players. He had to know everyone, by sight, right away—especially because so many of them were apparently family, or practically family.

Because wasn't that all anyone wanted—to be valued and respected?

"Thanks for covering for me with Miguel. It would've been embarrassing if he'd known that I spent a good half hour with his cousin and didn't connect the dots."

She nodded. "Well, giving you the benefit of the doubt, I guess there's no way you could've known she's a Mendoza. But don't worry, as long as you pull your weight, I've got your back. And I know that you've got mine, too."

A strangely protective feeling swept through him. "Of course I do. We're a team."

Somehow he didn't think she needed his help as much as he could benefit from hers. Beauty aside—

and she didn't seem to realize how stunning she was—he was in awe of her strength and people skills. She was young to be so self-possessed, so stalwartly sure of herself, yet it was all tempered with a vulnerability that made him want to gather her in his arms and promise her the world.

They sat in amiable silence for a moment, sipping their drinks and watching the people on the dance floor.

"So, Kinsley Aaron, tell me about yourself," he said.

She shook her head. "I seem to recall that we had a deal. You promised if I would have dinner with you tonight, you would tell me *your* story. So don't try to turn the tables, Mr. Fortune."

"There you go with the formalities again." He smiled so that she knew he was kidding.

"What's wrong? Does it make you feel like your father when someone calls you Mr. Fortune?"

He almost laughed. "Absolutely not. As a matter of fact, it has pretty much the opposite effect."

"Really? Do tell."

He took a long swallow of his beer, trying to think about where to begin.

"Obviously, you have a misconception that I'm someone that I'm not."

"Are you not a Fortune, or have you been impersonating one for the past two months?"

If she only knew how close to the truth that really was....

"Not exactly."

Thank goodness Miguel chose that moment to bring

the food. He set the plates and another round of drinks in front of them.

"Can I get you anything else?"

The food smelled delicious and the company was perfect.

Christopher looked at Kinsley. "I think we're all set," she said. "Thanks for everything, Miguel."

Miguel gave them a salute and hurried off to attend to other customers.

For a weeknight, the place was really rocking. It was great to see it doing such a healthy business.

As they ate their burgers, Christopher told Kinsley about growing up in Horseback Hollow with his mom and dad and six siblings. She was surprised to learn that they had little money and none of the advantages of the Fortune family she knew.

"Are you kidding?" Her wide blue eyes reflected sincere surprise.

"No, I'm not kidding. I had a very humble upbringing. When you have that many kids to feed and clothe, a rancher's income doesn't go very far."

She put down her burger and looked at him with true concern.

"Was your childhood difficult?"

"That depends on how you define *difficult,*" Christopher said. "I mean, we never went hungry or wanted for the necessities. But do you know what it's like to be lost in a crowd of strong-willed siblings, always having to fight for attention and approval, even the last piece of fried chicken?"

She shook her head. "I was an only child. So, no, I don't."

"Being an only child sounds like a little piece of

heaven," he said. "But I guess the grass is always greener when you're looking over the picket fence at someone else's life."

He shrugged. "To be fair, I guess I wouldn't trade my siblings. In fact, that was my brother Toby and his new wife, Angie, who stopped by the office the other day. They were on their way back from their honeymoon and stopped in to see me before they headed back to Horseback Hollow."

And he'd screwed that up, too. He and Toby hadn't spoken since that day. His brother had left the ball in Christopher's court, and Chris hadn't moved on it. What was he supposed to do? Toby had clearly come to do Deke's bidding. His sole purpose was to talk him into coming home. It wasn't going to happen. Not anytime soon.

Christopher laughed a humorless laugh. "My siblings are great at making life more challenging."

"How?" Kinsley asked.

"Compared to them, I guess you'd say I'm the black sheep of the family. My little sisters are sweethearts, but my brothers are hard acts to follow. We're just different. I'm the youngest of the boys. They all seem to be cut from the same cloth. They're right at home on the ranch, exactly where Deke wants us all to be."

"Deke is your father?"

Christopher nodded. "Good old Deke just can't understand how I could want more than spending my entire life in Horseback Hollow and working on the ranch. He clings to that broken-down place like it's life support. And he won't take a word of advice from me on how to make it more profitable."

Kinsley sat there with attentive wide eyes, but remained mostly silent. So, Christopher continued.

"Then my mom, who grew up thinking she was an only child—" he gave Kinsley a knowing look "—discovered not only did she have siblings, but she was one of a set of triplets who had been put up for adoption when they were very young. So then my uncle James, who is one of the triplets along with my aunt Josephine, who lives in England, felt bad that he had so much and my mom had grown up with so little, and he gifted her with a bunch of money."

Kinsley's jaw dropped.

Christopher shrugged. "It seemed like our lives would finally get a whole lot easier. But then, as fast as Uncle James had given Mom the money, she decided she couldn't accept it. She gave it back.

"Every stinking penny of it," he said.

Kinsley was leaning in, rapt. "Oh, my god, this sounds like a movie."

"I know, right?"

"Why?" Kinsley asked. "Why did she give it back if he wanted her to have it?"

"She didn't want to be the cause of any tension between Uncle James and his children. She said discovering that she had this huge family she never knew about was a big enough gift."

Christopher forced himself to leave it at that, because suddenly revealing his ill feelings over getting and then losing the money felt…selfish and narcissistic.

"But on the bright side, between my mom and her three siblings there are twenty-four cousins."

"Wait, you were just complaining about being lost

in a family of nine. How could adding eighteen cousins to the mix make it better?"

"My cousins—most of whom are the Fortunes that you know, or at least resemble what you think a Fortune should be, are a bit more... How do I put this tactfully... They're a bit more worldly than my humble family."

Christopher held off telling her about the fight he'd had with Deke the night he left Horseback Hollow for good.

Equal parts shame and regret washed over him as he thought about the harsh words he'd exchanged with his father that night. But what the hell was he supposed to do? If he'd listened to Deke, he wouldn't be sitting here with this incredible woman right now. If that in itself wasn't proof that he'd made the right decision to come to Red Rock, then he didn't know what was.

Kinsley shook her head. "I can't imagine having that many relatives. That would just be... I mean it would be cool, but no wonder you have a hard time remembering names. What's your mom like?"

"She is the sweetest person you could ever imagine meeting," he said. "She's all about her family and kids. But I wish she would be stronger when it comes to standing up to Deke. He can be the worst kind of bully," Christopher snorted. "Talk about someone who could benefit from a bully prevention program."

Empathy colored Kinsley's beautiful blue eyes.

"I understand what it's like to have father conflict," Kinsley said. "I was close to my mom, too. Your mom must be a good soul if she is content to build Fortune family relations with none of its monetary perks."

Christopher shrugged. "Are you saying I'm wrong

for wanting a different life than the ranch has to offer?
As far as Deke is concerned, my birthright is in Horseback Hollow."

"Why don't you go visit your dad and talk things
out?"

Chapter Seven

Why was she trying to give Christopher advice on family relations? Kinsley knew she was certainly in no position to do that. She'd run away from problems with her own father, and in the process had left her mother high and dry. Obviously, she was no expert on making things right.

"I'm not ready to go home yet," Christopher said, answering her question after a long pause.

"Why not?" Kinsley asked.

"It's complicated."

Kinsley shrugged. "Yeah, life gets that way sometimes."

She was speechless, listening to this man who was turning out to be nothing like the shallow, glad-handing guy who on his best days had irritated her... and on her worst days had tempted her.

She didn't want to think about that right now. In fact, she felt a little guilty about the preconceived notions she'd formed.

She wanted to know more about his life at the Horseback Hollow ranch, more about what he'd been like before he'd discovered his Fortune relatives. Even though she only knew a few things about his life before he'd moved to Red Rock, she sensed she knew his heart better now.

Everyone struggles with something, even if they hide behind a smile. Or in Christopher's case, expensive clothes and a fancy car.

Her mask was work and school.

She knew that, but she wasn't ready to do anything to change. If she wasn't willing to amend herself, why should she expect Christopher to present a different face than the one he showed?

She had to give the guy credit. At least he seemed to understand how fortunate he was to have been, given a leg up to starting his new life.

His upbringing explained a lot: his need for attention, his tendency to show off and his penchant for the ladies.

Yes, there was that, she reminded herself. If she knew what was good for her, she would keep that firmly in mind.

Christopher was charming and charismatic. Kinsley was willing to bet that this revolving door of women was as new to him as his red BMW.

Even if he'd always been popular with the ladies, if Horseback Hollow was as small as he'd made it sound, he'd probably never had the smorgasbord available to him now.

Despite that, her esteem for Christopher had risen. She could tell that he had genuine affection for his mother, brothers and sisters. She had to admit that she was just a little bit envious of his big, boisterous family. When she was little, she used to long for a big brother to watch out for her. Maybe if she'd had one, things would've been different. Maybe her mother would still be alive today.

"It sounds like Toby was trying to entice you to come home when he dropped by the other day."

He shifted in his seat and his face closed. "I wish it were that easy."

"I know it's a big trip," she said. "But maybe you could take a long weekend. I'm sure Mr. Jamison would understand."

As Christopher looked at her, she could see him choosing his words. "It's not the distance. I could fly there and back in less time than it would take to get to the airport. I'm just not in a very good place with my father right now."

"I know there's more going on between you and your father than what you've told me, and I understand if it's a private thing. You don't have to tell me. But logic does dictate that he must be a pretty good man to have raised such great kids."

Again Christopher shifted in his seat. This time he moved away from her and turned his attention to his beer.

"Christopher, nobody's perfect. But please take my advice. Sometimes it seems like the people who have taken care of us will be around forever, but the truth is life is short."

Her mother had been just forty-six years old when

she'd died. Way too young. It sounded ridiculous to say—she couldn't even say the words out loud, and she could barely admit them to herself—but it never occurred to her that her mother could die. Her mother, the one who had always looked out for her, the one who had thrown herself between Kinsley and that horrible man who just happened to be related to her by genetics.

Kinsley had been far too wrapped up in her own life, in getting out of the abysmal, abusive situation she was born into and starting the life she knew she was meant to have.

What she wouldn't give to go back and do everything differently. She would've insisted that her mom come with her. The man who had abused them both and cheated on her mother could've rotted in hell for all she cared.

Surely he was burning there now.

But there were no do-overs. She could only look forward and hope that she might be able to honor her mother's memory by helping some other unlucky woman who was caught in an unfortunate situation. More immediately, maybe she could help teenage girls realize that they didn't have to settle for someone who treated them poorly. That by the virtue of being born they were princesses—even if they never had a father to tell them so.

"Hey," said Christopher. "Where'd you go?"

She blinked at him, unsure what she had missed.

"You were somewhere far, far away," he said. "Would you care to share?"

This was one instance when she was glad she had never been able to cry about her mother and the whole sorry situation. She had always worried that if she let down the floodgates she might never stop crying. At that very moment, she vowed that she would never put her theory to the test.

The way Christopher was watching her she had a feeling that because he had shared his story, he was going to expect reciprocation from her. That was something else that wasn't going to happen.

The music changed to a medium-tempo Blake Shelton tune.

"I love this song," she said. "Dance with me."

She was on her feet and headed toward the dance floor before Christopher could refuse and before she could change her own mind.

By the time she'd wedged her way into a spot on the dance floor, Christopher was right there next to her. Only then did it dawn on her that he would probably hate this song that talked about red dirt roads and doing manual labor.

Oh, well.

The dance floor was small, hot and crowded, forcing them into close proximity even though it wasn't a slow dance. But that was okay because the music was even louder over here, and it seemed to keep Christopher from asking questions. Some couples tried to do a slow two-step around the perimeter of the close confines, but Christopher kept his hands to himself and didn't try to pull her into that kind of dance.

Given the kiss they'd shared, he'd proved himself unpredictable enough that she wouldn't have been shocked if he had pulled her close, but this was fine.

Really, it was.

After three glasses of wine, she would probably melt in his arms. She wasn't drunk, just nicely loos-

ened up. Once they had established their dance M.O.,
she let herself be swept away by the pounding rhythm
of the music. It felt good to let her hair down and lose
herself.

Christopher looked as if he was enjoying himself,
too, moving unselfconsciously to the beat. Maybe it
was the wine talking, but suddenly she wondered why
she didn't go out more often. Christopher smiled that
endearingly cheeky smile as he moved next to her. It
struck her that it was a pretty darn attractive quality
for a guy to be willing to dance. So many of the guys
she'd known had refused to let go like this.

As she took in Christopher's subtle moves, she
couldn't help but wonder what he would be like in
bed. She hadn't had that much experience, and really
none of it was notable, but she'd always heard that the
way the guy danced gave a lot of clues as to how he
would make love.

If that was the case, Christopher seemed to be proving himself *quite* capable.

Lord have mercy.

She was glad the music was so loud because she
felt a giggle bubble up and escape. It must have come
across as a smile because Christopher beamed at her.

The two of them got into the spirit, communicating
with only their eyes and expressions.

Again, this guy, who she'd been so quick to dis-
miss, was showing her another side. Here he was in
his white dress shirt with the sleeves pushed up past
the elbows getting down as well as any of the cowboys
in the place. She was tempted to tease him about his
ranch upbringing coming out on the dance floor, but
that was for later.

This was now.

This was fun.

This was a high she wished would last…and last… and—

An overzealous couple two-stepped right into Kinsley, knocking her into Christopher. He caught her, holding her close in his strong arms. The two of them stood breast to chest, staring into each other's eyes, vaguely swaying to the song's refrain.

Then, right there in the middle of the dance floor, he didn't ask permission; he simply lowered his head and kissed her unapologetically, ravenously. And she kissed him back shamelessly, completely taken by their mutual hunger.

The kiss bypassed slow and soft, immediately igniting into a voracious fire that had her parting her lips and deepening the kiss. Her arms found their way around his neck and her hands fisted into the cotton of his shirt. They leaned into each other as if they depended on this intimate contact for their life's breath.

The whole world disappeared—Mendoza's, the dance floor, the music. She didn't care who was there or who might be watching them. The only thing that mattered was the way he was holding her so tightly against him, staking his claim, in this wordless confession of desire.

The taste of his beer mingled with her wine and merged with hints of the truffle salt from the fries. And then there was that familiar hint of *him* that she had tasted when they'd kissed in his office. But that was then. Now, she tasted a hint of the forbidden mixed with the temptation of right now.

A moment ago she had convinced herself that this

was taboo, and now he was kissing her so thoroughly that she didn't want to stop. Feelings inside her that had awakened when he'd kissed her the first time were now laced with a passion that threatened to consume her.

She'd forgotten the once logical rationale for protecting her heart. Or maybe she no longer cared. The reasons had shifted and transformed *why not* into *oh, yes* were promising to be so worth the risk.

Kinsley had no idea how much time had passed as they held each other and kissed as people whirled around them on the dance floor.

As they slowly came up for air, Christopher held her face in his palms, his forehead resting on hers. Maybe it was the liquid courage talking, but this kiss felt right, and the way he was holding her seemed to say he felt it, too.

"Oh, my God, Christopher, what are we going to do now?"

No matter what Kinsley said today, he wasn't going to let this go. They couldn't go back to being purely platonic, not after last night's kiss. They were definitely in a different place now. And he liked it.

Christopher smiled to himself as he picked up the phone.

His gut told him that after he'd dropped her off at her apartment last night she'd probably overthought everything.

He dialed Red and made a lunch reservation for two at his favorite table, then sat back in his leather chair, glancing at the putting green. One kiss might have been a mistake. But two? There was no denying the fire that blazed between them last night.

Even if she resisted, he was going to prove to her that there was something special between them. Something worth fighting for.

He hadn't seen Kinsley yet today, but when he did, he wanted her to know beyond a doubt that last night meant something to him. What better way than to go back to when everything seemed to start—that day that Toby and Angie had arrived and he'd asked Kinsley to make a lunch reservation at Red. He hoped she'd see the meaning behind this lunch date.

He started to pick up the phone again to call her and ask her to lunch, but then he thought better of it. He got up and walked to her office.

The door was open, so he rapped lightly on the door frame.

"Good morning," he said when she looked up from her computer.

"Good morning." Her tone was neutral. She finished typing whatever it was he had interrupted before she said, "Come in."

He walked in and sat down in the chair across from her desk.

"I'm glad you're here," she said.

He smiled and quirked a brow, but she carried on business as usual.

"I realized this morning that we need to come up with a calendar of deadlines so that we make sure we get everything done in time for the Spring Fling. Do you realize it's less than two weeks away?"

What?

"That's not what I came in here to talk to you about, but sure. We can do that."

Her expression remained neutral, but her voice held

the faintest notes of exasperation. "Would you please close the door?"

Christopher complied. When they were safe behind closed doors, he said, "I enjoyed last night."

She tensed and closed her eyes a blink that was a few beats too long before she opened them again. "About that.... Listen, I appreciate you being so nice about it, but I think we both had a little bit to drink last night."

"We did and it was a great time. I hope we can do it again. In fact, I made reservations for us to have lunch at Red today at twelve-thirty. Of course, it might not be a good idea for us to drink as much as we did last night, since we have to come back and work on these things that you're putting on the calendar." She was sitting there staring at him blankly. "And I had hoped you might catch the meaning in me making the lunch reservation instead of asking you, but..."

He thought he saw her wince ever so slightly as she continued to regard him with that neutral expression. He reminded himself that he had expected her to react this way. *See, he knew her.* And he had also been prepared for the possibility of having to take things slowly as she came to terms with the fact that this was right—and good.

And very real.

"Okay, so why don't we discuss this calendar and everything we need to put on it at lunch today? At Red."

He winked at her. Then promptly realized that was probably not a good move.

"Or if you have a few minutes now," she said, "we can talk about it and get everything all squared away."

He saw what she was doing.

He stood. "Sorry, I don't have time right now. I'll pick you up at 12:15 and we can discuss everything over lunch."

He flashed his most charismatic smile and was pleased to note that some of her bravado seemed to wither away in front of him.

"Okay. Fine. We can have a working lunch."

He opened the door. "See you soon." He left it open, exactly the way he had found it.

As he walked back to his office, he was more determined than ever to make Kinsley see just how good they could be together.

"Hello, Mr. Fortune. It's nice to see you," said the tall, thin, pretty hostess at Red. "A table for two for you and...your girlfriend?"

"Oh, no. I'm not his girlfriend. We're not... We just work together."

The hostess regarded Kinsley with a subtle air that suggested she was just being polite and hadn't been convinced they were even a couple to begin with.

"Well, that's very good to know." The hostess smiled and boldly looked Christopher up and down.

Kinsley's cheeks burned.

How rude and unprofessional.

A little voice in the back of Kinsley's mind reminded her that it was a lot more professional than she had been when she'd made out with Christopher on the dance floor at Mendoza's. Anybody in town could have seen them acting like a couple of hormone-driven teenagers who couldn't keep their hands off each other.

Even though common sense told her that nobody

was looking at them as she and Christopher followed the hostess to their table, it felt as if every eye in the place was on watching them.

Once they were settled and the hostess had managed to tear herself away, Christopher looked her squarely in the eyes and said, "Kinsley, we make such a good team, in and out of the office—"

"That's why we need to pretend like nothing happened last night," she said.

"That's what we said after our first kiss," he countered. "And we see where that got us. Why are we fighting this? I think we could be very good together if you would just give us a chance."

Kinsley's heart pounded an insistent staccato in her chest. It was almost like a finger tapping her chest urging her to do the right thing—to set the record straight with Christopher, to make sure he understood exactly where they stood.

As long as they both worked at the Foundation, all they would be were platonic coworkers. Since she didn't plan on leaving her job anytime soon, apparently that was all that fate had in store for them.

Christopher would be free to fully enjoy all the perks of being a young, good-looking guy with too much money and a tendency to flash it to get whatever and whomever he wanted—like the hostess who had given Kinsley the stink eye when they'd arrived.

Women like that might throw themselves at him, but Kinsley would not be his conquest, and that was at the heart of why they would never work. The two of them came from different worlds. He might think he'd had it bad off being lost in the chaos of a large family where money had once been tight, but he had no idea what it was like to have lost the only person in the world who had ever shown unconditional love.

Kinsley had witnessed firsthand the pain her mother had suffered at the hands of her womanizing father, who couldn't or wouldn't stop himself when it came to the ladies. No matter how her mother had cried and threatened to leave him, he would simply turn the tables on her and somehow manage to blame her mother for his own philandering. Even after her front-row seat for this cautionary tale, in college Kinsley had still been stupid enough to put her faith in a man who ended up proving himself as verbally abusive and faithless as her own father. In her studies she had learned that victims of abuse often unwittingly fell into the trap of falling for abusive partners.

She wasn't convinced that Christopher had abusive tendencies, but he sure did have an eye for ladies. That was enough to make Kinsley put on the breaks. It was clear that Christopher still had oats to sow. She wasn't going to fall into the same trap that her mother had suffered or repeat the same mistake she'd already made....

Last night was her last dance with Christopher Fortune.

Chapter Eight

Thursday night was ladies' night at Mendoza's. That's why Christopher was surprised his cousin Sawyer Fortune who was in town for the day, suggested that they meet there to discuss a fund-raising opportunity for the Foundation over a beer and a quick bite to eat.

Ladies' night didn't officially start until nine o'clock, so even though it was nearly eight o'clock, Mendoza's still had the air of a restaurant. The lights were a little brighter than they would be later on, and the music was much softer and less honky-tonk than it would be when the clock struck nine. So they had time to wrap up their business before the party overtook the place. Sawyer would be long gone before then, anyway, because he had to fly to Horseback Hollow before it got too late.

Sawyer was happily married to Laurel Redmond, had been since New Year's Eve. After the wedding, they had moved to Horseback Hollow to open a branch of Redmond Flight School and Charter Service. The operation was headquartered out of Red Rock, so Sawyer still came to town occasionally. Today, Sawyer had been involved in nonstop meetings all day and had suggested that the two of them grab a couple of Mendoza's famous tacos before he flew home that evening.

Whether they were talking business or not, Christopher was always glad for a chance to visit with his cousin because he hadn't really had the opportunity to get to know him very well before his own move to Red Rock. This was not only a good chance to spend time with him, but also a chance to discuss a way for the flight school to make a charitable contribution to the Foundation.

Christopher had asked Kinsley to join them, but she had her statistics class tonight and after that, she was attending a Lamaze class with a teenage girl she had agreed to help.

Kinsley had so much on her plate that Christopher didn't know how she handled it all. But working all day, going to class and then finding the energy to help this girl were just a few of the many reasons Christopher found her so amazing.

She had said she would text him when she was free so that he could fill her in on the details of what he and Sawyer had come up with. She had mentioned that she should be finished shortly after eight o'clock. Christopher found himself glancing at his phone, alternately checking the time and making sure he hadn't missed a text from her.

Nothing yet.

"Are you expecting a hot date?" Sawyer kidded.

"Nope. Not tonight," Christopher said as he clicked off his phone yet again.

Sawyer gestured to the phone. "You keep checking that thing. I thought maybe you were waiting for someone to call you."

"Actually, I'm waiting for Kinsley Aaron, my colleague, to text me so I can fill her in on how you're going to help us raise all kinds of money."

Christopher and Sawyer had discussed the possibility of having an air-show fund-raiser to benefit the Foundation's bully prevention program. Unfortunately, the date of the Spring Fling was too close for them to get something together, but the event was definitely a possibility for the future. In fact, it was probably best to do it as a separate experience, anyway, because it would be another opportunity to raise awareness for the cause.

"Just tell Kinsley not to get too excited yet," said Sawyer. "I need to run all this by Tanner and Jordana before we can give it the official green light. But I have a feeling they will be just as thrilled as I am about having the chance to help with this worthy cause."

Tanner Redmond and his wife, Jordana Fortune Redmond, owned and operated the Red Rock branch of Redmond Flight School and Charter Service.

"I'm sorry Tanner and Jordana couldn't be here tonight to discuss this," Christopher said.

The Redmonds were out of town. That was one of the reasons Sawyer had flown up for the day, to cover some meetings, check on the Red Rock office and make sure everything was running smoothly.

"I am, too," said Sawyer. "Later on, after they give me the thumbs up, we'll all get together and discuss everything. Maybe your Kinsley will be able to join us then, too."

Your Kinsley. If Christopher had anything to say about it, next time Sawyer was in town, she *would* be his. Something intense flared inside him at the thought, and the sensation made him double his determination to make that so.

But the feeling was interrupted by a shapely brunette who slid into the seat next to Christopher.

"Hello?" Christopher said. "May I help you?"

The young woman looked familiar, but he couldn't place her.

"You don't remember me, do you?" she said, smiling as she twisted a strand of long dark hair around her finger.

Christopher darted a glance at Sawyer, who was watching them, in the off chance that the woman might be a friend of his. Christopher knew it was highly unlikely, though.

"I'm Crystal?" she said. "I seated you at Red for lunch the other day? And the time before that when you were in with the newlyweds?"

Crystal was pretty enough, but she seemed to have an annoying habit of turning every sentence into a question. Still, he didn't want to be rude.

"Right, I remember. Hello, Crystal. I'm Christopher Fortune. This is Sawyer Fortune, my cousin."

"Ooh," she said. This time it wasn't a question as much as an exclamation. She looked Sawyer up and down, her gaze lighting on his wedding ring. She turned back to Christopher.

"It's your lucky night. I'm going to let you buy me a drink."

Her question-phrasing was strike one. Strike two was calling him Chris. No one in Red Rock called him Chris.

Still, he played along. "Oh, you are, are you?"

Crystal nodded. "Yeah. And if you play your cards right tonight? I will make it very worth your while."

Christopher had gotten used to bold women, but this was the first time he had encountered someone who was downright carnivorous. He glanced at Sawyer, who looked as befuddled as Christopher felt, then he turned back to Crystal.

"Well, you're a very beautiful woman…and that sounds like an offer that would be hard for most men to refuse. But I'm right in the middle of a business meeting here."

At least he didn't have to ask her to leave. She scooted out of the booth. "Well, you come find me after you're done here, okay?" She blew him a kiss and tottered away in high heels and a short miniskirt that didn't look as alluring tonight as they had that first time he'd seen her.

Sawyer whistled under his breath. But it wasn't an appreciative sound; it was more the sound somebody made when they had witnessed a train wreck.

"Looks like someone's celebrating ladies' night a little early," said Christopher.

As he watched the woman walk away, he realized he wasn't interested. Not the least bit. Maybe he had finally had his fill of the pretty-girl smorgasbord. Or maybe he really did have standards when it came to women. How many other men had found it *worth their while* to buy her drinks? He really didn't want to know.

What he did know is that he wanted a woman with more substance.

As if right on cue a message from Kinsley flashed on his phone.

Just got home. How was the meeting?

Christopher picked up his phone and typed, Still with Sawyer. It's going well. A lot to tell you.

She returned, Good to hear. Fill me in when you're done?

He typed back, You bet!

"So, is your *colleague* back?" Sawyer asked.

"She is."

Sawyer took a long sip of his iced tea, then set the glass down on the table. "You seem pretty happy to hear from her."

Sawyer laced the words with insinuation. Christopher shrugged but couldn't hide his smile.

"Yeah, well..." He shrugged again.

Sawyer nodded. "Are you two dating?"

Christopher glanced at his phone again to see if Kinsley had responded. She hadn't.

"Why do you ask?"

"Well, I was just about ready to get on my way to Horseback Hollow so you could *make the night worth your while*. But I'm sensing you're not into that." Sawyer nodded toward the general area where Crystal waited.

Christopher didn't dare look over there for fear of sending her the wrong message. He really wasn't interested.

"It's complicated," he answered.

"It doesn't have to be," Sawyer said. "When it's right, it's the most uncomplicated feeling in the world. That doesn't mean things are always easy, or that in the beginning you don't have to fight the good fight. But when it's right you'll know."

Christopher weighed his words. He really didn't need to explain. In fact, there really wasn't anything to explain. He and Kinsley were in limbo right now, but something told him to stay quiet.

"Okay, then, let's just say, I'm fighting the good fight right now."

Sawyer nodded, a knowing look in his eyes. "Good luck, man. I hope she's worth it. Not to say she's not."

Another text flashed on Christopher's phone. His gut contracted but then released when he saw it was from his buddy Joe.

Art and I are headed over to Mendoza's for ladies' night. See you there.

Christopher considered typing, *Already here,* but Sawyer said, "Are you concerned at all about dating someone you work with? I know a lot of people caution against it, but Laurel and I work together and Tanner and Jordana do, too. We might be the exception to the rule, but at least we're proof that it can work. If you have feelings for this woman, don't let being colleagues scare you off."

Christopher pushed his phone away. "I have to admit I've wondered how Uncle James would feel about workplace dating. She's important to me, but I don't want to rock any boats at work."

Sawyer made a *pffff* sound. "If you only knew

how many Fortunes met their spouses on the job, you wouldn't be worried. The only thing you might need to keep in mind is if things don't work out, you can't let it get in the way of anything."

Christopher crossed his arms in front of him. "Of course not."

"Well, since you said Kinsley is important to you, I say go for it. You seem to have your priorities straight and a level head on your shoulders. Just use good common sense."

Sawyer looked at his watch. "It's getting late. I'd better get out of here so I can get home at a decent hour. I'm not going to lie. It's pretty nice to have someone to come home to."

Sawyer reached for his wallet, but Christopher held out a hand. "You came all this way. I've got the tab."

He was relieved that he hadn't seen Miguel tonight. Although it was generous of the guy to cover the bill the night he was there with Kinsley, Miguel's comment about Christopher's money not being any good there made him uncomfortable. He was perfectly prepared to pay his own way. He didn't want to seem like a moocher. In fact, even though he greatly appreciated Miguel's hospitality, he had to admit the thought of Miguel doing so in the future made him uneasy about hanging out at Mendoza's. Christopher's eyes darted back to the phone. Still no response from Kinsley. Then again, his response had been sort of closed-ended. He'd told her he would text her after Sawyer left, which was happening now.

Sawyer stood and so did Christopher. The two shook hands.

"It was great seeing you," said Sawyer. "And thanks for dinner. Next time it's on me."

Christopher clapped him on the back as he walked with him toward the entrance. "Next time, you bring me good news about the air-show fund-raiser and I'll not only buy you dinner, but I'll also throw in a bottle of champagne."

Sawyer laughed. "You better start chilling that bubbly because I'm pretty confident I'll have good news for you soon. Good luck with the girl."

As they were walking out to the parking lot, Christopher ran into Art and Joe, who were on their way inside.

Christopher introduced his cousin to his buddies and after quick small talk Sawyer said good night and excused himself.

"Should've known you'd already be here," said Joe. "You get an early start on the night? So what are we waiting for? Bring on the ladies."

Funny thing, for the first time ever, Christopher wasn't in the mood to party. He was more eager to get to a quiet spot where he could write down all of the ideas that he and Sawyer had come up with and text Kinsley.

"Actually, I was here for a business meeting," he said. "It's been a long day. I'm beat so I think I'm just going to hit it." He gestured toward the exit.

"Oh, come on, man," said Art. "Just one drink."

Joe elbowed Art. "If we can get a drink down him, he'll start talking to the ladies and end up closing down the place. What do you bet?"

Christopher usually had a good time with these guys he'd met them through a local men's pick-up basketball league and they'd hit it off straightaway. Maybe it was just his mood, but he really wasn't feeling it tonight. And he didn't like being pressured into staying.

Across the room, he saw Crystal. She looked up, saw him and waved. Then she got up and started walking toward him. Even stranger than not being in the mood to stay, he wasn't in the mood to deal with her tonight, either.

The thought actually made him do a mental doubletake. What the hell was wrong with him? His buddies were ready to have a good time. And here was a woman who, for all intents and purposes, was a sure thing.

And he wasn't in the mood for any of it.

"Hey," said Crystal. "I see you finished with your business meeting. Come dance with me."

Joe and Art were standing there pretending to be cool, like they weren't watching him interact with Crystal. And Christopher was willing to wager that if he didn't go home with Crystal tonight, one of them would.

"Normally, I'd love to dance with you," he said to Crystal. "But I have more business I need to take care of. These are my friends Art and Joe. Joe, Art, this is Crystal. I'm sure one of these guys would love to buy you a drink." He dug his car keys out of his pocket and handed his friends a fifty-dollar bill. "Enjoy yourselves, everyone. First round is on me."

Kinsley had just finished washing up her dinner dishes when her cell phone rang at about 8:45 p.m. She knew it would be Christopher before she even looked.

Still, her heart leaped a little bit when she saw his

name on her phone's display screen. She didn't even bother to dry her hands before she picked up the phone and accepted the call.

"Hello?" she said, taking care to keep her voice as level as possible.

"I hope I'm not calling too late." His deep voice was like sex. The thought made her blush. Where the heck had *that* come from?

Well, she knew where it came from; she just wished she could put it back in its box so that she could put the lid on tighter and ensure that thoughts like that never got out again.

Remember, last dance. Over. Done. Finito.

Good luck, said an impudent little voice that was probably responsible for unleashing the thought in the first place. *You know you want him.*

"Of course not," she said. "How did the meeting with Sawyer go?"

"The only way it could've gone better is if you would have been there."

"What? And miss all the fun of my statistics class and being a Lamaze coach? Actually, the Lamaze coaching is pretty cool. I'm glad I can be there for Tonya. She doesn't have anybody."

"You've got a really great way with kids, you know?"

She found herself smiling in spite of herself. "Thanks." She didn't quite know what else to say to that. She heard what sounded like a car horn in the distance.

"Are you in your car?" she asked.

"I'm sitting in Mendoza's parking lot."

She hated herself for it, but her heart sank. "Oh, that's right. It's Thursday—ladies' night at Mendoza's."

She did her best to put a smile in her voice. "Listen, I won't keep you. Why don't we talk about this tomorrow at the office? Oh, wait, I'm going to be out most of the day. I'm going over to the high school to work with the advisory board and the kids in the Cornerstone Club to finalize the plan for their part at the Spring Fling. I really want them to take ownership of this program. If they do, it will stand a much better chance of taking hold. But listen to me blabbing on. I'm sure you want to get inside. I'll talk to you tomorrow."

"Kinsley, wait. I'm actually leaving Mendoza's. I'm not staying for ladies' night. Sawyer wanted to go there for the tacos. I figured I'd let him choose where we ate since he doesn't get to town very often."

Why was she so relieved to hear this? "Is ladies' night canceled?"

"Canceled? No, why?"

"Well, I can't imagine it going on without you there. I thought you always closed the place down."

He laughed. "No reason to since you're not there."

Against everything she knew was prudent and good for her, she melted a little bit inside.

"Contrary to your etched-in-stone thoughts of me, I'm really not a player," he said. "I don't know what I have to do to make you believe that."

She walked over to the couch and sat down, curling her bare feet beneath her. She was still in the gray skirt and white blouse she'd worn to work. Her apartment suddenly felt stuffy. She reached up and unbuttoned the top two buttons on her blouse.

"I'm not quite sure what I'm supposed to say to that," she said.

"What you can say is that you had as good a time

dancing with me at Mendoza's as I had dancing with you."

Her hand fluttered to her throat, lingered there.

"You could say that maybe we could try it again. Say, maybe Saturday night?"

Her fingers pushed aside her blouse's cotton fabric and traced the line of her collarbone. She wasn't sure if it was his voice or his words that made her shiver a little…in a good way…with an anticipation that made her feel naked and vulnerable, that had her rethinking every reason why it was a bad idea to get involved with him.

"Christopher…"

"Yes, I'm here. And since you didn't say no, I'll consider it a yes."

Even though it was after four o'clock, Kinsley headed back to the office after finishing up with the kids at the high school. She could've gone home. She'd already put in an eight-hour day, but… Okay, if she was going to do this, she at least had to be truthful with herself.

She was going back with the hopes of running into Christopher. After all, if he had been serious about taking her out on Saturday night—tomorrow night— she needed to know where they were going and what they were doing, what time he would pick her up, all the details so that she could get ready. She played a crazy little game with herself when she found herself in a situation and was unsure of what she should do— and she still wasn't quite sure going out with him was such a good idea. After all, what happened at Mendoza's had happened by chance. If he picked her up on

Saturday night and took her someplace purely social, it would be a date. Even though their date wasn't until tomorrow, she decided to toss everything up to fate: if it was a good idea to see Christopher socially—to go out with him tomorrow—he would still be at the office. If he wasn't there, well that meant it was not a good idea. If he wasn't there she would cancel the date and explain to him that they needed to keep things platonic. She was usually such a practical person that she only used the toss-it-up-to-fate method of decision-making on the rarest occasions. It was like flipping a coin to help her decide what to do on occasions like this, when her head was telling her one thing and her heart was insisting on another. On one hand, if she got involved with him, it could end in disaster. On the other hand, what if this could be the start of something good. He sure had been trying hard, and she needed to give credit where credit was due.

And there was the fact that she just couldn't stop thinking about him.

When she turned into the Foundation parking lot and saw his car in his reserved parking space, she couldn't breathe for a moment.

There was her answer. She should keep the date. And she was so relieved that she almost shook with joy. Before she got out of the car, she took her compact and lipstick out of her purse and touched up her makeup, then ran her fingers through her hair, gave herself a once-over in the rearview mirror and decided that was as good as it was going to get.

She let herself out of the car, feeling as giddy as a girl who had just been asked to the prom by the captain of the football team. As she walked toward the entrance, she contemplated her strategy—she would go to his office under the guise of discussing what she had accomplished at the high school today and ask him about the fund-raising idea that he and Sawyer had come up with last night.

She actually had a spring in her step as she emerged from the elevator into the third-floor reception area.

"Hi, Bev," she said to the young woman who looked as if she was already starting to pack up and head home for the weekend. But Bev was young and she would learn that when you got a job you really cared about sometimes you had to put in longer hours to get where you wanted to go.

Or you had to come back to the office to find out whether or not you were going to go anywhere that weekend, said the snarky voice in her head.

In the movie in her mind, she reached up and stuffed a sock in her doubting mouth.

"Oh, hey," Bev said. "What are you doing back here? It's nearly five o'clock."

"I know. I need to talk to Christopher. Is he available?"

Kinsley started walking toward his office before Bev had the chance to answer.

"I don't think you should go in there," she said. She looked around the office as if confirming nobody else was within earshot. Still, she lowered her voice to a stage whisper. "He has a woman in there. And she's really, really pretty. She just got here about fifteen minutes ago. I don't know that it's a business thing. But don't you dare say that I said that."

Kinsley's whole body tingled. And not in a good way. It was more like a pang of regret that was trying to undermine her confidence. She took a moment to put things in perspective. Sure it was Friday evening, but why would Christopher have a date meet him at the office? The woman could be a donor. She could be his sister. He had told her he had a sister. Two, in fact. If she stayed out here when the two of them came out of his office he would probably introduce her.

No, that would look contrived and desperate. A little stalker-ish. Instead, she would wait in her office and when she heard them come out she would grab her things and just happen to meet them at the elevator.

Yes, that plan would work.

"Hey, Kins," Bev said. "Could I ask a huge favor? It's like ten minutes to five and I have a date tonight. Is there any way you could cover the phones for me? Since you're gonna be here, anyway...?"

"Sure," Kinsley said. "Just forward the main line back to my office. But answer a question for me. What did she look like?"

Bev pressed some buttons on the phone, then stood there with her purse on her arm, her cell phone in her hand and a baffled look on her face. "I don't know... really pretty...really classy...like she has a lot of money...like somebody he'd take to the symphony or ballet with on a Saturday night. You know, that kind of woman."

"Do you think she's here to donate to the Foundation?"

Bev was already edging toward the elevator. "I don't know.... She seemed to be kind of into him."

Bev pushed the elevator button and the door opened immediately. She backed into it. "I've got to go," she said. "Let me know what you find out. Maybe she's his new girlfriend?"

As the elevator doors closed and carried Bev away, Kinsley replayed in her head the conversation she'd had with Christopher last night. He had said that he wasn't staying at the night club because she wasn't there. He'd said that he wanted them to go out again. When she hadn't answered he'd said he would take that as a yes.

Given all that, why would he bring another woman he was interested in to the office? It just didn't make sense.

Kinsley went into her office, left the door open, settled herself at her desk and waited.

About fifteen minutes later, she heard laughter coming from the reception area. She stood and started to grab her purse so that she could go out and make the *accidental* meeting at the elevator happen, but something stopped her—something in the tone of their voices. Something in the way they seemed to be laughing intimately at a private joke...

She dropped her purse on her desk chair and edged her way to the door. She peeked out, hoping Christopher wouldn't see her. If he did she would just say she thought that she was the only one left in the office and... She looked just in time to see Christopher with his hand on the small of a very beautiful woman's back.

"Our dinner reservation is at seven," he said. "We should have time for a drink before they seat us."

As the elevator doors opened, his hand stayed there as he ushered her in. Kinsley ducked back inside her office so that they wouldn't see her when they turned around to face the front.

Standing there alone in the empty office on a Friday night, Kinsley suddenly felt like the biggest fool in the world. So she'd gone against her better judgment and had agreed to go out with Christopher tomorrow night. Here was proof positive that she was simply one of a string of women.

Her rational mind reminded her she had no right to be upset or jealous. She had known all along that this was his M.O. But she couldn't help the way her heart objected. Tomorrow night obviously meant something completely different to her than it did to him.

If she let herself fall for Christopher Fortune any more than she already had, she was setting herself up for a world of heartbreak. She'd grown up with a mother who had been so desperately in love with a man who treated her wrong. Her mom's love for her dad ended up killing her.

Even though Christopher had certainly given no signs of being physically abusive, his fickle ways, his seeming to want only the things that were out of his reach—and then abandoning them when he was finished toying with them—did not make Kinsley feel good.

If she invested any more emotion in him, she would be mentally abusing herself. That wasn't going to happen.

She forwarded the office phones to the answering service, gathered her purse and turned off the office lights, realizing that fate had given her the answer she'd been looking for earlier that evening.

Christopher Fortune had been in the building, but he was emotionally unavailable.

Chapter Nine

Okay, she was avoiding him.

She had been most of the week.

It was Thursday morning and she hadn't seen him in the office since she'd watched him leave with that woman on Friday. She admitted it was a little childish. But she felt a little burned and very foolish for letting her heart control her usually clear head. She needed to put space between them.

When he'd called her, she'd responded by text— except for Saturday and Sunday. She carefully avoided personal topics of conversation—such as *What happened to our date on Saturday? Didn't we have plans, tentative as they were?*

She hadn't bothered to explain that if he wanted to take her out he needed to firm up plans sooner than the day of—and not parade his Friday night date through the office.

Even if their relationship was casual, that was simply bad taste.

Oh, who was she kidding? If she hadn't seen him with that woman she probably would have overlooked his lax planning. But it didn't matter now. It was better that reality, the inconvenient interloper it was, crashed the party sooner rather than later. Now, she was intent on locating the silver lining in the gray cloud that she refused to let rain on her career.

This near miss had been fair warning that dating someone she worked with was simply a bad idea.

It wasn't that every man who took her out had to commit to exclusivity before the first date. But she realized—too late—that what she felt for Christopher was different. She should've known better than to let herself lose control. Playing with Christopher Fortune was like playing with fire. She knew who he was and what he was all about. She knew that she couldn't play by his rules.

It was best to keep their relationship strictly business. That way, no one misunderstood and no one got hurt.

Monday and Tuesday she had conveniently scheduled herself to be out of the office. With a little investigating, Kinsley learned through Bev that Christopher would be out of the office on Wednesday and today. That should be enough time to clear her head and regain her equilibrium. She was professional and she knew she couldn't avoid him forever. After all, the Spring Fling was on Saturday. But everything was in place. She had done her tasks and had discreetly followed up to ensure that he had taken care of everything on his list.

She wasn't surprised to discover that he had.

That's why she chose to focus on the good, the professional side of their relationship, the part that worked. She just needed to remember to not let herself get snared in Christopher's charismatic web.

She had the rest of the day to collect herself. Because he was supposed to be back tomorrow, she planned on emailing him later today and asking if he had time to meet at the fairgrounds Friday afternoon to do a walk-through and preliminary set up for the event. They would be so busy with their booth preparations there would be no time for personal talk. Plus, Christopher was a smart guy—he seemed to catch on quickly. Surely by now he understood that their relationship had been relegated to the "professional zone."

She printed out her to-do list and had just begun checking off items and making notes when she sensed someone standing in the doorway of her office.

Christopher.

Her stomach did a full-fledged triple gainer, and as much as she hated it she audibly inhaled. She bit the insides of her cheeks hard to get her emotions in check.

Act like a professional.

"Hey, stranger," said Christopher. "Just wondering if there's room for the putting green under the tent?"

Kinsley couldn't look him in the eyes. It wasn't very professional, and she knew it. But neither was the way his gaze seemed to be burning into her. She straightened a stack of paper on her desk. She put a few loose pens into her desk drawer. Aligned her coffee mug on the coaster on the edge of her desk.

"The putting green?" Good. Her voice was neutral. "Christopher, you know I was only joking when I suggested you bring it to the Spring Fling. You don't have to do that if you don't want to."

"I know I don't have to," he said.

She picked up her pen and circled an item on her list.

"I figured we could just have a raffle. The kids can put their name into a drawing for prizes when they sign the bullying prevention pledge card—"

"The raffle sounds great. But let's bring the putting green, too. It will be an active visual. We can use it to draw people in. Oh, hey, and I wanted to tell you that I got word earlier this week that not only is Redmond Flight School offering a couple of prizes for us to give away—a couple of glider flights, which the kids should really love—but also everyone over there is behind doing an air-show fund-raiser in the fall. And Susan Eldridge and Julie Fortune were able to snag some gift cards from some of the local restaurants and merchants for us to use as prizes. I'm just blown away by how great and helpful everyone has been. It's a great team, don't you think?"

"Of course. I've always found everyone here to be exceptionally helpful."

"I know. But good teams are hard to find." Something in his voice changed. "When you have one, you should hang on to it."

Oh, no. Here it came.

She decided to head it off before he could shift things into the personal.

"Yes, we are lucky to have such great coworkers, aren't we? And if you'll excuse me, I'm going to go talk to Hank in maintenance about getting some extra chairs for the tent."

She stood, but Christopher closed her office door.

"I called you on Saturday and Sunday, Kinsley. Did you get my messages?"

"I had to go out of town."

"If I didn't know better, I might think you've been avoiding me. We had plans over the weekend. Or so I thought."

"Well, you should have thought about that before you brought your Friday night date to the office. Christopher, you shouldn't have kissed me if you were involved with someone else." The words slipped out before she could stop them. Now she had no choice but to look him square in the eyes.

The sight of him completely upended her equilibrium. She fisted her hands at her side, digging her nails into her palms. It was supposed to distract her from how she always seemed to get drawn in simply by looking at him. Even now, as he stood there looking baffled.

Wow, not only was he a player, but he was a good actor too.

"I don't know what you're talking about," he said. "I'm not involved with anyone else."

Maybe *involved* was overstating it. "Well, you shouldn't have kissed me if you were even dating other people."

"Kinsley, I really have no idea what you're talking about. I mean, sure, I've dated other women in the past, but nobody seriously. You are the first woman I've even considered dating exclusively."

She suddenly felt claustrophobic. Hearing him say the words but knowing they were encased in a lie made her want to run. How could he stand here, look her in the eye and tell her she didn't see what she knew she saw? At that moment, she realized just how different she and this man who was playing with her heart really were.

"Please don't, Christopher. Don't insult me. I saw you with that woman here at the office on Friday."

Confusion contorted his face. "Nora?"

And now he was going to try and change his tune, try to explain it away, but she wasn't going to have it.

"I have no idea what her name is, but she is beautiful. You have great taste in women—at least outward appearances. But what you don't seem to understand is that *Nora* and I are obviously cut from different material. Women like her might be fine with kissing and keeping it casual, but I'm not. I don't *give myself away*. Not even a kiss. Kisses are intimate, and I don't take intimacy casually."

She seemed to have struck him dumb because all he could do was stand there and stare at her, his lips pressed into a thin line.

"Since we have to work together," she said, "we have to keep things strictly professional, Christopher. Unlike you, I don't have family who can come to my rescue. My contacts aren't unlimited. I need this job."

Christopher looked taken aback, but there was a new light in his eyes.

"Kinsley, Nora Brandt is an etiquette coach. I hired her because I took your advice to heart. I was thinking about how I needed to get better at learning people's names, and that made me wonder about my other social and professional deficiencies. Nora and I went out to dinner Friday night so she could see me in action."

For the love of God, she wanted to believe him.

"But I saw you with your hand on the small of her back. That's pretty intimate."

"Apparently so. She told me as much when we were in the elevator. Honestly, the entire night was pretty humiliating. I'm not good at this...this." He gestured with both hands, at her, around the office. "I was raised on a ranch. My role models were my buddies and my brothers. We hung out at The Grill and flirted with the same handful of girls who didn't know any better than we did. I have no idea what I'm doing. Sometimes I feel so far out of my element I feel like a total buffoon. So, I hired an etiquette coach to help me. You are so smooth and polished. You deserve to be with someone who is your equal. Someone who doesn't embarrass you like I would."

Kinsley was so stunned that her mouth actually hung open.

Christopher held up a finger.

"Wait just a moment. I can prove it to you."

He pulled a business card from his wallet and handed it to Kinsley. The card had Nora Brandt's photo on it. Sure enough she was the woman Kinsley had seen him with on Friday.

"You can call her if you want. She'll confirm everything."

Now Kinsley was the one who felt like the total buffoon.

"And just so you know, she's married. And even if she wasn't, *she's* not my type at all. There's no other woman in the world I'm interested in right now besides you."

* * *

Kinsley had been jealous.

The thought made Christopher smile as he filled the last helium balloon and tied a knot in the stem. Because if she was jealous, that meant she had feelings for him. Even though she was still keeping him at arm's length, the chill had thawed.

There was still a chance, he thought as he tied a ribbon to the balloon and added it to the bunch that would join its twin at the entrance to the tent.

He fully intended to seize that chance and make things work between them.

Today was the day of the Spring Fling. He and Kinsley had met at the fairgrounds early to get everything in place inside the white tents. Hank from maintenance had generously agreed to transport the putting green in his pickup truck. The guy had even taken it upon himself to build a wooden platform to keep the green out of the dirt.

Christopher made a mental note to get Hank a gift card to Red or something else he would enjoy. He had gone out of his way transporting the putting green on his day off. Building the platform was above and beyond.

But Christopher was beginning to learn that was how everything worked at the Foundation. They were all one big family. They helped and supported each other.

After he finished getting the balloons in place, Kinsley introduced him to a young pregnant woman named Tonya Harris who had agreed to help them today. He realized she was the teenager Kinsley was coaching through Lamaze.

Along with their anti-bullying message, the Foundation was also teaching self-esteem. The two went hand-in-hand. If a teen had low self-esteem, he or she might be more apt to fall prey to bullies. Bullies didn't all come in the same package. Sometimes the bully was the enemy. Other times the bully might be the boyfriend who pressured his girlfriend to have sex against her better judgment.

If they could save even one young woman from ending up pregnant and alone like Tonya, then he would consider this program a success.

He admired the way Kinsley spoke to the teenager like a friend, asking her advice on the placement of chairs and even entrusting her with manning the table where kids would pick up information and sign the anti-bullying pledge cards.

By the time the Spring Fling was open and running at nine o'clock, they actually looked as if they knew what they were doing. Music was playing from a sound system he had secured through one of his contacts. The putting green, which he was in charge of, looked pretty cool on its custom-made, green-painted plywood perch. Kinsley had wrapped a large rectangular box, where the kids would enter the drawing for the various prizes they were offering.

He thought back to Thursday when he'd been talking about what a great team they made. It was the truth. Look at everything that they had accomplished working together in such a short time. They seemed to have the same vision. There was a synergy between them, and if he had to spend an entire year proving himself to her, he would.

She was worth it.

As Christopher was demonstrating proper putting technique to a young boy who was frustrated because he couldn't seem to sink a hole in one, Lily Cassidy Fortune, who had created the Foundation in memory of her late husband, Ryan, who had succumbed to a brain tumor nine years ago, walked up and beamed at him, just as the boy sank his first putt. The kid let out a cheer and Lily clapped for him. After Christopher handed him his prize of two movie tickets and directed him to the table where Tonya could help him with the pledge card, Lily greeted Christopher as warmly as if he were part of her own family. It dawned on him that they actually were related somewhere down the line.

"I came over here purposely to shake the hand of the person who has been doing such a great job getting the word out to the community about the Foundation," she said. She gestured around the tent. "This is just magnificent. It's exactly the direction that I am proud to see the Foundation going. I know my Ryan would've been proud of this, too."

A pang of guilt spurred on by her genuine affection and appreciation stabbed Christopher. He glanced over at Kinsley and saw her helping a kid fill out an entry form for the drawing. There was no way he could stand here and take all the credit, especially when she was over there doing all the work.

"I appreciate you coming by, Mrs. Fortune," he said.

She put a hand on his arm. "Oh, please, do call me Lily. All my family does."

Christopher smiled at her generosity. "I would be honored to, thank you. If you have a moment, I want you to meet somebody who has been instrumental in putting together what you see here, and, I suspect,

everything you've heard about the community outreach program."

"I absolutely have time."

Christopher motioned her over to the table where
Kinsley sat with Tonya. Kinsley looked up and smiled
at the two of them, genuine warmth radiating from
her eyes.

"Lily Cassidy Fortune," he said, giving Kinsley a
significant look. "I would like for you to meet Kinsley
Aaron. She is an outreach coordinator for the Foundation and has tirelessly worked to put together everything you see today and more."

Christopher saw a faint hint of pink color Kinsley's
cheeks as she stood and offered her hand to Lily.

"It is such an honor to meet you, Mrs. Fortune,"
she said. "I'm proud to work for such an incredible
organization. The Foundation took a chance on me
when I had very little experience—I'm still going to
school. Their faith in me has made me want to work
even harder to connect the Foundation with the Red
Rock community. However, you need to know that this
guy right here is doing incredible work. He is making
a real difference. He has a great vision and nice way
about him that everybody seems to love."

Kinsley's eyes sparkled good-naturedly, but the real
meaning of what she said wasn't lost on Christopher.
He smiled back at her and quirked a brow, sending a
message that she was the only person he wanted to
love.

Chapter Ten

Christopher was right—they had been working hard. The turnout at the booth had been better than Kinsley had ever dreamed it would be.

When they started, she was afraid they were going to have prizes to spare. But because of the fabulous response, they were having to tell the kids that they would do the drawings on the hour and that they had to be present to win. At the start of each hour, kids of all ages would cluster around the tent to hear the name of the lucky person whose name had been drawn from the box.

Each time a name was announced the crowd would cheer wildly. It struck Kinsley that even this was bringing the kids together. There seemed to be no rivalry or resentment from those who didn't win. Of course, Kinsley always made sure to announce that they could win prizes, like T-shirts, rubber brace-lets and water bottles, instantaneously by signing the pledge card. Maybe these kids just needed a common meeting ground.

The crowd was dispersing after the most recent drawing, and for the first time since they had arrived Kinsley had a chance to step back and look around. Every single volunteer who had signed up to work the booth had shown up. Most of them were even hang-ing around after their shift was over. In fact, right now they had a plethora of help.

So when Christopher suggested that they take a break, she only hesitated for a moment. She was thirsty and what she wouldn't give for a bite of the cotton candy that she had seen the kids enjoying.

"Okay, but only if you promise we can go get some cotton candy," she said.

"Ahh, cotton candy. The way to Kinsley's heart."

She tried to ignore the butterflies that swarmed when he said that. She was beginning to realize he was an insufferable flirt. He couldn't help it any more than he could help the fact that his hair was blond and his eyes were a shade of blue that matched the clear spring sky.

She couldn't seem to help the fact that she noticed things like that about him. But what she had also no-ticed, she thought as they walked away from the Foun-dation tent, was that he had a much bigger heart than she had initially given him credit for. A lot of his bra-vado was to cover the insecurities of his upbringing.

She silently vowed to never judge another person until she learned their story. After all, who would've known that slick-dressing, fancy-car-driving Christopher Fortune had actually come from very humble roots? He may have been a Fortune by name, but his modest upbringing really was at the heart of everything he did.

After they grabbed some cotton candy to share, Christopher won her a giant teddy bear at the arcade shooting gallery.

"You surprise me every day," she said. "I never imagined that you'd ever even held a gun, much less that you knew how to use one. You're a pretty sharp shot."

"And that's just the start of my good qualities," he said, wiggling his eyebrows comically. "If you don't believe me, just give me a chance to prove myself."

His free arm, the one that wasn't holding the teddy bear, lightly brushed against hers as they walked side by side through the fair. The skin-on-skin contact made her shudder with a strange anticipation and an emotion that she couldn't remember ever feeling.

"You know what I've always wanted to do?" Christopher said.

"What's that?"

"Ride on the Ferris wheel with a beautiful woman," he said.

Kinsley rolled her eyes at him. "You are too cheesy for words sometimes," she said.

He laughed and and nudged her with his arm. This time the contact was on purpose. She couldn't help but wonder if he'd felt the same electricity the last time their arms brushed.

They made small talk as they made their way over to the Ferris wheel. By a stroke of luck the line was negligible. They were seated and the ride was in motion in less than five minutes.

With the giant teddy bear at her feet, the warm sun on her face and Christopher sitting next to her, Kinsley couldn't remember ever feeling so content or so free. When their car stopped at the top of the wheel, she felt as if she could see all the way to San Antonio. It was magical up there.

The car rocked a little and Kinsley gripped the safety bar that stretched across their legs.

"Don't worry," he said, stretching an arm around her and pulling her to him. "I'll keep you safe."

It was as if they were alone in their own little world. Kinsley leaned into Christopher, relishing how they seemed to fit so perfectly together. And when Christopher lowered his head to taste her lips, she didn't resist. In fact, she met him halfway.

All too soon, the car was moving again, breaking the spell and propelling them back into the real world. The only thing different was that Christopher did not remove his arm from around her shoulder until they stepped off the ride.

She wished that they could continue strolling around the fair hand in hand, stealing kisses and sharing cotton candy. But work called. They strolled back to the booth, not touching, looking as platonic as two coworkers ever looked walking with a giant teddy bear between them.

"You're an only child, right?" Christopher asked.

"Yes."

"How did you get to be so good with kids? You really are a natural. I thought only children were supposed to have a hard time empathizing with others. And that was supposed to be a joke but it didn't come out very well."

She smiled as he pretended to knock himself up the side of his head with the palm of his hand. "Just because I was an only child doesn't mean I can't relate to people, Christopher."

"What I'm trying so ineloquently to say is that I love watching you with the kids. They really listen to you and respect you. I think kids have a natural B.S. meter. They can tell when someone is sincere and when they're not. You're really good at what you do."

Her natural inclination was to make a joke out of his compliment or to spit out some snarky retort. But the words got caught in her throat. All she could manage was a choked "Thank you."

She cleared her throat. "I feel so lucky to do what I do, to have a job where I have an opportunity to make a real difference."

Christopher smiled. "Only-child anomaly number two—you're not selfish, either."

She felt her cheeks warming. "Would you stop with the compliments, already?" She shot him a smile so that he knew she was kidding. "Thank you. But good grief, if you keep this up my head is going to swell as big as the bouncy castle over in the kids' area."

"If it does, you'll have good reason."

"Christopher…"

"How did you meet Tonya?"

She smiled at the mention of the sweet teenage girl. "I met her at the high school a few months ago when I was there doing a presentation for Principal Cramer. She had just found out she was pregnant. Her parents had kicked her out of the house, and she really didn't have anywhere else to go. The boyfriend lives over in San Antonio and dumped her as soon as he found out they were going to be parents. She had slept at the bus station the night before and had almost gotten on a bus to San Antonio to try to talk to the boyfriend. The only thing that stopped her was that she didn't have enough money for a ticket. She went to school the next day because she didn't have any place else to go. I feel like it was divine intervention that I was there for her."

Christopher raked his hand through his hair. It wasn't a gesture of vanity as much as what seemed to be an expression of disbelief. The astonishment in his eyes spoke volumes.

"She broke down that day and cried and cried, right in my arms. I cried with her. And then I told her that she was allowed to have a twenty-four-hour pity party, but after that she needed to be strong for both her sake and the baby's. She stayed at my apartment that night and I went with her to talk to her parents the next day. They let her come back and that's where she is now. Her grades are good and she'll miss a little school when she has the baby in about three months, but I've already talked to the principal and we've arranged for her to do schoolwork while she's out. Her mother is going to watch the baby during the day, and she might have to get an after-school job to afford diapers, but she should be okay. I just keep telling her the most important thing is that she can't get behind on her schoolwork and she can't just give up. If she doesn't, everything will be fine."

Kinsley shrugged at a loss for what else to say.

"Isn't that what everybody needs sometimes?" Christopher said. "For somebody to tell them that they can do it? That the road ahead may be hard, but if they're persistent everything will be fine. Kinsley, you may have saved that girl's life. You helped her smooth things over with her family so that she has the support she needs until she graduates and gets a full-time job."

She didn't know what to say. So she didn't say anything for a long while as they walked. Then she identified one of the feelings knotted in her belly. It was shame.

"I meant what I said to Lily Fortune earlier. You really have done a good job. I didn't give you enough credit when you first started. I thought you were just trading on your name and your good looks."

"Oh, well, you've got to cut a guy a break in the trading-on-his-looks department." He shrugged and did a Justin Bieber-ish shake of his head, despite the fact that his close-cropped hair didn't move.

She knew he was kidding, but she couldn't resist egging him on. "And here I thought you were the humble Fortune—"

Her words were eclipsed by a commotion coming from the Foundation tent. She and Christopher exchanged a concerned glance and jogged over to the tent to see what was happening.

A sluggish-looking teenage boy was standing in an aggressive pose over Tonya, who was still seated at the table. The two were exchanging heated words. When Tonya stood and backed away from the guy, he reached out a hand, grabbed the back of her T-shirt and pulled hard. Tonya stumbled and immediately put her hands up, as if to shield herself from a blow. That's all it took for Kinsley to break into a sprint and put herself between Tonya and the boy.

"What the heck do you think you're doing?" she said to the guy. She got right in his face, determined to prove that she wasn't afraid of him. She looked the thug square in the eyes but kept her voice level and low as she spoke with authority. "You need to leave now. *Now.* Or I am going to call the police and have them escort you out of here."

A cocky sneer spread slowly over the guy's face. He was tall, but he was skinny. And although she didn't want to lay a hand on him, she was perfectly prepared to practice a few self-defense moves that she had learned over the years.

"I'm just here to talk to my baby mama," he said.

"It didn't look like you were talking to her. It looked like you were upsetting her."

"I don't need you interfering with me and my family," the thug said.

Kinsley sneered right back at him. "Oh, then you must be Jared. I've heard about you, Jared."

The kid seemed to flinch at the revelation that Kinsley knew him. "I think Tonya's dad would like to have a conversation with you. In fact, he's supposed to be stopping by any minute. Why don't you have a seat over there and wait for them?"

Kinsley could honestly say it was the first time she had seen all the blood drain from a person's face. Jared didn't say another word. He turned and sprinted away. It was only then that Kinsley realized that Christopher was standing right next to her, looking as if he was ready to spring into action if Jared had made one false move.

He squeezed her arm. "Why don't you see to Tonya? I'll deal with the crowd." He motioned with his head to the knot of onlookers that had gathered to watch the confrontation.

"Thank you," she said, giving him a squeeze back.

Tonya was huddled in the far corner of the tent, sobbing.

"Honey, I'm so sorry. Did he hurt you?"

Tonya shook her head as tears streamed down her face.

"What did he want?" Kinsley asked this question only to find out if Jared had been coming around other times or if this happened to be a chance encounter.

"Nothing," Tonya said. "He was just being disgusting. He's here at the Spring Fling with his buddies and he just wanted to act like a jerk."

And nobody had stepped in to help her.

"How long had you been standing there before I got back?"

Tonya shrugged as she swiped at her tears. Kinsley reached into her pocket and handed the girl a tissue. The girl blew her nose.

"He first saw me about ten minutes after you'd gone on break. He and his friends came up to me. I thought he wanted to say hi, but he called me a whore, asked me why I was here. He said they didn't allow whores at the Spring Fling. Then he walked away laughing with his friends. He came back just before you did."

Kinsley's mouth went dry.

"I'm so sorry this happened. But I don't think he's going to bother you anymore. If he does, you need to tell someone."

A dozen questions darted through her mind—at the top of the list was whether this was the first time she'd seen him since she told him about the baby and whether he had ever hit her in the past. His aggressive posture and Tonya's reaction made Kinsley wonder, but now wasn't the time to ask her. She gathered Tonya in her arms and let her cry on her shoulder, gently patting her on the back the same way she had the first day they'd met.

When Tonya's father arrived, she would let him know that Jared had been hassling her.

The girl needed to know she didn't have to put up with that kind of treatment. She needed to know she deserved better. Once she had calmed down, they would talk about that.

But there was one thing she needed to know right now. "Sweetie, did anyone try to help you? Did any one tell him to go away?"

"No."

That was the crux of the matter. That's why they needed to educate people about taking a stand to help others. Kinsley focused on the clinical side of it because if she thought about all those people standing there looking on and no one caring enough to get involved, she would be sobbing as hard as Tonya was. How could people be so heartless? To stand there while an innocent girl was being verbally attacked. Who knows what might have happened if she and Christopher hadn't come back when they did.

She squeezed her eyes shut to dam the tears that were welling and to try and erase the image of her father swinging and hitting her mother when she had jumped between them, just as she had jumped between Tonya and Jared.

A few hours later, it was time for the Spring Fling to close. The booth was empty except for Christopher and Kinsley. Tonya's father had come to get her as soon as Kinsley had called him. She had sent home all of her volunteers after they had put in such a long day's work. There wasn't much to break down now, only the chairs and the tables, which they just needed to fold up and set aside so that Hank could come by tomorrow morning and load it along with the tent into his truck.

"What did Tonya's father say?" Christopher asked.

Christopher kept a respectable distance when Mr. Harris had come by to collect his daughter.

"He said he was going to talk to the sheriff about a restraining order," Kinsley said. "I think that's a good idea."

Her voice cracked on the last words. It was probably the combination of fatigue and the letdown after the adrenaline rush, but suddenly all the tears that she'd been able to contain while she was comforting Tonya threatened to break through. If they did, she was afraid she might not stop crying.

"You were the epitome of grace under pressure," Christopher said.

Kinsley opened her mouth to say, "No," but the words lodged in her throat as tears broke free and rolled down her cheek. She turned her head, hoping that Christopher wouldn't see.

"Hey—" he said, putting a gentle hand on her shoulder. "Everything is going to be okay."

She wished she could believe him, but for girls like Tonya and for women like her mother, nothing ever turned out okay. The tears crested and streamed. The harder she tried to stop them, the harder she cried.

The tables and chairs could wait.
Kinsley could not.

Christopher had to get her out of there and to a place where she felt safe enough to let out whatever it was that had her so tied up in knots. The episode with Tonya and Jared was upsetting, but she'd handled it well. However, it had obviously brought up something else.

He hoped she would let down her walls and trust him enough to let him help her.

He saw two boys who had been helping at the Foundation tent that afternoon. Now they were just hanging around. He offered to pay them twenty dollars each if they would stack the chairs and break down the tables and leave them over by the tree. The two jumped at the chance to make an easy buck, freeing Kinsley and him to leave.

She seemed much too upset to drive, so Christopher was relieved when she allowed him to take her home. He told her he would pick her up in the morning and they would come and get her car then. Just to ease her mind, he phoned the fairgrounds security office and informed them they would be back to get the car tomorrow.

By the time they had gotten to her apartment, Kinsley had composed herself. Even so, he tenderly helped her upstairs, but just as he expected, once they were inside, she tried to downplay what happened.

The walls were firmly back in place.

"Kinsley, you don't have to do this with me," Christopher insisted. "You're not an island. You don't have to go this alone—whatever it is that is torturing you. Haven't we gone beyond that?"

He reached out and tucked a strand of hair behind her ear.

"Talk to me," he said.

She was silent for a moment as they sat together on the couch. Christopher was determined to not fill the silence. It worked.

"I told you that both of my parents are dead," Kinsley said in a small voice.

Christopher nodded.

"It was my father's doing. Well, mostly. He drank himself to death, and my mother never recovered. It's as if she died from a broken heart. Not because she loved him. Her heart broke because of the way he had treated her. He was the quintessential bully, made her believe that she was worthless. No one should have to live that way."

Listening to the words, Christopher felt all the blood drain from his face. He reached out and took Kinsley's hand in silent support.

"I couldn't do anything to help her," she said. "I guess I thought she would heal, that her life would get better after he was gone. But she didn't, she just wasted away. And died. As I was growing up, as far back as I can remember my father always belittled my mother, and she was defenseless against his words— and sometimes his fists. He had such an anger problem. He thought I had a smart mouth when I would stand up for her, so he'd come at me, and my mother would put herself between us and bear the brunt of his anger so that I could get away. She just let him treat her that way."

He squeezed her hand and shut his eyes for a moment. When he opened them, he said, "Kinsley, I am so sorry."

She shook her head. "Please don't feel sorry for me.

I don't want anyone's pity. Sure I wish I could've done things differently. I wish I could go back and force my mom to move out, to get away from him, but I can't and I know that. I made a decision long ago, Christopher, not to let my past define me. But it does inform my choices."

"Is that why you were so quick to put yourself in between Tonya and Jared?"

And why you tend to keep people at arm's length.

She nodded.

He pulled her into his arms and held her, just held her, for the longest time.

"I am so sorry for what you went through," he whispered in her ear. "But I'm not sorry for who you've become. You are one of the strongest, most amazing people I have ever met in my entire life."

He leaned his head in so that his cheek was on hers. The next thing he knew her mouth, soft, warm and inviting, had found his.

It vaguely registered that he shouldn't be doing this—she was vulnerable right now. But he was kissing her and she was kissing him back.

Her lips tortured and tempted him more than they satisfied his craving for her. As he sat there with his arms around her, the feel of her lips on his urged him to lean in closer. Raw need swirled inside him, as if taking possession of her might bind them and fix everything that was broken.

A moan deep in his throat escaped as desire coursed through him, a yearning only intensified by the feel of her lips. His one lucid thought as Kinsley melted into him was the taste of her: sweet as spun sugar and candy apples and something warm…like cinnamon and sunshine.

It made him reel.

For a few glorious seconds he never wanted to breathe on his own again. He could be perfectly content right here with her in his arms for the rest of his life.

His hands slid down to her waist and held her firmly against him as his need for her grew and pulsed.

He slowly released her, staying forehead to forehead while the heat between them lingered, drawing him to her almost magnetically. He reached out and ran the pad of his thumb over her bottom lip.

"I'd better go," he whispered. "If I don't…you know what's bound to happen."

"I know," she said. "And I want you to stay."

Caught in the twilight between craving and clarity, he claimed one more kiss of her lips but knew this was as far as they should go. As much as he wanted her, it wouldn't be right.

"I don't want to force things," he said, his lips still a breath away from hers.

"You and I both know we've been moving toward this moment for weeks—for months," she said. "Probably since the first moment we saw each other."

Her words, the nearness of her, sent heat rippling through his body. As she gently nipped at his bottom lip, he had to fight the desire to take her right there, right now, but in a way that would reach back through space and time and make right all the wrongs and ugliness that had ever darkened her world.

Tonight felt different.

This *thing* between them felt deeper and undeniably

right. For the first time in a long time—maybe ever—his heart was no longer his own. Her essence had infused his senses. All the Fortunes' money couldn't buy what he'd found in her.

Then those lips that had been driving him crazy took possession of his once again, and he knew there was no turning back from what was about to happen.

They were inevitable.

Chapter Eleven

Kinsley got to her feet and took Christopher's hand. If this was going to happen, she was going to have to prove to him she wasn't simply seeking sanctuary in his body. She needed to show him that she was truly ready.

She led him to the bedroom.

It had been a long time since she'd allowed herself to fully want, to fully trust, but all that mattered was how she needed this man. His evident need for her made her feel powerful and desirable. Strong and beautiful. No one had ever made her feel like this before.

Piece by piece their clothes fell away until they stood naked in front of each other in the dim light of the bedroom lit by moonlight filtering in through the sheer curtains. His gaze searched her face as if he were giving her one last chance to protest.

Not a chance.

As if reading her mind, he walked her backward to the bed and lowered her onto it. Climbing in beside her, he stretched out, propping his head on his free hand to look into her eyes.

She rolled over to face him so that their lips were a whisper away. She wanted him to see that this was exactly what she wanted. He reached out and smoothed her hair away from her face, then traced a finger down to her breasts. He smoothed his palm over the sensitive skin, making her inhale sharply.

"You are so beautiful," he said. "I can't tell you how long I've wanted this…wanted us."

He closed the distance between them, allowing no room for doubt. Her lips were still swollen and tender from kissing him earlier, but still she opened her mouth to let him all the way in.

He responded by rolling her onto her back and gently nudging her legs apart. He covered her with his body as she ran her hands down his arms, then up his back as he settled himself on her, positioning himself so that his hips were square to hers. The feel of him on top of her released all the desire and longing that had been bottling up in her since the day she'd first realized that she wanted him.

She tried to stifle a groan that bubbled up in her throat as she savored the heat that coursed between them. She reveled in the feel of him, in the anticipation of the imminent joining of their bodies.

It had been such a long time since she'd felt this way about anyone, since she'd allowed herself to lose control and trust someone like she trusted him.

It was good that they'd talked tonight, that she'd

opened up to him. It was cathartic, as if trusting him with her past had cleared a path to the future.

She wasn't sure what was going to happen after tonight, but she wasn't going to think about that now. All she cared about was the tender way he was kissing her neck as she lolled her head to the side to give him easier access. Now, his lips were trailing a path over her collarbones, then dipping down into the valley between her breasts.

One thing she had learned from Christopher was that you had to seize every moment, every opportunity and live. Until now, she hadn't been able to do that. But tonight she was in the here and now. Tonight, she intended to make love to him as if there would never be another moment like this one.

His kisses had found their way to her abdomen and were circling her belly button. Then he took a detour and kissed the insides of her thighs. She inhaled sharply and her eyes widened.

"Why did we wait so long for this?" Her voice was soft and breathless in the darkness.

"I don't know, but I can promise you it will be worth the wait." He flashed a wicked smile at her as he climbed back toward her. With a firm, quick move he pulled her on top of him. She could feel the hard length of him and she had to fight the urge to slide her body down and take him inside of her.

She drew in a jagged breath, determined to not rush things. Determined to savor every last delicious second of their first time together.

"But if you've changed your mind, I can stop," he said. "Are you sure about this?"

She nodded, then kissed him lightly on the mouth.

"I want you so badly, I can't think of anything else. So, if you're sure, then—"

"Shhh…" She pressed her finger to his lips. "I'm sure. Kiss me. Make love to me. Let's let what's in the past stay in the past. We can worry about tomorrow…tomorrow. Because tonight, I'm really glad we're right here."

He kissed her softly, then he slowly spread his hands over her breasts before gently cupping them. She was beautiful, all curves and legs and porcelain skin. He marveled at the ivory breasts in his hands and reverently closed his mouth over a nipple.

The sound of her sigh made him want her all the more.

He stretched out on top of her, gently nudging her legs apart with his knee. But then he felt her stiffen. She bit her lip and looked at him as if there was something she needed to say but couldn't find the words.

Had she changed her mind?

"What's wrong?" he asked, smoothing the back of his hand over her cheek.

She bit her bottom lip. "It's been a long time since I've been with anyone. So I'm not on birth control."

He bit back a curse. How could he have been so damn stupid? He was always cautious. He never had unprotected sex. It was a chance he wouldn't take for so many different reasons. Reasons that could justify a whole new division at the Foundation. Yet, tonight, being here with her so unexpectedly…wanting her as badly as he did, he'd pushed toward this coupling without thinking things through. Mainly because he hadn't been so presumptuous to think that he'd find himself in her bed.

"Oh...well...wow." He pulled himself off her and shifted onto his side so that he could look at her. He definitely needed some space, some room to cool off. "I don't have anything, either."

He cursed silently for not being prepared because he wanted her so much it almost caused him physical pain. He hoped it didn't show on his face as he stared into her beautiful, tormented blue eyes.

As she lay there illuminated by the moonlight filtering in through the slats in the plantation shutters, he realized he'd probably never seen her look quite so beautiful. That's when he knew...being here with her like this...holding her, feeling the warmth of her against him was all he needed.

"We don't have to make love tonight. We can just hold each other...or do other things. I can pick up some condoms tomorrow."

Never in her life had she experienced the perfect blend of euphoria and disappointment.

Euphoria because Christopher didn't have protection ready and waiting in his wallet or wherever grown men kept them these days. It meant that he wasn't prepared for a spur of the moment encounter, which put her mind at ease, and it showed that he cared about her and about his own health. He wasn't willing to have unprotected sex.

But she was also disappointed because she wanted him so badly that she... Okay, now she was blushing.

"So, here we are," he said, drawing in a deep breath.

Clearly, this sudden one hundred miles per hour to zero stop was just as jarring for him as it was for her.

He made a pained noise as he adjusted his position on the bed.

"So, here we are," she said.

He raked his hand through his hair. "Not to bring up a sore subject, but does this prove to you that I'm not as big a player as you think I am?"

She ran her fingers over the hair on his chest. His perfectly natural chest was almost as sexy as his broad shoulders, which she touched appreciatively.

"Honey, if I still believed you were a player, you wouldn't be here naked in my bed."

"Touché."

He looked almost edible lying there propped up on his side, watching her with his sexy eyes. She didn't feel the need to cover up or hide from him. In fact, she loved the fact that, judging by his body language, he obviously liked what he saw.

"So I gather you must not have been a Boy Scout," she said.

He grinned. "Ahh, because I'm not prepared." He laughed. "Actually, I *was* a Scout, way back when. I guess I'm a bit rusty in the preparedness department these days. But don't tell anyone because I may have to give back my merit badge."

"You can always earn that badge back."

"Oh, yeah? Exactly what did you have in mind?"

She ran her hand down the length of his body until she found his manhood. She touched him, happy to see that he was still every bit as ready to go as he had been before they'd been forced to stop.

"How do you feel about going and getting something for us? There's a twenty-four-hour drugstore two blocks from here. Will you do it? Please?"

He pursed his lips, and at first he seemed uncertain. For a moment she thought he might say no. But then he leaned in and feathered a kiss onto her lips before he lifted himself off the bed and got dressed.

He was back within ten minutes.

While he was gone, Kinsley opened a bottle of wine and lit some candles.

She handed him a glass when he came into the bedroom. "I was going to say that this deed deserved another kind of merit badge," he said as he sat on the edge of the bed, "but I see that you're way ahead of me."

She smiled. "So kiss me."

He complied, kissing her for a long time. Leisurely and thorough kisses that had her wondering, once again, if he had changed his mind while he was out and decided to take things slowly. He was still dressed even though he was stretched out beside her on the bed.

She ran her hand along the waistband of his blue jeans, tearing at the fabric of his shirt until her fingers struck gold...bare skin. He helped her by drawing it up and over his head.

She sighed as she drank in the raw beauty of him. When she straddled him, she could feel his erection through his pants. The thought of his body—so sexy and large—moving inside her ignited a slow burn in her belly. She wanted him more now than when he'd first touched her.

She ran both hands over his abs, up his chest and out onto his well-defined biceps. And, hello, there were those shoulders. They were broad and ropy, making his torso taper into a manly vee that disappeared beneath the waistband of his jeans. Those jeans.

They were the only thing that still stood between them.

She inhaled sharply.

Pace yourself.

She steadied herself by allowing her hands to travel back down over his abs, memorizing his form and the feel of the muscles under her hands.

She was so caught up in the beauty and feel of him, of his skin on her skin, that she was a little startled when he rolled her over and his hands did the exploring. They glided over her hips, down to her thighs and dipped between them.

This was really going to happen. She was ready and hyperaware of every breath, every kiss, every touch. When his hand found her most vulnerable spot, she shivered with anticipation. She noticed that his body seemed to tremble, too.

She put a little space between them and slowly unzipped his jeans. Together they got him out of his pants and his underwear. Finally, when nothing stood between them, she reached out and brushed her fingertips over his manhood. His body shuddered. He inhaled a sharp breath and his body arched slightly. Even though she'd already gotten a good look at him, she devoured his male glory with her eyes, from his flat, muscled stomach…up farther to his biceps and his shoulders…to his throat and the chiseled planes of his face. She stroked him and learned every inch of him, committing his body to memory, but he didn't let her linger for long. He pulled away and picked up the condom packet, ripping it open. As she watched him put the condom on the generous length of his maleness, she thought she would go over the edge before they'd even began. Once everything was in place, he settled himself between her legs. She welcomed him by opening her thighs so that their bodies could join.

The physical sensations of what was happening made her shudder with excitement. He entered her with a tender, unhurried push. The heat that radiated from him seeped into her. His body was stiff as he gently inched forward, going so very slowly and being so careful. As her body adjusted to welcome him, she joined him in a slow rocking rhythm.

"Christopher," she whispered. "Oh…Christopher…"

Her sighs were lost in his kiss. He touched her with such care and seemed to instinctively know what her body wanted.

Pleasure began to rise and she angled her hips up to intensify the sensation. Their union seemed so very right that she cried out from the sheer pleasure of it.

She wanted him to feel good, too. She needed to touch him, to give him the same pleasure he was giving her. So she slid her hand between their bodies, reaching for him, wanting to heighten his pleasure. But he grabbed her wrist and held her hand firmly.

"Not yet," he said.

"Why?" she asked.

"Because. Just…not…yet." His breathlessness matched her own. "When you touch me, you make me…crazy. And this…this time is for you."

He stretched her arms up over her head and held them there as he rocked her toward her first release.

As spasms of ecstasy overtook her body, his lips reclaimed hers.

The gentle, almost reverent way he touched her proved that he had been worth waiting for…but his hunger for her was never so evident as when he came up for air and devoured her with voracious eyes.

She couldn't get enough of his touch. As if he read her mind, he drove into her with such intensity she fisted her hands into the bed sheets and gasped, arching against him, propelled by the pulsing heat that was growing and throbbing inside her.

"Let yourself go," he said, his voice hoarse and husky. "Just let go, Kinsley."

Maybe it was the heat of his voice in her ear; more likely it was the way he made her body sing with his touch, but the next thing she knew he had driven her over the edge for the second time that night.

Again, he wrapped his arms around her, holding her tightly, protectively, until she had ridden out the wave.

She buried her face in his chest, breathing in the scent of him, of their joining, needing to get as close to him as possible. He continued to hold her tight. She lost herself again in his broad shoulders and the warmth of his strong arms.

"How was that?" His voice was a throaty rasp.

When she lifted her head and looked at him, his eyes searched her face.

"It was great. Really, breathtakingly great."

He smiled. "And I'm not finished yet."

The feel of his bare skin against hers almost put her into sensory overload.

She was so aware of him, of the two of them fused so closely that it seemed they were joined body and soul.

Christopher buried his head in the curve of her neck and let out a deep moan.

She eased her palms down his back, kissed him hard and fast and then things got a little crazy as she wrapped her legs around his waist and dug her nails into his shoulders. He didn't seem to mind how tightly she was clinging to him. So she held him in place by the shoulders and shifted under him. The way he groaned was so delicious that she arched beneath him again, drawing him deeper inside.

At that moment, staring down into her clear eyes, his body joined with hers, Christopher felt the mantle of his life shift. All of a sudden, without explanation, everything was different.

How could that happen now when it had never happened before?

Because he'd never been in love before now.

He was in love with Kinsley's laugh and her mind and the way she was able to set him straight without making him feel as if he'd been lambasted. He loved the way she felt in his arms right now, the smell of her smooth skin and the way she gazed up at him with a certain look in her eyes that was equal parts courage and vulnerability. It was everything he already knew about her and all the things he had yet to discover. He wanted to be the first face she saw in the morning and the last face she saw before she closed her eyes and drifted off to sleep at night. He wanted to be the shoulder she cried on and the lips she kissed.

He wanted to prove to her that all men weren't like

her father, and she deserved someone who was crazy about her, someone who adored her the way she deserved to be loved.

He wanted to show her that love didn't have to hurt. The only problem was the prospect of doing that, rendering his heart that vulnerable, leaving it in someone else's hands, scared him to death.

But it was too late now. Judging by the way he felt, he had a feeling he'd already passed the point of no return.

"Christopher?" Kinsley's eyes searched his face. "Are you…okay?"

"I am absolutely better than okay." He kissed her deeply, pulling her to him so tightly that every inch of their bodies were merged. He hadn't particularly cared how close he'd felt to other women he'd been intimate with. But as he built up to the pace that would simultaneously transport Kinsley and him to nirvana, he wanted to see her face. He needed a one hundred percent connection. Not just body to body, but eye to eye and soul to soul.

It didn't take long before their bond, coupled with the rhythmic motion of their bodies, carried them over the edge together. As he lay with her, sweaty and spent, he cradled her against him.

As they'd made love, three words had been darting around inside his head. Now they'd somehow found their way to the tip of his tongue.

Oh, man…. Don't do that, he thought. *You're caught up in the moment. Don't say things you don't mean.*

The problem was, he did mean it. With all his soul.

Even so, meaning it and following through with the implications of *I love you* were two very different things.

Kinsley rolled over onto her stomach and looked up at him. "Are you really okay?"

He wanted to tell her exactly how he felt. Except when he opened his mouth all that came out was, "I've never been better."

Christopher wasn't used to being in this position of vulnerability. Since he'd been in Red Rock, he'd been used to being in command. But this woman lying in his arms had changed everything.

Frankly, it scared him to death.

Chapter Twelve

Christopher didn't find his way home until late Sunday night. And that was only because he didn't have any suitable work clothes over at her place.

Once he was at home, with a little space to digest what had happened between them, he realized two very important things about himself: that he was in love with Kinsley, even if he didn't know how to tell her, and that he needed to be the one to reach out to his father and set their relationship on the road to right.

Funny, last week if someone had told him that falling in love would change him so much that he'd be willing to extend the olive branch to Deke, he would've told them to go to hell.

But here he was, at nine o'clock on Sunday night, staring at his cell phone as he dialed his parents' number.

He had to do it now before he changed his mind or the spell that Kinsley had cast on him wore off.

Somehow, he didn't believe that this call would do any good. His old man was as stubborn as a bulldog that had clamped down on a stick. Once Deke sank his teeth into something there was no prying it loose. Everything in his world was black-and-white. He wasn't about to change his mind about his son.

How his sweet mother had put up with him all these years was a mystery. As he listened to the phone ring two-three-four times, the realization washed over Christopher that the reason he had decided to be the one to reach out and try to make amends was so he could know in his heart that he had done everything in his power to not be like his father.

Good, bad or indifferent, it had taken him a while to realize that. And it had taken the childhood experiences of a great woman to help him reframe his situation and see his family with a new appreciation. Kinsley was right, the family you took for granted wasn't going to be there forever. Having lost both of her parents within a one-year period, Kinsley was living proof of this.

Her father sounded like a monster. While Deke could be difficult, the old coot had never emotionally or physically abused his family. Sure he was hard on them. You could say a lot of things about Deke Jones, but he always did right by his family. Or at least, his version of right.

Wasn't that something to hold on to? Something to focus on? Because when he put it all into perspective, Christopher knew his upbringing could've been a whole lot worse.

It was probably too late to call the house on a Sunday night, anyway. Deke, the creature of habit he was, had probably been in bed for a good half hour.

Maybe, subconsciously, he'd known that and that was the reason he'd decided to call...or maybe he shouldn't overthink it. He could try again tomorrow.

Christopher had just pulled the phone away from his ear, when he heard a craggy voice grunt and gruff, "Hello?"

Hesitating, Christopher drew in a breath as he brought the phone to his ear.

"Hello?" the man repeated, the irritation in his voice mounting.

Deke and Jeanne Marie didn't have caller ID so there was no way he would've known it was his son. In his mind's eye Christopher could see Deke giving the phone a dirty look before he slammed the receiver back into the cradle.

"Pops? It's Chris."

Silence answered him. For a moment he wondered if Deke had already hung up. But then the old man said, "Son?" His voice was so soft, it was barely audible and most un-Deke-like.

"Yeah, Pops, it's me. Is this a good time? I hope I'm not calling too late."

Christopher waited for Deke to cut him off at the knees as he was so fond of doing. The old man had had two months to stew on his anger at Chris for abandoning the ranch to take a desk job pushing papers, for disassociating himself from the Jones name, moving to Red Rock and surely a plethora of other sins real or imagined of which he had found Christopher guilty.

"You can ring this house at midnight and I would take your call, son. It's good to hear your voice."

As Deke's positive response registered, Christopher exhaled a breath he didn't realize he'd been holding. On the other end of the line, he heard his father call to his mom. "Jeanne, it's Chris on the phone. Get in here."

"Chris, it's ladies first. Talk to your mama and then she'll give me the phone."

His mother was her usual, sweet, unconditional self, saying how much she and the family had missed him but that they all understood that he was making a nice life for himself in Red Rock.

"I do wish you would come home to visit soon," she said, her voice a little wistful. "You don't know what I'd give to hug you."

Christopher made noises about being busy at work but promised that he would see what he could do about arranging some time off for a visit. He thought about telling her that she and Deke were always welcome in Red Rock but decided against it. Deke would never hear of making the trip. Not even if it was his wife's dying wish— Christopher stopped himself from tumbling down the path of negativity that he usually traveled when he conversed with his father. Old Deke had started the conversation off nicely enough. Even though it raised his hackles, Christopher forced himself to take the high road and not instigate an argument…and to refuse the invitation if Deke invited him to one.

"I got the photo album you made for me, Mama. I really appreciate it."

"I wanted you to have some pictures from Toby and Angie's wedding. We all missed you. It was a beautiful day, but it would've been even better if you had stood up with your brother."

A pang of guilt stabbed Christopher right in the heart. He grabbed the album off the end table where it had been hidden under a stack of magazines and financial newspapers since he'd brought it home from the office.

He opened it to a page featuring a five-by-seven photo of the smiling bride and groom. He flipped the page and saw another of the entire family—minus him, of course—gathered around his brother and his new sister-in-law.

It really had been ridiculous and selfish to miss such an important occasion. But with the frame of mind he'd been in then and as mad as Deke had been at him, there was no way he was going to cast a dark shadow over his brother's big day.

He heard Kinsley's voice in the back of his head saying, *Don't dwell on things you can't change. Look forward and spend that energy on things that matter.*

Toby understood why he'd stayed away and that was all that mattered. Still, a funny feeling circled in his gut like a shark poised to attack.

"It was great to see Toby when he and Angie were here in town. Will you please be sure and tell him I called?"

"I sure will, honey. But I'm going to hand the phone over to your dad now. He's getting a little antsy waiting to talk to you."

Right. That would be the day the sky fell when Deke stood antsy with anticipation waiting to talk to his black-sheep son. Christopher wanted to snort, but he didn't. Instead, he told his mother he loved her and promised her one more time that he would do his best to make it home for a visit as soon as he could manage.

Then he put on his emotional armor and prepared for Deke to shoot him like a sniper poised and ready high atop a building.

"Well, now it's my turn," Deke said.

Christopher held his tongue, unsure if that was sarcasm or sincerity in his dad's tone.

"You made your mama really happy by calling tonight, son."

Oh. Okay. Could it have been sincerity? Or was it a verbal trap designed to lure Christopher into a false sense of security so that Deke could turn around and sucker punch?

He closed the photo album and set it on the coffee table, scooting forward so that he was sitting on the edge of the couch.

"It was good to hear her voice," Christopher said. In a split second he decided to stick to his original plan and play nice. "It's good to hear yours, too, Pops."

The words hung out there for a few beats before Deke answered, "I'm glad to talk to you, too. Son, I have a confession to make. I regret the way we parted when you took off for Red Rock. You and I have had our differences over the years, but we've never left things so badly between us."

The old Christopher would have quipped, "You regretted it so much that you waited for me to call so you could tell me." But from his view on the high road, he could see that this was a hard confession for Deke to make.

"I've regretted it, too, Pops. I'm...I'm sorry."

As soon as the words escaped Christopher clamped

his mouth shut, gritting his teeth so hard he could feel it all the way up to his temples.

"That's right big of you to say that, boy. To be the first one to apologize." Deke's voice sounded small and...humble? So much so that Christopher wasn't even sure it really was his father on the other end of the line.

"How's that job of yours going?" Deke asked.

So in the end his father couldn't bring himself to say the two little words that would have gone such a long way toward healing them...reuniting their family. Then again, maybe this was Deke's version of an apology. Christopher swallowed his pride and decided it was.

"It's great. I'm really enjoying it. Working for the Foundation is giving me a lot of opportunities to do some good in the community."

And that was as far as he was going to justify what he did for a living.

"That's what I hear. James has been in touch with your mama and he's had a lot of good things to say about you. He bragged about you, saying that you have a great work ethic and a real creative head for business. He says you've been such an asset to the Foundation, he would've hired you even if you weren't a blood relative. I'm really proud of you, son."

Proud of you, son.

Christopher fell back against the couch cushions so hard it knocked some of the air out of his lungs in a *whoosh*.

For the first time in his life, his father had told him he was *proud* of him. Christopher had a hard time hearing the rest of what his father said because of the blood rushing in his ears.

Family could be the most amazing people in your life while simultaneously being the most exasperating.

If an apology was gold, the words that had just passed from Deke's lips and traveled four hundred miles through the phone line were platinum.

No, they were priceless.

What was the Foundation's policy about fraternizing with a superior?

As Kinsley flipped through the employee handbook, she silently chastised herself. *Now was a heck of a time to worry about that.*

Still, for her own peace of mind she needed to know. After Christopher left her on Sunday evening, Kinsley had fallen back to earth with a terrifying awareness of her vulnerability.

She'd decided when she saw Christopher again, it should be business as usual. If they were going to work together, they had to keep their emotions (and libidos) in check.

Or at least *she* had to.

That sounded like common sense, but it was easier said than done. Now she was having a hard time keeping her mind on work when she knew Christopher was right across the hall.

That was the problem. He sat right. Across. The hall. And that's where he'd been, holed up in his office, for the better part of the day Monday.

Now it was midday Tuesday and he hadn't come into the office yet, which was no big deal. Before things had *changed* between them, she hadn't felt it necessary to know his schedule. They had never checked in with each other. Why should they do that now? It was a ridiculous thought.

Yet every time she heard a deep voice in the reception area she looked up, hoping to catch a glimpse of him.

To no avail.

He was acting as if nothing had happened between them. He wasn't exactly avoiding her. Or maybe he was…she wouldn't know because she hadn't seen him except for late yesterday afternoon, when she'd run into him as she was on her way out and he was on his way in. He'd held the elevator door for her, and he had acted like the same old Christopher—the "before sex" Christopher. After the initial exchange of hi-how-are-yous, he'd mentioned that he had the germ of a wonderful idea for educating people on how to intervene when they saw someone being bullied. He had been saddened and inspired by what had happened to Tonya at the Spring Fling.

"Maybe we can talk about it soon?"

"Absolutely," she'd said, trying to figure out if he had run with the idea because he knew how important the cause was to her. Then again, adding another leg to the bullying prevention campaign would reflect well on him, too.

Although she hadn't expected him to kiss her at the elevator, she had wished for a little more. A whispered *Saturday night rocked my world;* a *Let's do it again soon;* or even better, *What are you doing for dinner tonight?*

He looked as if he was about to say something, but the elevator had buzzed, scolding them for holding the doors open too long.

He'd simply said, "Don't let me keep you," and she'd answered, "Good night," and had gotten into the elevator...alone with her pride.

She wasn't about to let herself appear needy because at that point, weren't his feelings pretty clear?

Today, after paging through the handbook no fewer than five times, she still couldn't find the answer to her question about superior/subordinate relationships. Did that mean there was no policy? And why wasn't there one? Probably because not sleeping with your superior/subordinate was common sense—something every savvy professional knew.

Instead of driving herself crazy dwelling on it, she busied herself doing something more productive: polishing the recap of the Spring Fling event for the staff meeting next week.

As she was reading through her draft, her mind drifted. Maybe she should call him and ask him where they stood?

And maybe she should just stamp the word NEEDY on her forehead.

Stop it.

She had two choices. She could talk to Christopher about it, or be confident that things would turn out the way they were meant to be.

She had always prided herself on being confident. She had never obsessed over things she couldn't control, and she wasn't going to start now.

Realizing that her eyes had been scanning the recap but her mind had been thinking about Christopher and nothing of what she had just read had registered, she started back at the top of the page and forced herself to focus.

Bev buzzed her phone.

"Hey, Kinsley," she said. "Sawyer Fortune is on line one for you."

Sawyer Fortune?

"Thank you, Bev."

She pressed Line One.

"This is Kinsley Aaron."

"Hi, Kinsley, it's Sawyer Fortune. Am I catching you at a good time?"

"Absolutely, Sawyer," she said. "How can I help you?"

"I've been trying to reach Christopher today, but he seems to be unavailable. When I met with him the last time I was in town, he mentioned that the two of you worked closely in the community relations department, so I thought I would run it by you."

Sawyer went on to tell her about possible dates for the air-show fund-raiser that would benefit the Foundation. She assured him that she would talk to Christopher today and make sure he got back with Sawyer as soon as possible to reserve the date.

So, Christopher had even been unavailable to Sawyer.

That shed a new light on things. Something was up. Maybe that meant he wasn't avoiding her.

She was about to hang up with Sawyer when he said, "Oh, and, Kinsley, thanks for talking Christopher into calling his father. When I last spoke to Christopher, he said he had talked to Deke and that you were the one who had urged him to do so."

A knot of emotions formed in Kinsley's stomach as she mumbled something to Sawyer, then hung up the phone. He had called his father. That was great, a true breakthrough for him. He had told Sawyer that he had done so at her urging. That was tremendous, especially because he had mentioned her to Sawyer yesterday. She could let her mind go in all sorts of directions, imagining what he had said about her to his cousin.

But why did there always have to be a qualifier? If she had been the one who convinced him to take such an important step, why hadn't he shared the news with her? It was pretty important. He could've said something when they were standing at the elevator.

A cold, prickling realization settled around Kinsley. Maybe he hadn't shared this personal news with her because it was *personal*.

Maybe she needed to take a hint from his lack of communication over the past day and a half.

A bubble of laughter escaped, but the sound was dry and devoid of humor. Despite Christopher's claims to the contrary, he had a love-'em-and-leave-'em reputation. Facts were facts. She had put too much stock into their night together. Their...liaison.

Oh, God. That was all it had been.

Icy hot humiliation settled around her. She bit her lip until it throbbed in time with her pulse. She sat there—just sat there—for several long minutes, letting reality seep into her pores, flogging herself with I-told-you-sos.

You knew this was a very plausible outcome. Whenever she violated her gut instinct, she always lived to regret it.

Now, if she knew what was good for her, she'd get herself together. No moping. No sniping at Christopher. No looking back with regret.

She would not let this interfere with her work.

Because in her work, she would find the solidity that would distract her and camouflage the despair that colored everything in sight.

For what must've been the hundredth time, Kinsley reminded herself that the Fortunes considered blood thicker than water. She didn't want to chance losing her job should someone disapprove of her affair with Christopher. Or worse yet, if talk started around the office that Kinsley was attempting to sleep her way to the top, Christopher might see her as a burden and decide the office would be better off without her.

If she had learned one thing growing up in an abusive home, it was that the less attention you drew to yourself, the better off—the safer—you were in the long run. That meant no more jealous outbursts like the time she thought he was dating his etiquette coach.

From this moment forward, she would put a smile on her face and it would be business as usual.

Good thing, too, because when she looked up, Christopher was standing in her doorway smiling and holding a big presentation board.

Christopher was simply flat-out scared to fall in love. He recognized that but had no idea what to do, besides stop hiding and acting like a child. Kinsley deserved better than that.

He knew he had been distant, using the excuse that he had been immersed in work, busy coming up with a plan for them to use as a follow-up to the initiative that they'd started at the Spring Fling.

But if he were completely honest with himself, he had been avoiding Kinsley. By doing so, he didn't have to face his feelings.

Why could he analyze so easily, but he had no idea what to do with it?

He had been heartened by his father's newfound respect and bolstered by his uncle's good report.

With this newfound support system, in a day and a half he had managed to outline the basics of the follow-up program. His initial reaction had him wanting to involve Kinsley, but fear caused him to back away. He simply needed a cooling-off period, time to put things into perspective and remember how to be her colleague without wanting to undress her and lay her flat across his desk.

But seeing her at the elevator yesterday, he knew that his silence was hurting her. Hell, it was hurting *him*. But last night he'd decided that in a similar way that he'd reached out to Deke, he needed to break the ice with Kinsley.

He thought the best way to do that—at least, for starters—was to ask her opinion on the new idea.

As he stood in her office doorway, gripping the presentation board, he felt the same pull of attraction that he felt every time he looked at her.

"May I come in?" he asked.

Her blue eyes looked wary as she smiled at him. Her professional smile. He recognized it.

"Sure," she said.

He left the door open on purpose, to discourage the conversation from veering off on a personal path.

"Remember how I told you yesterday that I had come up with a new plan for us to use in the schools?"

She nodded. Yep. Her wall was up. He recognized that, too.

"This is intended as a tool for school guidance

counselors to use." Damn, this was harder than he had expected. The way she was looking at him…it was more like she was staring right through him. "I hope that it will help kids remember to not just stand there when someone is in trouble, but to act."

He realized that he was nervous as he turned the board around, showing her the acronym GET IN-VOLVED. Each letter of the words stood for an element of the program.

Christopher watched Kinsley as she read the board, her lips pressed into a thin line.

When she was finished, she simply nodded and said, "Get Involved, huh? That's good advice. Even if it is a little ironic coming from a man who seems to do everything in his power to avoid doing exactly that."

Chapter Thirteen

On Wednesday morning, Christopher still couldn't get Kinsley's face out of his head. The way she'd looked as she'd read the GET INVOLVED acronym.

She'd had good reason for looking so upset. The words obviously hit home.

Sitting at his desk, he rested his forehead on his palm. He was such an idiot. How could he not have seen the irony of the message before he brought it to her?

As soon as she'd read it, he'd seen it in her eyes. Sure, she kept a professional poker face, but she couldn't disguise the hurt. She'd told him it was perfect and then excused herself, saying she had a lunch engagement.

She'd walked out, leaving him sitting there with his presentation board on the desk and his foot in his mouth. He needed to practice what he preached.

GET INVOLVED?

His problem was that he was too afraid to get involved. So ridiculously terrified—of what? He had
better figure it out because his fear was going to cost
him the best thing that had ever happened to him.

They needed to talk about this. Even if he didn't
know what to say. He needed to let her know it wasn't
her; it was him. That she was smart and beautiful and
deserving of so much more than he could offer.

He picked up the phone to call her office. But then
he put it back down in the cradle. Maybe he should just
go talk to her. Common sense told him he should wait
until after work. He didn't want to upset her, but that
seemed as though he wasn't giving her enough credit.

He got up from his desk and made his way into the
reception area, but before he could get to Kinsley's
office, Bev intercepted him.

"Mr. Jamison just called," she said. "He wants to
see you in his office right away."

Christopher made his way to Emmett Jamison's
wing of the building. His administrative assistant,
Clara, was expecting him.

"Oh, good, there you are," she said. "He wants
to see you but he has another meeting at 10:30." She
glanced at her watch. "Oh, no problem. You have
plenty of time. Go right in."

As Christopher walked toward Emmett's door, he
heard Clara inform him that Christopher was on his
way in.

For a fleeting second, he wondered if this had to
do with the talk he had had with his father. But then
that gave way to the guilt he felt over how things had

turned out with Kinsley. Surely, she wouldn't have lodged a complaint against him, would she?

No, that would be completely out of character for her. But he couldn't ignore the little voice that jabbed at him and said she would be completely within her rights. He should've been stronger and not taken advantage of her while she was vulnerable, even though that's not at all what he had intended.

The same jabbing voice brought up words like love and feelings, but he ignored it as he rapped on Emmett's door.

"Come in."

Christopher opened the door and stepped inside. He was immediately set at ease by the broad smile that graced Emmett's face.

"Just the man I wanted to see," Emmett said. "Have a seat, please." He gestured to a chair in front of his desk.

Christopher complied.

As soon as he was settled Emmett picked up the display board that outlined the GET INVOLVED program. He tapped it with his finger.

"This is good work."

He paused, as if letting the praise ring in the air.

"You have done some impressive work in your short time here at the Foundation. I'm not the only one who has taken notice. But before I tell you what I have in mind, let me ask you, are you happy with what you're doing? Because you sure are doing a good job."

"I love what I'm doing. I truly feel like I've found my calling here at the Foundation."

"Great, that's exactly what I was hoping you would say. I have an opportunity I would like to talk to you about. We have discovered the need for a presence in New York City. I know New York is very different than Red Rock, but the work would be similar. We—the board, your uncle James, Lily and I—were hoping that you would be willing to take on the challenge. How would you feel about relocating to New York City and opening that office for us? We would love for you to be the man in charge. If anyone can do it, you could."

Emmett's offer caught Christopher so off guard, he couldn't even answer for a moment. He was truly stunned.

New York City? They wanted him to move out there and open the office?

But what about Kinsley?

"Would anyone else be in the office with me?" he asked. "Would I have a staff?"

Emmett steepled his fingers. "Not right off the bat. We would have to make sure that the new office was up and running and self-sustaining, of course—there's no mission without margin—before we could fully staff the office. But don't worry. We would pay to relocate you and give you a salary increase and housing allowance that would allow you to live comfortably in the city."

Of course, it would mean leaving behind everybody he had come to care so much about.

Kinsley's face was the first to flash in his mind again. Even before his newfound relatives and all the friends he had made since moving to Red Rock.

It was a tempting offer. It meant that they trusted him. It meant that they respected him and appreciated his vision. Uncle James, Lily and Emmett were the first people who had truly believed in him.

That inappropriate voice piped up inside him and reminded him that Kinsley had once believed in him too.

"I realize that this is a lot to think about," said Emmett. "I will have Clara draw up the specifics and get them to you by the end of the day. Why don't you take a few days to think about it before you let me know your answer? The sooner we can get you there, the better."

Christopher cleared his throat. "I want you to know how much I appreciate your confidence in me. I am greatly honored and humbled that you would entrust me with this position. I'll look forward to reviewing the details."

Emmett stood and offered Christopher his hand. Christopher stood and accepted it. What would Deke and Jeanne Marie think of this? His father had had a conniption when Christopher had accepted the job in Red Rock. If his father had thought this place was highfalutin, what in the world would he think of his son moving to New York City?

But Christopher reminded himself not to get too far ahead. He hadn't seen the offer yet. He had no idea what they intended in terms of dollars and cents.

Even though he wasn't anywhere close to making up his mind, he knew one of the biggest sacrifices he would be making would be leaving Kinsley behind.

Suddenly everything that had been so muddled and tentative seemed to snap into sharp focus. This job was everything he had ever wanted, except it didn't include Kinsley. But maybe time away from her in a place where he could focus on his job and not be distracted by her full lips and the way their bodies fit so perfectly together that it drove him nuts to even catch a glimpse of her in the office hallway was a good thing.

Maybe putting some distance between them was exactly what he needed. Then again, maybe this opportunity would cost him the one woman he had ever loved. But maybe that was case in point why he should go and not look back.

That evening Christopher sat at his desk reading— for the fifth time—the details of the generous New York City relocation offer that Clara had delivered to him just before five o'clock.

Among other perks, they were offering him nearly twice his current salary and a housing allowance that would afford him a comfortable apartment in Manhattan.

It was a far cry from Horseback Hollow and the life sentence on his family's ranch. This offer was a dream come true. And more than that, it was validation that he was good at his job. The board could've chosen anyone to head up this project, but they'd put their faith in him.

Christopher closed the file and leaned back in his leather chair, stretching his feet out in front of him and looking around his office. When he'd first gotten here, he'd thought this place was the be-all and end-all with its paneled walls, living room furniture and that view.

Now, he'd been handed the chance of a lifetime to write his own ticket.

So why was he hesitating?

The numbers checked out. It would be a long time before a chance like this would come along again, much less be dropped into his lap.

He needed to think about it. Sleep on it. Even if Emmett was pushing for a fast answer, Christopher needed a few hours to process everything. Then maybe this uncertainty would sort itself out.

In his head it was a no-brainer: only idiots passed up the chance of a lifetime for a woman. Especially when he'd had trepidations about their relationship before the deal was on the table.

However, now that the deal was on the table, his head and his heart were at odds.

He'd have to sort that out, and fast.

He put the file in his briefcase and clicked off his desk lamp.

It was after 6:30 p.m. The sun was painting the Western landscape outside his window in shades of gold and amber. Everything looked a little different in the light of this offer. As Christopher headed toward the elevator, the light that was still on in Kinsley's office drew him like a moth.

She was completely engaged in whatever it was she was reading on her computer screen. He stood there watching her, wanting to memorize the way she looked right now with her guard down and her hair hanging in soft curls around her shoulders. He owed it to her to tell her about the offer before she heard it from someone else.

"Don't you ever go home?" he said.

She startled and looked up at him. "Oh, Christopher. I didn't realize anyone else was still here."

"Just you and me," he said, his heart compressing at the words. "Do you have a minute?"

She pushed her mouse away and angled her body toward him. "Sure, come in."

He settled himself in the chair across from her.

"Everything okay?" she asked. Her hand fluttered to her blouse collar and she fidgeted with the top button, which, as always, was buttoned up tight.

Despite everything, he had to resist the urge to reach out and undo it and all the others and pull her into him so that he could lose himself in the Nirvana that was her.

And that was exactly why he needed to distance himself. He couldn't even think straight when he was with her. It was his own fault. Yep, it was all on him, and he needed to do something to regain his equilibrium.

"Everything is fine. More than fine, actually. I got a job offer today."

Her expression remained neutral. "Really? Where?"

"New York."

He told her how Emmett had called him into his office earlier.

"It's great money, and such an opportunity I can't see how I can refuse."

For a split second he thought he saw a flicker of regret flash in her blue eyes, and in that same split second he knew that if she said, "Don't go," he wouldn't. He'd turn down the offer and he'd take her home and make love to her until they'd finally figured out that this complicated thing between them didn't have to be so—

"How wonderful for you," she said, verbally slapping the sense back into him. "When do you leave for New York?"

* * *

Kinsley was happy for Christopher. Truly, she was.

And she had told him that yesterday when he stopped by her office. She said it with her most genuine a smile.

She wanted him to be happy.

Really, she did. And if she kept telling herself how happy she was that he was leaving, maybe she would start to believe it.

Even though she hadn't seen the specifics of the offer yet, Kinsley knew he would take it. The Fortunes were generous with their compensation. There was no way he would turn it down.

His leaving was probably the very best thing that could happen to both of them. He would relocate to a place where he could steep himself in big city, sophistication. She could keep her job here and maybe regain her concentration…and her heart.

Of course it would end up this way. Of course it would. This proved that it really was best that they hadn't committed to each other.

It was hard enough to know that he didn't want a relationship with her. The only thing that might've been harder was knowing that he did want a relationship and then him having to choose between her and his dream job.

She laughed to herself as she realized she had gotten it wrong. Women weren't Christopher's mistress; his work was.

She sat there trying to convince herself that this really was the best thing for both of them. If she said the words enough, surely she would begin to believe it. If not now, maybe by the time he made the move. Just then an email popped up in her computer inbox. Kinsley sat up a little straighter when she realized it was from Lily Cassidy Fortune.

The subject line read Surprise party for Christopher.

Kinsley clicked on the email.

Hello, Kinsley, I am calling on you for a rather large favor. Since you seem to be the colleague closest to Christopher, would you please take on the task of organizing a surprise going-away party for him? I was hoping we could do something nice for him— something a touch sentimental? I will leave it in your capable hands as I'm sure you will know exactly what to do to make Christopher realize how much he means to us and how grateful we are that he has accepted this challenge. We were hoping to have the party tomorrow, as he will be making the move this weekend. I know this is all terribly fast, but I'm sure Beverly will be happy to assist you with anything you need.

Kinsley fell back against her chair and her breath rushed from her lungs.

So it was official.

And he was leaving this weekend?

Christopher was leaving *this* weekend?

Her heart cracked open and filled with a leaden dread.

She wasn't surprised that he had accepted it. He'd all but made up his mind when they'd talked last night. She just hadn't realized he would leave so soon.

She fought the sudden urge to cry, blinking back the

unwelcome tears that clouded her vision. There was
no use getting emotional. It was for the best.

Really, it was.

She needed to treat this the same way one would rip
off a bandage—the faster the better. The sooner Christopher got on with his new life, the sooner she could
get on with her life here in Red Rock without him.

She sat there for several minutes in her quiet office, listening to the whir of the air conditioner and
the hum of her computer. Now that the tears were at
bay, a strange numbness had overtaken her.

She picked up the phone and called Bev.

They had less than twenty-four hours. They would
have to get this party planning rolling as soon as possible if they were going to pull it off.

The sooner they started planning, the sooner it
would be over.

Chapter Fourteen

"*SURPRISE!*"

The chorus of voices rang out when Emmett opened the conference room door and ushered Christopher inside.

Christopher blinked once, twice, three times as he looked around at all of his coworkers who had crowded into the conference room, surrounded by streamers and helium balloons.

"What the heck is this?"

His uncle James stepped forward and clapped him on the back. "This is your party, son. We wanted to give you a good sendoff on your last day here in the Red Rock office."

A surprise party?

He glanced at Emmett and murmured something unintelligible. Emmett grinned back at him, obviously proud that his paper-signing ruse had worked to get him to the conference room.

Christopher *was* surprised. Surprised and genuinely touched that everyone would gather on a Friday afternoon—just for him.

There were steaming covered chafing dishes in the middle of the conference room table being tended to by catering staff in uniforms with the Red logo. His stomach growled as he inhaled the delicious aroma of Red's Mexican food—a mélange of savory dishes blending with the aroma of fresh corn tortillas, chilies and spices. There were platters of Red's famous corn roasted in the husk stacked on platters which were next to the biggest cake he had ever seen in his life. And there was champagne.

That's when he realized that everyone was raising a glass toward him. Lily stepped forward and handed him and Emmett each a flute, too.

Emmett and James, who were flanking Christopher, simultaneously touched their glasses to his.

"I would like to propose a toast," said James. "To Christopher Fortune, our golden boy. May you shine in the city as brightly as you do here."

"To Christopher!" someone shouted and everyone raised their glasses a little higher, then took a sip.

Christopher glanced around the room, taking in his family, friends and coworkers: Miguel and Marcos Mendoza were there. So was their cousin Sierra Mendoza Calloway. Standing next to her was Emmett's wife, Linda Faraday. She was talking to Susan Fortune Eldridge and Julie Osterman Fortune. Nicholas and Jeremy Fortune were there. Then he saw Tanner and Jordana Redmond and Sawyer and his wife, Laurel—

had they come all the way from Horseback Hollow to be here just for him?

As people surrounded him, offering handshakes, high fives and fist bumps, he realized how much he truly cared for these people.

It was a bit overwhelming.

Funny, before he got here, when he had first taken on the Fortune name, he had imagined them all to be so different than they had turned out to be. Not in a bad way. In fact, they were better than he could've ever imagined. They were all warm, loving, family-oriented people, and he was proud to be one of them.

And when Sawyer came over and shook his hand, Christopher experienced an inexplicable pang of homesickness for his immediate family in Horseback Hollow. Even Deke.

Especially Deke.

As the good wishes continued and people rallied around him—it was a good thing he wasn't claustrophobic—he found himself craning his neck searching for the one person he was desperate to see.

Finally, he saw Kinsley standing by the table with the champagne, refilling glasses, doing what she was so good at—helping other people.

His gaze was drawn to her like a pin to a magnet. He drank her in, trying to take a mental snapshot of her gorgeous face, her blue-blue eyes that were framed by eyebrows a few shades darker than her sun-streaked blond hair. Her finely chiseled cheekbones. The delicate slope of her neck. Her full lips.

He could still feel those lips on his. He could feel the way their bodies had fit so perfectly, as if they were made for each other. A surge of longing so deep and fraught with desire for her consumed him.

It was as if he were seeing her for the first time. Through new eyes. Now he wanted her even more than he had the first time he'd seen her.

Why was it that he never really appreciated what he had when he had it? Why did he always wonder if something better was around the corner? Standing here in the midst of the crowd, among all these well-wishers, his heart spoke loud and clear: there wasn't a better woman in the world for him than Kinsley Aaron.

He had to tamp down the urge to fight his way through the crowd and pull her into his arms. His heart ached for her.

As much as he loved the attention and the accolades and the thought that his uncle James and Lily Cassidy Fortune trusted him—*him,* the guy who never seemed to have the capability to do anything right back in Horseback Hollow—with opening their satellite office in a city like New York, and even though they had been more than generous with the compensation and benefits package that they had given him, moving to New York would mean losing touch with everyone that mattered to him.

And it would mean losing Kinsley.

Suddenly his future flashed before his eyes in a crystal-clear vision: he would have the money and the dream job and the prestige and everything he could ever want at his disposal in a big city where the world would be his oyster, but it would never be enough. He would never be satisfied with all of that because it was empty. Well, the work had proved to be fulfilling, but all the money in the world couldn't replace what he had found in Red Rock.

Being here, he had learned how to go home again.

He had learned the value of everything money couldn't buy.

Was he really willing to give up everything for... emptiness?

He excused himself from his colleagues and made his way over to Emmett and James, who were standing with Linda and Lily.

"This is a fabulous party," Christopher said. "I can't thank you enough."

Lily set a slender hand on his arm. "Oh, honey, I wish we could all take credit for this party. But this is all Kinsley Aaron. Is there anything that woman can't do? Didn't she do a lovely job?"

"There is absolutely nothing she can't do," Christopher said. "She's even taught me a thing or two since I've been working with her. So I'm not at all surprised to learn that she is the one responsible for this."

Christopher watched Kinsley as she cut the cake and put small squares on the colorful party plates. He watched her as she worked while everyone else was enjoying themselves. She was always willing to go the extra mile for somebody else. Always willing to sacrifice even if it meant standing back while somebody else shined.

How could he have been such a damn fool?

How could he have been willing to let go of the only woman in this world he would ever be able to love?

Christopher turned to James and Emmett. "If you don't mind, I need to speak to the two of you privately."

Both men did a double-take.

"Right now?" asked James. "In case you didn't notice, son, there's a party going on. Rumor has it it's in your honor."

"That's exactly why I need to talk to you now," said Christopher. "This can't wait."

Just keep yourself busy and it'll be over faster.

Kinsley was not in the mood to party. But she sure was good at playing the role of the hostess.

She reminded herself that this was not about her. It had nothing to do with her. She needed to keep smiling and keep her eye on the light at the end of the tunnel.

It would all be over soon.

So, Kinsley refilled the tortilla platters and the water pitchers. She brought out extra bottles of soda and champagne and replenished the paper goods, cups and the plastic utensils.

As she looked around, she caught a glimpse of Christopher. He was talking to Mr. Jamison, Lily Fortune and James Marshall Fortune. She looked away but not before she felt the heat of his gaze on her.

But then, when she glanced back, he was gone. Probably hidden by one of the one hundred balloons in the room. She breathed a sigh of relief and moved around the chafing dishes the catering staff had just replenished.

Good grief, these people were tough customers. From the way they were devouring the food you would think they hadn't eaten in days. But who could blame them? Red prided itself on delicious food. Today they offered beef brisket enchiladas, chicken mole and spicy lobster tacos. She was having to hustle now, but the more they ate, the less she and the staff would have to clean up later.

And the more work she would have to keep her hands busy and her mind off the reason for the party.

Christopher. The mere thought of him made her chest tighten and her heart squeeze.

Stop it.

But what good did fighting it do? She kept her head down and allowed herself to switch over to autopilot. To let the thoughts and feelings come and go as they would. Maybe if she leaned into the emotions she'd have an easier time of it.

Or maybe she would break down into a heaping, sobbing mess and really humiliate herself. She took a deep breath and released it slowly.

No, it seemed that the thoughts and feelings were hidden deep enough under the surface. Even so, everyone else in this room was so convivial and having such a good time that no one had a clue that her heart was breaking.

Scratch that. Her heart had already broken. Past tense. For days, she had been carrying around a bunch of bits and pieces of broken heart that she knew would never be able to fit back together again.

That was okay. She didn't have any use for her heart anymore. She just hoped the pieces didn't rattle.

Stepping outside of herself, she had to admit that Christopher had seemed astonished. It was always nice when a surprise party went off the way it was planned.

That's right. Focus on the good. There you go.

She resisted the urge to look up and search the crowd for him. So far, playing caterer had helped her

to not moon over him, to not watch what he was doing
or who he was talking to. It just hurt too much.

Plus, the last thing she needed was for someone
she worked with to discover her secret: that she was
brokenhearted because had slept with Christopher and
the affair had gone horribly, disastrously wrong. *That*
could be misconstrued in so many ways.

Normally, she didn't care what people thought of
her. But this was a different case. She may have lost
her heart, but it was imperative for her to walk away
with her integrity and dignity intact. Because what had
happened between Christopher and her hadn't been
like that. She wasn't using him to get favors or a boost
up the corporate ladder.

It was...

Yeah, it was.

And it was over now. She needed to get over it. But
it had only been a week since she had given herself—
body and soul—to him; her heart still felt tender and
her pride was pretty raw.

What had she expected? She knew what she had
wanted. But what you want and what you get were
sometimes two entirely different things.

What she had gotten was a lesson. She didn't give
her heart away easily. And she wouldn't do it again
anytime soon. After all, who would want the bag of
broken pieces she stored in the place where her heart
had once lived?

She would feel better someday. It would just take
time. Right now she needed to keep her chin up.

Chin up, buttercup. Her mom used to say that when
they'd hit a rough patch. God, what she wouldn't give
to be able to go to her mother right now. Not for ad-

vice, but for a shoulder. For the shelter of her hugs. She had been the one person in whom Kinsley had found unrequited love.

And if she'd learned one thing from watching her mother it was that sometimes when you loved too much your generous spirit became your undoing.

Unlike her mother, she had a second chance to reclaim herself. Rather than mooning, she would embrace the blessing in this narrow miss.

Right…

Forcing herself to look up, she glanced around the room admiring her handiwork—not looking for Christopher. Everyone was chatting, and the buzz of convivial energy filled the room. The helium balloons she had procured did a fairly decent job of hiding her—or hiding him. Either way, because they were clustered in the area where she had been hiding out, she had to make an effort to look for him. As if blatantly defying her, her eyes swept the room looking for him, but before she could pick him out she came face-to-face with a giant yellow balloon…well, what better caution sign could a girl ask for?

She was running the risk of driving herself crazy, so she made another conscious effort to refocus. She scanned the food tables in search of something to distract her, but it appeared that everyone was finally slowing down. Nothing needed refilling or replenishing or replacing.

She picked up a couple of empty cups and plates, realizing if she felt like the hired help, it was because she had put herself in that position. The catering staff would take care of this. She swiped the back of her hand across her forehead, then tucked an errant strand of hair behind her ear.

Maybe she would have a glass of champagne. She didn't really feel like celebrating, but that was no reason to boycott the bubbly. In fact, looking on the bright side, she should celebrate the fact that she'd pulled this off.

Who would've thought that planning a party would be one of the hardest assignments she'd ever faced?

The old adage what doesn't kill you makes you stronger definitely applied here.

She had just poured herself a glass of champagne when Mr. Jamison called everyone in the conference room to order.

"May I have your attention, please? Everyone, please settle down and listen. Christopher has something he would like to say."

Oh, boy. Here we go.

The room quieted down and everybody turned their attention to Christopher. For the first time that afternoon, Kinsley stopped what she was doing and gave him her ears.

Mr. Jamison turned to Christopher and murmured, "Are you sure this is what you want to do?"

Christopher nodded. "Actually, I've never been so sure about anything in my life." He glanced at Kinsley, and their gazes locked. She wanted to look away, but she couldn't. "Well, maybe I've been that sure about one other thing, and she's a big part of the reason that I'm going to say what I have to say. I appreciate this party. I appreciate everybody gathering here to wish me well and to give me such a great sendoff. However, turns out a funny thing happened on the way to the cake table. I realize I won't be moving to New York, after all."

Kinsley was frozen in place, desperately pulling back on the reins of her heart, which was hopefully anticipating a preposterous turn of events that would surely never be.

So just stop it.

Audible gasps mixed with surprised murmurs and astonished glances, but Christopher's gaze didn't waver from hers.

"It's always been important to me to be respected and regarded as an intelligent man. But it took a party like this, a gathering of my family and friends and one hell of a party planner—everybody please give Kinsley a round of applause for the wonderful job she did to bring us all together—to clarify some things for me."

Her hand fluttered to her collar. *Oh, why did he do that?*

She finally broke their gaze and glanced around at the people who were clapping for her. She really wished they wouldn't do that.

When they quieted down, Christopher continued. "Today I realize that I love Texas too much to leave. I have just gotten to know my Fortune family, and quite frankly I'm not ready to put that much distance between us. But most of all, there is someone special here I simply can't bear to leave behind."

Kinsley's heart stopped beating for what seemed like an eternity. When it resumed, it picked up double time.

"She has made me a better person. I haven't quite figured out how this happened, and I'm pretty sure I don't deserve her. But I love her. I love her with my entire being, and I can't imagine my life without her."

Kinsley's gasp was audible, surprising even herself. Heat crept up her neck and fanned across her cheeks as every gaze in the place turned to her.

She wasn't sure if she wanted to cry tears of joy or crawl under the table to escape scrutiny. The tears of joy definitely won out. This unusual proclamation of love certainly wasn't what she had expected when she thought about Christopher declaring his love, but had Christopher Fortune ever done anything by the book?

"I wouldn't blame Kinsley if she killed me right now," Christopher said, hoping he hadn't gone too far with this workplace pronouncement. "So if you see me with a piece of cake smashed in my face, it probably doesn't mean we've gotten married. It probably means she simply smashed that cake in my face, which I suppose I would deserve."

He was relieved when everyone laughed.

He couldn't quite see Kinsley, who had gradually worked her way to the back of the room. Hell, he didn't blame her—he probably shouldn't have gotten so carried away. It would serve him right if she told him to take a hike.

He remembered his initial vow to win her over no matter what. He fully expected to have to work harder than he'd ever worked his entire life to get her to commit to him. He'd never looked so forward to a challenge. Speaking of challenges, he still owed everyone the rest of the explanation. He turned back to the group and continued.

"Plenty of folks right here in this room are probably

better qualified than I am to open an office in the Big Apple. I was thinking about that while I was standing here enjoying everyone's company. So I offered Emmett, James and Lily a new proposal for the Fortune Foundation, but this one hits a little closer to home. With their blessing, I will be opening a satellite office of the Foundation in Horseback Hollow, with an anti-bullying/GET INVOLVED initiative. I will split time between Horseback Hollow and Red Rock. So, I'm sorry to say that you haven't gotten rid of me yet."

As his family and coworkers applauded this news, Christopher scanned the room for Kinsley, wanting to gauge her reaction, but he didn't see her. He wanted to go find her, but people approached and started the whole process all over again of shaking his hand, slapping him on the back and congratulating him—on the satellite office and on falling in love with a wonderful woman. They all seemed genuinely pleased for him. It was very moving, but he was starting to get a little anxious over Kinsley's absence.

Had she left?

He wouldn't blame her if she'd walked out. But if she had, he would fix it.

If it was the last thing he did, he would fix things between them.

He excused himself again from the knot of well-wishers and went to look for her.

He found her in the reception area standing quietly gazing out the window. It was a similar view as from his office, the one that had captivated him from the start. He'd thought the south Texas landscape couldn't look more beautiful. But he'd never seen it as a backdrop to Kinsley.

"I meant what I said in there," he said. "I'm in love with you. I may have changed my mind about the job, but I'm not going to change my mind about you. All I need to know is do I even stand a chance after all I've put you through?"

She turned and met his gaze. Her beautiful eyes were brimming with tears. In that instant he knew everything was going to be okay.

He walked over to her, pulled her into his arms and reached up and brushed a tear off her cheek.

"Don't worry," she said. "They're happy tears. I love you, too."

Kinsley was never so happy to leave a party— even one she'd planned. But she knew the two of them would have a much better time at the after party—in Christopher's bed.

With him, she was home, even amid the partially packed boxes that would now need to be unpacked. Yes, she was more than happy to help him with this task. It was the packing and the goodbyes she couldn't bear.

They spent a long, luxurious evening making love and snuggling and making love and snuggling. She couldn't tell if they were making up for lost time or living in the moment, but it didn't matter. They didn't need to define it. They already had when they had exchanged those three precious words that even twelve hours ago she feared she would never hear cross his lips.

If she had learned one thing about Christopher it was that when he said something he meant it. His word was golden, and Kinsley basked in the glow of it as he held her.

She splayed her hand across his chest, reveling in the downy-soft feel of his chest hair.

"So, speaking of being the last to know…" she said.

He pulled her closer, as if he were afraid she would get away.

"Oh, hell…here we go." He smiled and pretended to roll his eyes before he kissed her soundly. "I knew there would be hell to pay for what I did. May I make it up to you…again? Because I am perfectly willing to make love to you until you fully understand just how much I love you."

He shifted her to the side and then rolled on top of her.

"Oh, you have no idea how much trouble you are in, mister." She kissed his neck and then nipped at his earlobe as he nudged her legs apart and entered her again.

After they were spent and breathless, she managed to catch her breath. "As I was saying, I had to hear through the grapevine that you called your father. And that the two of you had a good talk."

He did a double-take. "Oh, yeah? Who is spreading such rumors?"

"I'm not telling."

He grinned at her slyly. "I thought we promised that there would be no secrets between us. Am I going to have to assign you penance?"

"Please do. I could be a very happy woman doing atonement with you." She traced his lips with her index finger, getting momentarily lost in the mix of masculine strength and male beauty that was Christopher.

She swallowed around a lump of love and gratitude that had settled in her throat.

Or maybe it was her heart that was so full it was spilling over. Whatever the case, she never wanted it to go away. She wanted it to keep bubbling up like a fountain.

She settled into the crook of his arm and rested her head in that place on his shoulder that seemed to be made just for her.

"Actually, it's not a rumor," he said. "I did call my dad. Deke said to tell you hello."

"Really?" she asked.

"No, but I do want to take you home to Horseback Hollow so that you can meet him and my mother. I know she'll love you. They will all love you. Maybe not quite as much as I do, but I don't know that that's humanly possible. But I digress.

"The call went great. Better than great. I underestimated my father. I learned that he and I are two different men, but that's okay. We have finally come to the point where we accept that and respect each other for who we are."

"I'm so glad," Kinsley said.

Gently, he rubbed her back in a slow, rhythmic motion that was almost hypnotizing. She couldn't remember the last time she had been this relaxed.

"I might not have called him—or at least not so soon—if not for you. Thank you for that. Thank you for always seeing the best in me."

"Well, not *always*— Remember, you still have a lot of penance before you're completely redeemed. But I can assure you that I do love what I see."

They were quiet for a moment. The air-conditioning

clicked on. Somewhere out in the world, outside the snug cocoon that had become their universe, a car door shut and a dog barked.

"So, who do you look like—your mom or your dad?"

"Everyone says I take after my dad. In looks and personality. My brothers say that's why Deke and I butt heads so often. That we're too much alike."

"I'd love to see a picture of him sometime. He must be a good-looking guy."

Christopher stretched. "My mama thinks so. She's stuck with him for forty years. Can you believe they've been married that long?"

"I think that's wonderful."

"Maybe that gives you a little hope for me. I don't commit easily, but once I do, I'm sort of like gum on your shoe."

"That's *so* romantic."

They laughed. She loved the way they didn't take themselves too seriously.

"At least I think I'll be the gum on your shoe. I've never loved someone enough to be their gum."

"Wow. How did I get so lucky?"

They laughed again, and when they stopped, she lost herself in his sigh of contentment.

"So, now, tell me again, how many brothers and sisters do you have?"

"I'm one of seven."

"Holy cow. Your poor mother."

"Nah, Mama loved her children. There are two girls and five boys, including me. A handful."

"Sounds like your mother should be canonized."

"Yup, pretty much. Wait—" he said sitting up suddenly. "I want to show you something."

Kinsley enjoyed watching him walk from the bed to the bedroom door.

"What a fine specimen you are, Mr. Fortune."

When he returned he was holding a photo album. The one she remembered seeing in his car that night they went to Mendoza's.

The night everything started.

"What's that?" she asked as he climbed back into bed beside her.

"It's a photo album my mother sent me to remind me of where I came from."

"And you're letting me look now? Remember that night before we went to Mendoza's? I thought you were going to smack my hand away from it."

He looked at her solemnly, momentarily sobering. "Besides loving you for the rest of your life, the other thing I can promise you is that I will never, ever raise a hand to you."

She inhaled sharply and nodded.

In that moment, she sensed that her mother was with her. That her mother, the angel, had quite possibly sent Christopher to watch over her. The kind of man she should have, rather than the kind of bad example her father had set.

Everything is going to be all right, Mom. Everything is fine now.

"Here," said Christopher. "Look at this picture. Here's my dad when he was about my age."

Wrapped in the sheet, Kinsley scooted up and sat next to Christopher on the bed.

She studied the picture, loving this new window into her love's world. "Wow, you do look like him."

"My dad's name is Jones. Deke Jones. I'm going to start using Jones in my name again. How would you feel about being part of the Fortune Jones family?"

"Hmm...Kinsley Aaron Fortune Jones," she said. "That's a mouthful. But it sounds like poetry to me."

When Christopher leaned in and kissed her. She knew that she was home, that she had finally found her family at last.

* * * * *

FORTUNE'S PRINCE

BY
ALLISON LEIGH

There is a saying that you can never be too rich or too thin. **Allison Leigh** doesn't believe that, but she does believe that you can *never* have enough books! When her stories find a way into the hearts—and bookshelves—of others, Allison says she feels she's done something right. Making her home in Arizona with her husband, she enjoys hearing from her readers at Allison@allisonleigh. com or Po Box 40772, Mesa, AZ 85274-0772, USA.

For all the Fortune Women
As always, it is an honor to be among you.

Chapter One

He stopped cold when he heard a faint rustle. The only light there was came from the moonlight sneaking through the barn door that he'd left open behind him.

Standing stock-still, Quinn Drummond listened intently, his eyes searching the black shadows around him. He'd built the barn. He knew it like the back of his hand. He knew the sounds that belonged, and the ones that didn't. Animal or human, it didn't matter. He knew.

He reached out his right hand, unerringly grabbing onto a long wooden handle. He'd prefer his shotgun, but it was up in the house. So the pitchfork would have to do.

This wasn't some damn possum rooting around.

This was some*one*. Someone hiding out in his barn.

He knew everyone who lived in his Texas hometown. Horseback Hollow was the polar opposite of a metropolis. If someone there wanted something, they'd have come to his face, not skulk around in the middle of the night inside his barn.

His hand tightened around the sturdy handle. His focus followed the rustling sound and he took a silent step closer to it. "Come on out now, because if you don't, I promise you won't like what's gonna happen."

The faint rustle became a scuffling sound, then the darkness in front of him gathered into a small form.

His wariness drained away. His tight grip relaxed. Just a kid.

He made a face and set aside the pitchfork. "What'd you do? Run away from home?" He'd tried that once, when he was seven. Hadn't gotten far. His dad had hauled him home and would have tanned his butt if his mother hadn't stepped in. "Never works, kid," he advised. "Whatever you think you're running from will always follow."

The form shuffled closer; small, booted feet sliding into the faint moonlight, barely visible below the too-long hem of baggy pants. "That's what I'm afraid of," the shadow said.

Forget wariness. The voice didn't belong to a child. It was feminine. Very British. And so damn familiar his guts twisted and his nerves frizzed like they wanted to bust out of his skin. A runaway would have been preferable to this. To *her*.

Amelia.

Her name blasted through his head, but he didn't say a word and after a moment, she took another hesitant step closer. Moonlight crept from the dark boots up baggy pants, an untucked, oversize shirt that dwarfed her delicate figure, until finally, *finally,* illuminating the long neck, the pointed chin.

The first time that he'd seen her had been six months ago on New Year's Eve, at a wedding for one of her newly discovered cousins, right there in Horseback Hollow. Her long dark hair had been twisted into a knot, reminding him vaguely of the dancers at the ballet that his mom had once dragged him and his sister to. The second time that he'd seen her months later at the end of April, had been at another wedding. Another cousin. And her hair had been tied up then, too.

But that second time, after dreaming about her since New Year's, Quinn hadn't just watched Amelia from a distance.

No.

He'd approached her. And through some miracle of fate—or so he'd thought at the time—later that night, he'd taken the pins from her hair and it had spilled down past her shoulders, gleaming and silky against her ivory skin.

He blocked off the memory. He'd had enough practice at it over the past two months that it should have been easy.

It wasn't. It was the very reason he was prowling restlessly around in the middle of the night at all when he should have been sleeping.

"What the hell'd you do to your hair?"

She made a soft sound and lifted her hand to the side of the roughly chopped short hair sticking out from her head. She'd have looked like a boy if her delicate features weren't so distinctively feminine. "It's lovely to see you, too." She moved her hand again, and it came away with the hair.

A wig. It was stupid to feel relieved, but he did.

She scrubbed the fingers of her other hand across

her scalp, and her hair, the real stuff, slid down in a coil over one shoulder, as dark as the night sky. "It's a wig," she said, stating the obvious. Her voice was unsteady. "The second one, actually. The first was blond, but there were reporters at the airport, and—" She shook her head, breaking off.

That night—the night he'd twisted his hands in her hair and thought he'd tasted perfection on her lips—she'd talked about the reporters who had dogged her family's footsteps for as long as she could remember. How she hated being in a fishbowl. How her life felt claustrophobic. How she envied his life on a ranch; the wide-open spaces, the wind at his back when he rode his horse.

Again, he pushed away the thoughts. He shoved his fingertips into the pockets of his jeans, wishing he could wipe away the memory of her silky hair sliding over his chest as they'd made love. "What are you doing here?"

"In your barn? Proving I'm better at remembering a Google Map than I thought." She let out a nervous sound that was maybe supposed to be a laugh but could have been a sob.

"Not my barn," he said tightly. *"Here."*

She took a quick, audible breath. She was young. Seven years younger than his own thirty. Practically a girl. Except she wasn't a girl. She was full-grown. Self-possessed. Aristocratic.

And now, she was hiding in his barn, stumbling around for words.

"Amelia," he prompted sharply. He couldn't pretend her unexpected appearance didn't make him tense. Any more than she could hide the fact that she was clearly nervous. The way she kept shifting from one foot to the other, almost swaying, told him that.

"Yes. Right. The, um, the last time we spoke—"

"*What* are you doing here?" He didn't want to rehash that phone conversation. It had been nearly two months ago. He didn't want to think about what had precipitated it. Didn't want to think about it and damn sure didn't want to feel anything about it. Not that conversation, or whatever was making her so skittish now.

Her lips moved again but no sound came out. She lifted her hand to the side of her head again. Swayed almost imperceptibly.

And pitched forward.

He let out an oath, his heart nearly jumping out of his chest, and barely caught her limp body before it hit the ground at his feet.

He crouched beside her, carefully holding her. He caught her chin in his hand. She felt cold. And was out cold. "Amelia!"

Dim light or not, he could see that her lashes, so dark against her pale, pale cheeks, didn't so much as flicker.

He rose, lifting her in his arms. It was easy. He routinely tossed around hay bales that weighed more than she did, and she seemed even thinner now than the night he'd replaced her fancy gown with his hands. She was neither short, nor tall. Pretty average height. But that was the only thing average about Amelia Fortune Chesterfield.

Everything else—

He shook his head, blowing out a breath and carried her out of the barn, not even bothering to pull the door closed though he'd likely come back in the morning to find that possum taking up residence there again. He aimed for his truck parked up by the house, about a hundred yards away, his stride fast and gaining speed as he went. The moonlight shone down on her, painting her face an even whiter hue, and her gleaming head bounced against his arm as he ran.

He could hardly breathe by the time he made it to his truck, and it wasn't because he was out of shape. It was because the nearest hospital was in Lubbock, a good hour away.

He could deal with a lot of minor medical emergencies.

He couldn't deal with an unconscious Amelia Fortune Chesterfield.

Adjusting his grip beneath her, he managed to get the door open with one hand and settled her on the seat.

Her head lolled limply to the side, quickly followed by her lax shoulders.

"Come on, princess," he whispered, gently situating her again, holding her up long enough to get the safety belt clipped in place. The chest strap held her back against the seat and he started to draw his hands away from her waist and her shoulders so he could close the door, but her arm shifted slightly. Then her hand. Sliding over his, lighter than a breath but still enough to make the world seem to stop spinning.

"I'm not a princess," she whispered almost inaudibly.

He exhaled roughly. She'd said the same thing *that* night, too.

Only then she'd been looking up at him through her lashes; a combination of innocence and sexiness that had gone to his head quicker than the finest whiskey.

Maybe she wasn't a princess. But she was still the youngest daughter of Lady Josephine Fortune Chesterfield and the late Sir Simon John Chesterfield. And since it had come out last year that Horseback Hollow's own resident Jeanne Marie Jones was a long-lost sister of Lady Josephine, the Chesterfield family was officially one of the town's hottest topics. Even Quinn's own sister, Jess, usually practical and definitely down-to-earth, had been struck royal-crazy. It had gotten so bad lately that he'd pretty much avoided her whenever he could, just so he wouldn't have to listen to her jabber on about the latest news from across the pond.

And for the past few months, particularly, he couldn't even visit the Superette in town to pick up his weekly milk and bread without seeing a magazine on the racks that mentioned Amelia in some way.

He took her hand and set it away from him, backing away to slam the truck door closed. He strode around the front and got in behind the wheel, not wanting to look at her, yet not being able to stop himself from doing so. The dome light shining on her face was more relentless than the moonlight, showing the dark circles under her eyes.

She looked ill.

He swiftly turned the key and started the engine. "I'm taking you to the hospital in Lubbock," he said flatly.

She shifted, her hand reaching for his arm again. Her fingertips dug into his forearm with surprising strength for someone who'd nearly face-planted in the dirt. "I don't need a hospital," she said quickly. "Please." Her voice broke.

"You need something." He shrugged off her touch and steered the truck away from the house. "And you won't find it here."

She sucked in an audible breath again and even though he knew he was in the right, he still felt like a bastard.

"You fainted. You need a doctor."

"No. I just... It's just been a long trip. I haven't eaten since, well since Heathrow, I guess."

He wasn't going to ask why. Wasn't going to let himself care. She was just another faithless woman. He'd already graduated from that school and didn't need another course. "First-class fare not up to your standards?"

She ignored his sarcasm. "I was in economy." She plucked the collar of her shirt that was mud-colored in the truck's light. "I was trying not to be noticed." She turned away, looking out the side window. "For all the good that did. I managed to lose Ophelia Malone before I left London, but there were still two more photographers to take her place the second I landed." She sighed. "I lost them in Dallas, but only because I changed my disguise and caught a bus."

He nearly choked. "You rode a bus? From Dallas to Horseback Hollow?" It had to have taken hours. On top of the flight, she'd probably been traveling for nearly twenty-four hours. "You have no business riding around on a bus!"

She didn't look at him, but even beneath the rough clothes that dwarfed her slender figure, he could tell she stiffened. "It's a perfectly convenient mode of transportation," she defended.

Sure. For people like him. He was a small-town rancher. She was *the* Amelia Fortune Chesterfield. And since the day she'd returned to England after her night dabbling with Quinn—after making him believe that she was going back to London only to attend to some royal duties and would quickly return to Horseback Hollow—she'd become one half of the engaged couple dubbed "Jamelia" by the media that dogged her steps.

Amelia Fortune Chesterfield was to marry James

Banning in the most popular royal romance since the Duke and Duchess of Cambridge. *Lord* James Banning. A viscount, whatever the hell that was. A man who was her equal in wealth and family connections. A man who was slated for an even higher title, evidently, once Amelia was his wife. Earl something of something or other.

His sister had talked about it so many times, the facts ought to be tattooed on his brain.

His fingers strangled the steering wheel. "Wedding plans becoming so taxing that you had to run away from them?" He didn't wait for an answer. "Never mind. I don't want to know." He turned through the overhead arch bearing the iron Rocking-U sign and pressed harder on the gas. The highway was still a fair piece away, but once he hit that, it'd be smooth sailing. He'd leave her in capable medical hands and wash his hands of her, once and for all.

Somewhere inside his head, laughter mocked the notion. He'd been doing that so-called washing for the past two months and hadn't gotten anywhere. There had to be something wrong with him that he couldn't just file her away as a one-night stand where she belonged and be done with it.

"*Please* don't take me to Lubbock," she said huskily. "I don't need a doctor. I just need some sleep. And some food." She reached across as if she were going to touch his arm again, but curled her fingers into a fist instead, resting it on the console between their seats. "Drop me on the side of the road if you must. I'm begging you. Please, Quinn."

He ground his molars together. Would he have had more resistance if she hadn't said his name? "I'm not gonna drop you on the side of the damn road."

He should take her to Jeanne's. Recently discovered family or not, the woman was Amelia's aunt. Jeanne would take her in. Even if it *was* the middle of the night.

He muttered an oath and pulled a U-turn there on the empty highway.

Maybe Amelia wouldn't mind Jeanne's questions, asked or unasked, but Quinn would. Particularly when he had unanswered questions of his own.

He didn't look at her. "I'll take you back to the Rocking-U. And then you can start talking."

His voice was so hard.

His face so expressionless.

Amelia wrapped her arms around herself and tried to quell her trembling. She was so, so tired.

She'd foolishly thought that once she got back to Horseback Hollow, once she saw Quinn in person, everything would be all right.

She could explain. And he would understand.

He would take her in his arms, and everything would be perfect and as wonderful as it had been the night of her cousin Toby's wedding. Quinn would know that there was only him. That there had only ever been him.

It had been the single thing keeping her going throughout the dreadful ordeal of getting to Horseback Hollow.

"You can start—" Quinn's deep voice cut through her "—with explaining why you came to the Rocking-U at all."

"I wanted to talk," she whispered.

He gave her a long look. Animosity rolled off him in waves, a stark contrast to the tender warmth he'd shown her just six weeks earlier. "Yet so far you haven't said anything new."

She wanted to wring her hands. Such a silly, naive girl to think that her presence would be enough to make up for everything she hadn't said that she should have. For everything she hadn't done that she should have.

"What did Banning do? Disagree over china patterns? So you run away again to the States to bring him to heel? Your last trip here was pretty effective. Ended up with a royal engagement the second you got back home. Or maybe you're just in the mood for one more final fling before the 'I do's' get said."

"I told you weeks ago that there's no engagement," she reminded carefully. After a week of the frantic telephone messages she'd left for him once she'd arrived in London, he'd finally returned her call. She'd tried to explain to him then about the media frenzy that had greeted her at the airport when she'd returned from Toby's wedding.

Reporters shouting their congratulations on her engagement to James. Cameras flashing in her eyes. She'd been blindsided by the unwanted attention as much as she'd been blindsided by news of an engagement she and James had discussed, but had never agreed to.

He grunted derisively. "And I don't believe you any more now than I did when you said it the first time. You came to Horseback Hollow two months ago and you had sex with the poor dumb cowboy who didn't know enough to recognize things for what they were. Your little walk on the wild side, I guess, before settling down all nice and proper with the English earl."

"James isn't an earl yet." Which was the furthest thing from what she wanted to say.

"I don't give a damn what he is or isn't." He slowed to make the turn through the iron archway, but the tires still kicked out an angry, arching spit of gravel. "He's your fiancé. That's the only thing I have to know. And as good as you were in the sack, princess, I'm not interested in a repeat performance."

She bit down on her tongue to keep from gasping and stared hard out the side window until the tears pushing behind her eyes subsided. They hadn't ever made it to a "sack," as he so crudely put it. They'd made love under the moonlight in a field of green, surrounded by trees, singing crickets and croaking frogs. She'd slept in his arms under the stars and wakened at dawn to chirping birds and his kisses.

It had been magical.

"It was six weeks ago," she whispered.

He still managed to hear. "Six. Eight. Whatever it was, it no longer matters to me. You want to screw around with a cowboy, do it on someone else's ranch."

She snapped her head around, looking at him. Even though it was dark as pitch, and the only light came from the glow of his pickup truck's instrument panel, she still knew every inch of his face. Every detail. From the dark brown hair springing thickly back from his sun-bronzed forehead to the spiky lashes surrounding his hazel eyes to his angular jaw. She knew his quiet smile. The easy way he held his tall, muscular body.

"Don't do that," she said sharply. "Don't cheapen what we had."

"What we had, prin*cess*—" he drew out the word in a mocking British accent "—was a one-night stand. And the next day, you returned to the loving arms of your intended. Poor bastard. Does he know what he's getting?" He pulled to a stop in front of a modestly sized two-storied house and turned off the engine. "Or maybe he doesn't care. Maybe he's just happy to merge one highfalutin' family with another and fidelity doesn't matter one little bit."

"He's not my fiancé!"

"And that's what you came all the way here to talk about," he said skeptically. "To claim that he's not your fiancé? While every newspaper and trashy tabloid in print, every gossipy website that exists, is dissecting the great 'Jamelia' romance. If he's not your fiancé, why the hell aren't there any quotes from you saying *that?* Everything else about the two of you has been chronicled across the world. Seems to me there have been plenty of opportunities for you to state otherwise." He stared into her face for a long moment, then shook his head and shoved open his truck door. "We had this same conversation two months ago on the phone." His voice was flat. "Should have saved yourself a ten-hour flight in coach." He slammed the door shut and started walking toward the house.

"Six weeks ago," she whispered again

But of course he didn't hear her this time.

Chapter Two

Amelia finally got out of the truck and headed slowly toward him. Quinn watched only long enough to assure himself that she wasn't going to collapse again, before he turned toward the house once more. He wanted her in his home about as much as he wanted holes drilled into his head.

It was hard enough to forget about her when she'd never stepped foot in his place. Now she was going to do just that. And his need to keep her out of his thoughts was going to become even more impossible.

He shoved open the front door and waited for her to finish crossing the gravel drive. Her dark hair gleamed in the moonlight, reminding him of the last time. Only then the long strands had been fanned out around her head, and her face bathed in ecstasy.

He clenched his teeth and looked at the scuffed toes of

his leather boots. The second she crossed the threshold, he moved away. "Close the door behind you."

His steps sounded hollow on the wood floor as he headed through the house to the kitchen at the back and he heard the soft latch of the front door closing behind him.

He slapped his palm against the wall switch, flooding the kitchen with unforgiving light, and grabbed the plastic-wrapped loaf of bread from where he'd last tossed it on the counter. He yanked open a drawer, grabbed a knife, slammed the drawer shut and yanked open the fridge. Pulled a few things out and slammed that door shut, too.

None of it helped.

She was still in his damned house.

Another woman he'd let himself believe in.

Didn't matter that he knew he was to blame for that particular situation. He'd barely known Amelia. And he'd known his ex-wife, Carrie, for years. Yet he'd made the same mistake with them both.

Trusting that he was the one.

The only one.

He carelessly swiped mayonnaise on the two slices of bread, slapped a slice of cheese on top, followed by a jumble of deli-sliced turkey.

Every cell he possessed knew the minute Amelia stepped into the kitchen behind him, though she didn't make a sound. She was as ghostly quiet as she was ghostly pale.

He dropped the other slice of bread on top of the turkey and managed not to smash it down out of sheer frustration. He tossed the knife in the sink next to his elbow and it clattered noisily.

He turned and faced her, choking down the urge to take her shoulders and urge her into a chair.

She looked worse than ill.

The shadows under her eyes were nearly purple. The oversize shirt—an uglier color than the contents of his youngest nephew's diaper the last time he'd been stuck changing it—had slipped down one of her shoulders and her collarbone stuck out too sharp against her pale skin.

It wasn't just a day of traveling—by means he damn sure knew she wasn't used to—taking its toll.

"What the hell have you done to yourself?"

Her colorless lips parted slightly. She stared up at him and her eyes—dark, dark brown and enormous in her small triangular face—shimmered wetly. "You're so angry," she whispered.

Angry didn't begin to cover it. He was pissed as hell. Frustrated beyond belief. And completely disillusioned with his judgment where women were concerned.

Especially this woman, because dammit all to hell, there was still a part of him that wanted to believe in her. Believe the things she'd said that night. Believe the things she'd made him feel that night.

And he knew better.

"I should have taken you to the hospital," he said flatly. "Have you had the flu or something?" God forbid she was suffering anything worse.

Her lashes lowered and she reached out a visibly unsteady hand for one of the wood chairs situated around his small, square table. But she only braced herself; she didn't sit. "I haven't been sick. I told you, I just need food and a little rest."

"A little?" He snorted and nudged her down onto the chair seat. A nudge is all it took, too, because her legs folded way too easily. He would have termed it collapsing, except she did even that with grace.

As soon as she was sitting, he took his hand away, curling his fingers against his palm.

Whether to squeeze away the feel of her fragile shoulder, or to hold on to it, he wasn't sure.

And that just pissed him off even more.

He grabbed the sandwich, and ignoring every bit of manners his mom had ever tried to teach him, plopped it on the bare table surface in front of her. No napkin. No plate.

If she wanted to toy around with a cowboy, she'd better learn there weren't going to be any niceties. He almost wished he chewed, because the notion of spitting tobacco juice out just then was stupidly appealing.

She, of course, not-a-princess that she was, ignored his cavalier behavior and turned her knees beneath the table, sitting with a straight back despite her obvious exhaustion. Then she picked up the sandwich with as much care as if it were crustless, cut into fancy shapes and served up on priceless silver. "Thank you," she said quietly.

He wanted to slam his head against a wall.

Every curse he knew filled his head, all of them directed right at his own miserable hide. He grimly pulled a sturdy white plate from the cupboard and set it on the table. He didn't have napkins, but he tore a paper towel off the roll, folded it in half and set it next to the plate. Then, feeling her big brown eyes following him, he grabbed a clean glass and filled it with cold tap water. She was surely used to the stuff that came in fancy tall bottles, but there was no better water around than what came from the Rocking-U well. Aside from water, he had milk and beer. He wasn't sure the milk wasn't sour by now, and she definitely wasn't the type to drink beer.

"Thank you," she said again, after taking a long sip of the water. "I don't mean to put you to any trouble."

He folded his arms across his chest and dragged his gaze away from the soft glisten of moisture lingering on her full, lower lip. "Shouldn't have gotten on the airplane, then." Much less a bus.

She looked away.

For about the tenth time since he'd found her hiding in his barn, he felt like he'd kicked a kitten. Then ground his boot heel down on top of it for good measure.

"Eat." He sounded abrupt and didn't care. "I'll get a bed ready for you."

She nodded, still not looking at him. "Thank—" Her voice broke off for a moment. "You," she finished faintly.

That politeness of hers would be the end of him.

He left the kitchen with embarrassing haste and stomped up the stairs to the room at the end of the hall. He stopped in the doorway and stared at the bed.

It was the only one in the house.

It was his.

"You're a freaking idiot," he muttered to himself as he crossed the room and yanked the white sheets that were twisted and tangled and as much off the bed as they were on into some semblance of order. He'd have changed the sheets if he owned more than one set.

Once she was gone, he'd have to burn the damn things and buy different ones. For that matter, he might as well replace the whole bed. He hadn't had a decent night's sleep since learning she'd gotten engaged to that other guy within hours of leaving his arms. He was pretty sure that sleeping was only going to get harder from here on out.

He realized he was strangling his pillow between his fists, and slapped it down on the bed.

It was summertime, so he hadn't personally been bothering with much more than a sheet, but he unearthed the quilt that his mother had made for him years earlier from where he'd hidden it away in the closet after Carrie left him, and spread it out on top of the sheets. It smelled vaguely of mothballs, but it was better than nothing.

Then he shoved the ragged paperback book he'd been reading from the top of the nightstand into the drawer, effectively removing the only personal item in sight, and left the room.

He went back downstairs.

She was still sitting at the table in his kitchen, her back straight as a ruler, her elbows nowhere near the table. She'd finished the sandwich, though, and was folding the paper towel into intricate shapes. Not for the first time, he eyed her slender fingers, bare of rings, and reminded himself that the absence of a diamond ring didn't mean anything.

When she heard him, she stood. "I should go to Aunt Jeanne's."

"Yes." He wasn't going to lie. She'd already done enough of that for them both. "But it's after midnight. No point in ruining someone else's night's sleep, too. And since Horseback Hollow isn't blessed with any motels, much less an establishment up to your standards," he added even though she was too cultured to say so, "you're stuck with what I have." He eyed her. "Bedroom's upstairs. Do you have enough stuffing left in you to make it up them, or do I need to put you over my shoulder?"

Her ghostly pale face took on a little color at that. "I'm not a sack of feed," she said, almost crisply, and headed past him through the doorway.

His house wasn't large. The staircase was right there to the left of the front door and his grandmother's piano. She headed straight to it, closed her slender fingers over the wood banister and started up. The ugly shirt she wore hung over her hips, midway down the thighs of her baggy jeans.

He still had to look away from the sway of her hips as she took the steps. "Room's at the end of the hall," he said after her. "Bathroom's next to it."

Manners might have had him escorting her up there.

Self-preservation kept him standing right where he was.

"Yell if you need something," he added gruffly.

She stopped, nearly at the top of the stairs, and looked back at him. Her hair slid over her shoulder.

Purple shadows, ghostly pale and badly fitting clothes or not, she was still the most beautiful thing he'd ever seen and looking at her was a physical pain.

"I need you not to hate me," she said softly.

His jaw tightened right along with the band across his chest that made it hard to breathe. "I don't hate you, Amelia."

Her huge eyes stared at him. They were haunting, those eyes.

"I don't feel anything," he finished.

It was the biggest lie he'd ever told in his life.

Amelia's knees wobbled and she tightened her grip on the smooth, warm wooden banister. Quinn could say what he wanted, but the expression on his face told another story.

And she had only herself to blame.

No words came to mind that were appropriate for the situation. Even if there *were* words, she wasn't sure her tight throat would have allowed her to voice them. So she just gave him an awkward nod and headed up the remaining stairs. Because what else was there to do but go forward?

There was no going back.

He'd made that painfully clear more than once and her coming to Horseback Hollow to see him face-to-face hadn't changed a single thing.

At the landing, the room he spoke of was obvious. Straight at the end of the hall.

The door was open and through it she could see the foot of a quilt-covered bed.

She pushed back her shoulders despite her weariness, and headed toward it. If she weren't feeling devastated to her core, she would have gobbled up every detail of his home as she walked along the wooden-floored hallway. Would have struggled not to let her intense curiosity where he was concerned overtake her. Would have wondered how each nook and cranny reflected Quinn. The man she'd fallen head over heels in love with on the foolish basis of a few dances at a wedding reception.

And a night of lovemaking after.

The thought was unbearable and she pushed it away. She'd deal with that later.

She stopped at the bathroom briefly and shuddered over her pallid reflection in the oval mirror that hung over a classic pedestal sink when she washed her hands. It was no wonder he'd stared at her with such horror.

She looked hideous.

Not at all the way she'd looked the night he'd stopped next to her at Toby's wedding reception, smiled quietly and asked if she cared to dance. She'd looked as good that day as her gawky self was capable of looking.

But when Quinn took her in his arms and slowly circled around the outdoor dance floor with her to the croon of Etta James, for the first time, she'd felt beautiful. All because of the way he'd looked at her.

Tears burned behind her eyes again and she quickly left the bathroom behind, hurrying the remaining few feet into the bedroom. She shut the door soundlessly, leaned back against it and slid down it until her bottom hit the floor.

Then she drew up her knees and pressed her forehead to them.

He believed their lovemaking had been some sort of last fling for her, before settling down with Jimmy, whom she'd been seeing during the months before she'd spontaneously attended Toby's wedding. Quinn had accused her of that during that dreadful phone conversation. In the weeks since, he'd obviously not changed his opinion.

So how was she ever going to be able to tell him that she was pregnant?

With *his* child?

If he accused her of lying about that, too, she wasn't sure she could survive it.

She sat there, her sorrow too deep for tears, until her bottom felt numb. Then feeling ancient, she shifted onto her knees and pushed herself to her aching feet. The boots she'd borrowed from Molly, one of her mother's junior secretaries whom Amelia trusted, were too wide and too short. They, along with the ill-fitting jeans and the shirt, belonged to Molly's teenage brother as had the other set of clothes she'd started out in. They'd been left, shoved deep in the rubbish, at the airport in Dallas alongside the blond wig and the knapsack in which she'd carried their replacements.

She dragged her passport out of the back pocket and set it on the rustic wooden nightstand. Even though Molly had helped with the disguises, neither one of them had been able to think of a way around traveling under Amelia's own name. Not with security standards being what they were. All she'd come with had been the passport, her credit card and a small wad of American currency tucked among the well-stamped pages of her passport. Molly had insisted on the credit card, though Amelia had wanted to leave it behind. She knew cash was untraceable, while a credit card wasn't, and she'd stuck to it. The only thing she'd purchased had been the bus fare from Dallas. Once she'd reached Lubbock, she'd hitched a ride with a trucker as far as the outskirts of Horseback Hollow. Then, using the directions she'd memorized from Molly, she'd walked the rest of the way to what she'd hoped was Quinn's ranch. But in her exhaustion and the darkness she hadn't been certain. So she'd hidden in the barn, intending to rest until daylight.

Her head swam dizzily and she quickly sat at the foot of the bed, the mattress springs giving the faintest of creaks. She closed her eyes, breathing evenly. She didn't know whether to blame the light-headedness on pregnancy or exhaustion. Aside from her missed period, she hadn't experienced any other signs that she was carrying a baby. And if it hadn't been for Molly who'd suggested that her irregularity might *not* be a result of stress as Amelia had believed at first, she probably wouldn't know even now that she was carrying Quinn's baby. She'd still be thinking she was just stressed over the whole engagement fiasco.

Why, oh, why hadn't she spoken up when those reporters greeted her at the airport six weeks ago, clamoring for details about her engagement to James? Why had she just put up her hand to shield her face and raced alongside her driver until reaching the relative sanctuary of the Town Car? She hadn't even dared to phone James until she'd gotten home because she feared having her cell phone hacked again. Even though it had happened well over a year ago, the sense of invasion still lived on.

If she'd only have spoken up, denied the engagement to the press right then and there, she wouldn't be in this situation now. After the initial embarrassment, James's situation with his family would have ironed itself out in time.

Most important, though, Quinn wouldn't have any reason to hate her.

She would have returned to him weeks ago exactly as they'd planned while lying together atop a horse blanket with an endless expanse of stars twinkling over them. Then, learning she was pregnant would have been something for them to discover together.

If only.

Her light-headedness was easing, though she really felt no better. But she opened her eyes and slowly pulled off the boots and socks and dropped them on the floor next to the bed. She wiggled her toes until some feeling returned and flopped back on the mattress.

The springs gave a faint squeak again.

It was a comforting sound and, too tired to even finish undressing, she dragged one of the two pillows at the head of the bed to her cheek and closed her eyes once more.

Things would be better in the morning.

They had to be.

When there were no more sounds, faint though they were, coming from his room upstairs, Quinn finally left the kitchen where he'd been hiding out. He left the house and walked back down to the barn with only the moonlight for company. He closed the door and even though there'd be endless chores to be done before the sun came up and he ought to be trying to sleep the last few hours before then, his aimless footsteps carried him even farther from the house.

But he kept glancing back over his shoulder. Looking at the dark windows on the upper story that belonged to his bedroom. Amelia had eaten the sandwich. But did that really mean anything?

If she fainted again how would he even know?

She'd been raised in the lap of luxury. First-class flights and luxury limousines driven by guys wearing suits and caps. Not economy class and bus tickets and God knew what.

Clawing his fingers through his hair, he turned back to the house. It wasn't the house that he and Jess had grown up in. That had burned nearly to the ground when Quinn was fifteen, destroying almost everything they'd owned. The same year his dad had already succeeded in literally working to death on the Rocking-U, trying to prove himself as good a rancher as the father who'd never acknowledged him. Jess, five years older, was already off and married to Mac with a baby on the way.

Ursula, his mom, would have sold off the ranch then if she'd have been able to find an interested buyer other than her dead husband's hated father. But she'd only been able to find takers for the livestock.

Despite Quinn's noisy protests, she'd moved the two of them into a two-bedroom trailer on the outskirts of town and there they'd lived until Quinn graduated from high school. Then she'd packed him off to college, packed up her clothes and moved away from the town that had only ever seemed to bring her unhappiness. Now she lived in Dallas in one of those "active adult" neighborhoods where she played bridge and tennis. She had a circle of friends she liked, and she was happy.

Not Quinn. The moment he could, he'd headed back to Horseback Hollow and the fallen-down, barren Rocking-U. He'd had a few years of college under his belt—gained only through scholarships and part-time jobs doing anything and everything he could pick up—and a new bride on his arm.

He was going to do what his father had never been able to do. Make the Rocking-U a real success.

At least one goal had been achieved.

He'd built the small house, though it had cost him two years and a wife along the way. He'd had his grandmother's piano restored and the dregs of the old, burned house hauled away. He'd shored up broken down fences and a decrepit barn. He'd built a herd. It was small, but it was prime Texas Longhorn.

He'd made something he could be proud of. Something his father had never achieved but still would have been proud of and something his father's father could choke on every time he thought about the people he liked to pretend never existed.

And when Quinn had danced with Amelia at a wedding reception six weeks ago, he'd let himself believe that there *was* a woman who could love his life the same way that he did.

All he'd succeeded in doing, though, was proving that he was Judd Drummond's son, through and through. A damn stupid dreamer.

He went back into the silent house. He had a couch in the living room. Too short and too hard to make much of a bed, but it was that or the floor. He turned off the light and sat down and worked off his boots, dropping them on the floor.

He couldn't hear anything from upstairs.

He stretched out as well as he could. Dropped his forearm over his eyes.

Listened to the rhythmic tick of the antique clock sitting on the fireplace mantel across the room.

What if she really was sick?

"Dammit," he muttered, and jackknifed to his feet. Moving comfortably in the darkness, he went to the stairs and started up. At the top, he headed to the end of the hall and closed his hand around the doorknob leading into his bedroom.

But he hesitated.

Called himself a damned fool. He ought to go back downstairs and try to redeem what little he could of the night in sleep.

Only sleeping was a laughable notion.

He'd just glance inside the room. Make sure she was sleeping okay.

He turned the knob. Nudged open the door.

He could see the dark bump of her lying, unmoving, on his bed. He stepped closer and his stockinged toes knocked into something on the floor. They bumped and thumped.

Her shoes.

It was a good thing he'd never aspired to a life of crime when he couldn't even sneak into his own bedroom without making a commotion. He'd probably been quieter when he'd found her in his damn barn.

Despite the seemingly loud noise, though, the form on the bed didn't move. He ignored the sound of his pulse throbbing in his ears until he was able to hear her soft breathing.

Fine. All good.

He had no excuse to linger. Not in a dark room in the middle of the night with another man's fiancée. There were lines a man didn't cross, and that was one of them.

It should have been easy to leave the room. And because it wasn't, he grimaced and turned.

Avoiding her shoes on the floor, he left the room more quietly than he'd entered. He returned to the couch. Threw himself down on it again.

He'd take her to her aunt's in the morning. After she woke.

And what Amelia did after that wasn't anything he was going to let himself care about.

Chapter Three

Quinn stared at the empty bed.

Amelia was gone.

It was only nine in the morning, and sometime between when he'd left the house at dawn and when he'd returned again just now, she'd disappeared.

If not for the wig that he'd found on the ground inside his barn door, he might have wondered if he'd hallucinated the entire thing.

It didn't take a genius to figure out she'd beat him to the punch in calling her aunt. One phone call to Jeanne, or to any one of the newfound cousins, and rescue would have easily arrived within an hour.

He walked into the bedroom.

The bed looked exactly the way it had when he'd tossed the quilt on top of it, before she'd gone to bed. Maybe a little neater. Maybe a lot neater.

He'd also thought her presence would linger after she was gone. But it didn't.

The room—hell, the entire house—felt deathly still. Empty.

That was the legacy she'd left that he'd have to live with.

He tossed the wig on the foot of the bed and rubbed the back of his neck. He had a crick in it from sleeping— or pretending to—on the too-short couch.

It shouldn't matter that she'd left without a word. Snuck out while his back was essentially turned. He hadn't wanted her there in the first place. And obviously, her need to "talk" hadn't been so strong, after all.

"Gone and good riddance," he muttered.

Then, because he smelled more like cow than man and Jess would give him a rash of crap about it when he showed up at his nephew's baseball game in Vicker's Corners that afternoon, he grabbed a shower and changed into clean jeans and T-shirt.

In the kitchen, the paper towel that he'd given Amelia was still sitting on the table where she'd left it, all folded up. He grabbed it to toss it in the trash, but hesitated.

She hadn't just folded the paper into a bunch of complicated triangles. She'd fashioned it into a sort of bird. As if the cheap paper towel was some fancy origami.

I have lots of useless talents.

The memory of her words swam in his head.

She'd told him that, and more, when they'd lain under the stars. How she had a degree in literature that she didn't think she'd ever use. How she spoke several languages even though she didn't much care for traveling. How she could play the piano and the harp well enough to play at some of the family's royal functions, but suffered stage fright badly enough that having to do so was agonizing.

He pinched the bridge of his nose where a pain was forming in his head and dropped the paper bird on the table again, before grabbing his Resistol hat off the peg by the back door and heading out.

He paid Tanya Fremont, one of the students where Jess and Mac taught high school, to clean his house once a week and she'd be there that weekend.

She could take care of the trash.

"Aunt Jeanne, *really?*" Amelia lifted a glossy tabloid magazine off the coffee table where it was sitting and held it up. "I can't believe you purchase these things."

Her aunt's blue eyes were wry as she sat down beside Amelia on the couch. She set the two mugs of herbal tea she was carrying on the coffee table and plucked the glossy out of Amelia's hands. She spread it over the knees of her faded blue jeans and tapped the small picture on the upper corner of the cover. "It had a picture of you and Lucie," she defended. "You and your sister looked so pretty. I thought I'd clip it out and put it in my scrapbook."

Amelia was touched by the thought even though she deplored being on the magazine cover. The photo was from the dedication of one of the orphanages her mother helped establish. Amelia recognized the dress she'd worn to the ceremony. "I don't even want to know what the article said." Undoubtedly, it had not focused on the good works of Lady Josephine or Lucie's latest accomplishments, but the pending nuptials of Amelia and Lord James Banning, the Viscount St. Allen and heir apparent to the Earl of Estingwood.

"No article," Jeanne Marie corrected. "Not really. Just a small paragraph from *close friends*—" she sketched quotes in the air "—of 'Jamelia' that the wedding date had been set, but was being kept under wraps for now to preserve your and James's privacy."

"There *is* no wedding date," Amelia blurted. She slumped back on the couch.

"Oh?" Jeanne Marie leaned forward and set the magazine on the coffee table. She picked up her tea and studied Amelia over the rim of the sturdy mug with eyes that were eerily similar to Amelia's mother.

That was to be expected, she supposed, since Josephine and Jeanne Marie were two thirds of a set of triplets. What wasn't the norm, was the fact that the siblings had only recently discovered one another. Amelia's mother hadn't even known that she'd been adopted until she'd met Jeanne Marie Fortune Jones and their triplet brother, James Marshall Fortune. He was the only reason the trio had found one another after having been separated as young children. There was even another older brother, John Fortune, to add to the new family tree.

Amelia realized her aunt wasn't gaping at her over the news there was to be no wedding. "You don't seem very surprised."

Jeanne Marie lifted one shoulder. "Well, honey. You *are* here." And again, even though her words were full of Texas drawl, her mild, somewhat ironic lilt was exactly the same as Josephine's entirely proper Brit would have been.

It was still startling to Amelia, even after meeting her aunt nearly a year ago.

"I'm assuming you have a good reason for not announcing you broke things off with your young man in England?"

"It's complicated," she murmured, even as she felt guilty for leaving her aunt under the impression that there had ever been something to break off in the first place. James had been as much a victim of their supposed engagement as she, since the presumptuous announcement had been issued by his father. But once it had been, and Amelia hadn't denied it, James had been doing his level best to convince her to make it a reality. Under immense family pressure to make a suitable marriage, he'd given up hope of a match with the girl he really loved—Astrid, who sold coffee at the stand in his building—and tried giving Amelia a family ring in hopes that she'd come around, though she'd refused to take it. "Jimmy and I have known each other a long time."

While she really only knew Quinn in the biblical sense. The irony of it all was heartbreaking.

"Sometimes a little distance has a way of uncomplicating things," Jeanne said. "And as delighted as I am to have you here, it does tend to raise a few questions. Particularly havin' to get you from Quinn Drummond's place practically before sunup. And havin' you dressed like you are."

Amelia's fingers pleated the hem of the oversize shirt. "I was trying to avoid paparazzi."

"So you said while we were driving here." Jeanne Marie finally set down the mug. She was obviously as disinterested in her tea as Amelia was. "What's going on between you and Quinn?"

"Nothing." She felt heat rise up her throat.

"And that's why you called me from his house at seven in the morning. Because nothing is going on between you two." Jeanne Marie's lips curved. "In my day, that sort of *nothing* usually led to a shotgun and a stand-up in front of a preacher whether there was another suitor in the wings or not."

Amelia winced.

Her aunt tsked, her expression going from wry to concerned in the blink of an eye. "Oh, honey." She closed her warm hands around Amelia's fidgeting fingers. "Whatever's upsetting you can be worked out. I promise you that."

Amelia managed a weak smile. "I appreciate the thought, Aunt Jeanne. But I grew up with my father always telling us not to make promises we couldn't keep."

Jeanne Marie squeezed her hand. "I wish I'd have had a chance to meet your daddy. Your mama says he was the love of her life."

Amelia nodded. Her father had died several years ago, but his loss was still sharp. "He was." She couldn't contain a yawn and covered it with her hand. Despite having slept several hours at Quinn's, she still could hardly keep her eyes open. "I'm so sorry."

"I'm the sorry one," Jeanne Marie said. She patted Amelia's hand and pushed to her feet. "You're exhausted, honey. You need to be in bed, not sitting here answering questions."

It took all the energy Amelia possessed to stand, also. "Are you certain I'm not imposing?"

Jeanne Marie laughed. "There's no such thing as imposing among family, honey. Deke and I raised seven kids in this house. Now they're all off and living their own lives. So it's nice to have one of those empty rooms filled again."

"You're very kind." She followed her aunt along the

hall and up the stairs to a corner bedroom with windows on two walls. Amelia remembered the room from her first visit to Horseback Hollow six months ago, though it had been her mother who'd been assigned to it then. It was obviously a guest room. Simply but comfortably furnished with a bed covered in a quilt with fading pastel stitching that was all the lovelier for its graceful aging, a side table with dried cat's tails sticking out of an old-fashioned milk bottle, and a sturdy oak wardrobe. White curtains, nearly translucent, hung open at the square windows and moved gently in the warm morning breeze.

"This used to be Galen's room," Jeanne Marie said. "Being the oldest, there was a time he liked lording it over the others that he had the largest room." She crossed to the windows to begin lowering the shades. "Would have put you in here back when you came for Toby's wedding in April, but James Marshall and Clara were using it."

"Leave the windows open," Amelia begged quickly. "Please."

"The sunlight won't keep you awake?"

She self-consciously tugged at her ugly shirt. Light was the least disturbing thing she could think of at the moment. And better to have sunlight than darkness while the memories of the last time she'd been at her aunt's home were caving in on her. "The breeze is too lovely to shut out."

Jeanne Marie dropped her hands. She opened the wardrobe and pulled out two bed pillows from the shelf inside and set them on the bed. "Bathroom is next door," she reminded. "I'll make sure you have fresh towels. And I'm sure that Delaney or Stacey left behind some clothes that should fit you. They might be boxed up by now, but I'll try to scare up something for you to wear once you're rested."

Her welcome was so very different than Quinn's, deserved or not, and Amelia's eyes stung.

She cried much too easily these days. "Thank you." She sat on the foot of the bed and tried not to think about sitting on the bed at Quinn's.

She'd thought that had been a guest room, too. Until she'd awakened early that morning and had gone looking for him. She'd done what she hadn't had the energy for the night before. The rooms upstairs were spacious and full of windows and nothing else. Almost like they were stuck in time. Waiting for a reason to be filled with furniture. With family. Downstairs, he had a den with a plain wooden desk and an older style computer on it. The living room had a couch, a television that looked older than the computer, and a gleaming black upright piano. She'd drawn her fingers lightly over the keys, finding it perfectly tuned.

What she hadn't found was Quinn. Not only had he been nowhere to be found inside the two-story house, but she'd seen for herself that his home possessed only a single bed.

Which, regardless of his feelings, he'd given up for her.

Jeanne Marie watched the tangled expressions crossing her new niece's delicate features and controlled the urge to take the girl into her arms and rock her just as she would have her own daughters. "We've got most of the crew coming for supper tonight. But you just come on down whenever you're ready," she said comfortingly. "And don't you worry about me spilling your personal beans to your cousins. You can do that when you're good and ready." Then she kissed Amelia's forehead and left the room, closing the door behind her.

She set out fresh towels in the bathroom, then headed downstairs to the kitchen again and stopped in surprise at the sight of her husband just coming in from the back. "I thought you'd be out all morning."

"Thought I could get the engine on that old Deere going, but I need a couple more parts." He tossed his sweat-stained cowboy hat aside and rubbed his fingers through his thick, iron-gray hair before reaching out a long arm and hooking her around the waist. "Which leaves me the chance for some morning delight with my wife before I drive over to Vicker's Corners."

Jeanne Marie laughed softly, rubbing her arms over his broad shoulders. How she loved this man who'd owned her heart from the moment they'd met. "We're not alone in the house," she warned.

His eyebrow lifted. "I didn't notice any cars out front. Who's come this early for supper? Can't be Toby and his brood." He grinned faintly. "Those kids've been coming out of their shells real nice lately."

"And they'll continue to do so," Jeanne agreed, slightly distracted by the way Deke's wide palms were drifting from her waist down over the seat of her jeans. "As long as no more hitches come up to stop Toby and Angie adopting them." Their middle son and his new wife were trying to adopt three kids he'd been fostering for the past eight months and the process hadn't exactly been smooth so far.

Her blood was turning warm and she grabbed his wide wrists, redirecting his hands to less distracting territory. "Amelia's here."

His brows pulled together for a second. "Amelia? Josephine's youngest girl?"

"We don't know another Amelia," Jeanne Marie said dryly.

His hands fell away. He leaned back against the counter and folded his arms over his chest. "Fortunes are everywhere," he murmured.

She knew his face as well as she knew her own. She had happily been Jeanne Marie Jones for forty years. But learning that she had siblings out there, learning that she had a blood connection to others in this world besides the children of his that she'd borne, had filled a void inside her that Deke had never quite been able to understand. Even though her adoptive parents had loved her, and she them, not knowing where she'd come from had always pulled at her.

And now she knew.

And though Deke hadn't protested when she'd added Fortune to her own name, she knew also that it hadn't been entirely easy for him. When their kids followed suit, it had gotten even harder for him to swallow.

No. The advent of the Fortunes to the Jones's lives hadn't been easy. And maybe it would have been easier if James had gone about things differently when he'd tracked her down. Her newfound brother was a self-made business tycoon used to having the world fall into place exactly the way he planned and he'd not only upset his own family in the process, he'd sent Jeanne Marie's family reeling, too, when he'd tried to give her part of his significant fortune.

She'd turned down the money, of course. It didn't matter to her that all of her siblings turned out to be ridiculously wealthy while she was not. She and Deke had a good life. A happy life. One blessed with invaluable wealth for the very reason that it had nothing to do with any amount of dollars and cents.

Convincing her pridefully suspicious husband that the only fortune that mattered to her was the *name* Fortune, however, had been a long process.

One that was still obviously in the works, judging by Deke's stoic expression.

"How long's she staying?" he asked.

"I have no idea. The girl came here to figure some things out, I believe." Because she always felt better being busy, she pulled a few peaches out of the basket on the counter and grabbed a knife. She'd already made a chocolate cake for dessert for that evening, but Deke always loved a fresh peach pie. And even after forty years of marriage, a man still needed to know he was in the forefront of his wife's thoughts. "Do you think she should stay somewhere else?"

He frowned quickly. "No. She's family." His eyes met hers. "I get it, Jeanne Marie."

Her faint tension eased. He might not exactly understand the way she'd taken on the Fortune name, but he did get "it" when it came to family. Nothing was more important to him, even if he didn't always have an easy time showing it.

"She'd been at Quinn Drummond's," she added. Then told him everything that had happened since Amelia had called. She pointed the tip of the paring knife she was using to peel the peaches at Deke. "I don't care what everyone's saying about her and that Banning fella." She deftly removed the peach pit and sliced the ripe fruit into a bowl. "There's definitely something going on between her and Quinn."

"I'd think Quinn's too set in his ways to be interested in a highbred filly like Amelia." Deke reached past her to filch a juicy slice. "'Specially after the merry chase that ex-wife of his led him on. She was a piece of work, remember?"

She did and she made a face. "That was years ago."

"Yup. Having your wife leave you for her old boyfriend leaves a stain, though. Least I think it would. Now he's interested in a girl the world thinks is engaged?" He stole another slice, avoiding the hand she batted at him.

"You keep eating the slices, I won't have enough left to make a pie for you," she warned.

His teeth flashed, his good humor evidently restored. He popped the morsel in his mouth and gave her a smacking kiss that tasted of him and sweet, sweet summer. It melted her heart as surely now as it had the first time he'd kissed her when they were little more than kids.

Then he grabbed his hat and plopped it on his head again. "I'll stop at the fruit stand on my way back from Vicker's Corners," he said, giving her a quick wink. "Replenish the stock." He started to push open the back screen door.

"Deke—"

He hesitated.

"You're the love of my life, you know."

His smile was slow and sweeter than the peaches. "And you're mine. That's what gets me up in the morning every day, darlin'."

Then he pushed through the screen door. It squeaked slightly, and shut with a soft slap.

Jeanne Marie pressed her hand to her chest for a moment. "Oh, my." She blew out a breath and laughed slightly at the silliness of a woman who ought to be too old for such romantic swooning.

Then she looked up at the ceiling, thinking about her young niece. Amelia was running away from something, or running to something. And she needed to figure out which it was.

Jeanne Marie was just glad that she was there to provide a resting place. And that she had a man of her own who could understand why.

Quinn had no intention of going by Jeanne Marie and Deke's place later that evening. But he ran into Deke at the tractor supply in Vicker's Corners before the baseball game and the man—typically short on words and long on hard work and honor—asked after Quinn's mom. That brief exchange of pleasantries had somehow led to Deke casually tossing out an invitation to come by for supper.

"Havin' a cookout," Deke had said. "All the kids're coming. And you know how Jeanne Marie always cooks more'n we need."

Quinn had wondered then if it was possible that Deke didn't know his wife's new niece was there. And then he had wondered if it was possible that Jeanne's new niece *wasn't* there.

Which had led to him poking at that thought all through the ball game, same way a tongue poked at a sore tooth, even though it hurt.

He ought to have just asked Deke.

Instead, here he was at six o'clock in the evening, standing there staring at the front of Jeanne and Deke's place.

He could smell grilling beef on the air and hear the high-pitched squeal of a baby laughing. Ordinarily, the

smell of a steak getting seared really well would have
been enough to get his boots moving. He didn't even
mind the babies or the kids much. He'd had plenty of
practice with Jess's batch, since she popped one out every
couple of years.

His reluctance to join them now annoyed him. He'd
had plenty of meals at the Jones's place over the years.
He'd been in school with the older ones and counted them
as friends. He'd danced at Toby's wedding. *With Amelia.*
Right here, in fact, because Toby and Angie had been
married out in back of the house.

Quinn hadn't been back since.

Muttering an oath, he grabbed the short-haired wig,
slammed the truck door and headed around the side of
the house. He knew they'd all be out back again and he
was right.

This time, though, instead of rows of chairs lined up
like white soldiers across the green grass and a bunch
of cloth-covered tables with pretty flowers sitting on top
arranged around the space, there were a couple of picnic
tables covered with plastic checked tablecloths, a bunch
of lawn chairs and a game of croquet in the works.

He spotted Amelia immediately and even though
he wanted to pretend he hadn't been concerned about
whether she had or had not sought haven with her aunt,
the knot inside him eased.

She was off to one side of the grassy backyard where
Toby's three kids were playing croquet, and talking with
Stacey, Jeanne's and Deke's second youngest. The two
females were about the same age and the same height, but
Stacey was as sunny and blonde as Amelia was moon-
light and brunette.

Both women were engaged, too, he thought darkly,

though only one of those engagements caused him any amount of pleasure. He was just a little surprised that Colton Foster, who was Stacey's fiancé, hadn't gotten her to the altar already. As he watched, Amelia leaned over and rubbed her nose against Piper's, Stacey's year-old daughter, who was propped on her mama's hip.

He looked away and aimed toward Deke where he and Liam were manning the grill. "Smells good," he greeted. "Would only smell better if that was Rocking-U beef."

Liam snorted good-naturedly. Horseback Hollow was dotted with small cattle ranches and all of them were more supportive than competitive with each other. "You got yourself a new pet there? Looks like a rat."

Quinn wished he'd have left the wig in the truck. He'd only thought as far as returning it to its owner so he wouldn't have the reminder around. He hadn't thought about the questions that doing so would invite. "It's a wig. Thought maybe one of Toby's kids might want to keep it around for Halloween or something." The excuse was thin and he knew it. "My sister's kids outgrew it, I guess," he improvised and felt stupid even as he did. He'd never developed a taste for lying. Anyone who knew Jess's brood would also know the five boys were hellions who wouldn't be caught dead wearing a wig.

Liam was eying him oddly, too. "Whatever, man." He grabbed a beer from an ice-filled barrel and tossed it to him. "Crack that open and get started. Maybe it'll soften you up before we get to dickering over that bull of yours I want to buy."

Despite everything, Quinn smiled. He tossed the wig on one of the picnic benches nearby. "Rocky's not for sale, my friend."

"Even if I paid you twice what he's worth?"

They'd had this debate many times. Quinn knew Liam wouldn't overpay and Liam knew Quinn wasn't selling, anyway. "That bull's semen's worth gold to me."

"Oh." The word was faint, brief and still filled with some shock.

The knots tightened inside him again and Quinn turned to see Amelia standing beside him.

Chapter Four

Her fragility struck Quinn all over again, like a fist in his gut.

The red dress that she was wearing was pretty enough, he guessed. But it was loose. And the straps over her shoulders couldn't hide the way her collarbones were too prominent.

She looked like she needed to sit at a table and stuff herself for a month of Sundays.

As if she read his disapproving thoughts, her cheeks were nearly as red as the dress.

The day of Toby's wedding, she'd worn a strapless ice-blue dress that ended just above her perfect knees, and a weird little puff of some feathery thing on her head. When they'd ended up sneaking off for a drive in his truck, he'd teased her about it. She'd promptly tugged it off, and plopped his cowboy hat on her head, where it had slipped down over her eyes, and said she was in the market for a new look, anyway.

His lips twisted, his eyes meeting hers. "You're going to hear words like *bull's semen* if you're going to play around cowboys, princess."

Stacey, standing beside Amelia, rolled her eyes. "Good grief, Quinn. Manners much?"

"It's quite all right," Amelia said quickly. She lifted her chin a little. "This is Texas, for goodness' sake. Cattle ranch country. I certainly don't imagine anyone stands around discussing tea and biscuits. Or, cookies, I guess you call them."

He nearly choked. Because they'd laughed together about that, too. Only she'd been naked at the time, and throatily telling him that she'd bet he'd enjoy teatime perfectly well if she served it up for him after making love.

"Depends on whose cookies you're talking about," Deke said. "Jeanne Marie makes some oatmeal peanut-butter deals that are the talk of three counties." His dry humor broke the faint tension. "Stacey girl, you wanna grab a tray for these steaks? They're 'bout ready."

"Sure."

"I'll take her," Amelia offered quickly, reaching out her hands for Piper, and Stacey handed her over. She settled the wide-eyed toddler on her hip and tickled her cheek, making Piper squeal and wriggle. "Who is the prettiest baby girl here, hmm?"

For some reason, Quinn's neck prickled.

He twisted the cap off his beer and focused on Liam. "Where's your better half, anyway?" There was no sign of his friend's red-haired fiancée.

"Julia's meeting with one of the suppliers over at the Cantina. She'll be here as soon as she finishes up."

"Is the restaurant still going to open on schedule?" Amelia asked.

Liam nodded. "Two weeks from now, right on track."

The Hollows Cantina was a big deal for their little town. It was owned and to be operated by Marcos Mendoza and his wife, Wendy Fortune Mendoza, who'd relocated all the way from Red Rock, a good four hundred Texas miles away. They'd hired Julia as an assistant manager and the establishment promised upscale dining that was intended to draw not only the locals from Horseback Hollow and nearby Vicker's Corners, but as far away as Lubbock. Considering the Mendozas' success with Red, a fancy Mexican food restaurant in Red Rock that was famous even beyond the state lines, Quinn figured they had a decent shot of success at it.

He was reserving judgment on whether that all would be a good thing for Horseback Hollow or not. He wasn't vocally opposed to it like some folks, nor was he riding around on the bandwagon of supporters, though he was glad enough for Julia. She'd always been a hard worker and deserved her shot as much as anyone did.

He, personally, would probably still choose the Horseback Hollow Grill over the Cantina. Even on a good day, he wasn't what he would call "upscale" material.

"My mother has the grand opening on her calendar," Amelia said. "I know she's looking forward to it. Not only is Uncle James going to be there, but Uncle John, as well. It should be quite a family reunion."

Quinn stopped pretending an interest in his beer and looked at her. Ironically, the British Fortunes seemed too upscale for the Cantina. "And you? Is it on your calendar, too, princess? Maybe you'll drag your fiancé along for the trip."

Amelia's chocolate-brown eyes went from her cousin's face to Quinn's and for the first time since he'd met her, they contained no emotion whatsoever. "I'm not sure what I'll be doing by the end of the month." Her voice was smoothly pleasant and revealed as little as her eyes did.

Her "royal face," he realized.

She'd talked about having one. Having had to develop as a little girl the ability to give nothing away by expression, deed or word.

He'd just never seen it in person before. And not directed at him.

Piper was wriggling on her hip and Amelia leaned over to set the little girl on her feet. She kept hold of Piper's tiny hands as the girl made a beeline toddle for the wig sitting on the picnic bench next to them.

"Keekee," she chortled, and reached for the wig.

Amelia laughed lightly and scooped up the wig before Piper could reach it and brushed the short thick strands against the baby's face. "That's not a kitty, darling. It's a wig."

She'd crouched next to Piper and while the child chortled over the hairy thing, she glanced up at Quinn. "There was no need to return the wig to me, Quinn," she told him. "You could have tossed it in the trash bin."

He really wished he would have.

Liam tilted his beer to his lips but not quickly enough to hide his faint grin. "Thought the rat belonged to your sis's kids."

"Here's the tray," Stacey announced, striding up with a metal cookie sheet in her hand that she set on the side of the grill.

She was also carrying a big bowl of coleslaw under

her other arm, and, glad of an escape route, Quinn slid his hand beneath it. "I'll put it on the table before you drop it." He turned away from the lot of them and carried it over to a folding table that had obviously been set out to hold the food.

Trying not to watch Quinn too openly, Amelia continued entertaining the sweet baby with the wig while everyone else seemed to suddenly spring into action organizing the food onto plates and the people onto picnic benches.

Though she tried to avoid it, she somehow found herself sitting directly across from Quinn. He was hemmed in on one side by Delaney, Jeanne Marie and Deke's youngest daughter, and Liam on the other. Amelia was caught between Jeanne Marie and Deke.

If she didn't know better, she almost would have suspected her aunt and uncle of planning it.

Judging by the way Quinn noticeably ignored her, he was no more comfortable with the seating plan than she was. Fortunately, his friendship with Liam was evident as the two men dickered over the issue of Rocky's studding abilities and whether or not the summer season would be wetter or drier than usual.

"Have some more corn bread," Jeanne Marie said, nudging a basket of the fragrant squares into her hands.

Amelia obediently put another piece on her plate, and managed a light laugh when Deke tried to talk her into another steak, though she'd only eaten a fraction of the one on her plate. "If I ate all this, I'd pop," she protested.

"So, Amelia," Delaney drew her attention. "What are you doing in Horseback Hollow, anyway?" Her eyes were bright with curiosity as she grinned. "Are you planning some secret meeting with your wedding gown designer? Texas has our very own Charlene Dalton. She's based in Red Rock and I hear she did Emily Fortune's gown."

"Delaney," Jeanne Marie tsked, handing the corn bread across to her daughter. "You're sounding like one of those nosy reporters."

Delaney made a protesting sound. "That's not fair. None of us expected to find ourselves family with *The* Fortunes. If you can't share some secrets among your own family, who can you share 'em with? It's not like I'll go tattling to the newspapers. And besides. I didn't get to see Emily's gown outside of pictures, 'cause she got married before we even knew we all were cousins!"

"It's all right," Amelia said quickly. Not only could she sense her aunt's sudden discomfort, but she was painfully aware of Quinn across from her. "I'm not…not planning any designer sessions." She was loath to discuss her personal business in front of everyone, even if they *were* family. That just wasn't the way she'd been raised. Even among her four brothers and sister, she didn't get into whys and wherefores and the most personal of emotions. She hadn't even divulged all the facts to her own mother about her "engagement," though she knew Josephine had her suspicions.

She tried not looking at Quinn, but couldn't help herself. "I'm not planning anything." It wasn't exactly a public admission, but since she'd discovered she was pregnant with his child, it was entirely truthful.

"'Scuse me." He suddenly rose and extricated himself from the picnic bench and the human bookends holding him there.

Amelia's fingernails dug into her palms as she

watched him carry his plate over to the table of food and make a point of studying the display.

"Getting a microphone stuck in your face or a camera flash blinding you every time you go out in public would be a pain in the butt," Deke said, as if nothing had happened. Then he looked around at the silence his unexpected input drew. His eyebrows rose. "Well. Would be," he drawled in conclusion.

And that seemed to be that.

Nobody else broached the subject about Amelia's unplanned appearance. Nor did the topic of the wedding come up again.

And Quinn never returned to their picnic table.

He stuck around long enough to have a piece of the three-layer chocolate cake when Jeanne Marie presented it, along with a peach pie that was so picturesque it might have come out of the kitchens at the Chesterfield estate. But whenever Amelia entered his vicinity, he exited hers.

It was so plainly obvious that he was avoiding her that she felt herself receiving looks of sympathy from Stacey, Delaney *and* Liam's fiancée, Julia, who'd arrived in time for dessert.

She didn't want sympathy.

She wanted Quinn's love.

In the absence of that, at least his understanding.

But clearly he wasn't going to offer that, either.

She saw him shake Deke's hand, drop a kiss on her aunt's cheek and exchange easily a half-dozen goodbyes with some of the others, without a single glance her way. And then he was walking away, heading out of sight around the corner of her aunt's house.

She swallowed and sucked all of her feelings inward until she felt reasonably confident that her expression was calm. She listened in on Toby and Angie's conversation as they talked about the difficulties they kept encountering trying to adopt the three Hemings children Toby had been fostering ever since she'd first met him, and knew she made the appropriate nods and sounds when she should have. But a portion of her mind was wondering if she could get back home again without drawing undue media attention.

Which was rather laughable to worry about now.

The attention she'd draw once word of her pregnancy got out would thoroughly eclipse what she'd already garnered.

And poor James. Instead of dealing with the embarrassment of a broken engagement, he would have to endure speculation over being the baby's father. It wouldn't matter that he wasn't. It wouldn't matter what statements were issued or what proof was given.

Forever on, people would whisper. Every time either one of them did something to draw the attention of the media, the scandal would be dug up all over again, regurgitated on the internet or on gossip networks.

They'd all pay the price and none more dearly than her and Quinn's innocent baby.

Her head swam dizzily and she excused herself, walking blindly. She instinctively followed the path that Quinn had taken, heading around the side of the house and away from all of the noisy gaiety.

Going home was as impossible as staying in Horseback Hollow would be.

The thought came over her in a wave and her knees went weak. She stopped, bracing herself with one hand against the side of the house.

"Are you going to pass out again?"

She nearly jumped out of her skin at the sound of Quinn's voice. He was standing a few feet away, his hazel eyes alert, as though he was ready to leap forward if he had to.

At least he didn't hate her badly enough to allow her to collapse flat on her face.

She let out a choking laugh at the thought, which only had him closing the distance between them, his expression even warier as he clasped her bare arms.

She shivered, looking up into his face. The night they'd danced, she'd felt as if they'd known one another for all their lives. "I think I'm losing my mind, Quinn." Even her voice sounded unhinged, shaking and pitched too high.

He made a rough sound. "You're not losing your mind."

Where was her dignity? Her self-control? Her throat tightened even more, her voice almost a squeak. "But you don't know—"

"Shh." His big warm hand slid around the back of her neck and he pulled her against his chest in a motion that felt both reluctant and desperate. "You're going to make yourself collapse again. Is that what you want?"

Her forehead rubbed against the front of his soft plaid shirt as she shook her head. She could feel the heat of his hard chest burning through the cotton. Could hear the rhythmic beat of his heart when she turned her cheek against him.

He was holding her, though not cradling her. But her ragged emotions didn't care. They only wanted her to burrow against him while he safely held everything that didn't matter at bay.

She'd never felt even a fraction of this need when she

was with James. If only she had, things wouldn't be in such a mess.

Her fingers twisted into Quinn's shirt lapel. "There's something I need to tell you."

"Well it's gonna have to wait." His hands tightened around her arms as he forcibly set her back a foot. "I only came back to warn you that there's an SUV parked maybe a hundred yards down the road that's not from around here. Has a rental car sticker on the bumper." His fingertips pressed into her flesh and his gaze, as it roved over her face, was shuttered once more. "It's probably nothing, but the strangers that've been coming around the Hollow these days usually stick to town. They don't traipse out onto private property and park off the side of the road half-hidden behind the bushes."

She grasped at the shreds of her composure and came up with threads. His thumbs were rubbing back and forth over her upper arms and she wondered if he even realized it. "You think it's a reporter." Maybe even that dreadful Ophelia Malone had managed to catch up to her. The young paparazzo had sprung from nowhere after Amelia's "engagement" and seemed determined to earn her stripes on Amelia ever since.

"All I'm thinking is that the car doesn't belong." His thumbs stopped moving. He still held her arms to steady her, yet managed to put another few inches between them. "But I don't figure any of the Joneses—*Fortune* Joneses," he corrected himself, "deserve their lives intruded upon."

"Whereas this Fortune Chesterfield does?"

His lips twisted and his brows lowered. "Don't make me feel sorry for you, princess."

"I'm not trying to!" Despair congealed inside her

chest and she lifted her palms to his face. She felt his sudden stillness and mindlessly stepped closer. "Please give me a chance to make things right, Quinn." Feeling as powerless as a moth flying into a flame, she stretched up on the toes of her borrowed sandals and pressed her mouth to his jaw. The hard angle felt bristly against her lips. "That's all I want. A chance." She stretched even farther, pulling on his shoulders, until her lips could reach his.

And for a moment, a sweet moment that sent her hopes spinning, he kissed her back.

But then he jerked away.

His hands felt like iron as he held her in place and took another step back, putting distance between them yet again. "Finish making one bed before you try getting in another." His voice was low. Rough.

"I was never in James's bed," she whispered. Her lips still tingled. "I'm not in it now. What can I do to make you believe me?"

A muscle worked in his jaw. "Walk out to that SUV and see if it's a reporter, and if it is, tell 'em what you told me. That the two of you aren't engaged. Never were."

She swallowed. "And that would make everything all right? Between you and me?"

He didn't answer and her stomach sank right back to her toes.

Of course it wouldn't.

He'd made up his mind where she was concerned and that was the end of it.

It didn't matter who was to blame for what as far as the "engagement" was concerned. James's father had precipitated everything by announcing they were engaged.

And she'd compounded the problem by not denying it when she could have.

By talking to the paparazzi now, all she would succeed in doing would be hurting James, embarrassing his family, and by extension, her own.

And in the process, she wouldn't gain a thing where Quinn was concerned.

She drew herself up. Lifted her chin. She was a Chesterfield. A Fortune Chesterfield. Even if her world was disintegrating around her, she needed to remember that fact. "That would be throwing James to the wolves."

His eyes flattened even more. "So?"

She exhaled, praying for strength. It was obvious that he wouldn't welcome hearing any defense of the other man. "An announcement like that needs to come through official channels, not some random gossipmonger on the side of the road. *Don't!*" She stared him down. "Don't look at me like that. Whether you want to believe me or not, it's true. Otherwise it would be just one more rumor tossing around among the flotsam."

"Even though it came from you."

She nodded. "Even though." This time, she was the one to put more space between them, though she had to force herself to do it. But it was enough to make his hands finally fall away from her arms. It took every speck of self-control she possessed not to clasp her arms around herself to hold in the feel of his touch. "James and I had been dating nearly a year when you and I—" She drew in a shuddering breath. "When I came here for Toby's wedding," she amended. "The...advantages of us marrying had come up a few times. I never lied to you about that."

"No, princess. Your lie was in pretending you weren't

going to bring those advantages to reality. You said you weren't in love with him. And that I did believe. Or there's no way we'd have ended up out in that field that night." His lips thinned. "Wouldn't have happened."

"Are you trying to convince me of that or yourself?"

The muscle in his jaw flexed. Once. Twice. Then it went still. His expression turned stoic and he didn't speak.

She realized she'd pressed her hands to her stomach and made herself stop. "And...and after I went back home to all that—" she waved her hand, trying to encompass the indescribable media storm that had greeted her "—and you made it plain once you finally deigned to speak with me that there was no...no hope for us—" Her voice broke and she stopped again, gathering herself. "James suggested we go on with the illusion. His father is in very poor health. For an assortment of reasons, he wants to see James married and pass on his title to him while he's still alive. We weren't the great romance everyone wants to make us out to be, but we *were* friends and, given time, he hoped we might be more." Her vision glazed with tears as she stared at him. "I didn't have you. So, yes. I made no public contradictions. I'd had one night of magic and I let it slip through my fingers. Maybe a life with him was the best I could expect after that. But then I—"

"Enough!" He slashed his hand through the air between them. "Enough of the fairy-tale bull, princess. I've been down this road before. I already know how it goes." His smile was cold and cutting. "I made the mistake of marrying the last woman who was selling a story like this. I am not in the market to buy it again."

Then, while she was frozen in speechless shock, he turned on his boot heel and strode back to his truck parked nearby.

Chapter Five

The next morning it was Quinn's sister, Jess, who saw the photograph first.

It was grainy. It had obviously been taken from a considerable distance and the subjects' faces weren't entirely visible, or even entirely clear.

But it was enough for Jess.

She slapped the piece of paper on Quinn's kitchen table in front of him and jabbed her finger at the image. "That's you." She jabbed again. "That's Amelia." Then she propped her hands on her hips and stuck her face close to his, wholly, righteously in big-sister mode. "What the *hell*, Quinn? They've already coined a nickname for you!"

Annoyed, because even though she was five years his senior, he was a grown man and not in the least interested in being called on her metaphorical carpet, he pushed her aside and picked up the sheet of paper that she'd obviously printed off her computer. "They who?"

Her arms flapped as she gaped at him. "It doesn't matter who! You've got eyes. You can read reasonably well, last time I checked. The caption is right there!"

Is this the end for Jamelia? Who is the tall, dark Horseback Hollow Homewrecker caught in a passionate clinch with England's own runaway bride?

He let out a disgusted sound and crumpled the thin paper in his fist. "You have five kids, a husband and a full-time job at the high school. When the hell do you have time for hunting up this sort of crap on the internet?"

"Summer vacation," she returned. "And obviously you've never acquainted yourself with internet alerts." She waved her cell phone that she seemed perpetually attached to under his nose, then shoved it back in her pocket.

He wasn't sure if she was more disgusted with the photograph itself or with his seeming ineptitude where technology was concerned. The only thing he kept a computer for was ranch records and he detested using it even for that. He'd rather be out in the open air than sitting in the office pecking at computer keys.

"That picture is everywhere," she added. "All this time and you never said *anything* about her to me! How long has this been going on?"

"There's no *this*." He opened the cupboard door beneath the sink and pushed the wad of paper deep into the trash can stored there.

"Please. Don't try saying that isn't you and Amelia in the picture. Where were you, anyway?"

Standing to one side of the Joneses' house, not as hidden from view as he'd thought.

He didn't voice the words. Just eyed his sister. "It's Saturday morning," he said instead. "Shouldn't you be at a soccer game or something instead of cornering me in my own kitchen?"

She pointed her finger at him, giving him the stink eye that she'd had perfected since she was a superior eight years old and didn't like him coming uninvited into her room anymore. "She's an engaged woman, Quinn."

It wasn't anything he didn't know and hadn't been tarring himself for. But that didn't mean he welcomed his sister's censure, too. And, he justified to himself, the photograph hadn't caught him kissing Amelia; it had caught *her* kissing *him*. "Engaged isn't married."

He scooped up a Texas Rangers ball cap and tugged it down over his eyes before shoving through the wood-framed screen door leading outside. For her, Saturdays were chock-full of squiring one kid or another hither and yon.

For him, Saturdays meant the same chores that every other day meant and he fully intended on getting to them. If he kept acting normal, sooner or later, things would be normal. It had worked that way when Carrie left. He had to believe it would work again now, or he might as well order up a straightjacket, size extra-large-tall, right now.

Amelia woke early the next day after yet another fitful night of sleep. She could smell the heady aroma of coffee wending its way from downstairs and she rolled out of bed, donning the robe that Jeanne Marie had loaned her. Downstairs, she found her aunt sitting at the kitchen table. Her silver hair—usually pinned up—was hang-

ing in a long braid down her back and she had a pair of
reading glasses perched on her nose as she perused a
newspaper.

When Amelia walked into the room, she looked over
the top of her eyeglasses and smiled. "Aren't you the
early bird this morning," she greeted. "Would you like
coffee?"

Amelia waved her aunt back into her seat when she
started to rise. "Don't get up." She wanted coffee in the
worst way, but had read that caffeine was something
pregnant women were supposed to avoid. "Water's all
I want." To prove it, she pulled a clean glass out of the
dish rack where several had been turned upside down
after being washed, and filled it from the tap. Then she
sat down across from her aunt. She was determined not
to think about Quinn for the moment.

She'd spent enough time doing that when she'd been
unable to sleep. She'd thought about him. And the fact
that he'd once been married. Something he hadn't shared
before at all.

"I need some clothes of my own," she said. "I can't
keep borrowing." It was something she'd never done in
her entire life. And she needed underwear. She'd been
washing her silk knickers every night, but enough was
enough.

"Well." Jeanne Marie looked amused. "You can, you
know. But a pretty girl like you doesn't want to keep
walking around in things two sizes too large." She adjusted her glasses and glanced at her newspaper again.
"Guess you already know you won't find much in the
way of clothes shopping here in Horseback Hollow."

"I know." Much as she loved the area, Horseback Hollow only consisted of a few small businesses. "I thought

perhaps Vicker's Corners." She hadn't been to the nearby town, but she'd heard mention of it often enough and knew it was only twenty miles away. "When I was talking to Stacey yesterday, she mentioned that there are a few shops there."

"Yes," Jeanne Marie agreed. "You'll find more of a selection in Lubbock, though."

She didn't want to go to Lubbock. She wanted to avoid all towns of any real size. Vicker's Corners was probably pushing it as it was. "I just need a few basics," she said. "I'm sure Vicker's Corners will suit." She chewed the inside of her lip for a moment. "I also ought to purchase a cell phone." Molly had called it "a burner." One that nobody—namely Ophelia Malone and her ilk—would know to track. "Do you think I'd be able to find one there, as well?"

"Imagine so. There's a hardware store that carries everything from A to Z." Jeanne Marie turned the last page of the newspaper and folded it in half. "I'd drive you myself, but I have to go to a baby shower my friend Lillian is giving her niece this afternoon. I can call one of the kids or Deke to drive you."

"I don't want to put anyone out." She'd sprung her "visit" on them uninvited. She certainly didn't expect them to rearrange their plans because of her. "I don't suppose I could hire a car around here? I have some experience driving in other countries."

Jeanne Marie's smile widened. "We're not exactly blessed with car rental companies," she said mildly. "But if you want to drive yourself, there's no problem. You can use my car and drop me off at Lillian's. Her place is on the way to Vicker's Corners."

Amelia hesitated. "I don't know, Aunt Jeanne. It's one thing to rent a car, but to impose—"

Her aunt waved her hand. "Oh, hush up on that imposition nonsense, would you please? Would you think your cousins were imposing if they came over to England to visit y'all there?"

"Of course not."

"This is about money, then."

Dismayed, Amelia quickly shook her head. "No," she lied. Because it was exactly about money. Her aunt and uncle had an undeniably modest lifestyle in comparison to the Chesterfields. The whole lot of Jeanne and Deke's family could visit their estate and they'd still have room to spare.

Jeanne Marie just eyed her.

Amelia's shoulders drooped. "Mum'll want to put me in chains if I've offended you."

Her aunt's lips twitched. "I'm not offended, Amelia," she assured. She propped her elbows on the table and folded her hands together, leaning toward her. "There are all kinds of wealth, honey. I have no problem whatsoever with the type of wealth I've been blessed with. I love my life exactly the way it is. A husband who loves me, kids we both adore and the opportunity to see them starting on families of their own. Just because we're not millionaires like my brothers and sister, doesn't mean we don't have all that we need." She tapped her fingertip on the table and her eyes crinkled. "And if I want to lend my niece my car, I will."

Amelia studied her for a moment. "Did you always know that this was the life you wanted?"

"Pretty much. I was only twenty-two, but I knew I wanted to marry Deke almost as soon as I met him." She chuckled. "Depending on the day, he might not necessarily admit to the same thing."

Her chest squeezed. She'd felt the same way about Quinn. "I'm a year older than you were then, and I don't feel half the confidence you must have felt."

Jeanne Marie rose and began puttering around the kitchen. She was wearing an oversize plaid shirt that looked like it was probably Deke's and a pair of jeans cut off at the knees. "Comparing us is as silly as comparing apples and oranges, sweetheart. I was learning how to be a good rancher's wife. You're out there establishing orphanages and dedicating hospital wings and such."

"Mummy's the one who gets those things done. I just—" She broke off and sighed. "I don't know what I just do." She made a face. "Maybe the media's right and the only thing I was perfectly suited for was being a proper wife for the future Earl of Estingwood."

"Which you've already admitted you're not planning to do," Jeanne reminded. "So *you* know you're not suited."

Her aunt had no idea just how unsuited.

She rose and restlessly tightened the belt of her borrowed flannel robe. "You really don't mind lending me your vehicle?"

Jeanne Marie smiled. "Just make sure you drive on the right side of the road."

Unfortunately, after Amelia had let off her aunt later that afternoon at her friend's home, she discovered driving on the right side was a task easier said than done.

Her aunt had told her that it was a straight shot down the roadway to Vicker's Corners. What she hadn't said was that the roadway wasn't, well, *straight*.

It was full of curves and bumps and dips and even

though there was hardly any other traffic to speak of, more than once Amelia found herself wanting to drift to the other side of the road.

By the time she made it to the quaintly picturesque little town of Vicker's Corners, her hands ached from clenching the steering wheel so tightly, and she heartily wished she'd just have waited until her aunt was available to bring her into town.

Which was such a pathetic, spoiled thought that she was immediately disgusted with herself. Back home, more often than not, she used the services of a driver. It was simpler. And as Jimmy had so often told her, it was safer.

But that privilege also came as part and parcel along with public eyes following her activities. And that was something she'd always hated. Growing up was difficult enough without having an entire country witnessing your missteps.

She didn't care what the supposed advantages were of being raised a Chesterfield. No matter what happened with Quinn, she was not going to raise their child in that sort of environment. It was fine for some.

But not for her. Not for her baby.

When she saw the way several cars were parked, nose in to the curb between slanted lines, she pulled into the first empty space she spotted and breathed out a sigh of relief. She locked up the car and tucked the keys inside the pocket of her borrowed sundress. It was the same red one from the day before because the other clothes from Stacey and Delaney that Jeanne Marie had found had been from their earlier years. It was either wear the slightly oversize sundress once more, or skintight jeans and T-shirts with the names of rock bands splashed in glitter across her breasts.

Even though she was the only one who cared about what she wore, the sundress was preferable.

Looking up and down the street, Amelia mentally oriented herself with the descriptions that Jeanne Marie had given her of the town. Her impetuously chosen parking spot was directly in front of the post office. Across the street and down a bit was the three-story bed and breakfast, identifiable by the green-and-white-striped awnings her aunt had described. Which meant that around the corner and down the block, she would find the hardware store her aunt recommended.

She waited for two cars to pass, then headed across the street. Her first task would be to secure a phone and then she'd check in with her mother. Amelia had instructed Molly to let Josephine know her plans once she'd left the country.

It wasn't that she'd been afraid her mum would talk her out of going. It was that Amelia didn't entirely trust everyone on her mother's staff to have the same discretion that Molly did. Someone had been feeding that Malone woman details concerning Amelia's schedule and the only ones who kept a copy were her mother's staff and James's assistant.

She reached the hardware store and went inside. There was a girl manning a cash register near the front door and she barely gave Amelia a look as she continued helping a customer, so Amelia set off to find what she needed.

The aisles were narrow; the shelves congested with everything from hammers and industrial-sized paint thinners to cookware. But she didn't see any electronics. She returned to the clerk who'd finished with the customer. "Do you offer cell phones?"

The girl chewed her gum and looked up from the magazine lying open on the counter. "Yeah." She jerked her chin. "Over on aisle—" She broke off, her eyes suddenly widening. "Hey, aren't you that fancy chick related to Jeanne Jones who's marrying this guy?" She lifted the magazine and tapped a photo of James Banning astride one of his polo ponies, his mallet midswing. "He is *so* hot."

"Jeanne Marie is my aunt." She managed a calm smile. "The phones?"

"Oh, yeah. Right." The girl slid off her stool and came around the counter. "I'll show you." She headed toward the rear of the store. "Keep alla that stuff on this aisle over here 'cause the only way out is back past the counter. Cuts down on shoplifting." She gave Amelia a quick look. "Not saying *you* would—"

"I know you're not." Amelia spotted several older-style cell phones hanging from hooks. They were generations away from the fancy device she was used to using. But then that fancy thing had been hacked.

She grabbed the closest phone. It was packaged in the kind of tough, clear plastic that always seemed impossible to open.

The girl snapped her gum. "Are you gonna want a phone card, too?" She gestured at the rack next to the small phone selection. It held an array of colorful credit-card-sized cards. "You pay for the minutes up front," she added at Amelia's blank look. "You know. Otherwise you gotta get a contract and all that."

Feeling foolish, Amelia studied the cards for a moment. Contracts were certainly something to avoid. "Do they cover international calls?"

"Yeah." The girl looked over her head when a jangling bell announced the arrival of another customer. Then she tapped one of the cards. "That one's the best value for your money," she provided as she backed away. "I've gotta get back to the register," she excused herself.

"Thank you." Amelia looked at the display. She wasn't going to use her credit card. Just the cash. Which meant, for now at any rate, she needed to use it wisely. She chose the card the girl suggested and flipped it over, reading the tiny print on the back. Not once in her life had she ever needed to concern herself with such details.

She carried the phone and the card back to the register, but stopped short at the sight of the young blonde woman standing there with the clerk.

Ophelia Malone.

Amelia ducked back in the aisle with the cell phones where she couldn't be seen. There was country music playing over a speaker and she couldn't hear what they were saying, but she didn't need to. There was only one reason why Ophelia would be in that store at that moment and Amelia was it.

She quickly returned the phone and the card to their places on the racks and scurried around the opposite end of the aisle, looking for an escape even though the girl had said there wasn't another way out. She discovered the reason quickly enough. There *was* another exit. But it was a fire exit and she knew from regrettable experience in similar situations that going through it would set off an alarm. Gnawing on her lip, she edged to the end of the aisle again and peeked around the racks toward the front.

Ophelia wasn't there. But the door hadn't jangled, meaning she was still in the store somewhere.

She felt like the fox in a hunt and that never ended well for the fox. She continued sneaking her way around the aisles, keeping to the ends because there was less chance of getting caught, hearing the door jangling periodically. When the urge to look grew too great, she held her breath, darting up the empty row next to her where she could see the entrance just as another customer came in.

She quickly backed out of sight again, then nearly jumped out of her skin when the clerk appeared.

"There you are," she said. "Your friend's looking for you."

"She's not my friend," she corrected, keeping her voice low. Feeling increasingly hemmed in, she grabbed the clerk's hands and the girl's eyes widened. "She can't find me. Is there another way out or an office where I can wait until she's gone?"

"Too late, Lady Chesterfield." Ophelia stepped into sight. Her green eyes were as sharp as her smile, and in a move she'd probably practiced from the womb, she deftly lifted her camera out of her purse.

Chapter Six

Amelia could hear the clicking whirr of the shutter even before the lens aimed her way and she wanted to scream in frustration.

"Any comments on Mr. Tall, Dark and Nameless you were kissing yester—" Ophelia broke off when a shrieking alarm blasted through the store, making all three of them jump. "What the bloody hell is *that?*"

"The fire alarm." The salesclerk waved her hands, looking panicked. "You have to leave the store."

"Oh, come on," Ophelia said impatiently.

"There are flammable items everywhere, ma'am. We don't take chances." The clerk pushed the reporter toward the aisle where a half-dozen other customers were jostling around the displays in the narrow aisle toward the front door.

Seizing the opportunity, Amelia dashed instead for

the fire exit in the rear. The alarm was going off already so what did it matter?

She hit the bar on the door and it flew open, banging against the wall behind it, and she darted out into an alleyway. Her heart pounding, she shoved the door closed behind her. The fire alarm was noisy even through the door, pulsing in the air and making it difficult to think straight. Could she make it back to Aunt Jeanne's car without Ophelia seeing her?

"Hey. Over here." A tall, dark-haired woman dressed in cutoffs and a tank top beckoned from one side near a large, metal trash bin. "They won't see you over here."

Amelia's didn't stop to question the assistance and her sandals slipped on the rough pavement as she took off toward her. She caught herself from landing on her bottom and hurried, half jogging, half skipping after her rescuer who set off briskly away from the hardware store. "*You* set off the alarm?"

"Yes, but if they try to fine me for it, I'm denying it. Already had to pay a few of them thanks to my oldest boy." They reached the end of the alley and the woman held up a warning hand as she cautiously checked the street. A fire truck, siren blaring and lights flashing, roared past. She waited a moment, then beckoned. "Come on. You need to get off the street before more people see you."

"How'd you—"

"Never mind." The woman grabbed her arm and tugged her out into the open. Amelia could see her aunt's car still parked in front of the post office down the street, but they didn't head that way. Instead, the woman pulled Amelia through the propped-open door of the bed-and-breakfast.

A teenager wielding a dust cloth across a fake Chippendale desk looked at them, clearly surprised. "Mrs. O'Malley. What're you doing—" her eyes landed on Amelia and widened with recognition "—here," she finished faintly. She pointed her dust rag at Amelia. "You're...you—"

"Yes, yes. She's her." The brunette—Mrs. O'Malley, obviously—nudged the teen's shoulder to gain her attention again. "You have any guests today, Shayla?"

Shayla shook her head and her wildly curling orangey-red ponytail bounced. "Not yet, but Ma's expecting some newlyweds t'night."

Mrs. O'Malley boldly stepped around the desk and grabbed an old-fashioned hotel key off a hook. "Gonna use number three for a while, then. Keep quiet about that, though, if anyone comes asking, all right?"

Shayla's lips moved, but no words came.

"All right?"

The ponytail bounced again, this time with Shayla's jerky nod. "Yes, ma'am."

"Good girl. Now come on." Mrs. O'Malley tugged Amelia toward a lovely staircase with a white painted banister and dark stained wood treads and started up. "Shayla's a student of mine," she said over her shoulder. "Her mother owns this place."

Thoroughly discomfited, Amelia followed. "You're a teacher?"

"High school English." The other woman turned on the landing and headed up another flight, her pace never slowing. "Better hurry your tush, hon," she advised.

Amelia grasped the banister and quickened her pace. Her head was pounding from the adrenaline rush. "Why did you set off the alarm?"

"Figured somebody needed to do something." She glanced over her shoulder. "I went in to buy paint for my youngest's room—the sweetest shade of pink you ever saw—and I saw that woman showing Katie your picture and asking about you."

"I should have tried Lubbock," Amelia muttered.

"You didn't get your paint and I didn't get my phone." They'd reached the top of the stairs and Mrs. O'Malley unlocked the only door there, pushing it open to reveal a cozy-looking guest suite.

They went inside and Mrs. O'Malley immediately crossed to the mullioned window and looked out. "Talk about the nick of time," she said.

Amelia shut the door before joining her, and keeping to one side of the window, looked down. She could see Ophelia marching up the street, her stride determined as she systematically went in and out the doors of each business until she disappeared beneath the striped awning over the B and B's front door.

Hoping she hadn't jumped from the pot into the fire, Amelia sank down on a white wicker rocking chair situated near the window and eyed the other woman. "What do you want out of this? If it's money, you'll be sorely disappointed. My family's dealt with more embarrassing situations than shopping for a discount cell phone."

Mrs. O'Malley didn't look calculating, though. If anything, her light brown eyes turned pitying. "Never heard of a Good Samaritan?"

Amelia's lips twisted. "I apologize for my suspicions, but lately helpful strangers have been in rather short supply."

The woman sat on the corner of the bed that was covered in a fluffy white duvet. "Not as much a stranger as you think. Doesn't seem fair for me to know who you are when you don't know me." She held out her hand. "I'm Jess O'Malley," she said.

Amelia shook her hand. "It's nice to make your acquaintance, Mrs. O'Malley."

"Jess'll do." The woman's lips quirked. "I'm Quinn's sister," she added meaningfully.

Amelia's mouth went dry. "Oh."

Jess shifted and pulled a fancy phone from her back pocket, tapped on the screen a few times then held it out.

Amelia warily took the phone.

The sight of herself in Quinn's arms on the display didn't come as a shock. Since her supposed engagement, she'd become almost numb to the existence of such photographs. The fact that she'd drawn Quinn into the mess, though, caused a wave of grief. "Where'd you find this?"

"It's all over the internet."

She scrolled through the image then handed back the phone. Her mouth felt dry. "Has he seen it?"

"My brother? Or your fiancé?"

Amelia tucked her tongue behind her teeth, gathering her wits. Jess pulled as few punches as her brother. "Quinn."

"He's seen it." Jess sat forward, her arms on her knees. Her eyes—hazel, just like Quinn's, Amelia realized—were assessing. "He doesn't need his heart broken again, Lady Chesterfield. Once was bad enough."

"Amelia," she said faintly. She loathed the courtesy title of "Lady" when she hadn't done a single thing to earn it. "I'm not trying to break anyone's heart. Quinn—" She swallowed and looked away from his sister's eyes. "Your brother hates me, anyway."

"Hate and love are two sides of the same coin, hon."

"Not this time." One corner of her mind wondered if she'd have been better off facing Ophelia than Quinn's sister. And another corner of her mind argued that she would probably get her chance momentarily, because she had significant doubts that any teenager would be able to hold up under the determined paparazzo, no matter how devoted she was to her high school English teacher.

The rest of her mind was consumed with Quinn.

It didn't take a genius to know it was Quinn's ex-wife who'd caused his heartbreak. She pressed her numb lips together for a moment but her need overcame discretion. "What exactly did his ex-wife do to him?"

"Cheated on him with her ex-boyfriend." Jess's voice was flat and immediate. She clearly had no reservations about sharing the details. "Got pregnant and left him for her ex-boyfriend."

Amelia felt the blood drain out of her head. She sat very still, listening as Jess went on, oblivious to Amelia's shock.

"They're still married, living right here in Vicker's Corners. Didn't even have the decency to get out of Horseback Hollow's backyard." Her tone made it plain what she thought of that.

"I haven't cheated on anyone," Amelia said. Her voice sounded faraway. "Least of all Quinn." No matter what he believed right now, six weeks ago, she had been nothing but honest with him. As for James, she'd never made any promises to him either before or after her night with Quinn. And when she'd returned to all the engagement commotion, she'd told him about the man she'd met in Horseback Hollow. The man she'd intended on returning to.

Only that man had said in no uncertain terms that her return was no longer wanted at all.

How would Quinn react once she informed him of her pregnancy?

Trying not to cry, she stood and looked out the window again. There were a few vehicles driving up and down the street. A young family pushing a stroller was walking along the sidewalk, looking in the shop windows. The cars on either side of her aunt's in front of the post office had been replaced by different ones. The fire engine siren had gone quiet.

Ophelia hadn't come pounding up the stairs, her camera whirring away.

"D'you mind if I ask what you're doing in Texas?"

Amelia laughed silently and without humor. Learning she was pregnant had changed everything. She could no longer remain in England actually considering marriage to a man she didn't love. Regardless of what Jess had revealed about Quinn's ex-wife, he still needed to know he was going to be a father. And she had to learn how to become a mother.

She blinked hard several times before looking at Jess, more or less dry-eyed. "Yes." Even that one word sounded thick.

Jess's eyes narrowed for a moment. Then she smiled faintly. "Well, at least that's honest."

Amelia's eyes stung all over again. She looked away. "I'm not a Jezebel."

"No." Jess sighed audibly. "I want to say you're a twenty-three-year-old kid. But that'd be ironic coming from me since Mac and I already had two babies by the time I was your age." She rose also. "Stay here. I'll see if your nosy gal-pal is still snooping around downstairs."

Amelia waited tensely until Quinn's sister returned. "Shayla says she doesn't know you're up here, but she checked in to the room downstairs anyway," she said. "Unfortunately, that room opens right onto the lobby. And there's no convenient fire exit this time."

Dismayed, Amelia could do nothing but stare.

"Yeah." Jess rubbed her hands down the sides of her cutoff denims. "I didn't expect her to check in, either," she grumbled.

"What am I going to do?" Amelia stared at the room around them. "I can't stay here! I have to get my aunt's car back to her."

Jess patted her hands in the air, obviously trying to calm her. "I'll figure something out." She made a face. "Shayla couldn't very well turn down a paying customer. There are only three rooms here. But she said she'd try to let you know if your fan heads out to look for you. If not, just be glad there's an entire floor between you with a newlywed couple expected to occupy it." She gave her a wry smile. "Maybe they'll make enough noise you can sneak out without anyone noticing."

Try as she might, Amelia couldn't prevent heat from rising in her cheeks.

"Wow." Jess eyed her flush openly. "Just how sheltered *were* you growing up?"

Amelia blushed even harder. She thought of the private schools. The tutors. The chaperones. There were days when she and Lucie had felt like the only thing they were being raised for was to become a pristinely suitable choice for a noble marriage. Something their mother had vehemently denied since *her* first marriage had been just that type. Arranged. And terribly unhappy despite the production of Amelia's half brothers, Oliver and Brodie.

Jess looked at the sturdy watch on her wrist and made a face. "I'm going to have to leave you here. Just for a bit," she assured quickly. "I've got to pick up my two oldest from baseball and drop off my middle at karate class. But I'll be back in an hour, tops. And, I'll, uh, I'll make sure Shayla keeps quiet in the meantime. At least the room's comfortable and it has its own bathroom, right?"

Amelia wanted to chew off her tongue. "The room's comfortable," she allowed. But a prison was still a prison. "My aunt's car—"

"I promise. It's my fault you're stuck up here and I'll figure something out," Jess said again. "Just hang tight for a little bit. Here." She handed Amelia her cell phone. "I'll leave that with you to prove I'll be back quickly. Everyone knows I don't go far without my cell. Quinn's always complaining about it."

"Fine." Amelia took the phone only because Jess seemed so intent on it and once the other woman left, she set it on the narrow dresser against the wall across from the bed and went back to the window. She saw Jess hurry out from beneath the striped awning a few minutes later and heartily wished that it was Ophelia Malone who was the one departing.

It was warm in the room and she figured out how to open the window to let in some fresh air. Then she sat back down on the wicker rocker.

She didn't even realize she'd dozed off until the buzzing of Jess's phone startled her awake. She had no intentions of answering the other woman's phone, and she ignored the ringing until it stopped. She used the bathroom and turned on the small television sitting on one corner of the dresser and flipped through the meager selection. Black-and-white movies, a sitcom repeat and an obviously local talk show. She smiled a little when the hostess with a helmet of gray hair talked about the buzz surrounding the Horseback Hollow Cantina slated to open in two weeks, and switched the telly off again just as Jess's phone began ringing again.

She picked it up, hoping to find some way of silencing it. But the sight of Quinn's name bobbing on the phone's display stopped her. Her thumb hovered over the screen almost, *almost,* touching it.

But she sighed and turned the phone facedown on the dresser instead. The ringing immediately stopped and she went back to stare out the open window. The street outside was undeniably picturesque with its streetlights shaped like old-fashioned gas lamps and big pots of summer flowers hanging from them. Her aunt's car was now the only one in front of the post office. Everything looked peaceful and lovely and on any other day, she'd be perfectly charmed by the town.

When there was a bold knock on the door, she went rigid, feeling panicked all over again.

She wouldn't put it past Ophelia Malone to go door-to-door looking for her. She looked out the window. There was plenty of space for her to climb out, but nothing to climb onto. No terrace. No fire escape ladder. Just the awning below her window that hung over the front entrance.

She'd never jumped out of a window onto an awning but she'd jumped out of plenty of trees. Now she was pregnant, though, so that option was out no matter *how* badly she wanted to avoid the reporter.

The knock came again. Followed by a deep voice that she would recognize anywhere. "Open up, princess."

Not Ophelia.

Shaking more than ever, she ran to the door and pulled it open, looking up at Quinn for only a second before dragging him inside. "Are you *crazy?* What if someone saw you?"

He was wearing faded blue jeans that hugged his powerful thighs, a plain white T-shirt stretched over his broad shoulders and he needed a shave. Badly. And even though his lips were thin as he looked down at her, he still made her knees feel weak. "If answering a phone wasn't beneath your dignity, you wouldn't have missed an opportunity to get out of here."

"What?"

"Your camera-toting friend went to the sandwich shop next door."

"How do you even know what she looks like? I didn't see her leave." She reached around him for the door. "If we're quick—"

"She's already back," he cut her hopefulness short. "And there aren't a lot of people browsing around Vicker's Corners with that sort of camera clenched in their hands."

"Shayla was supposed to let me know if Ophelia left!"

"Yeah, well, Shayla's a seventeen-year-old kid and her mom sent her out on an errand."

"How do you know that?"

His expression turned even darker. He crossed to the window and glanced out. "Because I heard them when I came in to see why the hell you weren't answering the damn phone."

Her head swam and she leaned back against the door for support.

He crossed to the window and glanced out. "Jess called me from the park where her boys play baseball. She got tied up there with the coach trying to keep the guy from kicking Jason off the team for fighting. For some unfathomable reason she was worried about you."

She winced. "You can return her phone to her, then." She'd have to take her chances with Ophelia whether the prospect nauseated her or not.

She was a grown woman carrying a baby. She shouldn't need rescuing. Maybe that was one of the ways she was supposed to start acting like one. "You might have gotten up here without Ophelia seeing you, but try not to be caught on camera when you leave again." She reached behind her and closed her hand over the doorknob. "I appreciate your…efforts…but I need to get my aunt's car back to her. I'm sure the baby shower she's attending is over by now."

He looked impatient. "Jess told me about the car. I already got hold of Deke. He's got Jeanne covered."

Amelia exhaled. At least that was something, though it didn't alleviate her anxiety over Ophelia, much less Quinn. "That was—" *unexpected* "—very good of you."

"Jess also told me she's the reason you're stuck here."

"*Ophelia*'s the reason. I never imagined that woman would go to these lengths for a few pictures to sell." Her stomach churned and her palm grew sweaty on the doorknob. "Regardless, you shouldn't have come."

"Afraid your fiancé'll find out?"

She strongly considered opening the door and walking out. Only the fact that she'd brought this on herself by not addressing the press—the legitimate press—straight-on from the beginning kept her from doing so.

She took her hand away from the doorknob and wiped it down the side of her borrowed sundress. "Insult me all you want. I still don't want Ophelia taking after you, too. Right now—" her lips twisted "—assuming she doesn't find us here *together,* all you are is a faceless man with dark hair. She's still focusing on me, and it's best to keep it that way."

"You'd prefer hiding out here on your own until she gives up and goes away?"

"If I confront her, she'll somehow use that for her own gain. I know how these people work, Quinn. She's not breaking any laws—"

"Yet. Or have you forgotten already about the ones who did when they hacked into your phone calls?"

She sighed. She would never forget. "Ophelia doesn't know for certain that I'm here. And she can't stay cooped up in this B and B forever. She's not gaining anything unless she has photos to sell."

Or a story.

And Amelia's pregnancy would be a whale of a tale. It would put the detestable woman's career on the map, at least until the next scandal came along.

"I'm just grateful your sister happened to be in the hardware store at the right time to provide a distraction." It was at least one thing that had gone her way.

His lips curled derisively. "Don't kid yourself, princess. My sister never *happens* to do anything."

"She was there to buy pink paint for her daughter's room!"

"Jess doesn't *have* a daughter. And I can promise you that none of my nephews would be caught dead in a pink room."

"But—"

"Don't try to figure it out," he suggested darkly. He paced around the room as if he found it as cagelike as she. "Jess is a law unto herself. She's just as infected with royal-fever as the rest of the people around here."

Except for him. He'd been fully vaccinated, courtesy of an engagement that didn't exist.

"I don't care why she was there," Amelia said abruptly. "Facing your sister, whatever her reasons, is always going to be preferable to Ophelia Malone. At least she's—" She broke off.

"At least she's what?"

Family. Amelia stared at him, the word she'd been about to blurt still alarmingly close to her lips.

Just tell him.

She'd wanted a chance to speak with him alone, and now she had it.

Just tell him!

Her mouth ran dry. She started to speak. "O-only trying to protect you," she finished, instead.

His eyes narrowed, studying her face so closely she had to work hard not to squirm.

"I wish I had another disguise," she said. "We could just get out of here. Even if Ophelia doesn't discover us, Shayla's mother probably will."

"We don't have to worry about her." He pulled something from his pocket and tossed it on the bed.

She eyed the old-fashioned key.

"I rented the room for the night," he added flatly.

Amelia's stomach hollowed out. "We're *both* stuck here?"

Chapter Seven

Quinn paced across the room, putting as much distance as he could between them. "I'm not the one who's stuck," he corrected.

The bed with the puffy white comforter loomed large between them. Particularly when she sank down on the corner of the mattress.

With the red dress and her dark, dark hair, she looked like she might have been posed there for an advertisement. If not for the fact that her face was nearly as white as the bedding.

He ruthlessly squashed down his concern.

"I can come and go any time I want," he continued. "You're the one who isn't supposed to be here."

"Right. Silly of me to forget," she murmured.

He exhaled roughly. "Maybe she'll want to go out for dinner later and we'll be able to get out of here."

Before morning.

Before they spent an entire night together in a room with only one freaking bed.

He pinched the bridge of his nose and sat on the rocking chair. The wicker creaked a little under his weight, sounding loud in the quiet room.

He cleared his throat. "How many times have you had to do this?"

"Hide out from paparazzi?" She pushed her hair behind her ear. "I have no idea. Lucie and I've been doing it since we were teenagers, I guess."

Lucie, he knew, was her older sister. "She doesn't seem to be in the news as much as you."

"That's just because nobody thinks she's marrying a future earl right now. We've always been in a fishbowl, but never as bad as the last several weeks have been." She rubbed her hands nervously over the bed beside her hips.

He looked away. Whether she looked terrifyingly fragile or not, imagining her hair spread out over all that white was way too easy and the effect it was having on him wasn't one he needed just then. "It's a first for me," he muttered.

She spread her hands, smiling without any real amusement. "Welcome to my world." Then even the fake smile died. "You didn't tell me before—" Her lashes swept down. "In April I mean, that you were married."

It was the last thing he expected to hear and as a cold shower, it was pretty effective.

"It was a long time ago," he finally said.

"How long?"

"Why does it matter?"

"Because you're painting me to be just like her."

His jaw tightened. Knowing she was right didn't mean that he was wrong. "History tends to repeat itself."

Her long throat worked. "You have no idea," she murmured.

The hairs on the back of his neck stood up and he sat forward. The chair creaked ominously. "What's *that* supposed to mean?"

She pushed off the bed and pressed her hands together. "Look, despite you trying to help me here, I understand that things are…are over between us. You've been more than clear about that. And no matter what I say I don't expect that to change. You are not under any obligation—"

His jaw tightened. "Amelia—"

She moistened her lips. Her dark brown eyes met his, then flicked away again. Her tension was palpable.

"I'm pregnant," she said in a low voice. "I came back to Horseback Hollow to tell you."

He stared at her. There was a strange, hollow ringing inside his head. "You're…pregnant."

She chewed her lip. "Keep your voice down. Who knows how thin the walls are."

"You're *pregnant*," he repeated, a little more softly, but no less incredulously.

"And saying it a third time won't change that fact." She went into the adjoining bathroom and returned with a glass of water. She pushed it into his hand. "Drink."

The kind of drink he felt in sudden need of came out of a bottle and was strong enough to put down a horse. He set the glass on the windowsill. "How do you know?"

She paced across the room again. "The usual way."

"You missed your period?"

A tinge of color finally lit her cheeks. She didn't look at him. "Yes."

"And you're saying its mine."

"Yes." The word grew clipped.

"Even though you're engaged to someone else."

She thrust her fingers through her hair and tugged. "I am *not* engaged!" She dropped her hands and sank onto the foot of the bed again. "And before you accuse me, I know this baby is yours because you're the only man I've ever slept with," she added in a flat voice.

He shook his head once, sharp enough to clear it of the fog that had filled it. "You expect me to believe you were a virgin? And I didn't happen to notice?"

Her cheeks turned bright. "I don't care what you noticed or not. That night with you was the only time I—" She broke off. "This baby is not James's," she said crisply. "What earthly reason would I have for being here—" she lifted her arms "—if it were? You think I like facing you and, and telling you—" her voice grew choked "—knowing how you feel about me?"

"Calm down."

"Easy for you to say." She rushed into the bathroom and slammed the door behind her.

He sat there, hearing his pulse pounding in his head. Remembering that April night. The dawn following.

She'd been shy, yes. At first. But he'd never suspected—

He shoved to his feet, crossed the room and pushed open the door.

She was sitting on the closed lid of the commode, tears sliding down her cheeks. And her jaw dropped at his intrusion. "What—"

"It's only been six weeks." He bit out the fact that

she'd been so careful to point out to him. "How can you be certain? Do you have any other symptoms? Have you seen a doctor?"

Her expression went smooth, her eyes remote. "I did a home pregnancy test."

"Sometimes they come back false." He grimaced when she just looked at him. "Another experience from my regrettable marriage." Before the "I do's" Carrie's test had been positive. After, the test was negative. But he couldn't even accuse her of lying about it, because at that point, he'd still believed she loved him and he'd been right beside her when they'd looked at those test results.

Carrie had been relieved.

He hadn't been. Not at that point, anyway. He'd built their house with a family in mind. A family that had never come. Not for him.

"Two years later she got pregnant for real," he added abruptly.

"With her ex-boyfriend's child."

He studied her for a long moment but could see nothing in her expressionless eyes. "Either you've been listening to really old gossip or my sister's got a big mouth."

She didn't respond to that. "I'll agree to whatever tests you want." Her tone was still cool.

He really, really hated that "royal" face of hers. "Another pregnancy test will do for starters."

Her brows lifted, surprise evidently overcoming remoteness. "I meant paternity tests."

"I know." He could only deal with so much at once. "When you arrived in my barn, you were worn out. Exhausted and full of stress. You collapsed, for God's sake. Let's just make certain there's a pregnancy to begin with."

She sucked in her lower lip for a moment. "I don't think now's a good time for me to stroll into a pharmacy to buy a test kit."

He stifled an oath. For a moment there, he'd managed to forget the very reason they were in the guest room at all. "After we get back to the Hollow," he said. "My sister's pregnant so often she's probably got a stockpile of tests."

As far as humor went, it fell flatter than a pancake.

Turning slightly, she swiped her hand over her cheek. As if he couldn't see perfectly well that she was crying.

"First things first," he said gruffly. "Sooner or later, your stalker downstairs will have to eat. Or sleep. And then we'll get the hell out of this place."

"Here." Several hours later, Shayla handed Quinn a set of keys on a key chain with a plastic heart hanging from it. "Mrs. O'Malley said to give these to you, too."

It was finally dark and Ophelia had left the B and B, presumably for dinner, though Shayla reported that she'd had her camera with her when she'd gone.

The teenager—who clearly thought she was taking part in an exciting adventure—had also delivered a knapsack much like the one Amelia had ditched in the airport restroom, filled with clothing and a long blond wig.

"Those are the keys to Mrs. O'Malley's van?"

The girl nodded, looking conspiratorial. "It's parked at the end of the block in front of the bar. You could see it from your window if you looked out."

The bar, Amelia knew, was O'Malley's and it belonged to Jess's father-in-law. She looked at Quinn. Aside from working out their escape plan with his sister and Shayla, he hadn't said much in the past few hours.

He hadn't done much except watch Amelia, leaving her to imagine all manner of dark thoughts he was having about her.

"I can just as easily drive my aunt's car," she argued not for the first time.

"Ophelia probably already knows it belongs to your aunt," he returned, also not for the first time. "It's been sitting there all day even though the post office closed at noon."

As long as Ophelia didn't spot them together, there was no reason for him not to drive his own pickup truck back to Horseback Hollow.

Her stomach was churning. The longer they'd waited in the pretty guest suite, the crazier she'd felt. The news that Ophelia had left the B and B on foot had been a relief, but it didn't mean the end of her problems.

Not by any stretch of the imagination.

"I'll change into the clothes then." It wasn't as if she had many options. She looked at Shayla. "You've been a big help, Shayla."

The girl bounced on her toes. "Are you kidding? Nothing interesting ever happens here! I'm just glad my ma's out on a date tonight. I love her, but if she knew *you* were here, so would the rest of the town. She can't keep anything a secret." Holding her finger to her lips, she slipped out the door and closed it behind her.

Amelia exhaled and, avoiding Quinn's gaze, took the clothing into the bathroom. She changed into the diminutive bandage of a skirt that was as bright an orange as Shayla's hair and the white V-neck shirt that came with it. Amelia wasn't wearing a bra and when she pulled the thin cotton over her head, she cringed at her reflection. The neckline reached midway down her chest and

the shadow from her nipples showed clearly through
the fabric.

If she asked for another blouse, though, they'd be
delayed even longer. And they had no idea how long a
window Ophelia was unwittingly allowing them. So she
swallowed her misgivings and wound her hair into a knot
on her head before pulling on the cheap wig that Shayla
had provided. The hair was synthetic and an obviously
false platinum blond. But it covered Amelia's dark hair
and reached down to her waist.

As a disguise, she decided she far preferred the boy
look she and Molly had attempted.

She kept the sandals on that she was already wearing. There was nothing distinctive about them and the
platform wedges that Shayla had stuck in the knapsack
were too small anyway. Then she zipped the discarded
dress inside the pack and, hauling in a steadying breath,
opened the door to face Quinn.

"Jesus," he muttered.

"I look like a tart," she said before he could.

"You look like jail bait." His gaze was focused on
her chest.

Flushing, she dragged the cheap blond hair over her
shoulders so it covered her breasts. "Are you ready to
leave or not?"

In answer, he opened the door and handed her the
heart-shaped key ring. "Like we agreed. You first. I'll
follow in a few minutes. We'll meet up at the Rocking-U.
You remember how to get there?"

"I got there on foot. I imagine I can get there by van."
Squeezing the hard metal heart in her fist, she left the
room.

This wasn't her first rodeo, as they said, when it came

to avoiding the paparazzi, but it was the first time she'd done so as a scantily clad teenage girl. Even when she'd *been* a teen, she'd never dressed like this. Her parents wouldn't have allowed it.

She encountered no one on the stairs between the third and second floors. On the second, she could hear music coming from behind the door of the honeymooners who had arrived a short while ago. On the last flight, she descended more gingerly.

But Shayla, dusting again though there was surely no need for it, caught her eye and quickly nodded. "All clear, Lady Amelia," she whispered loudly.

Resisting the urge to look back up the staircase to see if Quinn was watching, Amelia skipped down the rest of the stairs and sailed across the small lobby and out into the night air. She turned left, walking briskly to the end of the block, waiting with every footstep to hear a camera shutter clicking or see a camera flash lighting the night.

But there was nothing.

And soon she was jogging. Then running flat out, the knapsack bouncing wildly against her backside, until she reached the green van right where it was supposed to be. Her heart was pounding in her chest as she fumbled with the keys, nearly dropping them, before managing to unlock the door and climb inside. Once there, she worked the knapsack free and tossed it behind the seat before fitting the key into the ignition.

The engine started immediately and she cautiously drove away from the curb. She hadn't been accustomed to her aunt's car and the van—considerably larger—felt even more unwieldy to her.

She drove around the corner, then the next and the next until she was right back where she'd begun the day, near the post office. She waited for a car to pass, then turned again and headed out of town. Back to Horseback Hollow.

Going from one fire into the next.

Amelia was sitting at Quinn's piano, rubbing her fingers over the keys but not really playing anything, when he arrived. He walked over to the piano and deliberately closed the lid on the keys as if he couldn't stand the idea of her touching it.

"Here." He tossed her a small white sack. "I stopped at the drugstore on the way back."

She dumped out the contents on her lap.

A three-pack of pregnancy test kits.

Evidently, he *really* wanted to be certain.

"Decide you didn't want to let your sister know?"

His smile was thin. "Something like that."

She dropped the paper sack on top of the discarded blond wig sitting on top of the piano and turned the box over, pretending to read the instructions on the back, but not seeing any of the words.

She'd been waiting nearly an hour alone at his home before he got there. He'd told her the door wouldn't be locked, and it hadn't been. Only the fact that she needed the loo had made her go in, though.

Otherwise, she would have just sat in his sister's van and waited.

It wasn't as if he truly wanted her in his home, after all.

"You weren't followed?"

He shook his head once.

She pressed her lips together and rose. "I suppose you want me to do this now?" She waved the box slightly.

"You want to wait until morning?"

She wanted to turn back the calendar six weeks and do things right. She wanted the warm, tender man back that he'd been the night they'd made love.

Her eyes burned. Not answering, she walked past him and down the hall to the bathroom there. When she was finished, she put the cap back on the stick and left it sitting on the bathroom counter.

She opened the door to find him standing on the other side and heat ran up under her cheeks. "Two minutes."

He lifted his hand and she realized he was holding a pocket watch.

"My father used to carry a pocket watch," she murmured.

He crossed his arms and leaned back against the bathroom door, his hooded gaze on the test stick. "So did mine. This one." He dangled the watch from the chain. "One of the few things the fire didn't take. This and the piano." He could have been discussing the weather for all the emotion in his voice.

She chewed the inside of her lip.

Never had two minutes passed so slowly.

When finally it had, he picked up the stick and studied it silently. Then he flipped it into the little trash can next to the cabinet.

"It's late," he said, walking past her. "You need to eat."

Amelia's throat tightened.

Even though she knew, she *knew* what the test would show, she plucked the plastic stick out of the empty can and looked at the bright blue plus sign.

Tears slid out of her eyes and she dropped it in the trash once more.

She turned on the cold water and splashed it over her

face until her cheeks felt frozen. Then she dried her face and followed him.

He was in the kitchen. Just as he had been the night he'd found her in his barn.

Only this time the sandwich was sitting on a plate, and a glass of milk sat next to that.

Her stomach lurched. Whether from a sudden attack of morning sickness-at-night or from the horrible day it had been she didn't know. But the thought of choking down any kind of food just then made her want to retch.

She forced herself to sit down, though, in front of the plate. He, however, remained standing by the window, looking out into the night. "Aren't you going to eat?" He had spent nearly as much time cooped up in the B and B as she had.

"We'll go to the justice of the peace on Monday." He didn't look at her. "Unless you want a minister. It'll be more complicated that way, but—"

"A *minister.*" She pushed aside the plate and stared at his back. "What are you suggesting?"

He turned, giving her a narrow look. "What do you think? My kid's not going to be born without my name."

Her jaw went loose. "So," she said with false cheer, "now you magically believe it's yours?"

His lips twisted. "Don't push me, princess."

She shoved back from the table so abruptly the chair tipped over and crashed to the tiled floor. "Don't push *you?* I can't believe I ever thought I—" She broke off, grasping for some semblance of self-control even though she wanted to launch herself at him, kicking and screaming. Which was altogether shocking, because she never lost her temper like that. "If I wanted a marriage without love, I could have stayed in England and married Jimmy! It certainly would have been easier than this!"

"That—" he pointed toward her midsection "—changes things."

She lifted her chin, channeling her mother at her most regal. "It doesn't change the fact that I won't be arranged into a convenient marriage. I've done a lot of things in my life purely for propriety's sake, but not this."

He swore and planted his boot on one leg of the upturned chair and kicked it away from her.

She gasped as it slammed against the wall.

"Next time you give me that royal face, I'll put you over my knee." He leaned over her, tall and furious. "And I won't let you take *my kid* back there to be raised by another man!"

Shocked to her very core, she stood there frozen. "I wouldn't do that."

A muscle ticked angrily in his jaw and his eyes raked over her face.

"I swear to you, Quinn." She stared into his eyes, wishing with all of her heart that he'd just take her in his arms the way he had six weeks ago. "I would never do that," she finished hoarsely.

"Then you can prove it on Monday in front of the JP."

She hauled in an unsteady breath. Marriage to Quinn Drummond was something she'd dreamed about since they'd made love. Since they'd unknowingly created the baby inside her.

But not this way.

Not ever this way.

"No."

Then she retrieved the chair, turned it upright and tucked it under the table and walked out of the kitchen.

Chapter Eight

When he heard the front door open and close, Quinn bolted after her, catching her at the bottom of the porch steps. "Where the *hell* do you think you're going?"

She yanked her arm out of his grasp and gave him a glacial look. "Where I go is not *up* to you."

"You wanna strut out to the highway and hitch a ride, princess?" His lips twisted as he looked her over. "Imagine a trucker will go by eventually. Depending on what sort of guy he is, he might or might not stop for someone looking like you."

She gave a futile yank down on the hem of the skirt that showed nearly every inch of her gloriously God-given stems. "You are *not* the man I thought you were," she said through her teeth.

"And you aren't the woman I thought, either," he returned.

She turned on the heel of her little sandals, her hair flying around her shoulders and started walking away, her sweet hips swaying.

He cussed like he hadn't cussed since he was fifteen and his mom had washed out his mouth with soap. "You're not going anywhere, princess." In two long steps, he reached her and hooked her around the waist, swinging her off her feet before she had a chance to stop him.

Her legs scissored and he slid her over his shoulder, clamping his arm over the back of her legs before she could do either one of them physical damage. "Cut it out."

She drummed her fists against his backside, trying to wriggle out of his hold. "Put me *down* this instant," she ordered imperiously.

"I warned you," he said and swatted her butt.

She pounded his back even harder. "You...cretin."

"Yeah, yeah. Sweet nothings won't get you anywhere, princess." He stomped back into the house and into the living room. He lifted her off his shoulder and dumped her on the sofa.

She bounced and tried scrambling away, but he leaned over her, pinning her on either side with his hands. "Stay," he bit out.

She glared at him through the hair hanging in her face. "I. Don't. Take. Orders." Her chest heaved.

He didn't move.

Didn't do a damn thing even though he should have, because she was there, in his house and she was pregnant with his kid and he didn't want to ask for a polite dance or gentle, moonlit kisses.

He just *wanted*.

With a need that was blinding.

She suddenly went still.

A swallow worked down her long, long throat and the glint in her eyes shifted to something else entirely.

She moistened her lips. "Quinn," she whispered.

And then her hands weren't pushing at him, they were pulling.

At his shirt that he ripped off over his head.

At his belt that slid out of his belt loops with a loud slither.

"Hurry," she gasped, squirming beneath him as she yanked his fly apart and dragged at his jeans, nearly sending his nerves out the top of his skull.

He reached under that excuse of a skirt and tore her panties aside. She was wet and hot and she gasped when he dragged her closer and drove into her.

He let out a harsh breath, trying to slow down, get some control, get some sanity, but she wrapped her lithe legs around his hips, greedily rocking. And then she was shuddering deep, deep inside, her body clutching at him and her lips crying out his name.

And he was lost.

Every cell Amelia possessed was still vibrating when Quinn silently rolled away. She felt like they'd just been tossed out of a tornado.

The night they'd made love had been magical. Tender. Sweet.

This was...raw. Most assuredly not sweet.

And every bit as powerful.

She let out a shuddering breath, knowing that if he touched her again, she'd welcome him just as wantonly. "Quinn—"

"This shouldn't have happened." He sat up and slid

off the sofa. He didn't look at her as he fastened his jeans and his voice was low. "Did I hurt you?"

She caught her breath, aching inside. "No," she whispered honestly. "Did...did I hurt you?" She dimly recalled her nails sinking into his flesh while pleasure exploded inside her.

He looked over his shoulder at that, genuinely surprised. His gaze raked over her and she trembled, muscles deep inside her still clenching. The thin cotton shirt felt rough against her agonizingly tight nipples and she tugged the skirt down where it belonged. She had no idea what had become of her underpants.

"No," he said gruffly. "You didn't hurt me." He leaned over and picked up his T-shirt. The neckline was nearly torn right out of it. He looked at it for a moment, then bunched it in his fist. "I'll get you something to put on."

She sat up, curling her legs to the side. "Thank you."

The roping muscles defining his strong shoulders seemed to tighten when she spoke. He went up the stairs and returned in minutes with a button-down shirt. "You still need to eat," he said evenly, handing it to her. "And decide if you want a minister or not."

Then he turned and went into the kitchen. Through the doorway she could see him readjusting the chair.

Her eyes stung.

She didn't know what she was going to do.

But she knew she was not going to marry Quinn Drummond without his love.

Swiping her cheeks, she stood on legs that felt as insubstantial as candy floss. The shirt he'd given her was clearly a dress shirt but it definitely wasn't the one he'd worn to Toby's wedding. That one had been stark white while this one was a pale gray with an even paler pinstripe. When she unbuttoned it and found a tag still attached to the collar inside, she realized it was new. Never been worn.

She'd have preferred something he'd worn. At least she'd have been able to take a little comfort from it. And she wouldn't be wondering who'd bought the shirt for him because it looked too fancy for anything he'd have chosen for himself.

She removed the tag and pulled the shirt over the one she already had on. New or not, there was something very intimate about wearing his shirt. She needed all the barriers against that feeling that she could get.

She buttoned it up, then folded the long sleeves over several times until they didn't hang past her wrists. She spotted her panties and picked them up. The thin silk was torn in two.

Thank goodness the shirttails reached her knees, though just thinking why that was a good thing made her cheeks hot and her stomach hollow out.

She toed off the one sandal that she was still wearing, blushed some more over that as well, then hurried down the hall to the bathroom, the ruined silk bunched in her fist.

She washed up, dropped the panties in the trash next to the test stick, and tried to restore some order to her tangled hair with her fingers. Finally, with no other excuses remaining, she returned to the kitchen.

The sandwich was still there on the plate.

He was sitting in the chair opposite it, his long legs stretched out across the floor, a dark brown bottle propped on his hard, tanned abdomen.

She ignored the curling sensation inside her belly at the sight and sat down. Unlike earlier, she was suddenly famished, but she cringed a little when she picked up the sandwich, because the bread hadn't even had an opportunity to grow stale while they'd been…been—

"Don't think about it," he said abruptly and she jumped a little.

"I beg your pardon?"

"You're thinking about what we just did on the couch." His hazel eyes were hooded and unreadable. "My suggestion is don't." He lifted the bottle to his lips and took a long drink. "Safer that way," he added when he set the bottle down again. The glass clinked a little when it hit the metal tab still unfastened at the top of his jeans.

She dragged her eyes away and took a bite of the sandwich. For something that had transpired in a span of minutes, she was quite certain *not* thinking about it wasn't going to be as easy as he made it out to be.

"I didn't have anything but peanut butter and jelly," he said.

She chewed and swallowed. "I like peanut butter."

His lips twisted a little. "So do my nephews. They go through a jar every time they're here."

She gingerly took a sip of milk. On a good day, she didn't much care for it, and now was no exception. She slid out of the chair and saw his eyes narrow. "I prefer water," she said quickly, lifting the glass. She dumped the milk down the drain, rinsed the glass and refilled it from the tap then sat down again to the sandwich. "Your sister really doesn't have a daughter?"

"She really doesn't," he said evenly.

"How old are her boys?"

"Fifteen, thirteen, nine, six and two."

"Goodness." She toyed with the water glass. He might not have told her before about an ex-wife, but he had talked about his family. The death of his father. The fact that he had only one older sister.

"Who else knows you're pregnant?"

She looked at him quickly, then back at the sandwich. "Just, um, just Molly." She tore off a tiny piece of crust. "She's one of my mother's secretaries."

He bent his knees and shifted forward, setting the bottle on the table. "You told a *secretary?* Not a friend or your sister?"

"Molly is a friend. And Lucie—" She shook her head. "Lucie's busy with her own issues. Besides, we've never exactly shared secrets."

"Thought you were close in age?"

"We are. She's only two years ahead. But—" She shrugged. "We've all had our responsibilities growing up. Some more than others." She smashed the tidbit of crust between her thumbs. "Mostly, mine has been to provide window dressing at my mother's events."

"You pulled together the companies who funded that last orphanage. That's a little more than window dressing."

She looked at him and it was his turn to glance away and shrug. "I can read," he muttered. "And Jess was yammering on about it not too long ago."

In other words, don't get excited thinking he'd been following her activities. She wondered how impressed he'd be if he knew the companies she'd been able to pull together for the funding were all controlled by the Earl of Estingwood, and took another bite of the sandwich.

The peanut butter and jelly stuck to the roof of her mouth, reminding her of the sandwiches she used to beg off their cook when she was a little girl. "Well—" she swallowed it down with another drink of water "—speaking of reading. We might have avoided Ophelia Malone for now, but I doubt she'll go quietly into the night."

"She got lucky with one photo," he dismissed.

"Sometimes one photo is all it takes to set off a firestorm."

"Afraid your—" he hesitated for a moment "—future earl is going to see it?"

She was certain he'd been going to say *fiancé*. Undoubtedly, James and his staff had already seen the photo and were organizing the appropriate damage control. But she didn't share that fact because Quinn wouldn't want to hear about it. "May I use your phone?" she asked instead.

He looked at the pocket watch he'd left earlier on the table. "Nearly eleven. Your aunt figures we're still in Vicker's Corners."

"I'm not calling my aunt." It would be early in London, but James always rose early. "I'm calling James."

His hazel eyes went flat. "Missing Lord Banning already?"

"If I didn't know better, I'd think you were jealous," she said sweetly. Of course he wasn't. He'd have to feel something other than reluctant lust and duty for him to be jealous. "May I use your phone or not?"

He picked up his bottle and gestured with the bottom of it. "It's right there on the wall, princess."

And he wasn't inclined to give her any privacy. That was more than apparent.

She went over to the phone that was, indeed, hanging on the wall just inside the doorway. Even though she knew Quinn had built the house within the past ten years, the phone was an old-fashioned thing with a long coiled cord tethering the receiver to the base. She plucked the receiver off the hook and punched out the numbers she knew by heart. After a number of clicks and burps, the line finally connected and James answered.

"It's Amelia," she greeted. She could feel Quinn's eyes boring holes in her backside. "How's your father?"

"Amelia! Where the bloody hell have you been? The media here is going mad. Not even your mother knew you were leaving. Are you all right?"

"I know. And I…I'm fine." She absently worked her finger into the center of the coiling phone cord. "You've got to issue a statement that we're not being married."

Even across the continents, she could hear his sigh. "You're back with that fellow, then."

She didn't know how she'd describe the situation with Quinn, but "back with" wouldn't be it. "I know what you'd hoped, Jimmy, but you've got to trust me. It's better to come from you. And the sooner the better." She looked over her shoulder when she heard a scrape on the floor.

Quinn had pushed back his chair and he walked past her, leaving the room.

"Ophelia's been hunting me around," she said into the phone, wanting to laugh a little hysterically because there was a gun rack containing several rifles attached to the wall above the doorway.

"If you hadn't given her something to find, she'd have had to give up," James returned. "You let her catch you kissing that man."

She exhaled, pressing her forehead to the cream-colored wall for a moment. "Just tell your father the truth," she said. "Tell him you're not in love with me. You never were!"

"Father doesn't care about love. He cares about blood-lines and he decided a year ago that yours was the right one."

"A marriage between us would be a disaster." She said the same thing she'd been telling him for months, ever since the whole idea of a union between them had come up. "You're in love with Astrid and I'm—"

"In love with your Horseback Hollow rancher," he finished and sighed again. "Father's condition is worse. He's home still. Refuses to go to hospital. Says there's no point alerting the vultures and he wants to die in his own bed."

She exhaled. "I'm so sorry, Jimmy." For all the earl's faults, he thought he knew what was best for his son. "How's your mum?"

"A rock, like always. Can you just hold on a few more days, Amelia? That's what the doctors have told us he has left. Days." He cleared his throat. "Once father is… gone…I'll issue a statement. You won't come out looking badly. I'll blame it on my increased duties or something. Mutual decision and all that."

She knew his request wasn't because of the Earldom he'd inherit. It was because, despite the problems between them, he wanted his father to die in peace, believing his son was on the track he'd laid.

"A few days," she agreed huskily.

"Thank you. You've been a good friend, Amelia." She heard him speaking to someone in muffled tones, then he came back. "I have to go. Take care of yourself. And look out for Ophelia Malone."

"I will." The line clicked, going dead and she unwound her fingers from the cord and replaced the receiver. She left the kitchen, thinking that Quinn would be in the living area. But he wasn't. Nor was he upstairs.

She went to the window and pulled up the blinds, looking out. She could see a light on inside the barn and she pushed her feet back into the sandals and went outside. The night air was balmy and quite a bit warmer than it had been six weeks earlier, and it smelled earthy and green.

He'd parked his pickup truck next to where she'd left his sister's van and she walked around them as she headed toward the barn. Unlike the house, which he'd built not so long ago, the barn looked like it had stood there for generations and in the dark now, with gold light spewing out the opened doorway, it looked almost medieval. She stepped inside.

Quinn, still shirtless, was stacking bales of hay against one wall.

She pulled in a soundless breath at the sight of him, entirely too aware of her lack of undergarments beneath the shirttails.

Her sandals scuffed the hard packed ground and he looked at her.

"I, um, I would have been much less nervous the other night had I known there were lights in here," she said, gesturing with her hand toward the row of industrial looking fixtures hanging high overhead.

He turned his back and tossed another bale into place. She wasn't sure why. To her, it looked as if he were just moving the stack from one spot to another.

She rubbed her damp palms down her thighs. "James will issue a statement in a few days."

He just kept working. "Why the wait?"

She hesitated and saw the way his lips twisted as if she'd done exactly what he expected.

Annoyed, she walked across the barn, feeling bits of straw and grit crunching beneath her shoes. "I told you James's father is in poor health. He's also been hiding that fact because, in addition to being the Earl of Est-ingwood, he is head of Estingwood Mills."

"The textiles."

She wondered if he'd learned that courtesy of his sis-ter, or if he'd found out on his own. "James has been run-ning the company in his father's stead and fending off a takeover bid by one of their competitors. If the earl's health was made public it would endanger their hold. Once James succeeds his father, that will no longer be the case. The mill will be safe, as will the hundreds of people it employs."

"Again, why the wait?" His tone was hard.

"The title is passed on at the earl's discretion during his lifetime, or to his son upon his death which, accord-ing to James, sadly is fairly imminent. Before now, he's insisted that James be married to an appropriate mate before receiving the title and had been doing his best to see that happened."

He tossed another hay bale and turned to her. "So the old man was yanking Banning's strings."

"I suppose it might look that way." Sweat gleamed across his broad chest and she looked away, shocked at how badly she wanted to press her mouth against that salty sheen. "Lord Banning's not a bad man. He just has very traditional expectations where his family is con-cerned. You behave suitably. You marry suitably."

"Fine. The old man kicks the bucket in a few days. So which is it going to be? Justice of the peace or a minister?"

Stymied, she just stared. "Your callousness aside, re-gardless of what announcements James makes, I'm still not marrying you like this!"

He tugged off the worn leather gloves he'd been wearing and grabbed the shotgun she hadn't even noticed leaning against the wall.

"I've heard of shotgun weddings," she said, smiling weakly, "but this is taking it too literally."

"I've got a possum."

She blinked. "Excuse me?"

"A possum," he repeated with exaggerated care. "It's raiding my feed."

She grimaced. "And you want to shoot it?"

"I don't want to make it a pet," he drawled. "Ranching, princess." He dragged the leather gloves beneath her chin and flicked her hair behind her shoulder. "It's not fine linens and sidesaddles."

Fine linens had their place, but she was just as happy sitting in the kitchen with a peanut butter and jelly sandwich. "I've never once sat sidesaddle," she said with a cool smile. "Some of the Chesterfields are champion riders. I do know what manure smells like."

"You'll get even more familiar with it." He smiled, too, but it was fierce-looking and dangerous. "Along with the stench of branding and the mess of castrating. JP or minister?"

Her smile wilted. Her stomach lurched more alarmingly than ever before and she suddenly knew it wasn't going to go away so easily this time.

She whirled on her heel and barely made it outside of the barn before she leaned over and vomited right onto the dirt.

Quinn came up beside her.

"This is the most humiliating moment of my life," she managed miserably. "Please, *please* just leave me alone."

He carefully gathered her hair behind her shoulders. "Not a chance in hell, princess."

Chapter Nine

"There you are!" Jeanne Marie waved her hand from the window of her car and pulled up alongside Quinn's pickup truck. She got out quickly and strode across the gravel, a wide smile on her face.

Even though Amelia had gotten a few hours of actual sleep after tossing her cookies the night before, her stomach still felt rocky half a day later. She gingerly pushed out of the porch chair where she'd been sitting, soaking up the fresh afternoon air while Tanya, the teenager Quinn paid to clean his house, worked inside, and went down the three steps to greet her aunt. "I'm so sorry about the car."

"Oh." Jeanne Marie waved her hand. "These things happen." Then she laughed. "Well, not exactly *these* things. Nobody around here has ever had to hide out from the paparazzi before. But it turned out perfectly

convenient for me. After church, Deke dropped me off
in Vicker's Corners and was able to go back home rather
than waiting around while I browsed the shops for you.
Which made him a very happy camper." She gave Amelia a quick, squeezing hug. "And I'm glad that you didn't
go to church this morning. That woman with the camera was there asking questions about you." She sniffed.
"Not that *anyone* gave her the time of day."

"A fine churchlike attitude," Amelia said wryly,
though she was glad the citizens of Horseback Hollow
were showing some discretion, even if it was only because of loyalty to her aunt.

Jeanne Marie laughed again. "Now. Shall we discuss
this *nothing* going on between you and Quinn?" She
looked over Amelia's head at the ranch house behind her.

Amelia assumed her aunt didn't know about the internet photograph or she would have mentioned it. And she
was glad for that. "Something is going on. I'm just—"
she tugged at the red sundress that she'd pulled on yet
again that morning "—not ready to say exactly what
that is."

Her aunt's eyes narrowed a little, studying her. "At
least you don't look quite like the whipped puppy that
you did last week, so I'll give you a pass for now. Have
you spoken with your mother?"

Amelia nodded. She'd called Josephine that morning
and told her that the false engagement was over, though
not the entire reason why. She wasn't ready to share her
pregnancy with anyone other than Quinn, though she
knew she'd need to sooner rather than later. She couldn't
very well wait until she was round as a house. Her mum
had been glad to hear about the pretense coming to an
end, but Amelia wasn't so sure how she'd react to having

another grandchild. Her brother Oliver had little Ollie already, but at least he'd been born *before* Oliver and his wife divorced.

Amelia could be married before her baby arrived, too, if she were willing to marry a man who didn't love her.

"She's really looking forward to coming for the Cantina's grand opening," Amelia told Jeanne Marie. "She hinted that she might be able to stay a few days longer than she expected."

"That would be marvelous." Jeanne turned back to her car and opened the back door. She pulled out a plastic shopping bag and handed it to Amelia. "Whatever doesn't fit can be returned," she said. "I made sure of that."

Amelia peeked inside the bag, seeing a couple T-shirts, a skirt and a package of white cotton underpants. "Perfect," she breathed. "Thank you so much, Aunt Jeanne." She carried the bag up onto the porch and set it on the wooden rocking chair and her aunt followed. "Where's Quinn?"

"Off doing chores," she said vaguely. She wasn't entirely sure, because she'd been giving the man a wide berth since he'd insisted she take his bed the night before.

She'd been as wary of instigating another episode that led to torn panties as she was finding herself weakly admitting that she preferred a minister over a justice of the peace.

And her cheeks heated just thinking of panties and a minister in the same thought.

She realized her aunt was watching her thoughtfully, and quickly plucked the receipt for the purchases out of the bag. She drew a couple folded bills to cover the amount out of her sundress pocket and handed them to her aunt.

"All right now," Jeanne Marie said, tucking the cash in her own pocket. "Can you and Quinn come for dinner later? Christopher and his gal, Kinsley, will be there. You know he's opening a branch of the Fortune Foundation here."

Amelia smiled. "I know you're excited about that, but I suspect it's more because Christopher's moving back here from Red Rock."

"It was hard when he was gone," Jeanne Marie admitted. "When he left, there was such turmoil between him and Deke. All came to a head because of that darned money James Marshall wanted to give me." She let out a huge sigh as if she were dismissing all her bad thoughts and smiled again. "The important thing is our boy is coming home. Kinsley will be a beautiful wife for him and he's happier than he's ever been. He's finally found his niche with the Foundation."

"Tell me again how we're all connected to it?"

Jeanne Marie leaned against the porch rail, her expression bright. "Chris could tell you far more than I ever could since he works there, but it was founded in memory of Ryan Fortune who was a distant cousin of ours. They have all sorts of community programs and they help fund clinics and—oh, just bunches of good things for people. Having a branch in Horseback Hollow is going to mean so much. It'll be jobs, it'll be aid for those who need it—" Her eyes sparkled as she focused on Amelia's face. "Where was I? Oh, yes. Ryan's cousin William Fortune—he used to have a business in California—is married now to Lily, who was Ryan's widow and they're in Red Rock. I know it sounds scandalous, but it really wasn't. And then there are the Atlanta Fortunes—John Michael is our oldest brother, then James Marshall and your mama and me."

Amelia chuckled. "I need a map."

"I know." Jeanne Marie laughed merrily. "And they all have grown children and some of them are starting families, and it's just... Well, I hit the mother lode in family when I grew up with none except my adoptive parents."

Amelia smiled. It was hard not to let her aunt's delight infect her as well. "And to answer your question, yes, I'd love to join you all for dinner." She wasn't going to speak for Quinn.

Jeanne Marie glanced at her watch and tsked. "Speaking of, I've got to get the roasts in the oven or we'll be stuck eating at the Horseback Hollow Grill. Come by anytime. Food'll be on around six." She kissed Amelia's forehead and went back down the steps, briskly returning to her car.

Amelia watched her drive away, then jumped a little when Quinn appeared around the side of the house.

He was wearing a white T-shirt covered in sweat and dirt, multi-pocketed cargo shorts, heavy work boots and had a tool belt slung around his lean hips.

And he still needed a shave.

She felt heat gather inside her and dug her fingernails into her palms as a distraction.

It failed miserably, particularly when he spotted her hovering there on the front porch. It felt as if his gaze saw right through her dress to the sum total of nothing that she wore beneath it.

She pulled the strap that kept slipping off her shoulder back into place and snatched up the bag of clothes that Jeanne had delivered. "My aunt played personal shopper," she said.

The top rail surrounding the porch was chest high to him and he dropped his arm over it before tipping back the bill of the ball cap he wore. Throwing up in front of him may have been excruciatingly embarrassing, but it had served to break *some* of the tension.

At least he didn't have accusation clouding his eyes every time he looked at her.

"Guess you're wishing you'd have had her do that in the first place," he said

The bag crinkled in her fingers. "It would have been easier," she allowed. The memory of the way his T-shirt had torn the night before taunted her, and she focused instead on the dirt covering the one he was wearing now. "What, um, what have you been doing?"

He lifted his arm off the rail again and tilted his head. "Come on. I'll show you."

Surprised by the invitation, she squeezed the bag again. "I should, uh, probably change."

His lips quirked and he plucked his dirty shirt. "What for?"

She dragged her eyes away from his chest. "Aunt Jeanne invited us for dinner later."

"Nice of her. S'pose you want to go."

"Christopher will be there. I haven't seen him since Sawyer's wedding over New Year's. He's engaged now."

"I heard."

It wasn't an answer of whether *he* wanted to go. "So?"

He smiled faintly. "I generally don't turn down a meal cooked by someone else."

She didn't know if she was relieved or not. But she left the porch anyway.

He waited until she reached him before turning and heading away from the house and the barn and the antique-looking windmill beside it that stood motionless in the still summer air. They passed several pens, all empty and fenced in by round metal rails, following a path that was more dirt than gravel with a strip of grass growing down the center.

He kept to the dirt part and puffs of dust rose around his sturdy boots as he went and he eyed her when she moved to the grassier strip and shook one foot then the other to get out the grit that had worked its way into her sandals.

"These boots aren't made for walking," she said wryly.

"I could toss you over my shoulder," he deadpanned.

She flushed and continued walking. "I don't think so," she said primly.

He laughed softly.

Something in her stomach curled, and it was not morning sickness.

She stared ahead at the land. It seemed more covered in scrubby bushes and wild grasses than anything. And the horizon seemed to stretch forever. "Don't you have fences to pen in your cattle?"

"There's fence. Just can't see it from here."

"What about your horses?"

"We're getting there."

She moistened her lips. "It's, uh, it's very warm today, isn't it?"

He shot her an amused look. "Probably close to ninety. 'Bout average for this time of year. Be glad there's air-conditioning in the house. The one I grew up in didn't have it. Probably just as well that shack burned down. Made tearing down what was left easy."

"You told me back in April you were very young when it happened."

He shrugged. "Fifteen." The hammer hanging from his tool belt made a soft brushing sound against his khaki-colored cargos with each step he took and she realized her steps had slowed, intentionally or not, allowing her an excellent view of his backside.

She picked up her pace again, skipping a few times until she was level with him once more.

He didn't seem to notice.

"Same year my dad died," he added.

She studied his profile. The night of Toby's wedding, they'd talked about everything under the sun. But he hadn't told her that he'd been married. Or that the fire had happened the very same year he'd also lost his father. "That must have been devastating."

"You lost your dad, too."

"And it was horrible," she murmured, "but we still had a home."

"The Chesterfield estate," he drawled.

Her nerves prickled at his tone. "Yes."

He stopped. Propped his hands on his hips and stared out. "Lot different than this place, no doubt."

She continued forward a few steps and turned until she was facing him. "Yes," she agreed. "But, like the Rocking-U, it has been in the Chesterfield family for generations. I understand ancestral ties to one's land."

His lips twitched again.

"What?"

"Just listening to you talk, darlin'." He shook his head. "Kills me."

She huffed. "There is nothing wrong with the way I speak. *You* are the one who's all...all...drawly." Had he really called her *darlin'*?

"Drawly." His smile stretched. "That some grammatical term they taught you in those fancy schools you attended?" He shook his head again, then started walking once more, brushing past her since she was standing right in his path.

Wholly bemused, she turned and followed and shortly, the road began descending and she realized his house and his barn were positioned on the top of a ridge. "There's a river!"

"That's like calling a mosquito an eagle. It ain't a river, but it's a decent creek. The Rocking-U always had water and thank God it still does since Texas has been drying up around our ears for too damn long." He headed for the trees and the grass growing lush and thick alongside the glittering water.

She hurried after him. Several horses were grazing contentedly, barely even giving a flick of their tails at their approach. "It's beautiful down here."

He pointed at an enormous oak tree. "That is what I've been doing."

Confused, she walked toward the tree, feeling the coolness its shade provided. She had no idea how tall it was, but it was *huge,* with a trunk so wide not even Quinn could have circled it with his arms. "Pruning the tree?"

"Nah. Nature prunes that beast. Even lost a couple limbs during a lightning storm when I was a kid." He closed his hand around her upper arm and moved her around to one side, pointing up into the canopy above them. "You can still see the scar there."

She couldn't see anything because her entire being seemed focused on the feel of his fingers. "Right," she said faintly.

"Figured I'd build it back up."

"Hmm?"

He was still pointing and she mentally shook herself, looking. She saw the healed over slash on the trunk, nearly hidden among the leaves. And then she saw the pieces of lumber a few feet above that, forming the frame for a floor. "You're building a *tree house?*"

"Rebuilding." He let go of her, circling the base of the tree where she realized he'd fastened fresh boards for a ladder. "The one my dad put up was about like everything he put up." He looked wry. "Half-assed and half-done," he murmured. "But the guy never stopped trying."

Quinn's efforts were half-done, too, but that was the only comparison she could see. "I used to love climbing trees. I'd go as high as I could and feel like I was flying. My mother didn't agree. She used to send me to the nursery as punishment. Since I considered myself much too mature as a teen for that, it seemed a fate worse than death." She eagerly placed her foot on the first foothold.

"No way, princess. You're not climbing up there."

She huffed. "I'm perfectly capable!"

"You were perfectly capable of riding a bus all the way from Dallas, too, and look what state you were in once you got here."

He closed his hands around her hips and she went breathless, her nerves vibrating. But all he did was lift her away from the tree and set her feet on the thick grass. "You're pregnant," he added. "You're not going up there. The floor isn't close to being finished. What if you fell?"

Her lips parted. Why hadn't she realized that herself?

"But I want to go up there." She craned her head back and studied the tree house. It wasn't complete, of course, but when it was, she could tell it would be magnificent. "I think you have a bit of Peter Pan in you."

His expression sobered. "I grew up a long time ago."

"Why are you build—*re*building this now?"

He looked back up into the branches. "It was a good place to be when I was a kid."

She chewed the inside of her cheek, watching him. "And you think it'll be a good place for—"

"Our kid." His hazel gaze slid over her. "Yeah."

She was melting inside. There simply was no other description for it. "It'll be years before he—"

"Or she—"

"—is ready for that," she finished huskily.

"Yeah, well, it's also a good way to burn off some energy. And lately, I have a lot of—" He suddenly tugged the strap that had slipped from her shoulder back into place. "Energy."

Her mouth went dry and breathing became an effort. She stared up at him, feeling the warmth of him sliding around her, through her.

"What's this?" He dragged his finger along her collarbone where her skin was faintly irritated.

Her heart lurched. "I think it's, um—" She moistened her lips. "From your beard."

Something came and went in his eyes. He abruptly turned away and slapped his palm against the tree as he walked around it, heading toward the stream. "It'll be a good tree house," he said briskly.

She actually felt herself sway and was glad he was looking elsewhere. She hauled in a soundless breath and pressed her hand to her heart, willing it to calm. She'd blame the effect he had on her on pregnancy hormones if she could, but he'd had the same effect on her from the very beginning.

It's the reason she was pregnant in the first place.

"You coming?" He'd taken off his tool belt and sat down on the grass and was unlacing his boots. "Might as well cool off in the water for a few minutes."

She knew the water wasn't deep enough to swim; she could see right through the crystal clear water to the rocky bottom.

No skinny-dipping here.

She held back a nervous giggle at the shockingly disappointing thought and started toward him, only to trip a little when he tossed his cap aside and pulled his T-shirt over his head.

He glanced her way. "You all right?"

She balled her fists in the folds of the dress at her sides and smiled brightly. "Just shoe… Just caught my, uh, my shoe. In the grass."

He looked away but not before she saw his smile and she knew she was turning as red as the borrowed, too-oft-worn dress.

Pressing her lips together, she crossed the grass purposefully and sat down beside him. "Would serve you right if I whipped *my* dress over my head," she said crossly.

He laughed outright, tossing his T-shirt behind him. "Darlin', if you're expecting a protest from me, you're dreaming. Unless you took to stealing boxers from my drawer, I know what all you *don't* have on under there so feel free to get naked as a jaybird. No telephoto lens in the world strong enough to spot you out here."

Flushing even harder, she slid her feet out of the sandals and stuck them in the water. "Whoa!" She just as rapidly jerked them back. "Cold."

"Refreshing," he countered, and tugged off his boots and socks. Then he stood and stepped into the creek. The water swirled around his strong calves, only a few inches below the bottom of his long shorts. "Come on." He held out his hand and beckoned.

"What if I slip and *fall?*"

He smiled faintly. "I'm getting the sense you were pretty spoiled growing up. You're the baby of the lot, right?"

"Yes. And I was not spoiled," she grumbled and pushed to her feet, stepping gingerly into the water, bunching the dress in one hand above her knees.

After the initial shock, the water was possibly more refreshing than frigid, though she wasn't going to admit it. She was glad for his hand, though, because the rocks littering the bottom of the creek were smooth and slick.

"If you start to fall *here,*" he said calmly, "I would catch you." He squeezed her free hand.

And her heart squeezed right along with it.

They walked quite a distance and he kept to the center of the creek which she quickly discovered was far less rocky and far more sandy and she was able to let go of his hand and walk unaided.

When he finally stopped, he swept his arm from one side to the other. "All Rocking-U land right up to there." He pointed. "That water tower over there is the eastern border."

She could see the structure well off in the distance across an expanse of unyielding looking red earth peppered with stubby trees, wild grasses in every shade from olive to straw, and lazy-looking cattle in just as many hues from yellow to black with horns that looked deadly even from a distance. And the blue sky overhead went on and on, without a single cloud in sight.

In her mind's eye, she pictured him on horseback, riding out there. Open and free. "It's no wonder you came back," she breathed. "Built your house. Built your herd." She looked up to find him watching her.

"This life isn't for everyone."

She wasn't sure if he was warning her, or remembering. In April he'd told her how his mother had been happy to leave this place. "Maybe your mum couldn't bear staying after losing your dad."

"She wasn't the only one who didn't like it here." He touched her elbow but she didn't want to take the hint that it was time to turn back.

"You mean your ex-wife," she said instead. "She didn't go far," Amelia added boldly. "Jess told me she lives in Vicker's Corners."

His eyes were narrowed against the bright sun. "Might not seem like it to you, but there's a big difference between Horseback Hollow and Vicker's Corners."

Yes. Horseback Hollow possessed a single main street with a handful of businesses, though that was already changing with the coming Hollows Cantina and Fortune Foundation office. For now, Vicker's Corners, while still small and quaint, was considerably more developed.

"I like Horseback Hollow," she said evenly and sloshed her feet through the water, her toes squeezing into the sandy bottom as she started back the way they'd come.

For how long?

The question stuck in Quinn's head though he didn't

voice it. He watched her walking in front of him. She was holding up the dress, but the back of it had still dragged in the water below her knees, and it trailed behind her, dark and wet. Her hair was tangled around her shoulders that were turning pink from too much sun.

Right now, she might want to be there.

But she didn't know how hard his life could be. Didn't know that sometimes there could be as many bad years as good. That's what had driven his dad to his early grave.

Ahead of him, Amelia leaned down and swiped her hand through the water, then splashed it over her head.

She looked young. And carefree and ungodly sexy.

He blew out a harsh breath and leaned over, cupping water to throw over his own face. It was cold.

But it wasn't enough to douse the heat.

It wasn't ever going to be enough to do that.

Chapter Ten

"I was getting used to the red dress."

Amelia smiled ruefully as she entered the kitchen. Once they'd returned from their walk, Tanya was finished, so while Quinn paid the teenager, Amelia had gone upstairs to shower and change into the clothes that her aunt had procured for her while Quinn headed into the barn.

"This isn't going to fit me for long," she told him now and twitched the skirt that reached her ankles. The light gray knit hugging her hips before flaring out loosely had wide black stripes angled across it and was much livelier than her usual taste, but she'd toned it down with a white T-shirt with a deep scooped neck and snug cap sleeves. She knew the second she developed a bump, it would show. "The sundress was roomy enough to last awhile."

He was sprawled at the kitchen table wearing jeans

and a black T-shirt. He'd obviously used the downstairs bathroom to shower as well; his hair was wet and darker than ever. He'd also shaved.

She nearly told him she'd been getting used to the ridiculously sexy stubble.

"Not that it matters," she blathered on. "I'll have my own wardrobe soon enough."

He didn't move, but his gaze sharpened. "Is it being shipped here?"

She had the sense to realize she'd just stepped right into a minefield. All because she obviously couldn't think sensibly when she was near him.

"No," she said cautiously. "But I can't stay here forever."

"Here." His jaw canted slightly to one side for a moment. "Rocking-U here? Horseback Hollow here?" His eyes narrowed and he rose. It was like watching a cobra uncoil. "*United States* here?"

She stood her ground though the desire to back up was strong. "I do have responsibilities at home. I can't avoid them forever."

"I told you, I'm not letting you take my child away from here."

"Actually, to be specific," her tone cooled, "you said you weren't going to let another man raise your child."

He slowly pushed the chair back into the table. "What did I tell you about pulling that royal face with me?"

A jolt shot through her from her head to her toes.

She wisely took that step back after all, only to find her spine against the countertop. "I'm not pulling anything," she attempted reasonably. "I'm not saying I intend to return to the UK permanently."

"You want to go back, you can go. After we visit the justice of the peace."

"I don't have the choice of a minister anymore?" Her smart question fell flat and she exhaled. "At least you seem to believe me about James," she muttered.

He snorted. "Honey, I don't give a goddamn anymore if you were engaged to the man for real." He stepped up to her and pressed his palm flat against her abdomen. "The second you told me you're pregnant with *my* kid, that no longer mattered."

She braced herself against the shudder that rippled through her.

He angled his head toward hers. But all he did was speak softly next to her ear. "I may not be some fancy-pants future earl with money and connections, but there is no way on this earth I will let my child grow up without me." He suddenly straightened and dragged his palm upward until it was pressed flat between her breasts. Then he spread his fingers, rubbing them pointedly over the stab of her nipple through the white fabric. "I'll use every advantage I've got."

She couldn't very well deny the fact that she was weak where he was concerned. She'd slept with the man after only a few dances, something she'd never once been remotely tempted to do even though she'd been squired around by suitable matches since she was sixteen.

But neither could he hide the fact that he was equally aroused by her.

"Is that a threat?" she asked evenly. "Or a promise?"

His eyes darkened. "Don't pull an animal's tail, princess. Even the most patient one'll eventually turn on you."

The man who'd counted stars on a magical April

night with her was the same one who was building a tree house, and the same one who was standing here now, she reminded herself, and she lifted her chin.

"You already turned on me," she reminded boldly. "When I didn't immediately deny the engagement stories." Her heart was thundering so hard in her chest he couldn't fail to notice. "And whether that was wrong or not, you obviously didn't care about me as much as I'd believed, or you wouldn't have mistrusted me as easily as you did. And you *still* don't trust me, only this time it's because you think I'll take your child away from you."

Instead of trying to pull away, she leaned into him until her breasts were pressed against his chest, his hand caught between them. "I am not your ex-wife," she said evenly. "No matter what you thought, or still think for that matter, I didn't betray you with anyone. And I have no intention of keeping you from being this baby's father." She went onto her toes until her mouth was only inches from his. "Using sex," she whispered slowly, "still isn't going to make me agree to a loveless marriage."

Then, taking advantage of the fact that he'd gone still as a statue, she shimmied out from between him and the cabinet and deliberately lowered her gaze to the hard length of him clearly evident behind his zipper. "Now, are we going to my aunt's for dinner, or do you have something else in mind?"

His eyes narrowed until only a greenish-brown sliver showed. His jaw flexed. And for a breathless moment that seemed to last an eternity, she was afraid he would call her bluff.

But he finally moved and the sound of his boot against the tile floor seemed loud. "Be glad there's hardly any food in the fridge," he said, and pulled open the kitchen door, stomping outside.

Her shoulders sank and she brushed her hair behind her shoulders with shaking fingers.

"You waiting for a pumpkin carriage or something?" he called from outside.

She pressed her lips together, lifted her chin and joined him.

Deke and Jeanne Marie's place was so packed inside with people when Quinn and Amelia arrived that, at first, their entrance wasn't even noticed.

But then Piper, half crawling and half walking, latched on to Amelia's leg and she chuckled, picking up the little girl and stepping into the crowd of family, leaving Quinn behind.

He couldn't seem to drag his eyes away from her. The shirt she was wearing hugged her lithe torso like a lover, and the skirt was just as guilty around her narrow waist and slender hips. It hardly seemed possible that she was sheltering a baby inside her.

"You going to stand there and drool or do you want a beer?" Liam stood beside him looking amused.

Quinn took the beer bottle and twisted it open. He nodded toward Liam's younger brother, Christopher, who seemed to be holding court in the middle of the parlor, his arm around a pretty blonde. "Guess your family's going to be having a lot of weddings in the near future."

Julia, Liam's fiancée, tucked herself under Liam's arm. "We might have to draw dates out of a hat," she said humorously. But then she looked stricken, looking from Quinn's face to Amelia and back again.

He pretended not to notice.

All of Jeanne Marie and Deke's offspring were engaged except for Galen and Delaney. The oldest and the
youngest. And Toby, as well. He and Angie had already
gotten hitched.

He finally managed to pull his gaze away from the
swell of Amelia's hips where she'd pulled the hem of
her snug T-shirt over the long, flowing skirt. As a teenager, he'd always been more preoccupied with the front
of a woman.

But the perfect sweep of Amelia's back, nipping into
her waist then flaring out again was enough to bring
him to his knees.

He chugged a little more beer. The front door was
open, but the room was still too warm thanks to all the
bodies. He asked the first thing he could think of. "Toby
and Angie get their adoption approved yet?"

"Not yet." Almost absently, Liam brushed his lips
against Julia's forehead as he looked over at his middle
brother. He was sitting on the couch with Kylie on his
knee, watching over the checker game that Brian and
Justin were playing.

Quinn hadn't been around the Hemings kids all that
much, but it was the quietest he'd ever seen them. "Never
thought adoption proceedings took this long. Toby was
already taking care of them for months before he filed."

"I don't think all adoptions have the challenges that
Toby and Angie have had," Julia murmured.

"You'd think learning we're Fortune-connected would
have made it easier," Liam added, even though Quinn
could remember a time when his buddy hadn't been remotely thrilled about that particular connection. He'd
been suspicious the Fortunes were invading Horseback
Hollow, throwing their moneyed weight around and mak-

ing too many changes. "Instead, the social worker's got some bug about the kids' safety *because* of it."

Christopher joined them, holding Kinsley's hand. "Yeah, well, there've been times over the years when being a Fortune was sort of like having a target painted on your chest. The stories I learned while I was in Red Rock—" He pursed his lips and blew. "Lot of history there. Some serious stuff."

"That was years ago," Liam dismissed.

"Tell that to Gabriella," Julia reminded. "She only came to Horseback Hollow to take care of her dad after his plane accident. And those anonymous letters to the post office, saying it wasn't an accident? That it was sabotage and the *Fortunes* were the target and not Mr. Mendoza at all?" She made a face. "You'd think people around here would be grateful your cousin Sawyer and his wife opened their flight school and charter service in Horseback Hollow instead of somewhere else. I'm sure the investigators will get to the bottom of things, but what a horrible business."

"You gonna let that scare you off of marrying me? My mama's a Fortune, too," Liam goaded lightly, clearly not afraid of any such thing.

Julia's eyebrows rose. "Oh, no," she assured. "You're not getting off the matrimonial hook, mister, any more than Jude is with Gabi."

Quinn sucked down half the beer. Everyone around him seemed as happy as pigs wallowing in mud. He wished he found it revolting.

Instead he just found it...enviable.

His gaze strayed back to Amelia. She was perched on the arm of her aunt's chair, still holding Piper on her lap and trying to untangle the kid's fingers from her long hair.

She couldn't be accustomed to gatherings like this. Nearly twenty people jammed into the front parlor of an old ranch house. The night they'd spent together she'd told him about the huge house where she'd grown up. The servants. The carefully orchestrated public functions.

What reason would be strong enough to keep her in Texas when she had *ancestral lands* and a family estate and God knew what else waiting for her back home?

It wasn't love.

She'd already said as much. No loveless marriages for her.

One small sliver of his mind kept listening to the conversation around him.

"Has Toby been able to find out who made that donation to him yet?" someone asked.

"Don't think he cares. That anonymous money'll go a long way to raising those kids. There's enough for college funds even."

"Must be nice," Quinn murmured. Generally speaking, there weren't too many packed into that parlor who'd been able to go to college at all. Or, like him, they'd had to scrimp and save and pray for every scholarship that came their way.

Not Amelia, though.

She'd gone to the finest schools that her family's money and position could buy.

Through no effort of his, her baby—his baby—would never want for anything.

He'd finished his beer and needing escape he excused himself, heading into the kitchen that was nearly as congested as the parlor. Jeanne Marie was at the center of things, giving out orders to her helpers with the precision of a master sergeant. She caught his eye with a smile as he continued right on through until he'd escaped out the back where Deke and Galen were hanging over the opened hood of an old pickup truck.

He joined them. "You still trying to keep this old thing running, eh?"

"Never get rid of something that still works." Deke's hands were covered in grease as he worked.

"*Works* being the operative word here," Galen said wryly. His hands weren't quite as filthy as his dad's but they were close. Quinn still shook the man's hand when he stuck it out, then propped his elbows on the side of the truck to watch them tinker.

"Guess that reporter girl has been making the rounds in town," Galen said. "Has she found her way out to the Rocking-U yet?"

Quinn grimaced. "Don't expect her to. She only knew to find Amelia here because it's no secret Jeanne's her aunt." He absently grabbed a hose that Deke couldn't quite reach and held it in place.

"What's going on between you two?" Deke pinned Quinn with a look. "Jeanne Marie's real fond of that gal. Do I need to ask your intentions?"

Galen laughed silently and lifted his hands up. "Good luck, bro. I'm outta here." He turned on his heel and strode away.

Deke's brows rose. "Well?"

"You don't need to ask," he said flatly.

"Recognize the side of my own house when I see it," the other man said.

He damned the heat rising in his neck. "Jeanne know about the photo, too?"

The other man's eyebrow rose. "Who d'ya think showed it to me?"

Quinn grimaced. "She's not engaged to that other guy."

"Heard that, too. Amelia 'fessed up on that score to Jeanne Marie right off," he added at Quinn's surprised look.

"She comes from a different world," Quinn said after a moment.

"Yup," Deke agreed, drawing out the word. He scratched his cheek, leaving behind a streak of black. "You worried about that?"

Quinn started to deny it but the older man's steady gaze wouldn't let him. "Yes, sir."

"Yeah." Deke's piercing gaze finally flicked past Quinn to look at the house behind them. "Jeanne Marie coulda bought anything her heart desired if she'd kept that money her brother wanted to give her. Clothes. New car. New furniture. Coulda travelled around the world a dozen times and stayed in the fanciest hotels there are. Hard to figure why a woman wouldn't care about those things but she says she doesn't." He pursed his lips for a second and scratched his cheek again.

"Deke Jones!"

They both looked back to see Jeanne Marie hanging out the screen door. "You get your hands outta that rust bucket and wash up for supper!"

Deke straightened and wiped his hands on a thin red rag he pulled from the back pocket of his jeans. He smiled a little at Quinn and tossed the rag to him. "All comes down to trust," he said and headed toward the house.

It was easy for Deke to trust Jeanne, Quinn thought,

wiping his hands and following. They'd been married longer than he'd been alive.

The first time he'd set eyes on Amelia had been six months ago. And he could count on his fingers how many actual days they'd spent together in the time since.

He pulled open the screen door and went inside. Jeanne Marie was smiling up into Deke's face, rubbing a dish towel over the black streak on the man's weathered cheek. "What am I going to do with you?" he heard her murmuring.

"Don't you want to be like them after forty years together?"

Startled, Quinn found Stacey and Colton standing behind him and he realized her words had been for her fiancé. He gave them a dry look.

"Considering the two of you can't look at each other without a besotted expression on your face, I'd say your chances are pretty good," Quinn said.

Colton chuckled and Stacey smirked, jerking her chin toward the doorway opening up to the dining room where Amelia was standing, talking to her cousin Jude and Gabriella. "Get out a mirror whenever you're looking *her* way," Stacey suggested smartly.

"Dishes, dishes," Jeanne Marie called out. "If you are standing in *this* kitchen, and your hands are empty, then grab something and take it into the dining room," she ordered. "Meal's not going to get onto the table by itself!"

Quinn grabbed the closest thing—a basket of fragrant, yeasty rolls—and escaped into the dining room.

They'd had to set up folding card tables on either end of the actual dining room table to accommodate everyone but they were covered with tablecloths. None of them matched. Some had colorful flowers stitched on the corners. Some didn't. But they were all crisply ironed and Quinn had a sudden memory of the way his mom had stood at an ironing board doing just the same thing before every Thanksgiving and every Christmas. The plates weren't all matching, either, nor were the glasses, but they were Jeanne's best.

She had all of her family home and it was obvious that she was celebrating that fact with all the finery she had.

She bustled in to the crowded room, pointing and directing and soon everyone's butt was in their designated chair. Deke at the head of the pushed-together tables. Jeanne Marie at the opposite.

Quinn and Amelia were situated midway down, next to each other. The chairs—another mixture of real dining room chairs, folding chairs and even the picnic table bench from outdoors—made for cozy seating, and there was barely two inches to spare between them and that, only because Amelia was as narrow and slender as she was.

Deke said the blessing and the dishes started passing. Quinn was relieved to see Amelia pile on the food for once. She was too thin as it was, and now she was eating for two. And fortunately, there were so many simultaneous conversations going on that nobody seemed to notice the fact that they were barely participating.

Her arm brushed his when they both reached for the cucumber salad at the same time and she quickly drew back. "Excuse me."

He grabbed the bowl and held it for her. "Go ahead."

Her gaze flicked over his, then away again. She scooped some of the salad onto her plate. "I feel like a glutton," she murmured as she handed him the handle of the serving spoon.

"It's about time you're finally eating more than a few bites." He dumped some of the cucumber and onion mixture on his plate. His mom made the same thing every time he visited her in Dallas. "Were you the one who gave that money to Toby for the kids?" He kept his voice low so only she would hear.

She blinked, looking genuinely surprised. "No." She looked across and down the tables. Toby's brood was surrounding one of the folding tables, with him and Angie on either side.

Supervising referees, he figured.

"Even if I'd wanted, *I* don't personally have that kind of money," she said quietly. "From what Aunt Jeanne told me, it was quite a large sum. It wasn't my mum, either. Aunt Jeanne asked her outright."

"How much money do you have?"

She let out a soft sound and gave him another quick look. "Why are you asking?"

He just eyed her. "Why do you think?"

Her soft lips compressed. "This is hardly the time, Quinn."

"Preacher or justice of the peace?" He waited a beat. "If you can't make up your mind, we could put it out for a vote right here. See what everyone else has to say."

Beneath the edge of the starchy white tablecloth, she dug her fingertips into his thigh. "You wouldn't dare."

He damned the heat collecting in his gut and closed his hand over her wrist, pushing her hand away. "Don't tempt me." The warning worked on all counts. Outing her pregnancy to the entire family all at once. Pulling her hand up to his fly despite sitting in the middle of that very family.

She twisted her wrist free. "I have a personal account

that I control," she said after a moment. "It allows me a comfortable existence."

"Comfortable's a subjective term."

"Comfortable," she repeated evenly. "Not extravagant. Then there are family trusts as well from both my mother's and my father's sides that my brothers and sister and I all come into at various ages. It's all managed and very secure, and frankly I haven't ever much thought about it." She speared a green bean with her fork and smiled tightly. "Does that answer your question?"

Enough to underline the differences between their worlds.

Even if he sold every acre of Rocking-U land, and every hoof that ran on it, he wouldn't be able to match the resources she had at her disposal.

Amelia suddenly grabbed his hand beneath the table and pressed it against her belly. "I am not taking him away," she murmured, sliding him a look. "Now, quit looking shocked and eat your supper."

Chapter Eleven

By the time they returned to the Rocking-U it was late.

Quinn parked where he usually did halfway between the house and the barn and turned off the engine. "Your aunt's a good cook," he said after a moment and felt the look Amelia gave him.

"Maybe she'll give me lessons," she said. "It'd be more useful than most of the other lessons I've had." She pushed open the door herself and got out, heading around the truck toward the house.

His neck prickled, though he didn't really know why and his eyes searched out the shadows of the barn and the windmill.

But there was nothing to see.

That's what came from studying every unfamiliar car he spotted. Every unfamiliar face. He was letting paranoia get the best of him.

He left the keys hanging in the ignition like always and caught up to her. "Let me turn on a light first." He went up the front steps and inside. Turned on the porch light and held the door open for her. His gaze roved over the porch. The two rocking chairs his mom had given him a few Christmases ago were in their usual spot. Nothing out of place.

Amelia slipped past him. "What's wrong?"

He rubbed the back of his neck and closed the door. "Nothing." He hit the wall switch again, turning on the light that hung over the small foyer.

"You should take the bed tonight." She folded her arms around herself. "It's your bed. And the sofa is too short for you."

The simple answer squatted like a fat elephant in the middle of the room.

Share the bed.

"I'll live." Once she was gone—and he was convinced she would be sooner or later—he'd need to get rid of the couch, too. Like the bed, it would be riddled with memories. "I'm gonna take a look around outside."

Amelia studied him for a moment. He was still rubbing the back of his neck. "Seriously, Quinn. What's wrong?"

"Nothing," he said again and went into the kitchen to retrieve the shotgun from the rack over the door. "Just want to check if that possum's rooting around again." He went outside before she could comment.

Sighing, Amelia wrapped her hand around the banister and dragged herself upstairs.

She'd never felt so tired in her life and wanted to blame it entirely on being pregnant. But feeling like she was on one side of a war with Quinn on the other was not helping.

She washed her face and cleaned her teeth—blessing her aunt who'd had the forethought to include some basic toiletries among the clothes—and pulled on the pinstriped shirt of Quinn's again for something to sleep in. She bundled up the quilt—it was warm enough that a person didn't need any covering but a sheet anyway—and carried it downstairs, along with one of the bed pillows.

She didn't care what Quinn said. He was over six feet tall and couldn't possibly stretch out comfortably on the sofa. He needed his own sleep, too.

She spread the quilt out on the brown cushions, then flopped down on it, bunching the pillow under the back of her neck. She yawned hugely and pressed her hands to her belly.

How long would it be before it was no longer flat?

Before her secret—*their* secret—was visible for anyone and everyone to see?

How long would it be before Quinn would trust her?

She flexed her toes against the arm at the end of the sofa, and yawned again before turning on her side, cradling the pillow to her cheek, and slept.

She didn't even wake when Quinn came in a while later and spotted her sleeping on the couch.

He hadn't found the possum, though the evidence it had been there was obvious thanks to the trash can it had upended and strewn across the ground in back of the barn.

He'd cleaned up the mess, slammed the lid back on the can and weighted it down again with a concrete block. He should've remembered to warn Tanya to do the same when she was cleaning.

Now, looking at Amelia's defiant possession of the couch, he debated the wisdom of carrying her upstairs and putting her in bed where she belonged.

Some remaining cells of common sense inside his brain laughed at that. There *was* no wisdom in carrying Amelia anywhere. He'd already proven that.

Sleeping in his own bed without her—now that she'd occupied it twice—held zero appeal but it was safer than the alternative.

He returned the shotgun to its rack, turned on the light over the stove so it wouldn't be completely dark if she woke, then turned off the foyer light and went upstairs.

Evidence of her was everywhere.

In the damp hand towel she'd folded neatly over the rack next to the sink

In the inexpensive clothes she'd folded and stacked on the top of his dresser in the bedroom.

For someone who'd grown up with servants at her beck and call, she was a whole lot neater than he was.

He flipped off the light and peeled out of his clothes, pitching them in the general direction of the hamper. It was stupid to be avoiding his own bed, but there was no denying that's what he was doing when he went to the window and fiddled with the blinds. Pulling them up. Letting them down. Tilting them until they were just so and then repeating the whole damn process again.

Finally, he gave up. He pulled on a pair of ancient sweatpants and went back downstairs and scooped Amelia off the couch.

She mumbled unintelligibly, turned her nose into his neck as trusting as a babe and slept on.

He carefully carried her upstairs and settled her on the center of his bed. It let out its faint, familiar squeak.

He started to back away, but she made a protesting sound and caught his arm.

Not asleep after all.

"I wish we could start over," she whispered.

So did he.

But he was afraid he wouldn't know how to do anything differently the second time around.

She pulled slightly on his arm. "Quinn."

He exhaled roughly and nudged her. "Move over."

She quickly wriggled over a few inches.

He lowered himself onto the mattress. "Come here." His voice was gruff.

She scooted back, until she was tucked against his side, her arm sneaking across his chest.

He stared into the dark. "We're getting a marriage license tomorrow." He wasn't sure if he said it to piss her off or to remind himself how adamantly opposed to marrying him she was.

She shifted slightly, but surprised him by not moving away. "Did your parents love each other?"

"What?"

"I always knew my parents loved each other," she whispered. "It was obvious in everything they did. He'd walk in a room and she'd light up. She'd smile at him when he was upset about something and place her hand on his chest, and everything would be all right." Her palm slid over his skin, leaving a trail of heat in its wake.

He steeled himself against it. "Get to the point, Amelia."

"That's what I want," she finished huskily. "The whole package. Can you give me that?"

His jaw was tight. "My father was illegitimate. I know that stuff doesn't matter these days, not like it used to.

But it mattered to his mother. It mattered to my old man. And it matters to me. You're having my kid. He's going to come into this world with my name. Nobody's going to steal that right from me. Not even you."

Pressing her hand against his chest, she levered herself up until she was half sitting. He could feel the weight of her gaze just as clearly as he could feel the long ends of her silky hair drifting over his ribs. "I'm not trying to steal anything, Quinn."

"Then prove it. Minister or justice of the peace?"

Her fingertips flexed against him with frustration, but only succeeded in sending heat through his veins.

"That's all marriage is to you? A means of legitimizing our baby? It has nothing to do with love?"

"Love's never been a friend of mine."

She was silent for so long he hoped she'd drop it.

But she didn't.

"If I said yes, what happens after the baby is born? What then? We live our separate lives? Passing the baby back and forth on what? Alternate weekends and holidays?"

His jaw went so tight it ached. "If that's the way you want it," he said stiffly. "You're used to a life that I won't ever be able to give you. Things I'll never be able to provide."

She was silent again for a long, long while before speaking, and when she did, her voice was husky. Careful. "I told you before that none of those…trappings… mattered to me. Did you…never believe me?"

"It's one thing to talk about it. It's another to actually live it."

Her fingers curled against him, then pulled away. "Be

glad I'm too exhausted to fight." She lay back down on the bed, her back to him.

Fighting was safer than making love.

He threw his arm over his eyes, grimly aware that there was no point in doing either.

And equally aware that it would only take a nudge, and he'd be ready for both.

He didn't expect to sleep, but eventually he did and when he woke it was only because his arm was going to sleep where it was tucked beneath Amelia's cheek and the rest of him was wide-awake thanks to her warm thigh tucked between his.

For a while, he stared at the sunlight streaking through the slats in the window blind. It had been years since he'd slept past dawn.

Then he carefully extricated himself, arms and legs, grabbed a pair of jeans and a shirt and left the room, quietly pulling the door closed after him.

He showered, letting the cold water pour over him, then pulled on his jeans and went downstairs. His mind consumed with the woman upstairs, he went through his usual routine by rote. Started water running through the coffeemaker. Dumped cereal into a bowl and ate it, standing in the back doorway, looking out over his land while it brewed. He had stock to check, horses to feed. Same things as every other day. Day in. Day out.

It was a life he loved. A life he knew he couldn't exchange for anything else, not unless he wanted his soul to shrivel up and die.

He heard a faint noise and looked back to see Amelia shuffling into the room, her eyes soft with sleep, her hair tangled and the shirt Jess had given him for his last birthday wrinkling around her bare thighs.

"Coffee smells so lovely." Her bare feet crossed the kitchen floor and she leaned over the coffeemaker, inhaling deeply.

The shirttails had climbed a few inches as she'd leaned against the counter and he dragged his eyes away from the smooth thighs and the tender spot behind her knees that he knew from experience was ticklish.

He knew his sister didn't drink any caffeine when she was pregnant. She also always gave up the margaritas she loved, and she'd complained often and long about that fact. Particularly since her husband, Mac, hadn't had to give up either.

"Sorry." He crossed the room and yanked the plug out of the outlet. The gurgling continued for only a moment before sputtering to a stop. "I'll quit making it."

She pushed her hair out of her face. Her gaze roved over his face. "You don't have to do that."

"Because you don't plan to be around?"

She tucked her hands behind her, leaning back against the counter. Unplugged and half-brewed or not, the scent of coffee filled the room. Same as her beauty shined through whether she was clothed in designer dresses or a man's wrinkled shirt.

"Because there's no reason for you to give up something you enjoy just because of me." She tucked her hair behind her ear. She wore no earrings. Didn't even have pierced ears at all. He knew, because he'd spent enough time kissing his way around her perfect earlobes to know there were no holes marring them. "There's no—" She broke off when there was a loud knocking on the front door.

He didn't want to answer it. Didn't much care who was out there, because he wasn't expecting anyone.

But she'd pressed her soft lips together and her lashes had swept down and whatever she'd been about to say was obviously going to go unsaid.

Particularly when the knocking continued, intrusively annoying and noisy as hell.

He left the kitchen and strode to the front door. "Cool your jets," he said, yanking it open.

He barely realized there were at least a half dozen people crammed onto his porch because of the cameras suddenly flashing and the microphone that was shoved close to his face.

"Do you have anything to say about your involvement with Amelia Chesterfield when her fiancé is reportedly sitting by his father's deathbed?"

Amelia suddenly raced up behind him and slammed the door shut on the words that just continued shouting through the wood.

Her eyes were huge in her face and she was visibly shaking. "How do they keep *finding* me?"

"I don't—" He broke off, because they were pounding on his door again and one of 'em—a guy with spiky hair and wide-lensed camera—was even peering through the unadorned front window.

Quinn grabbed Amelia's arm and steered her toward the staircase which was out of view from the window. "Stay."

"Don't aggravate them," she insisted, though she backed up several steps before sinking down onto one and hugging her arms around her knees. "It only makes them behave more outrageously." Her teeth were chattering and she'd gone white. "Did you tell anyone I was pregnant? Your sister? *Any*one? If that gets out—"

"I haven't told anyone," he said flatly.

The pounding and questions hadn't ceased and he stomped into the kitchen. He grabbed his shotgun off the rack above the doorway and loaded it with birdshot.

"What are you doing?"

She bolted to her feet and her huge eyes engulfed her entire face. They were the haunted eyes she'd had when she'd fainted in his barn.

And they made him want to string somebody up from the nearest tree.

"Getting rid of the vermin."

She shook her head rapidly. "Don't, Quinn. You have to ignore—"

"They're trespassing. Maybe they should've concerned themselves with aggravating *me*," he finished harshly.

Then he yanked open the door, greeting the intruders with the business end of the shotgun. "Get off my land."

Like cockroaches hit with the light, they scrambled off his porch, but only so far as to shield themselves.

He stepped out onto the wood porch and cocked the gun. It sounded satisfyingly loud and threatening. "Get."

"How long have you been sleeping with her?" some fool called out and Quinn swung the barrel toward the voice, finding the gel-haired guy who'd had the nerve to aim a camera through his front window.

"You're trespassing," he said coldly. "And I'm a real good shot." He met the man's eyes. At least he had the good sense to take a nervous step backward. "You want to test it out?"

"Lord Banning's a powerful man," someone else

yelled in a shrill voice. "You're not afraid of retribution for trying to steal his bride?"

He aimed beyond them where the vehicles they'd arrived in were parked every which way all over his gravel, and planted a load of shot exactly six inches from the front tire of the closest car. The noise was shockingly loud and gravel spewed, pinging against the car.

The roaches scattered even faster.

"Next one goes in the car!"

He had no intention of shooting anyone, but they didn't need to know that. There were seven of them, three men and four women, and he wondered which one, if any, was the Ophelia who'd plagued Amelia.

He eyed them each before cocking the gun again. *"Get off my land."*

They scrambled for the cars, nearly colliding among themselves as they poured into doors, gunned engines and spun tires.

Only when the last of them was nearly out of sight and the clouds of dust were starting to die did his grip on the gun relax.

And it was several minutes after that before the rest of him relaxed enough that he could go back inside the house.

He closed and locked the door, unloaded the rest of the birdshot and left the gun propped against the door.

Amelia was no longer huddled and hiding on the staircase.

She was pacing around the living room, looking agitated. "You couldn't have just *ignored* them? You had to go all...all Texas Ranger on them?" She sank down on the couch and clawed her fingers through her hair. "You may know ranching, Quinn, but I know the paparazzi.

There will be pictures of you on every network by the evening news." Just as fast as she'd sat, she shoved off the couch. "I have to phone my mother. Warn her." She laughed, sounding on the verge of hysteria, and her face was white. "If she hasn't already been treated to the same sorts of questions."

He caught her arms before she made it to the kitchen. "Calm down," he said. "You're going to make yourself sick again."

"Calm down?" She shook off his hands. "Would you feel calm if you knew you were causing nothing but embarrassment to the people you love?"

The words felt like blows.

"That's what involvement with me is. An embarrassment."

She looked stricken. "No! I never said that. I—I—" She broke off hugging her arms tightly around her. Her eyes turned wet. "I don't like being the cause of scandal. That's all."

"I don't believe you."

Her lips parted. She seemed to sway a little.

Then her face smoothed, though her eyes still gleamed, wet and glassy. "Of course you wouldn't," she said expressionlessly. "You haven't believed me about anything I've said yet. You just want to maneuver me into marriage to protect *your* interests. Same thing James wanted to do."

"You're gonna compare our baby to a textile company?"

She just shook her head, looking weary, and walked over to the stairs.

There was no phone upstairs. The only one inside the house hung on the wall in the kitchen.

"Thought you were calling your mother."

She didn't answer him. Just kept going up the stairs.

He was still standing there, rooted in place, when she came down a few minutes later.

She'd twisted her hair into a knot at the nape of her neck and pulled on a black T-shirt with the same striped skirt she'd worn the day before. The clothes were inexpensive. Hardly fancy. Yet she still managed to look untouchably elegant.

Her eyes didn't meet his. "If you'd be kind enough to drive me to Aunt Jeanne's, I would be grateful."

His hands curled into fists. "Aren't you afraid the vultures will be waiting?"

"I'm sure they will be." Her triangular chin lifted. "I'll handle it."

Unlike him.

She didn't say it.

But she didn't need to.

Chapter Twelve

"When is this going to die down?" Jeanne Marie fretted, and turned off the television and yet another gossipy tidbit on the morning news speculating about the most intimate details of Amelia's, Quinn's and James's lives while a silent video ran in the background showing Amelia, dressed only in Quinn's shirt slamming his front door shut on the photographers' cameras. "It's been a week already."

This time, the commentator—Amelia refused to call the vapid woman an actual reporter—had even dug up ancient stories about her mother's first marriage to Rhys Henry Hayes and even more ancient stories about King Edward's abdication of the throne for the woman he'd loved. Trying to manufacture out of thin air similarities where there were none at all.

"It's because of the funeral," Amelia said on a sigh.

James's father's funeral service had been held in London that morning and the timing made it a prime topic for the morning's national news shows. "The story will lose traction eventually, once something more interesting in the world comes along." She made a face. "Horrible of me to wish for a slew of natural disasters somewhere in the world."

Jeanne Marie squeezed her hand and sat down beside her. "Have you spoken with Quinn?"

Just the sound of his name caused a pang inside her and she shook her head.

Since he'd dropped her off at her aunt's home that dreadful morning a week ago, he hadn't tried to reach her once.

To be fair, she hadn't tried to speak with him, either. The only thing she'd been able to do was unleash threats of a lawsuit against the offenders who'd trespassed on the Rocking-U.

Only because her family had won the last suit they'd brought against the phone hackers a year ago had there been enough teeth behind the threat to encourage many of the pests to finally move on. Amelia wished that were true of Ophelia Malone, but the woman was still taking up residence at the B and B in Vicker's Corners. She was a freelancer, according to the sketchy information Molly had been able to unearth. She didn't have publishers keeping her on a leash they could retract when necessary.

"You're going to want to talk to Quinn sooner or later," her aunt said gently.

"I know." Amelia plucked the knee of her jeans. She just didn't know what she was going to say when she did. He'd had an up close and personal taste of the sort of things she'd had to deal with almost daily back in London.

Who would blame him for wanting no part of it?

For the past week, she'd lived in the seclusion of her aunt and uncle's house. Avoiding going outdoors in case there were still remaining telephoto lenses aimed their way. Avoiding all but the most necessary of phone calls. She'd even been careful not to find herself standing or sitting near windows.

It wasn't fair to burden her aunt and uncle with that sort of behavior, but they'd both been adamant that she remain with them. Even Amelia's mother had agreed that Amelia should stay in the States while she and James— now the Earl of Estingwood himself—dealt with the official media back home.

Everyone around her was taking care of her.

And she was heartily tired of it.

"I need a good solicitor," she said abruptly. "An attorney. Is there anyone you recommend? Someone you trust?"

Jeanne Marie looked thoughtful. "We haven't had a lot of need for attorneys, but Christopher once mentioned an attorney in Red Rock he knew through people at the Fortune Foundation. Or I can contact James Marshall. He surely has his own legal department at his company."

Amelia knew that JMF Financial was located in Georgia. Red Rock, though, was only four hundred or so miles away. "Would you mind calling Christopher for me?"

"Of course not." Jeanne Marie hesitated a moment. "Do you want me to call him right away?"

Now that Amelia had brought it up, she did.

In fact, she was suddenly impatient to do *something*.

"If you would. I need an appointment as soon as possible. Preferably before Mum arrives in a few days. I can call Sawyer Fortune and arrange for a charter flight to Red Rock." Until her latest escape from London and subsequent trek making her way to Quinn's, she'd used the flight service her cousin ran to get from Dallas to Horseback Hollow the other times she'd visited.

"You're ready to go out in public?"

Amelia made a face. "No," she admitted. "But the longer I hide out, the harder it will get. And I'd rather get used to it now than wait until the Cantina's grand opening this Friday." She followed her aunt into the kitchen and found herself looking out one of the windows at the picnic table and benches sitting on the grass.

But she wasn't really seeing them.

She was remembering dancing with Quinn out there on a portable dance floor.

He'd put his arms around her, and even though it was the first time he'd touched her, the first time they'd ever done anything but see each other from a distance really, she felt like she'd come home.

Her throat tightened and her nose burned with unshed tears.

Now, she feared that home was nothing more than a fantasy. A silly girl's romantic longing.

"Pour another." Quinn tapped the empty shot glass sitting on the bar in front of him. At seven in the evening, he hadn't expected the Two Moon Saloon to be entirely empty, even on a Tuesday. But he'd been the only one there for a good hour now.

He'd had no particular desire to go out at all, but Jess had nagged him into meeting up at the Horseback Hollow Grill for burgers with her family. He'd been avoiding her, like he'd been avoiding most everyone else in town for the past week. But he'd been sick of his own company, and since the paparazzi that had plagued him for most of the week since the whole shotgun incident had finally gone off for greener pastures, he'd agreed.

And even though, for once, his sister had wisely showed the good sense not to bring up anything to do with Amelia or the fact that his image—shirtless and brandishing a shotgun like some kind of madman—was all over creation thanks to the magic of the worldwide web and nonstop news services, he'd been glad when the meal was over.

While his sister and brother-in-law had corralled their sons out the door to go home, he'd just gone next door to the saloon that was attached to the grill.

He was sick of his own company, true. But he also wasn't in the mood for socializing.

Nor was he in the mood to hide out inside his own damn house because everywhere he looked, he saw Amelia.

One night last week he'd even slept out on the porch.

Damned pathetic.

He eyed the pretty bartender who was pouring him another shot of bourbon. "You're new." She had brown hair and brown eyes, just as dark as Amelia's, and was slender as a reed, also like Amelia.

And he didn't feel the faintest jangle of interest.

"What's your name?"

"Annette."

"Why'd you come to Horseback Hollow, Annette?" He tossed back the drink and clenched his teeth against the burn that worked down his throat. "Nothing going on in this place." He set the shot glass down on the wood bar with a thud.

She swiped her white bar towel over the wood. "Wouldn't say that, Mr. Drummond," she countered.

He narrowed his eyes, studying her while his fingers turned the small glass in circles on the bar. "How'd you know my name?"

She smiled faintly. "How d'ya think? I have a television." She lifted the bottle. "Another?"

He moved his hand away and she filled the glass, then set the bottle on the counter behind her and returned to her polishing.

"It wasn't as bad as it looked," he muttered.

"It looked like a man trying to protect what's his," she said calmly. "What's so bad about that?"

He lifted the glass, studying the amber-colored contents. The deputy sheriff who'd come calling about the matter had agreed with that notion and it'd been plain from the ample video coverage that Quinn hadn't tried shooting at anyone.

But that didn't change things for Quinn.

Amelia *wasn't* his. She'd made it plain she didn't want to be his. The only thing that *was* his was the baby she carried.

His chest tightened and hating the feeling, he put the glass to his lips. The liquor burned again, but brought no relief. No blurring of reality. No softening of the facts.

Amelia came from one world. He came from another.

"Send us over a round of margaritas and a couple a' waters, would you, darlin'?"

He realized that a group of people were coming in through the street-side entrance and glanced over to see Sawyer and Laurel Fortune coming in along with a few of the folks he knew were working for them over at their charter service. He lifted his hand, returning the greeting they sent him, then turned back to his solitude.

He quickly realized, though, that Sawyer and his group weren't cooperating with that notion, insisting that he join them as well.

Quinn had no desire to be among the Fortunes, but Orlando Mendoza was with them, and his daughter Gabriella was marrying Jude Fortune Jones, whom he'd known all his life. The new bartender was noisily scooping ice into margarita glasses with one hand and pouring tequila into a pitcher with the other so he reluctantly left his empty shot glass and moved over to their table.

"Y'all look like you're celebrating," he greeted.

"We are." Sawyer gestured to his companions. "You know everyone here, don't you, Quinn?"

"Some, more 'n others." Quinn gave a general nod, sticking out his hand to Orlando and the older man shook it. "Glad to see you're up on your feet again."

The pilot grinned. "Needed to if I'm going to be able to walk Gabi down the aisle and give her away when she and Jude get married. Glad to get the casts off at last. Things were itching me like crazy."

The bartender delivered the tray of waters and ice-filled, salt-rimmed glasses and set the margarita pitcher in the middle of the table before returning behind the bar.

"Broke my arm once." Quinn shook his head when Laurel started pouring out drinks and offered him one. "Couldn't stand the cast so bad I ended up cutting it off myself a week before the doctor said. Are you cleared for flying again?"

The salt-and-pepper-haired man nodded, looking relieved.

"That's what we're celebrating," Sawyer said. "That and the fact that the investigators have finally closed the case about the accident." He held up one of the glasses and waited while the others did the same. "No sabotage. No pilot error—" he gave a nod toward Orlando at that "—and no maintenance insufficiencies."

"So what happened?"

"Aircraft design," Orlando supplied.

"The plane's been recalled," Laurel added. She clinked her glass against her husband's and the others. "Just wish the manufacturer could have caught their error before people got hurt."

"Manufacturer is wishing the same thing," Sawyer said. "Not saying we're planning to, but it's a given that someone will bring lawsuits against them about it all."

Laurel looked at Quinn. "Speaking of lawsuits, is that what Amelia's planning?"

His skin prickled. "What do you mean?"

Orlando sat forward. He was the only one around the table drinking only water. "I flew Miss Chesterfield to Red Rock this morning. She was meeting with one of my cousin Luis's boys. Rafe's a lawyer over there. Told her she could've just waited until this weekend to talk to him, since he'll be in town for the opening of his brother's restaurant, but she was anxious to go now. I'll be picking her up again tomorrow afternoon."

Was she just adding on another layer of protection against more media invasions like they suspected? Or was she really laying the groundwork to keep his child away from him? "You'd have to ask Amelia what she's planning," he said abruptly and started backing away from the table. "I'll leave y'all to your celebrating. Congratulations." Not leaving them an opportunity to respond, he peeled a few bills off his wallet and dropped them on the bar.

Annette tucked the bills in the cash register. "You want some coffee before you head out, Mr. Drummond?"

He had never felt more stone-cold sober but to keep her satisfied and quiet about it, he told her to give him one to go, and then he went on his way, a foam cup of hot coffee in his hand. He was parked on the other side of the grill, so instead of leaving on the street side, he walked through the doorway separating the bar from the grill.

Only a few people were still sitting at the old-fashioned tables positioned around the ancient tiled floor. The little game room where his nephews always fought over playing the race car game was silent, the light turned off.

The coffee smelled bitter, like it was a day old by now, and his first sip confirmed it tasted that way, too.

The coffee still reminded him of Amelia.

He dumped the cup in the trash can next to the pay phone that hung in one corner of the diner and pulled out the thick phone book that was stuffed on the shelf below the phone. He paged through the yellow pages, finding the section he wanted. He tore out the first page of law firm listings, pushed the book back on the shelf and left.

Amelia paged through the agreement that Rafe Mendoza had sent with her and read through the paragraphs yet again. The attorney had tried talking her out of some of the stipulations that she'd wanted included, but she'd been adamant.

"You may change your mind," he'd argued. "You want to stay in Texas now, but there's no reason to sign away your choice of moving away later on." His dark eyes had been kind. "You're only twenty-three, Amelia. At least think about it."

"I won't change my mind," she'd told him. But she'd agreed to give it a day and had picked up the agreement that afternoon on her way to the Red Rock regional airport for her return charter to Horseback Hollow.

She closed the document and tucked it back inside the folder Rafe's secretary had provided with the custody agreement and then she climbed out of her aunt's car that she'd borrowed and walked past Quinn's truck toward the house.

It was the middle of the afternoon, so she wasn't particularly surprised when he didn't answer her knock. When she tried the knob and found it locked, though, she was.

A lesson learned from the paparazzi, she assumed with a pang of guilt. Once your privacy was invaded, it was hard to trust that it wouldn't happen again.

Carrying the folder with her, she walked down to the barn and found it empty. There were six horses standing around in the corral next to the barn, their long tails swishing against the heat of the day. She held out her palm over the metal rail and the nearest one nuzzled her palm, obviously looking for a tidbit.

"Sorry, girl," she murmured and rubbed her hand down the horse's white blaze. "Next time I'll bring a treat."

If she'd be allowed a next time.

Following the road with the grassy strip in the center, she kept walking until it began to dip and she could see Quinn's tree house tree in the distance. When she drew closer, she heard the distinctive beat of a hammer.

And even though she'd been gearing herself up for

the past twenty-four hours to see him, her mouth still went dry and her chest tightened.

She tucked the folder under her arm and smoothed back a strand of hair that had worked free from the chignon at her nape. She aimed toward the tree while the hammering grew louder and more distinct, and soon she was standing beneath the shady leaves.

She moved around to where the footholds were and tapped the lowest one with the toe of the Castleton cowboy boots she'd purchased while killing time in Red Rock. Since her whereabouts weren't remotely a secret, she'd also visited Charlene's boutique with her credit card, and stocked up on clothing, including a black silk dress for the Cantina's grand opening. She'd also had lunch with her cousin Wyatt and his wife, Sarah-Jane. And even though Amelia had found Red Rock surprisingly sophisticated and quite lovely, she knew she still preferred the rugged, much smaller Horseback Hollow.

"Fancy boots. You buy them before or after meeting up with that Red Rock lawyer?"

She looked from the detailed stitching over her toe up into the leaves and met Quinn's hazel gaze. "As usual, news is traveling at the speed of light." She ran her palm over the rough tree bark. "Can you come down?"

He swung down from the floor he was constructing and climbed down several footholds before jumping the rest of the way to the ground. He straightened and looked down at her, his expression unreadable. "You going to tell me anything I want to know?"

"I don't know," she said huskily and handed him the folder. "Considering everything that happened last week, you might not welcome anything to do with me."

His lips thinned and he made no attempt to open the

folder. "A hundred reporters camped out on my front porch wouldn't change the fact that you're pregnant with my baby."

"They didn't cause you any more problems, did they?" She tucked her hands in the front pockets of the narrow, black trousers she'd bought at the boutique. There'd been a small selection of delightful maternity clothes, though she hadn't had the nerve to purchase any. Not with the other customers there who'd watched her, somewhat agog, as she'd shopped.

"Guess you'd have seen it on the news if they had." His tone was flat. He gestured with the folder. "You bring this here to settle the fact I can't prevent you from going back to England? Already found that out myself from three different attorneys over in Lubbock."

A pang drove through her. "If that's what you think, you really don't know me at all."

"Saw your earl's press conference."

"Evidently not," she countered, "if you still have the impression that James is *my* anything."

"'Amelia Fortune Chesterfield's support during this difficult time has been steadfast,'" Quinn said, quoting almost verbatim the brief statement that James's staff had released. "'And though we are not betrothed,'" his lips twisted, "'we remain loyal friends.' Didn't exactly say you were never engaged to marry him in the first place."

"People in James's positions don't explain," she said. "They don't complain to the media and they never lend credence to speculation by commenting on anything that smacks of scandal. Which is not to say they won't use the media if it serves their purposes. James's father certainly proved that." She exhaled. "I didn't come here to talk about him." She nodded toward the folder. "I came here to give you that."

Looking even more grim, he flipped open the folder.

His eyes narrowed as he read, his frown coming and going as he flipped slowly through the pages.

"It's a shared custody agreement." Of course he could read for himself what it was, but his silence was more than she could bear. "With stipulations that the baby will bear your name and be raised here in Horseback Hollow."

He finally looked at her. "Why would you do this?"

She lifted her chin. "Why wouldn't I? I've told you more than once I don't want that life." She unconsciously pressed her hand to her abdomen. "I didn't want it for myself and I don't want it for our child. I don't know how else to prove it to you."

"You've already signed it."

"Yes. Duly witnessed by the appropriate individuals." She pressed her tongue to the back of her teeth, hunting for strength. "Go back to your Lubbock attorneys and have them review it. They'll tell you it's exceedingly fair. And once you sign it, there'll be no need for a justice of the peace or a minister."

His jaw canted to one side. He closed the folder and tapped it against the side of his jean-clad thigh. "You *really* don't want to marry me."

"No." She suddenly jabbed her forefinger into his unyielding chest. "*You* really don't want to marry *me*. You're stuck in the past with the one who did betray you. The only reason you want to marry me is to ensure the baby has your name." She gestured at the folder. "Well, happy tidings. Sign it and neither one of us need worry about that a moment longer."

"I don't have a pen."

She felt like her heart was turning to dust inside her chest. She looked up into the leaves above their heads.

He'd build a magical place for their child.

But he wouldn't let himself believe in love.

At least not love with *her*.

"I'm sure you'll find one somewhere," she managed. "You can send me a copy of the agreement once you do."

"And then?"

"And then I guess we'll figure out what to do next." She lifted her hands, feeling helpless. "At least things can't possibly get any worse."

Then she turned on her boot heel and walked away.

Chapter Thirteen

But Amelia was wrong.

Things could get worse.

And they did.

"She is *pregnant?*" Jess's screech could have been heard around the world.

It was certainly enough to wake Quinn from his stupor where he was sprawled on his couch, and he bolted upright, rubbing his hands down his face as his sister stormed into his house brandishing a magazine over her head.

"What?"

She slapped the glossy tabloid on top of Amelia's custody papers that were sitting on the coffee table and picked up the bottle of whiskey he'd tried working his way through the day after Amelia had left him. "Oh, my God." She was clearly disgusted. "You're drunk."

"No. I was drunk." He pinched the bridge of his nose. "Now the term would be *hungover*. So if you'd take your hysterics and leave me the hell alone, I'd appreciate it. And give me back your key to my front door while you're at it."

She sat down on the coffee table in front of him and caught his chin in her hand, giving him a look that was unreasonably similar to their mother's. "You're a grown man who's going to be a father," she tsked. "Start acting like it!"

He brushed her hand aside. The fact that she knew about Amelia's pregnancy was seeping into his throbbing brain. "How'd you find out?"

She shifted and tugged the magazine from under her hip and waved it in front of his face. "Same way everyone on the planet did."

He snatched it from her and stared at the cover of the international tabloid. It contained only a single photograph of a positive pregnancy test stick, with a question mark and the words The Real Cause Behind the End of Jamelia? superimposed over the top.

Disgusted, he threw it aside and shoved off the couch. "Why the *hell* won't everyone just leave her alone!"

Jess narrowed her eyes and studied him. "It's true, then. Amelia is pregnant."

"Whatever happened to people's right to privacy?"

"Privacy's an illusion," Jess said. "I think somebody famous said that. Or the government did. Or—" She shook her head. "Doesn't matter. I'm asking you, Quinn. Is that story true?"

He raked his fingers through his hair. "I didn't read the damn story."

She made a face and straightened. She tilted her head slightly, studying him. "Quinn."

"Yes," he said grudgingly.

"Is it yours?" She quickly lifted her hands peaceably when he glared at her. "I'm just asking!"

"It's mine."

"How do you know? I mean, a week and a half ago, she was supposedly engaged to marry Lord Banning."

"She wouldn't lie to me." His head was clanging and he headed blindly into the kitchen. There was still coffee in the pot from the day before and he dumped it in a mug and drank it cold and stale. Amelia wouldn't lie, yet how many times had he accused her of it, anyway?

Jess had followed him into the kitchen. Her eyes were concerned. "What are you going to do?"

"Not much I can do," he said wearily. "She won't marry me."

His sister's eyebrows disappeared up her forehead. "You, Mr. Never-Get-Married-Again, *proposed?*"

"She refused." More than once and the memory of each time felt engraved on his throbbing brain. He turned on the faucet and stuck his head under the cold water.

When he came up for air, Jess stuck a dish towel in his hand. "Did you tell her you loved her?"

He jerked. "This isn't above love."

"Oh, Quinn." Jess shook her head, looking disgusted all over again. "When it comes to a woman, particularly a pregnant woman, everything is *always* about love."

"Maybe for you." He ran the towel over his face and tossed it aside. "And Mac." His brother-in-law had grown up in Vicker's Corners. "You two've been together since high school. You're the same. Hell, you even teach together at the same school!"

"So? Carrie and you had the same backgrounds, too, and that wasn't exactly a stellar success!"

"There's no comparison between Carrie and Amelia." His voice was abrupt. Carrie had never made him feel half the emotion that Amelia did.

She gave him a look. "Well, duh. It's about time you realized it."

He shoved his fingers through his hair, slicking the wet strands back from his face. He hadn't been talking about the other similarities, despite what his sister obviously thought. "Where'd you see the tabloid?"

"It's front and center on the racks in the Superette."

He exhaled. "This'll send her off the rails." He reached for his Resistol and headed for the door, but his sister grabbed the back of his shirt.

"Hold on there, Romeo," she drawled. "Might want to at least brush your teeth before you go after the fair maiden."

He yanked away. "You're a pain in the ass, you know that?"

"Yeah." She patted his cheek like he was ten. "But nobody loves you like I do. And I kinda fancy the idea of getting some blue blood in our family gene pool." Then she shoved his shoulders, pushing him toward the living room. "And clean clothes wouldn't go amiss, either."

The fact that she was right annoyed the life out of him. He headed toward the steps. "I don't know how Mac puts up with you."

"He loves me," she assured blithely and patted her flat belly. "Which is why we're trying for a girl again." Her eyes were revoltingly merry. "According to that tabloid, your baby and mine will be born right around the same time next January."

Quinn squinted. "You're pregnant, too? Again?"

Jess smiled. "Isn't life grand?"

Amelia stared at the cover of the magazine that her mother had presented the second she'd walked into Aunt Jeanne's house.

The pregnancy stick in the picture was not the same brand Amelia had used either time, but some portion of her mind knew that it didn't really matter.

The message was still the same.

"Well?" Josephine propped her hands on her slender hips and raised her eyebrows. She'd arrived a full day earlier than expected because of the dreadful magazine, and her blue eyes were steely. "Is it true?"

Amelia rubbed her palms down the thighs of her cropped slacks and nodded. Then she gestured at the cover. "I don't know how they found out. Were you contacted for a comment?"

Her mother just gave her a look. "As if we would have offered one to such a disreputable publication? My senior social secretary gave me a copy when no one else on my staff seemed to have the nerve to show it to me." She sighed and sat down on the couch next to her. They were alone in the house only because Jeanne Marie and Deke had gone to see Toby and his crew for a while. "We'll have to release something officially at some point, but I wanted to see you for myself, first. Darling, why didn't you *tell* me?"

Amelia's throat tightened. "I was going to. I just wanted to clean up some of the mess I made after the whole Jamelia business exploded."

Her mother closed her cool hands around Amelia's

and squeezed gently. "Are you feeling all right? I hate knowing you've been dealing with this all on your own."

"It's about time I finally dealt with something on my own," she murmured thickly. She met her mother's eyes. "I'm sorry I've done such a poor job of it."

"Amelia." Josephine sighed. "I love you. The only thing I am concerned about is that you're happy. I knew you weren't happy in London even before this ridiculous betrothal business with James came about." She tucked Amelia's hair behind her ear the same way she'd been doing since Amelia was a tot. "Had you confided in me, perhaps we could have prevented some of this outrageous publicity."

Amelia chewed the inside of her cheek. "Molly knew," she whispered. "She's the only one other than Quinn who knew I was pregnant."

Josephine's expression cooled. "*My* Molly?"

Amelia nodded miserably. "I don't want to believe she would have said something, but who else was there?" James hadn't known she was returning to Horseback Hollow, much less that she was pregnant with Quinn's baby, so the information couldn't have come from his quarter.

"And your Quinn," Josephine said gently. "He wouldn't have—"

"No." Amelia shook her head, adamant. He might have threatened that one time to out her pregnancy during Jeanne Marie's and Deke's family dinner, but he never would have gone beyond that. Certainly not to the very type of strangers he'd threatened off the Rocking-U. She reached for the hateful tabloid and flipped it open to the main article that turned out to be only a few paragraphs, accompanied by two pages of photographs obviously meant to chronicle the rise and fall of her and James's supposed romance.

There were also a startling number of images of Quinn that had to have taken some effort to collect. One was even of him as a solemn boy, standing next to an easily recognizable Jess and a woman she could only assume was their mother, given the casket they were looking at. She trailed her fingertip over his young face then made herself look at the text.

"'Sources close to Amelia Fortune Chesterfield and her baby daddy, Horseback Hollow Homewrecker Quinn Drummond, confirm that the stick turned a big, positive blue,'" she read aloud. Then she made a face and flipped the magazine closed, tossing it aside. "Ophelia Malone finally gets her big payday," she muttered. "And Quinn didn't do a thing to deserve her trashy comments."

"I'll have to deal with Molly." Josephine rose and paced around the parlor. Her silver hair was immaculately coiffed and despite her day of travel, she looked impeccable in a black and white pantsuit. "I'll have Jensen look into her finances." She referred to Amelia's third-eldest brother. "If there's proof she was compensated, we can take her to court since it's a violation of her confidentiality agreement. Jensen knows how to be discreet."

"Whereas I don't."

Her mother sent her an exasperated look. "Stop reading between the lines, Amelia. I wasn't implying any such thing."

"I want it all to go away." She twisted her hands together. "You always said if we ignored rumors and gossip, they'll die of starvation."

"Well, that used to be truer than it is nowadays. People don't depend on news to come from reputable newspapers and the nightly news." She sighed. "It's become quite exhausting in the past few years." She brushed her hand down her silk sleeve. "Either that, or I'm just getting too old to want to put up with it."

"You're not old, Mum."

Josephine's lips twisted a little. "I'm sixty-two, darling. I've divorced one husband and buried another. Now I'm going to be a grandmamma again, and maybe I would like to slow down my schedule and enjoy that more this time around than I was able to do with Oliver Junior."

She sat down beside Amelia again and hugged her arm around her shoulders. "I don't want you worrying about Molly. She's my secretary and I'll see that matter is handled appropriately. In the meantime, you can tell me more about your Mr. Drummond."

Amelia's nose burned. "Quinn is anything but *my* Mr. Drummond," she said thickly.

"Do you love him?"

Amelia nodded. "I knew he was special the first time I saw him. When we were here for Sawyer's wedding. Remember?"

"I remember."

"I couldn't get him out of my head. When I came for Toby's wedding, I made the excuse that I just wanted some space from James pressuring me about marrying, but I had to see Quinn again."

Her mother smiled softly. She rested her head against Amelia's. "I felt the same way the first time I saw your father."

Tears collected and squeezed out her eyes. "He'd be so ashamed of me," Amelia whispered.

Josephine tsked. "He'd have been ready to put Quinn's head on a spike," she allowed, gently teasing. "Because you were his baby girl. But then he'd have come to his senses, the way Simon always did, and start campaigning for the baby to be named after him."

Amelia smiled through her tears. "Yes." She wrapped her arms around her mother's neck. "Yes, he would have. I love you, Mum."

"I love you too, darling." Josephine squeezed her back. "And everything is going to be all right. You'll see."

They both heard the crunch of tires from outside and Josephine stood again while Amelia swiped her cheeks. "Sounds like my sister and Deke are back already. I hope they have good news finally about Toby and Angie's adoption."

Only it quickly became apparent that it wasn't Amelia's aunt and uncle, when her mother looked out the window. "Oh, my." She turned and eyed Amelia for a moment, then picked up her suitcase that was still sitting near the front door where she'd left it upon arriving. "I'm going to go upstairs and get settled."

Amelia started to tell her that she was using the room her mother was accustomed to, but broke off when she spotted Quinn crossing in front of the window.

A moment later, he was pounding on the front door. "Open up, Amelia," he said loudly. "I saw you sitting in there."

She nervously tucked her hair behind her ears and moved to the door, waiting until her mother was gone before tugging it open.

His hazel eyes were bloodshot and they raked over her face. "Was that your mother I saw?"

She nodded. "She's a day earlier than I expected," she said inanely.

He brushed past her, entering the house even though she hadn't exactly issued an invitation. "Are you all right?"

He was looking at the magazine lying on the coffee table.

Dismay sank through her belly and her shoulders bowed. "You've seen it." She could tell by the lack of shock on his face.

"Jess brought a copy by."

"I'm sorry," she said huskily. "If I would have just stayed in London, you would never have been dragged into any of this."

"And I wouldn't know you're having my baby." His voice was flat. "Regretting the papers you had drawn up already?"

"No!" She lifted her hands. "I don't know what else to do, Quinn." She waved at the tabloid. "Thanks to that nastiness, every last bit of privacy we might have had is lost."

"I don't give a rip who knows about us," he said impatiently. "But I also don't want you working yourself up into a state over it."

Her lips parted. "You were worried about me?"

His gaze raked over her again. "That's my baby you're carrying. You think I want anything endangering that?"

She pressed her lips together, her hopes sinking yet again. Of course his concern would be for the baby. "As you can see, I'm fine."

"Suppose your mother wants to take you back."

"Actually, no." Her voice cooled even more. "I've

made it more than clear to you that I intend to remain in Horseback Hollow and raise our child here where he—"

"She—"

"—will have both parents in his life." She stepped closer to him, looking up into his face. She'd seen him just the day before when she'd left him the agreement, but he looked like he hadn't slept in weeks. "Why are you so insistent that the baby is a girl?"

He picked up the magazine and flipped it open to the article. "Got enough boys in the family," he muttered. "Little girl would be a change of pace."

Her throat tightened. How easy it was to imagine him holding a baby girl. Their child would succeed in wrapping him around a tiny finger.

He would love the baby. He just wouldn't love her.

She rubbed her damp palms down her thighs again, banishing the image before she started crying like a baby herself. "Did you consult an attorney about the, uh, the agreement?"

He tossed the magazine down again. "I don't need to consult anyone. And I haven't signed it."

"Why not? It gives you everything you wanted!"

His lips twisted. "You'd think."

Her head felt light in a way that it hadn't since she'd first arrived in Horseback Hollow. She thought about how many times he'd seemed stuck on the idea that she'd be happier back in London. "Do you *want* me to go back to London?"

His brows pulled together. "No."

Her hands lifted, palms upward. "Then what, Quinn?"

"I want to know I can protect you from crap like that!" He gestured at the magazine. "And I know I can't."

Her heart squeezed and she had to remind herself that

feeling protective wasn't the same thing as feeling love. "I wanted to protect you, too," she said huskily. "And I didn't do a good job of it, either. I confided in Molly—" She broke off and shook her head. "I shouldn't have trusted anyone but my own family. And you."

"You know for sure it was her?"

"Who else?" She sat down on the arm of the couch and held her arms tightly around her chest. "You said nobody saw you buy the test kit I used here. I know you didn't tell anyone. That just leaves Molly. You think you trust someone and they betray—" She broke off. "I don't want to think about it anymore." She watched him for a moment. "I thought I'd, um, speak with Christopher about volunteering at the Fortune Foundation office once he gets it up and running here. I could offer music lessons or something."

"Thought you didn't like playing in front of people."

"I don't like performing. But one-on-one? I told you once I liked working with children." She wished she wouldn't have brought it up, because it only made her remember that perfect April night when she'd talked about her life and he'd actually seemed to listen. "I…I have to do something to fill my days."

"You'll have a baby to fill your days." He waited a beat. "Or are you planning to hire some nanny to do that? That's what people like you do, right?"

"People like you," she repeated, mimicking his drawl. "I was born into a family that happened to have money," she said crisply. "It doesn't make me a different species than you!"

His jaw flexed. "People with your financial advantage," he refined. "That's what my dad's father's *real* family did. Hired…nannies."

She studied the fresh lines creasing his tanned forehead. He'd said his father was illegitimate but hadn't offered anything else about it. Only had used it as a reason why she ought to marry him. "What do you mean?"

"Baxter Anthony." He practically spit the name. "My grandfather. He had a wife. He had kids. His *real* family. The ones who lived in comfort on a big old ranch in Oklahoma. While my grandmother—whom he fired as one of those nannies after knocking her up—and my dad eked out a life in Horseback Hollow. Baxter's real family had nannies. They had private schools. They had everything that my old man didn't."

"I don't want a nanny," she said after a moment. "It never even entered my mind. But the baby won't be here for months yet, and I'm not exactly used to sitting around, whiling away my days waving a lacy fan and eating bonbons."

"You could use a few bonbons," he muttered. "You're still too thin."

"Gawky, skinny Amelia." She sighed. "Lucie got all the grace in the family."

"What the hell are you talking about?"

She shrugged dismissively. "It doesn't matter."

"You're the most graceful thing I've ever seen," he said in such a flat tone she couldn't possibly mistake it for a compliment. More like an accusation. "You're so far out of my league it's laughable. I still can't believe you danced with me that night, much less—" He broke off and shoveled his fingers through his hair, leaving the thick brown strands disheveled.

She tucked her tongue between her teeth, trying to make sense of his words. "You're the one who seemed out of reach to me," she finally said. Self-assured. Quietly confident. A man who'd held her and made her feel safe and beautiful and wanted.

His brows were pulled down, his eyes unreadable. "Baxter was the only one who wanted to buy the Rocking-U when my old man died." His lips thinned. "He'd buy it now, too, if I'd let him. Just so he could finally succeed in wiping away the evidence that anyone with his blood ever existed here."

"Forget about him! The man sounds hideous. And why would you want to sell the Rocking-U? That ranch is—" She broke off, trying to make sense of the nonsensical. "It's who you are," she finally finished and knew she had it right. Ranching wasn't merely something Quinn did. It was entwined with everything he was. The ranch was an extension of him just as much as he was an extension of it.

"It's the only way I can bring something equal to the table," he said through his teeth.

She pushed to her feet. "Let me get this straight," she said slowly. "You think the only thing you can offer this baby is *money?*" She laughed, but it sounded more hysterical than anything. "Money doesn't matter, Quinn! Good Lord, how can you think it would?"

"Because you've always had it," he said roughly.

"If I gave it all away would that make you happy?" Her voice rose. "Would that soothe your…your *ego?*" She swept out her arms, taking in the room around them. "How can you stand in this home that *love* so obviously built and talk that way?"

She snatched up the tabloid and threw it at his chest. "You should have sold the story," she said icily. "At least then you would have been the one to make a fortune on it. You know what? *Don't* sign the custody agreement.

I'd rather take this baby back to London than have him be raised by a man who can't recognize what's right in front of his face!"

Then, because tears were blinding her and her stomach was heaving, she fled upstairs.

Quinn started after her. She'd walked away the other day when she brought him that custody agreement and he wasn't going to let her walk off again.

He got to the top of the stairs just as she slammed the bathroom door shut and he started to reach for it.

"I would give her a little time," a calm voice said.

He looked from Amelia's mother, standing in a bedroom doorway, to the bathroom door. On the other side, he could hear Amelia retching, and his sense of helplessness made him want to punch a wall.

"Come." Lady Josephine walked toward him and tucked her hand around his arm, drawing him away from the door. "No woman wants to be overheard when they're in Amelia's state. Morning sickness is never fun." She smiled at him with unexpected kindness.

But he also noticed the way she subtly placed herself between him and the door.

"She's in there because of me." He wasn't only talking about her pregnancy. "She's upset."

"Yes." Lady Josephine's expression didn't change. Nor did her protective position or the steel behind her light touch on his arm. "It's been upsetting business. Come."

He reluctantly went with her back down the stairs and followed her into the parlor. She glanced out the window, then sat on the edge of a side chair, her hands folded in her lap, her long legs angled to one side. It was such an "Amelia position" that he had to look away.

"Mr. Drummond, please sit."

He exhaled and feeling like a kid called in front of the principal, sat on one end of the couch. "Call me Quinn. Lady Josephine," he tacked on hurriedly. Was it supposed to be Lady Chesterfield? Lady Fortune Chesterfield? He wished to hell he'd listened more to Jess's yammering about all that.

A faint smile was playing around the corners of the woman's lips. "And you may call me Josephine. We are a bit of family after all."

He could feel heat rising up his neck. "I suppose I should apologize for that. I wouldn't blame you if you wanted my head."

Her head tilted slightly. "Are you saying you took advantage of my daughter?" Before he could answer, she shifted slightly. "Amelia has a kind heart," she said. "She's always hated the attention our family is given back home. As if we're celebrities of some sort. Unfortunately, this business with Lord Banning got quite out of control and in hindsight, I wish I would have interfered early on. Perhaps I could have saved us all some of this embarrassment. But I've actually never witnessed Amelia allowing herself to be taken advantage of. In fact, she can be quite headstrong at times." Her blue gaze didn't allow him to look away. "I feel certain she was an equal participant in this situation."

"Lady—"

"Josephine."

"Josephine." He rubbed his hands down his jeans and stood, because just sitting there had his nerves wanting to jump out of his skin. "No disrespect, ma'am, but I'm not going to talk about that." He wasn't going to talk about having sex with Amelia to her mother. He wasn't going to talk about it with anyone.

"I've always thought that when two people who belong together are not, it's one of the saddest things there is."

He stared. "You think she belongs with *me*. I'm a small-town rancher, ma'am. I don't have a pot of gold. I've got one failed marriage and pots of cow manure."

Her lips twitched. "I forget how refreshingly frank you Americans can be." She rose gracefully. She was taller than Amelia, but no less slender, and Quinn knew when Amelia was her age, she'd be just as beautiful. "I had an unsuccessful marriage as well, Quinn. And then I met Amelia's father and I had a very, very successful one. I loved Simon with all of my heart and knew that he loved me equally. I want that for Amelia. I want that for all of my children. The past is past. And if you'll forgive an unintended pun, fortune isn't in gold. I hope you'll realize that for both your sakes."

She patted his arm as she passed him and pulled open the front door. "You don't have to love Amelia to be a good father to your child together. But if you don't love Amelia, be decent enough to allow her space to find someone who will."

Chapter Fourteen

"Come on." Jess dragged Quinn by the arm, pulling him toward the brightly lit building.

The Hollows Cantina was having its grand opening celebration and everyone in town seemed to have turned out for the festivities.

"Mac reserved a table for us," Jess continued, "and is waiting, and you are *not* getting out of coming just because you're a flaming idiot."

"Amelia's going to be there."

"No kidding, Sherlock." She dug her fingernails into his forearm the same way she'd done when she was an equally irritating teenager. "Maybe if you weren't so clueless when it comes to wooing a woman, you'd be with her instead of playing third wheel to me and my husband."

"I don't want to be here with you, either," he reminded. But she'd driven out to the Rocking-U and made it plain she wasn't leaving unless he came with her.

For the sake of a little peace and sanity, and only because he really didn't want to upset yet another pregnant woman, he had pulled on the only suit he owned and gone with her.

"I'll be just as happy to go back home again," he finished. There were strands of white lights strung around the Cantina's building, outlining not only the second story's open-air terrace, but the market umbrellas lining the street in front of it, and country music spewed out from inside. The festive atmosphere was the last thing he was in the mood for.

"Over my dead body," Jess raised her voice over the music and even though there were a couple dozen people lined up outside the entrance waiting to get in, she pulled him into the throng, waving at the familiar faces they passed. He knew everyone in Horseback Hollow, too, but she knew everyone from Vicker's Corners who was there as well, which made for slow going. But they finally reached the small table deep inside the first floor of the restaurant where Mac was already seated.

She slipped behind the table to sit next to her husband who shoved out the chair that had obviously been added to what should have been a two-person table for Quinn. He gestured with his half-empty beer mug. "Place is a madhouse," he said, leaning across the table so he could be heard above the noise. "Already put in orders for a beer for you."

Jess made a face and reached for her glass of fruit juice. "Some men might forgo alcohol in support of his pregnant wife having to abstain."

Mac grinned at her, obviously unfazed. "Baby, you're

pregnant so often, I'd never have another beer again if I gave it up whenever you're knocked up." He bussed her cheek. "I ordered you some hot crab dip," he added. "You can eat yourself silly on it."

Jess looked slightly mollified. "At least I know I won't have to share it with either one of you." Both Mac and Quinn detested crab. "You wouldn't know there had ever been any protests in town about this place opening." She was craning her neck around, openly gawking at the people crowded inside. "This is amazing!" She wriggled a little in her seat, clearly delighted. "I think every person from Horseback Hollow *and* Vicker's Corners must be here tonight."

Quinn was looking around, too, hopefully less noticeably than his sister.

But he hadn't spotted Amelia.

He knew she hadn't left town. Jess would've reported it.

A waitress wearing a stark white blouse and a black apron tied around her hips stopped next to their table and delivered a steaming crock of crab dip and crackers as well as two freshly frosted mugs filled with beer. "We have a special menu tonight," she told them as she dealt three one-page menus on the table. "Because of the grand openin' and all. I'll give you a chance to look it over and be back if you have any questions."

Quinn's only question was where Amelia was.

Not that he knew what he would say to her if he saw her. She was making a habit of walking away from him. The fact that he deserved it wasn't something he was willing to look at real closely.

And he was still feeling the bruises from her mother's velvet-over-steel dismissal the day before.

He lifted the beer mug, and angled in his seat so he could see around the restaurant more easily.

The staircase that led to the second floor was situated close to the center of the room; a wide iron and rustic wood thing that was as much a focal point as it was functional and the mayor, Harlan Osgood, was holding court at the base, recounting the steps taken to bring such a fine establishment to their little town as if he hadn't ever had his own doubts about it. Privately, Quinn figured it was a good thing Harlan's main job was as the town's barber, because a natural politician, he wasn't.

Marcos and Wendy Mendoza, the owners, were working the room, too. The young couple was eye-catching, to say the least. Wendy in particular looked more like she belonged on the cover of magazines than making the desserts that Julia claimed were out of this world. Quinn had to give the couple credit for seeming to give equal attention to everyone they stopped to speak with. They gave just as much time to Tanya and her folks, sitting at a table as crowded as Quinn's across the room, as they did the mayor.

"Mac, what are you going to have?" Jess was asking, tapping the crisp edge of her menu against the table. "I'm starving. I haven't had a speck of morning sickness in two days, and I am going to take advantage of it."

Mac chuckled. "I think I'm having whatever else it is you want to order so you can eat it, too."

Was Amelia still plagued with morning sickness?

Quinn pushed out of the chair.

Jess looked at him. "You're *not* leaving."

He leaned over her. "Stop bossing," he warned.

Then he kissed the top of her head and made his way toward the staircase. He knew the entire extended Fortune family was supposed to be there that night, and if they weren't on the bottom floor, maybe they were up top.

Getting there proved as slow-going as getting into the restaurant in the first place, though, because of all the people standing around on the stairs blocking the way. He could hear bursts of laughter coming from the upper floor and barely controlled the urge to physically move some of the roadblocks out of his way.

"Mr. Drummond!"

He looked over the side of the staircase to see Shayla waving at him excitedly, her orange ponytail bouncing, and he sketched a wave. But she was already worming her way around the mayor and up the steps until she was only a few below his position midway up. "It's so cool to see you," she gushed. "Is Lady Amelia here, too?"

The girl had helped them avoid Ophelia Malone in Vicker's Corners, so Quinn swallowed his impatience to get upstairs. "I'm looking for her now," he admitted. "How've you been? Do you still have a particular guest staying at the B and B?"

She widened her eyes dramatically. "Right? Miz Malone finally left this morning. My ma's not so happy—" she waved her hand behind her, presumably to indicate the presence of her mother somewhere in the madhouse "—'cause she paid the room on time and all, but I was glad to see her go. I can't believe what she got printed the other day." She wrinkled her nose. "So gross."

It was as good a definition as any and a lot milder than what Quinn still thought about the tabloid cover. "Did you and your mom already have dinner?"

"Nah. Not yet." She twisted her head around, looking

down on the patrons below. "Ma's over there talking to the Fremonts. They're all on the graduation committee for high school next year."

He automatically glanced over at the table he'd noticed earlier where Tanya sat with her parents. Shayla's mother's hair was just as orange as her daughter's. Either the color was real or they shared the same bottle of hair dye.

"Can't believe she did it," Shayla was babbling on. "Just so stupid, you know?"

He frowned. "What?"

"Tanya." Shayla rolled her eyes, looking disgusted. "Believe me, she's not one of *my* friends anymore."

God save him from teenage girl angst. He managed to edge up another step when the person in front of him moved slightly. "That's too bad," he said vaguely. Tanya had always been a hard worker for him and the dozen or so other people she also cleaned for in order to help supplement her family's strained income.

"Wow. You're nicer than I would be," Shayla was saying. She was practically shouting to be heard above the music. "Blabbing about your personal business to Miz Malone and all."

He went still, her words penetrating.

He went back down the step. "What did you say?"

Shayla looked suddenly nervous. "Uh—"

He nudged her to one side of the stairs so one of the servers carrying a stack of menus could get past them. "What do you mean about personal business, Shayla?" But he had the sinking feeling he already knew.

He'd tossed Amelia's pregnancy test in the trash.

Tanya cleaned his house.

Shayla shot a look toward the table below and Quinn

caught the pale expression on Tanya's face even from a distance.

"I don't think she meant to," Shayla said hurriedly. She might be willing to eschew Tanya's friendship, but she was obviously afraid of tossing her under the bus. "It's just Miz Malone kept talking to everybody and... and—" She lifted her shoulders. "Well, Tanya needed that car in the worst way or she's not gonna be able to get back and forth to Lubbock for school when she graduates next year and the money she gets cleaning houses is already used up on her ma's medicine. I thought you already knew."

Quinn sucked down his fury.

"I don't think she knew how bad it would be," Shayla finished. "Still." She made a face. "*I* wouldn't want her cleaning around my stuff. You're prob'ly pretty mad, huh."

Amelia's friend Molly hadn't done a single thing to betray her.

"It's okay, Shayla." He squeezed her shoulder and managed a smile even though he wanted to kick both Ophelia Malone and Tanya Fremont off the planet altogether. "I'm glad to hear the truth."

"Quinn!"

He looked toward the top of the stairs to see Liam beckoning.

"Go on and enjoy your dinner," Quinn told Shayla. "Once I find Amelia, I'll let her know you're here. I'm sure she'll want to say hello."

Shayla beamed. "You think?"

He nodded and started edging up the stairs again while she slipped through the people on her way down.

Liam clapped him on the shoulder when he finally

made it to the top. "Julia's done a helluva job here to-night with the Mendozas, hasn't she?" The man's face was proud. "We've got the whole family up here."

Suspicions confirmed, Quinn looked beyond Liam to the crowded tables spilling out onto the open terrace. Jeanne and Deke were sitting with Josephine and their brother, James Marshall Fortune. There was also another older couple sitting with them and he was pretty certain the man was the threesome's older brother, John. Which, according to Jess who always needed to know who was who, made him Wendy Mendoza's father. Aside from Jeanne and Deke's crew, spread out among the rest of the tables were a bunch of other faces he recognized from Sawyer and Laurel's New Year's wedding.

But Amelia was not among them.

"We've got extra reason to celebrate," Liam was saying. "Angie and Toby's adoption was finally approved."

His head was still banging with Shayla's news, but Quinn glanced at the man who seemed deep in conversation with his uncle James. Happiness radiated from his face. "That's great," he said. "Where's Amelia?"

Liam looked surprised for a moment, then glanced around. "Don't know, man. She was here earlier." He raised his voice even more. "Aunt Josephine, where'd Amelia go?"

In addition to Amelia's mother, Quinn suddenly found himself the focus of way too many eyes.

Josephine said something to her companions, then rose and worked her way through the tables toward him.

"I didn't mean to interrupt your dinner," Quinn said.

"You're not interrupting," she assured. She smiled slightly at her nephew. "Liam, I haven't had a chance yet to applaud your fiancée's efforts tonight. Is Julia going to be able to join us, or is she on duty all evening?"

"She's not on duty at all," Liam said, grinning. "But she can't keep from checking on things. She'll be 'round soon enough." He headed after the waitress that was circulating throughout the room with a tray laden with drinks. "Hey there, darlin', lemme take one of those off your hands."

Josephine looked back at Quinn. "I wasn't sure we would have the pleasure of seeing you tonight."

He wondered what she'd really like to say if she weren't so polite. Probably something more along the lines of hoping he wouldn't have the gall to show his face that night.

"I wasn't going to come," he admitted. He was glad he had, though, if only to hear what Shayla'd had to say. "Is Amelia all right?"

Josephine's expression was the same as it had been the other day when she'd essentially told him to put up or shut up. Calm. Seemingly gracious, yet still reserved.

"She's unhappy." She didn't attempt to raise her voice above the music to be heard, yet her words somehow managed to carry through anyway. "As are you, I believe." Then she sighed a little, her gaze following Sawyer and Orlando Mendoza as they moved among the tables. "I keep having to remind myself how entwined the Fortune and Mendoza families are," she murmured then looked back at Quinn again. "She went outside a short while ago. She said she needed some fresh air."

He stifled an oath. How had he missed her leaving the restaurant when he'd been on the damn stairs?

"Thank you." He started to turn and go back the way he'd come, but stopped. "La— Josephine."

She lifted her eyebrows, waiting.

"It wasn't Molly," he said abruptly. "You know. Who spilled the beans." He told her briefly about Tanya cleaning his place.

When he was done, he couldn't tell if she was relieved or not. He'd thought that Amelia's "royal face" was bad, but in comparison to her mother's, her expressive face was an open book.

"What do you plan to do about your young employee?"

"Fire her," he said flatly.

"Hmm." She nodded once. "Is that why you're anxious to see my daughter? To share this information?"

He could lie and say it was, even though he'd been looking for Amelia before Shayla's disclosure. As far as he was concerned, what went on between him and Amelia *was* between him and Amelia. "I don't know why I'm anxious to see her," he finally said truthfully. "I just know I have to."

It wasn't any sort of answer, but it seemed enough for her to smile just a little as she nodded once and headed back to her table.

He went down the stairs again where the sounds of celebration weren't as raucous, though the music was, and pretended he didn't see his sister trying to flag him down as he worked his way toward the entrance.

Once he got past the crowd still waiting to get in, he felt like he'd been shot from a noisy cannon into blissful peace.

The music was still loud. There were still dozens of people surrounding the tables beneath the colorful market umbrellas. But it was still *open* and he yanked off his suit jacket and hauled in a deep breath of fresh air.

The Hollows Cantina might well be bringing new jobs and new revenue to the area, and it wouldn't be crazy busy in the days to come like it was for the grand opening, but he was pretty sure he wouldn't be in any hurry to go back, no matter how good the food might turn out to be.

Bunching his jacket in one hand, he scanned the tables outside the restaurant. Amelia wasn't at any of them, so he walked past them until he reached the side of the building. She wasn't there, either, so he walked all the way around the building. And even then, he didn't spot her.

"Dammit, Amelia. Where are you?"

The whole of Horseback Hollow's businesses were contained in just a few short blocks and trying not to imagine her passed out cold in some shadowy corner, he started down the street, and then nearly missed her altogether where she was sitting on a bench in front of the mayor's barbershop.

The soles of his boots scraped against the street when he stopped in front of her and peered at her in the dark. Her skin looked white in the moonlight, her hair, eyes and clothing as dark as midnight. "You're not easy to find."

"I didn't know you were looking." She shifted slightly, given away only by the slight rustle of her clothes. "You've been in the restaurant?"

"Yeah." It was a warm night and he tossed his jacket on the bench beside her and started rolling up his sleeves. "It's a zoo."

She made a soft sound. "Yes. Too many people and too much noise for me."

"Were you feeling sick?"

She shifted again. "Not in the way you mean," she murmured. "What do you want, Quinn?"

"Molly didn't rat us out," he said abruptly. "It was Tanya. When she cleaned the house—"

"She found the test," Amelia finished slowly, dawning revelation clear in her tone. "Of course she did. I can't believe I never thought of that."

"I can't believe she talked to that woman," he said flatly. "I wouldn't have known if Shayla hadn't said something. Would've just kept paying the kid every Sunday to clean the bathrooms and mop the damn floors, never knowing any better."

"She's a girl," Amelia murmured.

"She talked about *our* business for the price of a car," he countered. "She won't be stepping foot in my house again. Or any others, if I can help it."

"Didn't you ever make a mistake when you were young?"

His lips twisted. "Why are you being so understanding? You were pretty upset thinking it was your mother's secretary."

"It's just all so...so sad, isn't it?" Her voice was soft. Oddly musing. "I'd say it was tragic except there are so many other real tragedies occurring every day." She sighed. "The press has been vilifying us ever since I came to Horseback Hollow. Ophelia used Tanya like a tool, no differently than she'd use a long-distance lens. Have you ever noticed how random it all is?" she asked abruptly.

He peered at her face but even though his eyes were becoming accustomed to the dark, he still couldn't tell if she was looking at him or not. "What's random?"

"If I hadn't decided to come to Horseback Hollow

with Mum for Sawyer's wedding over New Year's. If you and I hadn't danced when I came back again for Toby's. If James's father hadn't announced an engagement-that-wasn't. If any one of those things hadn't occurred, everything would be so different today."

"Maybe that's not random." His chest felt tight. "Maybe that's fate."

She shifted, her dark dress rustling. "You believe in fate." She sounded skeptical.

"I don't know what I believe, Amelia. Except I know I don't want you going back to London."

"I've told you and told you, you needn't worry about your place in the baby's life."

"What about a place in your life?"

She went silent for a moment, then slowly stood, walking closer to him until he could smell the clean fragrance of her hair and see the gleam in her dark eyes.

"Did you really want me to come back to Horseback Hollow after the night we shared? You said you did. And I…I thought you meant it. But maybe that's just what a person is supposed to say after a one-night stand. Protocol, if you will."

"It wasn't protocol," he said flatly. "I meant it."

He felt the weight of her gaze. "Why?"

The shirt button he'd left loose at his neck wasn't enough and he yanked another one free. "What d'ya mean *why?* I liked you. We had great—"

"Sex," she finished.

"*Chemistry* is what I was going to say."

"The end result is the same."

"Where are you going with this, Amelia?"

"I don't know." She sighed. "I've just been trying to

figure out how much I imagined about that night and what was actually real."

He didn't need light. He closed one arm around her waist and pressed his other hand against her flat abdomen, feeling as much as hearing the sudden breath she inhaled. "That is real."

"Yes." The one word sounded shaky. "But sex is not love. Having a baby doesn't mean love, either."

"Sometimes it does." He wanted to get out the words. But they felt stopped in his chest by a lifetime of disappointments. "Jess and Mac are having another baby. Trying again for a girl. So maybe she really had been in that hardware store to buy pink paint."

"I'm happy for them." Her voice was low. She gently patted his chest once. Then once more. "Think about it before you fire Tanya," she murmured. And then she stepped out of his arm and started up the street, disappearing into the dark.

Chapter Fifteen

Amelia's eyes glazed as she stumbled up the street.

"Amelia!"

Quinn was not going to come around. He wouldn't let himself, and she couldn't bear it.

"Don't walk away from me."

Her chest ached. She'd never understood that a heart breaking was a physical breaking, too. She could barely force herself to move when all she wanted to do was curl into a ball. She swiped her cheek and forced her feet to move faster. "What are you going to do? Throw me over your shoulder?"

"Please." Just one word. Rough. And raw.

Her feet dragged to a stop.

A block away, she could see the lights of the Cantina. Could hear the music playing on the night.

She didn't have to look back to see Quinn coming up

behind her. She didn't even need to hear his footfalls on the pavement. She could feel him.

"Toby and Angie's adoption was approved this afternoon. Did you know that?"

"Yeah. I saw him and your uncle James together. D'you think he's the one who gave him that money?"

"Aunt Jeanne wouldn't take the money he wanted to give her, so why not? He can afford it." She clasped her arms around her waist, trying to keep the pieces of herself from splintering on the road and nodded toward the festivities. "Everyone in there is celebrating," she said painfully. "Everyone in there is happy. Julia and Liam can walk into a room and light it up simply by looking at each other. Colton and Stacey are like two halves of a whole. I think Jude would lay down his life for Gabi and Christopher and Kinsley—" Her voice broke. "They're all happy. They're all in love. Is it so wrong to want that, too?"

"No."

She turned on her heel and looked up at him. "I could marry you, Quinn," she whispered. "Justice of the peace or a minister. It wouldn't matter. I could stand up in front of either and promise to love you for the rest of my days. And I wouldn't be lying." She sniffed but the tears kept coming. "But the marriage *would* be a lie, because I know you don't love me. And I can't live like that." She turned again, desperate to go somewhere, anywhere, for a little peace.

"And I can't live without you."

Had she gone so far over the edge that she was hearing things now, too?

"Don't leave me."

She sucked in a shuddering breath.

"Amelia." He closed his hands over her shoulders and turned her toward him. "Please." His low voice cracked. "Don't leave me." His fingers tightened, almost painfully.

"Quinn—"

He closed his mouth over hers, his hands moving to cradle her face. "Don't," he said hoarsely, brushing his thumbs over her cheeks. "I can take anything but that."

She could no more stop her hands from grasping his shoulders than she could stop loving him.

He kissed her again, lightly. Tenderly. The way he had that very first time. "If you leave me, I won't be able to take it. I love you," he whispered. "More than I've ever loved anything or anyone. And I am terrified. Okay?"

She wound her arms behind his neck, her heart cracking wide. "Nothing terrifies you."

"Not being good enough for you does." He dragged her arms away, holding them captive between them. "Not being a good enough father." He shook her gently, as if trying to convince her. "Not being a good enough husband. If I failed you or the baby—"

"You won't," she cried. "You can't fail me if you'd just love me. You think I'm not afraid? I don't even know how to make a baby's bottle. Infants can't eat peanut butter sandwiches!"

He folded her against him, tucking her head into his shoulder. "I know how to make a bottle," he said roughly. "Jess made me learn years ago. That's the easy stuff, Amelia. I'm talking about a life. What do I have to offer you?"

"Your heart," she said thickly. "Offer your heart! It's the only thing that matters. If you're afraid, be afraid with me. I can't bear it if you shut me out."

"Oh, my God," a voice said from nearby, startling them both. "Get a room or get on with it."

Amelia stared into the darkness, appalled when Ophelia Malone strolled closer. All of her pain, her uncertainty where Quinn was concerned, coalesced into a ball of hatred toward the paparazzo. *"You."* She started to launch herself at the dreadful woman, but Quinn held her back. "Haven't you done enough?"

"Evidently not." Ophelia sighed slightly. She held out her hands to her sides and Amelia spotted the camera she was holding.

She pulled against Quinn, but again he held fast. "She's not worth it." His voice was cutting.

"Why do you do this?" Amelia demanded of the woman. "Why do you go around making peoples' lives a misery? Is the money that good? Is it just that you enjoy tearing people's lives to shreds? What is it?"

"Oh, the money was good. Very, very good. But it didn't work anyway." Ophelia circled around them, giving Amelia's clawed fingers a wide berth. "Even knowing what sort of person you really are, Lord Banning *still* isn't giving my sister a chance."

Amelia shook her head, suddenly lost. "What?"

Ophelia sighed again. "You really are as dumb as a post," she mocked. "Your rancher there has more smarts than you do. At least he built that successful little ranch of his out of nothing but ashes. What have you ever done but smile pretty for the cameras while your mummy does all that charitable work that has people thinking she's such a saint?"

Quinn set Amelia to one side of him and snatched Ophelia's wrist with his free hand, making the other woman drop the camera. "Keep it up," he spat, "and I'll let her at you."

"Who's your sister?"

Ophelia shook off Quinn's hold and crouched down to pick up the two pieces of the camera. She held up the lens to the light from the Cantina, then tossed it off to the side of the road. "So much for that pricey little thing." She pushed to her feet. "Astrid," she clipped. She circled around Quinn until she was near Amelia again. "Astrid is my sister and if it weren't for *you* and your eminently suitable pedigree, Lord Banning would have chosen *her.* He would have gone against that decrepit father of his and married my sister whether she was a common shop girl or not!"

"You're insane," Amelia whispered, shocked to her very core.

Ophelia held out her arms. "Guilty as charged, no doubt." She suddenly tossed the camera at them and Quinn caught it midair before it could hit Amelia. "I don't have the stomach for this anymore. I'd like to say I hope you'll be happy together, but we all know I'd be lying." She turned on her heel and started walking down the street. "Taa taa, darlings."

Amelia pulled against Quinn's hold.

"Let her go," he muttered.

"She's. . .she's *vile!* I can't believe that woman is Astrid's sister."

He dropped the camera on the ground and turned her back into his arms, his hands sweeping down her back. "You know her?"

"Astrid? She sells coffee in James's building. And he's crazy about her. But he's had years to go against his family and marry her. Now that he's the Earl of Estingwood, he could do whatever he wants. But he won't."

"Why?"

"Because she's a commoner," Amelia said simply. "She's divorced. She has a child. Take your pick."

"I thought that stuff didn't matter anymore."

"It matters to the Bannings. And above all things, James is loyal to his family."

He pressed his lips against her temple. "I don't want to talk about James."

"Neither do I." From the corner of her eye, though, she kept watch of Ophelia, long enough to see the woman climb into an SUV and roar off down the street in the opposite direction.

Quinn suddenly pushed her away from him. "Where were we?"

Her throat tightened. "I don't know," she whispered.

"I do." Holding her hands, he abruptly went down on one knee, right there in the middle of the street. "I think this is the way it's supposed to go. Never did it before."

She inhaled sharply. "Quinn—"

"My heart is yours, Amelia Fortune Chesterfield. It has been from the second you agreed to a dance with a simple cowboy."

Tears flooded her eyes. "So is mine. Yours, I mean. My heart." She laughed brokenly. "I'm making a mishmash. And there's nothing simple about you."

"Will you marry me?"

She nodded and pulled on his hands. "Yes. I don't want you on your knees, I just want you by my side."

He rose and caught her close. "Preacher or a JP?"

She dragged his head to hers. "As long as it's soon, I don't care," she said thickly, and pressed her mouth to his. Joy was bubbling through her, making her feel dizzy with it. "Take me home?"

He cradled her tightly, lifting her right off her feet. "Kissing me like that is how getting you pregnant started off," he warned. And then he laughed a little and swore. "I can't. I don't have my truck. I rode here with Jess."

She groaned. "I want to be alone with you." She sank her fingers through his hair, reveling in the realization that she *could.* "I don't care how shameless that sounds. I need to be alone with you."

"You're killing me," he said gruffly, and kissed her so softly, so sweetly, that she would have fallen in love with him all over again if she hadn't already done so.

Then he gently set her back on her feet. Kissed her forehead. Her cheeks. "We'll go back and borrow some keys from someone."

"And then you'll take me home?"

He lifted her hand and kissed her fingers. "And then I'll take you home." They started back toward the Cantina, but Amelia suddenly ducked under his arm and ran back to retrieve Ophelia's camera.

"What do you want that thing for?"

She pulled his arm over her shoulder once more and fiddled with the camera as they continued walking back to the Cantina. "There's got to be a memory card in here somewhere." She held up the camera, squinting in the light from the strands hanging in the trees. "Ah." She spotted the storage compartment and freed the tiny square inside before handing the camera to Quinn. "Don't toss that aside either," she warned. "There might be internal memory or something that will need to be erased."

"Ophelia's gone." He brushed his hand down her hair. "Nobody else is going to care about that thing."

"Probably," she agreed, "But I'm not taking any chances." She went over to one of the umbrella-covered tables and reached for one of the candles burning inside short jars. "Mind if I borrow this for a moment?" she asked the people sitting there, and when there were no objections, carried it back to him.

Holding the jar between them, she dropped the memory disk onto the flame. "No more Ophelia Malone," she murmured, watching the thing begin to sizzle and melt, and feeling like the last load was lifting from her shoulders.

When the memory card was no longer recognizable as anything but a misshapen blob of plastic, she blew out the candle and carefully plucked it out of the wax.

Then she dropped it on the road and ground it fervently beneath her heel.

Quinn lifted the candle out of her hand and set it back on the table. "Remind me never to make you really mad," he said when she finally stopped grinding.

"I know how to fox hunt, too," she told him, looping her arm through his. She couldn't seem to get the smile off her face, but then she couldn't imagine a reason why she needed to.

Quinn Drummond loved her.

What she'd feared was only a dream was real. And she was going to treasure that for the rest of their days.

"Fox hunt," he repeated warily. But he was smiling, too, and he absently hooked the camera strap over his shoulder.

"My father taught us." She looked up at the balcony above the umbrellas and saw her mother there, talking with Orlando Mendoza and looking unusually animated. "Once upon a time my father was a pilot," she murmured, nodding toward the balcony. "The Royal Air Force."

Quinn pulled her close against his side once more, as if he couldn't stand even a few inches separating them. He tilted his head looking upward, his gaze sharpening slightly. "They look—"

"Cozy," Amelia finished.

"Interesting." He steered her toward the entrance of the Cantina that was no less crowded than it had been earlier. "Maybe Horseback Hollow will end up appealing to more of the Fortune Chesterfields."

As much as the idea delighted her, she was presently more interested in Quinn. "You promised something about keys?"

"Yes, ma'am," Quinn said softly and kissed her right there in front of the Hollows Cantina for all the world to see. Then he tugged her after him through the crowds. Jess and Mac were sitting all cozied up together at their small table, clearly unworried whether he ever returned or not. The stairs were still crowded and he exhaled impatiently. But Amelia dragged him through the swinging doors to the kitchen where there was another staircase.

Not grand. Not the center of attention. But entirely welcome. At the top, he threaded his way around the tables there.

Lady Josephine was sitting once more next to Jeanne Marie and Deke and her smile deepened when she saw them. "Have you figured out where your fortune is, then, Quinn?"

"Yes, ma'am," he said and lifted his hand linked with

Amelia's. "I surely have." His eyes met Amelia's. "Love's the fortune."

Her smile trembled and she leaned into him. "Keys," she whispered.

He threw back his head and laughed. "Keys." He spotted Liam. "Lend me your truck for the night and I'll *consider* selling Rocky."

Liam reached into his pocket and tossed the keys over several heads. Quinn caught them handily.

Amelia giggled, squeezing his hand.

And they raced for the stairs.

Epilogue

Quinn parked his truck near the tree house tree and went around to open Amelia's door. "Come on."

She tilted her head up toward his, a smile on her face below the bandana he'd tied around her eyes before they'd left the ranch house.

It had been a week since the Cantina's grand opening. A week during which they'd barely left one another's side. A week in which it was finally sinking in that Amelia was his.

She loved him. She wasn't going anywhere. She was filling the empty parts of him, and together they'd fill the empty rooms of their home.

"What are we doing?" Her voice was full of laughter.

"You'll see." He took her hands and helped her out of the truck.

"Not exactly." Her lips tilted. "Since you've blindfolded me." She turned her head from side to side as he drew her closer to the tree, obviously trying to get a sense of where they were. "Do I hear the creek?"

He moved behind her and slid his hands around her waist and kissed her neck below her ear, right where he knew it would make her shiver. "Good instincts."

She sighed a little, shimmied a little with that shiver, and covered his hands with hers, pressing them against her belly. She rubbed her head against his chest. "On occasion. I picked you, didn't I?"

"That you did." He kissed her earlobe. "Okay, you can look."

She tugged the bandanna off her head.

"I knew it," she said, laughing in her triumph. She peered up into the tree branches. "You've finished the floor! When did you have time to do that?"

He'd finished a lot more than that. "When you're lazing around in bed, snoring."

"I don't snore."

"You do." He kissed her nose. "Daintily. Like the lady that you are."

She rolled her eyes. "Oh, that makes it all right then."

He laughed softly. "It's safe for us to go up."

Her dark eyes roved over his face while a smile played around her soft lips. "*Us?* As in now you're going to let me climb a tree?"

His hands slid down her hips. "Only because I'm here with you. So do you want to go up or not?"

Her eyes sparkled. "What do you think?" She quickly yanked off the sandals she'd been wearing and tossed them onto the grass, then set her bare toes on the first foothold and deftly began climbing.

"Just go slow, okay? Be careful."

She looked over her shoulder at him, grinning and looking more like a teenaged girl than a pregnant woman. "Fine warning from the man who puts temptation in my path."

She continued up with Quinn standing below her, and between his distraction over the view of her bare legs beneath her summery pink dress as she went, even he had to admit that she seemed to know exactly what she was doing. "How often did you say you used to climb trees?"

She laughed. She'd reached the base of the tree house and pushed open the door in the floor. "Every day that I could get away with it." In seconds, she'd clambered through the hatch, and then there was only silence.

He imagined her up there, seeing the preparations he'd made early that morning while she'd been sleeping in his bed.

Their bed.

A moment later, she leaned over the high side boards that formed the walls of the tree house, her long hair hanging down past her shoulders. Her youthful grin was gone, replaced by a soft expression. "Are you going to stand around down there, or join me?"

He kicked off his own shoes and climbed up.

It didn't take him any longer than it had her, but in that brief time she'd still managed to slip out of her dress, and was laying on the thick blankets he'd spread out on one side of the structure.

He let out a breath.

She propped her head on her hand and smiled slightly, holding one of the daisies he'd stuck in a jar to her nose. She was wearing sheer panties and a bra the same pale blue color as the Texas sky. "This *is* what you had in mind, isn't it?"

He crawled through the door and dropped it back in place. "Yeah." He shucked his own clothes, pitching them in the corner.

Her lashes swept down and pink color touched her cheeks. "I'm wondering if Peter Pan ever got up to such mischief."

He knelt down beside her, and she rolled onto her back, her hair pooling out around her head. "Peter Pan was a boy," he murmured, sliding one strap off her shoulder and kissing the creamy skin there.

She ran her thigh against his as she bent her knee and dropped the flower in favor of closing her hand boldly around him. "And you're *no* boy."

He exhaled on a rough laugh and caught her hand in his, pulling it away. "Not so fast, Lady Fortune Chesterfield." He stretched out next to her and slid off the other bra strap, then unsnapped the tiny silver clasp between her breasts holding it together. "I have plans for you."

"That'll be Mrs. Drummond—" her voice hitched when he caught one of those rosy crests between his lips "—to you."

He smiled against her warm flesh. Already he could sense small changes in her body because of the baby inside her. Her breasts were fuller. Her nipples a deeper pink. "Soon as you finally say whether you want a minister or a justice of the peace, that's who you'll be." He kissed his way down her flat belly, anchoring her hips gently when she shivered and twisted against him.

"Minister," she whispered. Her fingers slid through his hair, clutching. "And soon."

He nuzzled his way beneath the sexy little panties that matched the bra. "Impatient to make this all legal?"

"Yes." She suddenly twisted, reversing their positions

and pinned him on the blankets. "And I want to say yes before I'm big as a house. But I want my brothers and sister here, too. And you'll need a suit since you lost your jacket at the Cantina the other night." She kicked off her panties and sank down on him, letting out a shuddering moan.

He clamped his hands over her hips. "You're not always gonna get your way like this, princess." He sucked in a sharp breath as she rocked her hips against him. "I'm only indulging this need for constant speed you've got 'cause—"

"You love me." She leaned over, rubbing her tight nipples against his chest, and kissed him.

"—you're pregnant and at the mercy of your hormones," he finished.

Then, wrapping his arm around her waist, he flipped her onto her back. Loving the color in her cheeks and the way her eyes went an even darker brown, soft as down and feeling like home.

"And because I love you," he said the words quietly. They were coming easier, but even when he didn't say them he wanted her to know he would never stop feeling them.

Her eyes turned shiny and wet. She laid her palm along his jaw and brushed her thumb over his lip. "If I'm a princess, you know that makes you my prince."

"I don't care what you call me, Amelia—" he sank into her "—as long as it means *husband*."

She gasped, and twined her legs around his hips, arching against him. "This…tree house is off-limits the second our son—"

"Daughter—"

"—hits puberty," she managed breathlessly.

He laughed and thumbed away the tears leaking from her big brown eyes. "Damn straight it is," he agreed. And then he kissed her and together, they flew.

* * * * *

MILLS & BOON®
By Request

RELIVE THE ROMANCE WITH THE BEST OF THE BEST

Just can't wait?
Buy our books online before they hit the shops!
www.millsandboon.co.uk

Also available as eBooks.

Join Britain's BIGGEST Romance Book Club

50% OFF your first parcel

- **EXCLUSIVE offers** every month
- **FREE delivery direct** to your door
- **NEVER MISS a title**
- **EARN Bonus Book** points

Call Customer Services
0844 844 1358*

or visit
millsandboon.co.uk/subscriptions

KCB3